Free Wind

Also by Keira Andrews

Contemporary

The Spy and the Mobster's Son
Honeymoon for One
Beyond the Sea
Ends of the Earth
Arctic Fire

Lifeguards of Barking Beach
Flash Rip
Free Wind

Holiday
The Christmas Deal
The Christmas Leap
The Christmas Veto
A Baby for Christmas
Only One Bed
Merry Cherry Christmas
Santa Daddy
In Case of Emergency
Eight Nights in December
If Only in My Dreams
Where the Lovelight Gleams
Gay Romance Holiday Collection

Sports
Kiss and Cry
Reading the Signs
Cold War
The Next Competitor
Love Match
Synchronicity (free read!)

Gay Amish Romance Series
A Forbidden Rumspringa
A Clean Break
A Way Home

A Very English Christmas

Valor Duology
Valor on the Move
Test of Valor
Complete Valor Duology

Historical

Kidnapped by the Pirate
Semper Fi
The Station
Voyageurs (free read!)

Paranormal

Kick at the Darkness Trilogy
Kick at the Darkness
Fight the Tide
Defy the Future

Fantasy

Barbarian Duet
Wed to the Barbarian
The Barbarian's Vow

Free Wind

by Keira Andrews

Free Wind
Written and published by Keira Andrews
Cover by Dar Albert
Formatting by BB eBooks
Editing by Cecily Green

ISBN: 978-1-998237-65-4
Print Edition

Content Warnings

- Depiction of the aftermath of a Traumatic Brain Injury
- Injury and blood

Acknowledgments

Thanks so much to Elaine, Karen, and Sharna for their help with the Aussie lingo and cultural references. Thanks also to Helen (eagle eye!), Lori, Mary, and Rai for excellent proofing and beta reading. And special gratitude to my editor, Cecily, for making this book so much better!

Author's Note

Anyone familiar with Sydney's Bondi Beach will recognize the similarities to Barking Beach, which I set south of Perth and Fremantle. While Bondi was absolutely an inspiration, Barking, its surrounding area, and its lifeguards are completely fictional.

Language usage and slang can vary widely across Australia depending on many factors including—but not limited to—age, location, and socioeconomic status. I've lived in Australia, and I love it dearly. I do my best to portray characters authentically with the understanding that experiences aren't universal, and that while one person in Perth might use a particular word or saying, someone in Melbourne might not. I use multiple Aussie beta readers to make the language as authentic as possible.

Glossary

AFL: Australian Football League

Aggro: aggressive or confrontational behavior

Alfresco: outdoor covered living or dining space

Ambo: ambulance OR a paramedic

Anzac: Australia and New Zealand Army Corps

Arvo: afternoon

Bait ball: small fish swarming together in a circle to defend against a predator

Bang on: to be exactly right

Barbie: barbecue

Bathers: swimsuit

Bench: a counter such as in a kitchen

Boardies: board shorts

Bogans: typically a derogatory term for an uncouth or uncultured person

Brekkie: breakfast

Brickie: bricklayer

Brissie: Brisbane

Brushed: brushed off

Cark/carked it: to die or stop working

CBD: Central Business District

Chockers: extremely full or crowded

Chook: a chicken

Chucking a sickie: calling in sick

Chuffed: pleased or delighted

Climbing the ladder: the actions of a drowning person trying to lift themselves out of the water

Clubbies: members of a surf lifesaving club (SLC) who volunteer as lifeguards

Coldie: cold can or bottle of beer

Cooked: exhausted or overwhelmed; could mean heavily intoxicated

Copped/copping it: to receive something very unwelcome

Crook: feeling ill

Dag/daggy: unfashionable or socially awkward; could be an endearment or mild insult

Doona: duvet or comforter

Duck-diving: surfing technique where a surfer pushes their board underwater to dive under a wave

Esky: portable cooler to keep food and drinks cold

Fair dinkum: genuine, real, true

Fin chop: severe laceration or cut caused by the fin of a surfboard

Firey: firefighter

Flash rip: a rip current that develops suddenly without warning

Flat stick: at top speed

Flat white: double shot of espresso with steamed milk

Footy: football, typically AFL

Freo: Fremantle

Frothin': extremely excited or enthusiastic about something

Galah: a bird known for flying into windows; used as an insult for a silly or stupid person

Goon bag: flexible plastic bladder or sack that holds wine sold in a cardboard box

Grommet/grom: a young person learning to surf

Hoon/hooning: reckless, dangerous, antisocial behavior; typically highspeed, irresponsible driving

Icy pole: popsicle

Kook: a surfer with an exaggerated idea of their skill level; they often get in the way of other surfers

Larrikin: mischievous, unruly but goodhearted young person who breaks rules

Lino: linoleum

Lollies: candy of all kinds

Mince: ground meat

Nippers: children participating in the surf lifesaving club's junior development program

Physio: a physio/physical therapist OR the physical therapy itself

Pommies: British people

Pressie: a present/gift

Rapt: very happy or delighted with something

Rashie: formfitting sun safety shirt worn in the water or outdoors to prevent sunburn; originally known as rash guards for surfers to prevent chafing from wetsuits or boards

Ratbag: stupid, untrustworthy or disagreeable person

Resus: resuscitation

Ripper: fantastic, excellent or great

Rock up: to arrive or show up somewhere

Rotto: Rottnest Island; a small scenic island off the coast of Perth, popular for day trips

Salvos: Salvation Army

Sausage sizzle: community fundraiser where sausages are cooked on a grill; often outside Bunnings, a home improvement/building store

Servo: gas station

Shore break/shorey: wave that breaks on a shallow bank close to shore or the shoreline itself

Shout: as a noun it's typically a round of drinks someone is buying; "my shout" is my treat, and you can also "shout" someone something as a verb

Silly season: Christmas and New Year holiday period

Smoked: as a verb, to get beaten or smashed by something like a wave

Snag: sausage

Southerly: wind coming from the south that's typically cooler

Spunk: an attractive person

Spray: to give someone a spray is to scold or lecture them

SRC: Surf Rescue Certificate

Stitch-up: to trick or prank someone; in more serious context to frame or falsely accuse

Strewth: exclamation expressing surprise, dismay or amazement

Stubby holder: Foam or neoprene cozy for beverage cans or bottles to keep them cold

Stubby/stubbies: glass beer bottle

Stuff up: mess up or ruin something; make a mistake

Sunnies: sunglasses

Swag: bedroll used while camping

TAFE: Technical and Further Education; community college offering job-related skills

Taking the piss: teasing or making fun of someone/something in a usually friendly manner

Thongs: flip-flops

Tinnie: can of beer

Togs: swimsuit

Tosser: unpleasant or obnoxious person

Trackies: trackpants

Tradie: general term for a skilled tradesperson such as a plumber, electrician, carpenter, etc.

Triple-0: equivalent of 911; 000 is dialed in emergencies

Ute: utility vehicle; a pickup truck

WA: Western Australia

Wanker: a loser or someone who shows off and thinks they're better than they are; a dickhead

Waterman: someone skilled and at ease in the water

Woolies: Woolworths grocery store

Chapter One

A S ANOTHER WAVE washed over the white sand at Barking Beach under a cloudless sky, Blake reminded himself he was supposed to be watching the water—*not* the lifeguards.

There was one in particular who always caught his attention with long blond hair, a lean swimmer's build, red sunnies, and a crooked smile. Even though he was only in his early twenties, he clearly knew the beach like the back of his hand.

It was impressive to watch him paddle out now, navigating the shore break flawlessly as he rescued a tourist who'd quite literally gotten in over his head. Blake could only hope to be half as skilled in the water eventually, but he was learning.

And he could only hope he might catch the lifeguard's attention one day.

He shifted on his white plastic chair under the sunshade he and his fellow Barking Surf Life Saving Club members had set up. It was a busy Saturday morning, and they were parked in front of the safe swimming area marked with red and yellow flags, keeping watch while the lifeguards spread out over the kilometer-long beach.

The official name was Barkininy Beach, but hardly anyone called it that. It was Barking or "Barkers" to the locals, and it still gave Blake a thrill that he could finally count himself as a bona fide local now.

It was early February, and the days had been hot and dry. It hadn't rained a drop since November, and Blake didn't think he'd seen a single cloud that week. The lifeguards had their work cut out for them. He loved that he and the other clubbies could help even a little bit.

Beside him, Kat pitched their voice higher. "Oh, Damo, you're so brave and handsome."

There was no point denying his little crush since Kat had clocked it the very first week Blake volunteered. He watched Damo bring in the patient, catching a wave that took them right onto the sand.

Blake smiled and muttered, "Yeah, yeah."

Kat lowered their voice an octave and flipped imaginary long hair over a shoulder to impersonate Damo. "It just comes naturally, bro. You're quite brave and handsome yourself. For a clubbie."

Blake and Kat both laughed. The surf lifesaving club had patrolled the beach on weekends and holidays since the nineteen-sixties—long before Barking was busy enough to warrant professional lifeguards. The lifeguards were in charge now, and the rivalry between the two groups was all in good fun. Mostly.

"As if he'd look twice at me," Blake said.

"I'm telling ya, he has."

"And I know you're having me on."

Kat sighed long-sufferingly as they gazed at the throng of people splashing and swimming between the flags. Taking off their red uniform cap, they ran a hand through their tumble of chin-length brown curls. They had dark skin and striking, thick-lashed brown eyes that were often crinkled in laughter.

Kat and Blake wore the same uniform: red cap and shorts and a yellow long-sleeved rashie to protect from the sun emblazoned with *Surf Rescue* in red.

"I've known Damo since we were nippers, and I'm telling ya—he might've only dated chicks when we were at school, but he's got eyes for blokes as well. And he definitely had an eyeful of your arse last week when you were helping that woman up."

Blake groaned. "Right, and I'm sure he was really impressed by me getting smoked by that next wave."

An older woman had struggled in the shore break, mired in sand and tumbled around by the incoming waves. Blake had bent over to help her when another wave broke. It took him off his feet, and what followed had been a comedy of errors as he tried to assist the woman only to have her pull him down more than once.

Kat grinned. "It was like one of those old slapstick routines my gramps loved. Black and white and everything. Except you've got a much hotter arse than those fellas."

"I'll be sure to add that to my profile on the apps."

Not that he'd been very active on them lately. He'd been eager for hookups when he'd first moved to Barking after living back home in the middle of nowhere for three years, but now...

He needed more. It'd been years since he'd had a proper boyfriend, and that was the next item on his plan that he needed to tackle. He needed to go on dates that were more than a few pleasantries—and sometimes not even that—before sex.

About ten meters up the sand amid the clusters of families, sunbakers, and a small group doing yoga headstands, Damo crouched beside the coughing man he'd rescued, speaking to him in what Blake imagined was a gentle tone.

Damo always seemed to wear a smile, that laid-back surfer attitude in place even when he had to be frustrated with patients ignoring the warnings to only swim between the flags.

Speaking of which...

Blake forced his gaze back to the water, watching a few kids splash safely in the shallows before looking out farther to where swimmers bobbed in the swells. Even though he was a volunteer, he still had to focus on his job, and he huffed softly, disappointed in himself for the attention lapse.

Kat said, "Talk to him."

"What? No. He's working."

"I don't mean right this second. Surely you've seen him here surfing? He practically lives at Barking."

"Yeah, but he's incredible. I've only been at it regularly for six months. I learned during uni, but I'm barely better than a grommet at this point."

"Fake it 'til ya make it. You're a fit, gorgeous guy. Ask him to come to Rodeo one night. Then we'll know if I'm right."

"And as soon as I do that, you and the others'll jump out from behind a sandcastle to take the piss. I know newbies get pranked. I—"

For a moment, they both watched a young woman wearing shorts and a T-shirt sputter and cough after mistiming the shore break and copping it in the face.

Then she got up and laughed with her friend, retreating to the sand. Tourists who couldn't swim often went in the water fully dressed, and it could have disastrous consequences. Blake exhaled, glad she was back on dry land.

Kat said, "You're not that new, mate. Been on the team a couple of months now."

"And I'm still waiting for the inevitable prank to happen."

When he'd moved to Barking six months before, the first thing Blake had done after finally finding an apartment was ring the life-saving club to ask when he could join. Now he'd finished his training, completed his certifications, and was a full-fledged clubbie—just like he'd planned.

Check! Another box ticked.

He hadn't just planned it—he'd *dreamed* of it. Barking was everything he'd imagined, from the soft white sand between his toes to the crystal-clear turquoise water under clear, cerulean skies.

To the brave, gorgeous lifeguards.

Blake allowed himself a glimpse of Damo, who was now watching the water, speaking into his radio.

Kat wiped their Aviators with a cloth and said, "If I was gonna prank ya, you'd've had to clean out the clubhouse storage closet and organize the contents alphabetically by now."

Blake frowned. "Does it need organizing? I can come early tomorrow and have a go." He could pull everything out and categorize into groups and subgroups…

Kat shook their head. "Glutton for punishment."

"But if I can help…"

They motioned to the water. "You're helping. You've volunteered both days every weekend *and* Chrissie *and* New Year's."

"I was happy to." He genuinely had been, since the thought of spending Christmas in particular alone in his apartment was decidedly not merry.

He'd have come down to Barking regardless, but being alone in a crowd wasn't much better. Getting to know the other clubbies and sharing a barbecue dinner that night under a starry sky had been magical.

Kat added, "Trust me—that storage closet is above our paygrade. Besides, that wouldn't be a prank. It would just be mean."

Considering they were all volunteers, Kat was probably right. They whistled sharply at a teenage boy. "Oi! Don't even think about leaving that empty bottle in the sand to get broken and stepped on. Yes, you. The one in desperate need of a haircut."

The kid sheepishly fetched the juice bottle and stuffed it into his rucksack before hurrying on.

Blake chuckled, and Kat said, "That's not mean. That's teaching a member of the community to take responsibility for his actions. Suppose I could've left out the commentary on his hair." They grew serious. "I wouldn't tell ya to ask out a bloke if I thought he was straight. We queers have to stick together."

They offered a fist to bump, and Blake did as Kat added, "It's not a stitch-up. Talk to Damo sometime. Bit of a knob, but he means well."

"He's not a knob!"

Kat grinned slyly. "It's adorable how you defend his honor when you don't even know him."

A girl of about eight in pink bathers and a short-sleeved white rashie approached through the growing crowd. Eager for the interruption, Blake jumped up.

"You right, sweetheart?" he asked.

Her chin wobbled, eyes glistening. "I, I—" She bit back a sob. "I can't find my dad." Tears tracked through the white zinc on her pale nose and cheeks.

Blake dropped to his knees, wishing he could give the poor girl a hug but needing to maintain boundaries. "We'll find him, no worries. What's your name?"

"Z—Zoe."

"It's okay. Here, come sit on my chair."

She did, sniffling and shivering even though the morning was so hot that Blake's hair was damp under his uniform cap just from sitting in the shade. She answered questions about her dad's appearance and clothing and when she'd seen him last while Kat radioed the information to the lifeguard tower, which sat at the middle of the beach with storage underneath and lifeguard headquarters and viewing windows up top.

A few of the other clubbies on shift gathered, then fanned out to search. In all likelihood, the man was looking for his daughter or unaware she couldn't find him, but any missing person could potentially be in the water.

Blake grabbed a cold bottle of water from the esky and gave it to Zoe, who sipped between quiet little hiccupped sobs. Crouching beside her, he asked a few questions about school and siblings and mates. Anything to keep her occupied.

"Is this Zoe?" a voice asked.

Blake looked up to see Damo's familiar red sunnies and crooked smile. His long golden hair was damp from the water, curling around his shoulders.

Throat gone dry, Blake forgot how to form words.

"Yes," Zoe said in a tiny voice, peering up at Damo with wide eyes.

"You look like me getting called into the boss's office!" Damo squatted down on the other side of the plastic chair, his bare knee under his black board shorts brushing Blake's for a fleeting moment. "You're not in trouble, I promise. I'm sure your dad's looking for ya. We'll track him down any minute."

Damo was actually *right there* beside Blake—like the surfer poster he'd had in his childhood bedroom come to life.

That poster, of a young Luke Stedman in the nineties carving a wave with his golden hair shining under a spray of water, might as well have been burned into Blake's retinas. He'd found it at Salvos and had carefully pressed out the creases and taped the torn corners.

For a reckless moment, Blake wondered what Damo's hair would feel like between his fingers before coming to his senses.

Kat, who was standing on a chair and searching the crowd, said to Damo, "She was swimming between the flags while her dad had a nap and held down the fort."

"And now you can't find the fort, hey?" Damo asked, giving Zoe a grin. "Happens to the best of us." He pushed up his sunnies, revealing sympathetic blue eyes. "One time when I was your age, I couldn't find my dad for the life of me. It wasn't even this crowded, but he'd vanished. Ended up running home to tell my mum. Meanwhile, poor ol' Dad was turning over every grain of sand."

Damo dug in the sand to illustrate, exaggerating as Zoe

laughed through her tears. Blake's chest filled with warmth as if his heart was actually swelling.

"You did exactly the right thing," Damo said to Zoe. "You came to the clubbies. And if they weren't here, you know to ask us, right?"

He motioned to his long-sleeved blue uniform shirt with *Lifeguard* on the front. While the volunteers were in a combination of red and yellow like the flags planted on the beach in the safe swimming area, the professional lifeguards wore blue and black.

Zoe nodded solemnly.

Damo motioned to Blake. "We're always here to help."

Blake filled with pride to be included as a colleague. To be a helper.

"Here's Dad!" Kat announced.

A lifeguard buggy drove up, beeping the horn to get through the crowd. In the passenger seat was a red-faced man who'd probably aged a decade in the last twenty minutes.

Blake could only imagine the terror of losing a child on a crowded beach. Even with lifeguards and safety flags, if he was ever lucky enough to actually have kids, he'd never let them go swimming without watching every second.

Unbidden, his mother's anguished cry echoed through his mind: *"What about children? Don't you want children?"*

He refocused as Zoe launched herself into her father's arms. The man thanked them all profusely. Presumably, he'd learned his lesson.

"Thanks for that," Damo said as Zoe and her father disappeared back into the crowd. "How ya going, Kat?"

"Can't complain. Have you met our new recruit?"

Blake's heart skipped, heat rushing as Damo's blue eyes swung to him. Wait—he hadn't planned for this! What was he going to say? What was the *right* thing to say? Kat's advice echoed.

Fake it 'til ya make it.

Deep breath. He could start with his name, obviously…

What was his name again?

Before Blake could say anything, Damo's radio squawked to life. "Central to Damo. Little flashy just popped up north of the flags. Don't reckon this bloke can get back to shore on his own. You might be in here."

"Copy, central," Damo said, turning away and peering at the water, all business in a blink. Then he was gone, weaving around sunbakers and returning to where his rescue board waited in a rack on the sand.

"Don't take it personally," Kat said. "Duty calls."

"Of course." Blake picked up the water bottle Zoe had dropped and stowed it in the recycling bag. He gulped from his own bottle, the battered metal familiar under his fingers. "What would I even say?"

Kat dropped their voice to a baritone. "Hiya, Damo. I think you're a spunk, and I reckon we should go for a drink at that new queer club. See where the night takes us."

He almost spit out the water. "A *spunk*? Who are you, my mum?"

Laughing, Kat dropped their growly tone. "You're from the outback. Bit behind the times."

"I went to uni in Melbourne!"

"Yeah, but didn't you move back after?"

Blake's smile tightened. "For a few years."

"Why'd ya go home after uni anyway?"

He waved a dismissive hand. "Family stuff." Straightening, he squinted at the shore break. "Hey, that kid has a body board." No boards were permitted between the flags.

"Go on, then." Kat nodded to two other clubbies nearing. "Billy and Trish are back from patrol anyway. I'll introduce you to Damo later."

"Forget it. It's just a little crush." He headed toward the water.

"We'll see about that!" Kat shouted.

Blake shook his head with a smile as he jogged across the hot sand. He'd accomplished so much on his to-do list since moving to Barking, but as much as he wanted to add *"Date hot lifeguard of my dreams"* to his plan, he'd always been a realist.

Chapter Two

A S PALE ARMS shot up from the turquoise water, waving madly, Damo groaned. When he was a kid, a Wednesday afternoon at Barkers would never be this busy, even at the height of summer. Too bad the clubbies didn't volunteer during the week.

The radio had been running hot with rescue after rescue, and he'd just paddled in with a tourist who'd ignored the warnings not to swim at the north end of the beach.

Now, here were two more—young men wrestling with their useless boogie boards they'd probably bought for ten bucks at Target.

Damo grabbed his radio from the buggy parked on the sand and tossed down the sunnies he'd only just put back on. "Central, I'm getting wet again. Croc's got two blokes out the back." He shielded his eyes from the glare, keeping track of them.

"Copy that—we see them. I'll send Cody down to help, but it'll take him a minute to get through the crowd."

Grabbing the long rescue board by its rope handle, Damo raced back into the surf. The tide was low, and the rip the lifeguards called the Croc was dragging out the boogie boarders at three meters per second.

On his knees, Damo paddled hard with both hands. He

punched over a swell in the impact zone, shaking saltwater and his hair out of his face. He used the power of the current to get him out to the two flailing men, who were full-on panicking.

One had the arm rope from the boogie board around his ankle as if it was a surfboard leash, and Damo choked down frustration. They had no business swimming outside the safe, flagged area. Even then, they should probably stay waist-deep, and those cheap pieces of Styrofoam wouldn't do shit.

But now that Barking had become a hot tourist destination after being named Australia's top beach, it was packed with people who had no bloody business in the water.

Damo kept his eyes locked on them as he neared, assessing which patient to grab first. Normally, the lifeguards went for the person farthest out, but the nearer man's ginger hair was plastered over his eyes, and he bobbed under, disappearing for long seconds. His boogie board had disappeared, finally torn away. He looked to have about two gasps left in him.

Then he wouldn't come up.

Paddling hard, Damo watched him go under again in the one-meter swells rolling by. Heart in his throat, he willed the man back above the surface. The bloke remained hidden, swallowed by the Indian Ocean, his mate beyond him shouting, trying to fight the Croc head-on instead of swimming sideways out of the rip.

Ten meters away from the closest man now.

Come on! Stay with me!

Five. Two.

Plunging an arm in and reaching for the blur under the clear water, Damo snatched the redhead up by the hair, hauling him over the rescue board. The man was deathly pale, his ginger freckles stark, but he gasped and muttered.

Damo had no time for relief—he still had to get the other patient. He glanced back to see if Cody was in the water yet. No sign. He knew Cody was coming as fast as he could, but for the moment, Damo was alone with two lives in his hands.

He struggled to get the hefty ginger man on the board fully, pushing his head down near the nose before paddling with the guy's arse in his face. Rescuing two adults with one board could go bad in a blink, but he had no choice. He stroked, yelling at the other patient in the water to stay calm. The man flapped and squawked something in a thick Irish accent.

Damo yelled, "You're okay! Grab my board. I've got ya!" He sat up and straddled the rescue board, reaching for the bloke's shoulder and—

They tipped, the Irishman in the water so panicked that he was going to drown them all. Damo sucked in a breath, keeping an iron grip on his board as he went under. He shoved at the panicking patient, trying to get a safe distance between them before he resurfaced, the stupid boogie board whacking him.

The thrashing man grasped blindly, pushing Damo under to keep himself afloat. Choking down the flare of fear, Damo held his breath, relying on his training and years of building his lung capacity. Punching at the bloke's balls, he hit close enough to his target, and the man released him.

Damo resurfaced, still gripping his board like the lifeline it was, his heart pounding. The panicking patient clutched at him again desperately, but someone was suddenly there on a surfboard, shoving hard at the man. Damo gulped in a grateful breath as he straddled the rescue board, blinking saltwater from his eyes.

"Stop!" he shouted at panicking patient number two while grabbing the dazed ginger man around the chest and keeping his head out of the water.

The surfer who'd come to lend a hand looked familiar, but he wasn't one of the locals Damo had known forever. Looking a few years older than Damo, he was white with a tanned, round face and short brown hair, and he was solidly built, dragging the worn-out ginger man sideways over his surfboard with a grunt. Swells lifted them all rhythmically under the sun's powerful glare.

Damo kept the nose of his board between himself and the Irishman, who clung to it as another swell rolled by. The nut-punch had apparently taken the edge off his panic, thankfully. Damo's heart still thumped, but he kept his voice even.

"You're safe now! Breathe." To the surfer, he said, "Thanks, mate."

"No worries." The surfer kept a strong hand on the whimpering, coughing patient's shoulder. "Guess even the lifeguards need rescuing sometimes, hey?" He smiled, but he wasn't being a dick about it. He had freckles across his cheeks and nose, and his lips were a pretty—

Stop thinking about that!

Damo nodded. "Yeah, I was in the shit there."

"Here's your backup." The surfer nodded his chin toward shore.

Damo sighed in relief as he watched Cody paddle hard toward them, a determined look on his face. He was small but mighty.

To the patient who'd freaked, Damo ordered, "Get rid of that boogie board." He leaned forward and tugged the leash free before tossing away the light board, which was decorated with a Teenage Mutant Ninja Turtle. "Trust me, cheap Styrofoam Michelangelo won't save ya, and it'll only get in our way. Get on my board. Head down the front." The man struggled to follow orders, first putting his head toward Damo at the rear.

Finally, Damo had him on, both of them flat on their stomachs. He angled to shore and caught a wave, nodding at Cody as Cody took the other patient from the surfer. Mia was waiting on shore with the medikit, her long, black ponytail dancing in the breeze.

On the sand, the patient who'd panicked collapsed on his arse. His face was bright red, and he gulped in a massive sob that shook his sunburned shoulders. Damo crouched beside him. "It's okay.

You'll be right."

"I c-could have killed you!" He trembled violently.

Damo gave him a few pats on the back. He wasn't stoked that he'd had to fight the guy off, but that was what panic did to people. "You were off your head. Next time swim between the flags. It's okay, mate. Take some deep breaths."

"I'm so sorry. Feckin' hell."

"No dramas," Damo said, watching Cody and Mia get oxy on the pale ginger man, whose face was too gray. "We'll have to call the ambo for your buddy from the looks of him. Should check you over too. Even if you feel okay, you could have inhaled some water."

The man nodded and apologized over and over, and Damo repeated that it was all right, staying with him while keeping an eye on the water until the ambos rocked up.

Cody stopped Damo from leaving with a squeeze of his shoulder, his expression serious. His brown hair curled over his sunburned ears, dripping water. He was wiry and compact and had a sure grip on Damo.

"You right? That looked hectic. Sorry it took me so long. Could barely get through the crowd." He nodded at the beach, which was chockers with tourist families under bright umbrellas and all sorts of people.

"It was intense, but that surfer backed up."

"Yeah, good thing." Cody nodded his chin at something behind Damo before giving his shoulder another squeeze and returning to the patients.

The surfer who'd helped was standing there with his mango-colored longboard under an arm, his half wetsuit that ended above his knees unzipped and peeled down to his waist. Water glistened on his bare skin in the summer sunlight.

He was a few inches taller than Damo and stockier. An average guy—not ripped, but sturdy and strong. Tattoos spread over his left ribs—four simple black birds in flight with wings wide. There were tan lines on his arms, and dark hair scattered over his chest and around his nipples.

Not that Damo *noticed*.

He definitely didn't notice a drop of water hanging on the end of one dark pink disc on the surfer's strong chest. Nope.

Stop thinking about nipples!

He realized with a jolt that he was standing there staring. But the surfer didn't seem to mind, watching him right back in a silence that should have been awkward but felt strangely…electric.

The surfer's eyes were light hazel-brown, and he eyed Damo with a quiet intensity that made his stomach flip like he was on his surfboard paddling hard for a set—anticipation zipping through him laced with a twist of nerves.

"They going to be right?" the surfer asked. A drop of water clung to his full lips, and he brushed it away. There was a bit of scruff on his face. Damo had never kissed anyone with scruff.

And you're not kissing him, you boofhead!

"Uh, yeah. Thanks for your help. You're a legend." Damo held up his hand for a slap-shake.

The surfer took it, squeezing firmly as he said, "Blake Holbrook." His voice was low, his hand work-rough and big, and there was no reason for Damo to notice that either. Or to kind of like it? But he'd been liking things lately that he hadn't thought about before.

Well, hadn't thought *much* about before. But these days, he couldn't stop noticing people in new ways. Bloody confusing ways.

"Damian Williams. Damo." He suddenly clocked the surfer as he let go of his big hand. "Hey, you're one of the clubbies, right? Thought you looked familiar."

Blake licked his lips, glancing around nervously for some reason Damo couldn't suss out. "Didn't think you'd really noticed me."

"You were looking after that lost kid on the weekend." He was pretty sure he'd noticed Blake volunteering before that too. Had he been the bloke with the—

He flushed. Right. The bloke with the nice meaty arse.

Blake seemed to want to say something else before finally nodding. Twitching his fingers and spreading his toes in the warm sand, Damo glanced over at the patients. The ginger guy seemed to be pinking up with the oxy.

"He was cooked," Damo said before taking a deep breath and blowing it out. The patients were back on shore. It hadn't been pretty, but he'd done his job.

"Must be scary. I haven't had to do a real rescue yet."

Damo tried to shrug it off. "Can be. That ginger bloke was as close to drowning as you ever want to be. Glad you were here to help. Did you chuck a sickie?"

"Nah, I'm a garbo. I do an eight-day fortnight, so three days off a week." Blake cleared his throat and stood straighter, putting on an official voice. "I should say I'm a waste services operator."

Damo laughed. "Sweet. Gotta love the council jobs." He gazed out at the water, spotting a head going out in the Croc. He'd be in again soon. "I always knew I'd be a lifeguard, so lucky for me council has the budget. Can't imagine anything else. Being in an office?" He shuddered dramatically.

"Yep. It's not glamorous emptying bins, but it pays well, and it's a steady job since people will always make heaps of garbage. And I've got surfing time. I'm really glad I was here." Blake nodded to the patient who'd panicked hard. "He could have drowned you. You were very kind to him just now."

Damo shrugged but secretly he was chuffed. Not that he had any reason to want to impress a clubbie he didn't even know.

He scanned the waves and said, "People will drown their own husbands and wives when they panic. Like I told him, he was off his head. I don't take it personally." He hesitated, then whispered, "And I admit, I wasn't feeling so kind when I was cursing them as

I paddled out."

"You hide it well."

Blake's voice was low and steady and…Damo liked hearing it. He tugged on the purple cord he wore around his neck, recently braided by his baby sister, Tabitha, as a lucky talisman to keep him safe on the job. "Say, where do you live?"

Blake blinked and licked his lips. They probably tasted salty… "North Barking."

"Are you new around here? Thought I knew all the locals." Blake was definitely Aussie judging by the accent.

"More or less. Moved here from South Australia in July."

"You're good in the water for a rookie. Maybe I'll see you around. I surf when I'm not working."

"I know."

The skin on the back of Damo's neck prickled, which was probably just the saltwater drying in the sun—though his hair brushed the tops of his shoulder blades. The sensation definitely wasn't a rush from being noticed.

Or from the intense way Blake watched him.

Damo realized he had to say something as he shifted more hot sand through his toes and glued his eyes to the waves. "Cool."

He could smell coconut tanning oil on the breeze, probably coming from the hot girls in bikinis stretched out nearby on colored towels. He scanned the water, too aware of Blake's eyes on him, his skin tingling. "Thanks again, mate. I owe ya."

"No, of course you don't. I'm glad I helped."

"I can still shout ya a beer sometime." He had plenty of friends. Why was he inviting out the new clubbie?

Nothin' wrong with being friendly!

Blake's thick eyebrows shot up. "Yeah?" He grinned, his cheeks dimpling.

Damo had to smile back as he shrugged, his shoulders weirdly tense. "Sure."

"I'll—" Blake hesitated, then said in a rush, "I'll be at Rodeo on Friday night in Freo if you're not doing anything."

"That new club? I think I heard it was good."

He didn't go out in Fremantle much at all these days, so he wasn't sure why he was pretending to be in the know. He actually wasn't much for dancing since he sucked at it. Sometimes his mates went to the clubs in Perth to pick up chicks, but Damo preferred pubs or parties.

"Yeah, it's a fun crowd. Diverse."

"Cool."

Wait, was it a gay club? Now that he thought about it, Damo remembered Cody trying to convince his boyfriend Liam to go with absolutely no luck.

"No dramas if you can't make it."

Damo was about to say, yeah, nah. He'd be at home Friday night with Tabby anyway. Instead, the words that came out of his mouth as he monitored a few swimmers were, "Maybe I'll see you there."

Waaaaaait. What? No, he wouldn't see anyone at a club! Where had *that* come from? Was it the power of this bloke's dimples? Not to mention his nipples…

Before Damo could take it back, Blake said, "Cool. I'll let you get back to work," and lifted a hand in a wave before disappearing into the crowd of umbrellas and endless people, at least twenty thousand of them cramming onto the beach.

Returning to the buggy he'd parked on the sand, Damo picked up binoculars to watch the swimmer out the back who was definitely not getting out of the Croc's grip without help. No point in putting his shirt back on.

He checked on a few other swimmers about to get into trouble and hopped on the megaphone to tell them to come back to shore.

Why had he said that to Blake? No way Damo was going to a dance club on Friday night. He'd be working that day, and it would probably be full on again since the forecast called for sun and heat.

Look, Blake seemed like a good bloke, but Friday night, Damo'd have a feed and a few beers, then hang out with Tabby and hear about the latest year-eight drama from school.

Still…

The idea of not spending the night at home, of actually going out, away from those four walls and everything inside it…

Guilt stabbed. If he went out alone, he'd be leaving Tabby to deal with Dad. She already did more than any kid should have to.

No chance. No, he wasn't going *dancing* at a maybe-gay bar with some cute clubbie he just met.

An undeniable thrill crashed the guilt party. Fine, yeah, the clubbie was cute, all right? Blake was cute. More than.

As he tracked the swimmer, Damo thought of how Blake had appeared out of nowhere, shoving away the panicking patient like something out of a movie.

Damo was the one who was supposed to be saving people, but he had to admit it felt amazing to have someone charge to his rescue for a change. Surfers often lent a hand, keeping patients afloat until lifeguards arrived, but this had been a little more…dramatic.

Butterflies flapped in his belly. Sure, it was normal to have that adrenaline rush after a big rescue, but he tingled all over thinking of Blake.

Guilt roared back to remind him that he had responsibilities and he couldn't just go swanning off to a club. Sure, it wasn't like he'd never gone out over the years. But things at home hadn't been like…this.

Thumb on his radio, he said, "Central, I'm gonna be in here."

Picking up the rescue board, he cleared his mind of everything but getting past the shorey and paddling as hard as he could.

Chapter Three

AFTER TRYING ON five different shirts, Blake cycled through them again. He was set on his black skinny jeans and Doc Martens, but if Damo did actually come to the club…

"He won't," Blake repeated to his reflection, eyeing the sleeveless black mesh shirt. It was fairly sheer, and in the bright light of his bathroom, his chest hair and nipples were extremely prominent.

A surge of confidence buoyed him, and as he rubbed a dab of pomade between his hands, he allowed himself to relive paddling over to help Damo.

Blake was grinning as he remembered shoving away the Irish tourist and making sure Damo was okay. Practically like a real lifeguard. He'd truly helped and been useful.

And Jesus, Damo was *gorgeous*. The swirl of memories played through his head like a movie: Damo's crooked smile, digging in the sand to make the scared little girl laugh, running into the surf to save lives, strong arms slicing through the water as he paddled out like one of the surfing gods Blake had daydreamed about…

Refocusing, Blake smoothed down a few stray hairs and examined his look again. Yes. Black mesh. Even if Damo didn't come tonight—which he wouldn't—there'd be other blokes to pick up if he was in the mood. Why go for subtlety?

With a nod, Blake returned to his bedroom and hung up the other shirts in his closet, making sure the hangers faced the same way. It was still far too early to be getting ready, but he couldn't just half-watch *MasterChef* and pace.

In the white-tiled bathroom, he pulled out his little blue makeup bag. He'd learned to put on eyeliner in uni with the help of his friend Ashley, who was now married with kids in country Victoria but still DM'd him makeup tutorials.

Wearing his garbo uniform of high-vis orange during the week left him keen to dress up when he went out for the night. He'd experimented in uni with different styles before settling on this look. It was simple—eyeliner and glossy lipstick paired with tight clothes—but it still felt...indulgent.

Maybe a little forbidden too.

After a swipe of lippy, he blotted and gave himself a smile in the mirror, examining the color choice. Hmm. Too dark? He wiped it off and tried another.

Dressing up was his little treat for himself. He didn't want to do it every day—if he wasn't at work, he was surfing or volunteering at Barking, and it was far too hot and wet for makeup at the beach.

Even if it wasn't, if he did it every day, it wouldn't be special somehow. It was perfect for going out. Satisfied with his red gloss, he uncapped his eyeliner and started penciling under his right eye. Though...

What would Damo think?

Blake hesitated, examining himself critically, his confidence faltering. He'd picked up plenty of blokes when he was in his glam outfits. Besides, Damo wasn't even going to show. Blake would see him again on the weekend at the beach, wave awkwardly, and go back to his sexy surfer daydreams.

His phone buzzed in his pocket with the rhythmic chimes of a video call, and he nearly dropped it in the toilet when he saw his mother's face on the screen.

Shit!

He couldn't answer wearing makeup, so she'd just have to wait until morning.

But what if something was wrong? What if she needed his help?

Groaning, Blake fumbled for his makeup remover and squeezed too much onto a cotton ball before scrubbing at the half line of charcoal under his eye.

He flipped on the tap and splashed water over his face, his eye burning from the remover. As he grabbed a towel with one hand, he swiped his screen with the other.

"Hey, Mum. You okay?"

"What? Fine, love." She gave Blake a wonderful view of her chin and up her nose.

"Is Dad—"

"Doing me head in like usual. Doc says he's not supposed to drink, and of course he won't listen to me."

The surge of adrenaline morphed into frustration. Why did he let her get him into a panic? He could have just kept his makeup on and rang her back without video. Everything was *fine*.

"Mum, lift up the phone," he snapped. It was clearly sitting on the kitchen benchtop.

"Hold your horses," she said, even though she'd been the one to ring him. "What's got your knickers in a twist? I'm finishing up another batch of potatoes."

He didn't have to ask what kind—it was Friday, which meant the pub was serving bangers and mash with whatever veg was in season or on sale that week. Dessert would be sticky date pudding with custard.

The rhythmic thudding of the potato masher was reassuringly familiar, and Blake breathed deeply, reminding himself his mother hadn't done anything wrong by wanting to talk.

With the camera still only showing the top of her worn green apron and right up her nose, Mum went on. "He says when a customer shouts the drink, he has to take it or he'll offend them. Like they have any place else to go in two hundred Ks."

"He could just add the cost of a drink to their tab and not drink it."

"And I told him—" Mum lifted the phone. Her bottle blonde hair was short as always, and the wrinkles around her mouth creased even more as she frowned. "Nah, can't do that. If the fellas pay for a drink, it has to be drunk. I told him Frank and Daryl will be thrilled to save the money if he says he's not allowed."

"Darl, the doc said I can have two drinks!" Dad said from a distance.

Mum stepped back, shouting, "Two a bloody *week*, and you know it!"

Dad replied something Blake couldn't make out, and he sighed as Mum shouted back.

The kitchen behind her was the same old metal shelving and banged-up brown cabinets. Blake could almost feel the worn lino under his feet as he washed endless dishes and listened to the twang of country music and loud murmur of conversation from the pub.

Her face filling the frame, Mum raised a hand to rub her eye, mashed potato stuck on her small diamond ring and wedding band that she never took off. "I wish you were here, Blakey. He listens to you."

That was…debatable, but warmth flowed through him to hear the endearment. When he was little, Mum had sung him a song at night to the tune of "Waltzing Matilda."

"Bedtime for Blakey, bedtime for Blakey, closing his eyes and going to sleep…"

"Can you have a chat to him soon?" she asked.

"Of course." He had to help, and he was pleased by Mum's

grateful smile.

"That's our boy." Her smile vanished. "And your sister's being a right you-know-what at the moment. Did I tell you?"

She hadn't—though it was the same argument as always—and he sat on the side of the bed, *mmm-ing* and agreeing with her when necessary.

"It was so much easier when you were here, love."

"I know, but I have to work." That old tug-of-war of guilt raised its head. There was no way he was living in Blinman again. Never. Yet the thought that Mum and Dad needed his help pulled at him.

"We would've been lost without you when I was crook. Such a good son."

The familiar tangle of love and guilt and undeniable pride battled in him. "Thanks, Mum."

"And I know that garbo gig seems to be a good one, but if it doesn't pan out, you know you can come back here in a blink. Always a place here, love."

He was determined to never live in Blinman again, but he nodded and smiled.

"Did I tell you we had to hire that useless Douglas girl since Camden Martin went off to uni like you did? With your brothers up in Queensland, and Ella in Adelaide, who'll run this place when we're gone?"

Not me. "Don't worry. We'll figure it all out."

She smiled tenderly. "You really should have become a doctor. I'm sure you could convince your patients to follow your orders."

"You need to be good at maths and science for that. My English lit degree wouldn't cut it."

"You *were* good at maths and science!"

"I was all right, but I didn't like it enough to do it in uni." He leaned over and reached for the glass of water beside his bed. "Look, Mum—"

She gasped, her voice rising. "What on earth are you wearing?"

Too late, he realized his sheer black shirt was visible. Guts twisting, he brought his phone closer. "Nothing." The way she could make him feel like a naughty child in an instant…

Her smile had vanished, and an awkward silence stretched out as she mashed again, still holding the phone in one hand. *Thud, thud, thud.*

Eyes downcast, she finally said, "What will they think at work?"

He tried to laugh. "I'm not wearing club gear to empty the bins."

Eyebrows raised, she said, "What kind of clubs are you—" She broke off, quickly adding, "Never mind!" as if he was about to launch into a description of S&M bondage.

"It's just a shirt, Mum."

"Barely." She mashed like her life depended on it, still not looking at him. She glanced sharply to her left and hissed, "Your father's coming. Don't let him see!"

Only Blake's face was visible now on the screen. "I have to go anyway."

Mum painted on a smile, still not actually looking at him. "All right, love. Have a good—" Her smile cracked, and she stared with imploring, tearful eyes. "Be careful. Promise me."

Part of him wanted to remind her it wasn't the nineties, and he was *fine*, but he couldn't bear the worry etched on her face. "I promise. Love you."

Shoulders slumping, he flopped back on the bed. He didn't feel like going out anymore. He'd text Kat to tell them he couldn't go, take off his silly mesh shirt, and have an early night. He could surf early before his volunteer shift. It wasn't as if Damo would actually show, and Kat had plenty of mates to hang out with.

Pushing to his feet, he returned to the bathroom to put away his makeup. He caught his reflection and stopped.

He really did look good in that shirt.

Taking a long, deep breath, he shook off the *ugh* and picked up the eyeliner. He'd moved away from home for the last time. Even if Mum and Dad needed help again, he wasn't living in Blinman. He was in Barking by the ocean like he'd dreamed about for so, so long.

And he *might* have a date with a hot surfer just like he'd dreamed about.

Even if Damo didn't show, Blake needed this.

And what would Damo think of the makeup? Maybe he'd think it was weird, but…

No, Damo seemed chill. Not that Blake knew him, but his gut told him it was okay. And if it wasn't, better to find out now.

Not that Damo would actually come.

〰〰〰

A COUPLE OF hours later, Blake buzzed from a gin cocktail and the pulsing beat. Damo hadn't appeared, but the disappointment was tempered by dancing with Kat and a few of their mates. He was slowly getting to know Kat's circle of friends well enough to chat to and have a few laughs.

Kat took a drink—then made a choking sound, eyes bulging. Before Blake could determine if they were having some kind of seizure, they gulped and yelled too loudly even on the dance floor, "He's here!"

"Who?" Blake spun around.

"The king of England. Who'd ya think?" Kat grabbed him and ducked behind a pole as if this was suddenly a spy thriller and they were taking cover from foreign operatives. "Ten o'clock."

"I thought it was eleven by now?"

"Not the bloody time!" Kat smacked his arm and nodded to the left.

Feeling ridiculous and a bit giddy, Blake peeked out from behind the pillar.

It was really him.

Damo stood a few meters inside the club with his hands stuffed into his pockets, gazing around anxiously. He wore skinny jeans and a short-sleeved button-down shirt in blue that matched his eyes and showed off the muscles in his arms.

"I told ya so." Kat grinned. "Now go get 'im, tiger."

Acid bubbled in Blake's stomach. "But…"

"No ifs, ands, or buts. You look fantastic, and he's here *for you*. Now go stand by the bar, show off your magnificent arse, and let him find you. You've got this."

"Fake it 'til I make it?"

With a decisive slap on said arse, Kat pushed him toward the bar.

Chapter Four

THE BASS FROM some Kylie remix reverberated through Damo's bones, rattling his skull. Throat dry, he searched for Blake, his armpits already damp.

The club had an ironic cowboy theme that explained the name, but he wasn't sure why they'd bothered. As long as there were cheap-enough drinks and a beat, what more did you need in a club? Not that he was an expert.

Damo didn't even know what the hell he was doing there, but he couldn't just not show up when he owed a shout to a bloke who'd possibly saved his life. No, it wouldn't be right, he told himself for the hundredth time.

All afternoon, he'd looked for Blake in the surf lineup in between scanning for trouble and hauling tourists out of the rips. If he'd spotted him, they might've been able to have a beer after Damo's shift, but he hadn't, so there'd been no choice but to show up to the club.

No sign of Blake now, either. Pulse matching the beat, Damo fiddled with the braided cord from Tabby as he scanned the club, feeling dressed up even though other people were wearing fancier.

After shifts at Barking, he normally went to the pub with other lifeguards wearing shorts, a tee, and thongs on his bare feet. Tonight, he'd put on suede Pumas. He'd fussed with his hair.

He'd ignored Tabby's teasing and insisted he wasn't going on a date.

Because he *wasn't*.

Guilt tugged, and he pulled out his phone. Tabby had proclaimed that at thirteen years old—and three-quarters—she was completely capable of watching TV, checking on Dad in his room, and going to bed by eleven before Mum came home from her shift at the hospital.

It was almost her bedtime, and Damo texted to make sure she didn't need him to come home. Her immediate reply was a string of eye-roll emojis that he took for a no. He sent her back his own eye-roll, quickly following it up with a heart.

Damo had asked Mia to come out for a drink, but she had plans with her new boyfriend. Once upon a time, he'd been bummed that she was utterly uninterested in him, but they were better off as mates. Mixing work and a relationship was a bad idea.

"Though really good mates wouldn't make you go to a club alone," he muttered. To be fair, he hadn't mentioned where he was going. He'd considered asking Cody, but he and Liam would be going to bed early since they were opening the lifeguard tower on Saturday morning.

And sure, Damo had plenty of other mates he could have asked. But he hadn't, and he wasn't sure exactly why. It wasn't like there was anything wrong with him meeting up with Blake. It wasn't a bloody date.

He elbowed through a crowd to get to the other side of the dance floor, swiping at a splash of beer on his arm. The floor was already sticky, and he was damn glad he hadn't worn his thongs.

Even if it *was* a date—which it wasn't—no one would care. He knew Cody and Mia wouldn't. After all, Cody was gay, so he definitely wouldn't judge Damo for being…curious.

And he owed Blake a drink!

Damo laughed at himself, the music loud enough that the

mob around him didn't notice.

Curious.

He was being a dickhead. Making a big deal out of nothing. Everyone was curious at some point, right? Didn't mean anything. He was there because he owed Blake a beer.

For all he knew, Blake wasn't even at the club after all. They'd only spoken for a minute or two. Blake had probably forgotten all about it when he'd disappeared into the throng of people on the beach that day.

The thing was, the thought that Blake wasn't there to meet him made Damo's heart sink with something he couldn't deny was disappointment.

"Such a dickhead," he whispered. Blake was still fairly new to the area—he was probably just keen for more mates. Which was great, because Damo dated chicks, not blokes.

And he hadn't even had a girlfriend in a year. Everything at home had gotten worse, and he didn't have the time.

As he scanned the club's shadows, blinking into flashing lights, he checked out a group of girls in short skirts laughing under the huge antlers on the wall. He could go chat one of them up if Blake didn't show, but fuck, he was tired.

"This is mental," he muttered. If he didn't spot Blake in a minute, he was leaving. He was—

Then he did spot Blake.

Or thought he did?

Damo picked out the wide shoulders and solid frame in the growing crowd by the bar. Though the sheer, sleeveless, skintight black shirt made him think twice. Black skinny jeans clung to the guy's strong legs like a wetsuit—and there was that meaty arse.

The man turned.

Air punched from Damo's lungs like it was his turn for a blow to the nuts. It was indeed Blake he'd spotted, and along with the black see-through shirt, he was wearing makeup. Not, like, full drag—not that there was anything wrong with that—but his lips were dark and shiny and that looked like eyeliner?

Damo supposed it was guyliner. Whatever it was, it gave Blake a fierce, focused look. And he was staring right at Damo, a slow, sexy smile spreading over his face.

Wait—*sexy?*

A silver disco ball spun overhead, and lights bounced around in time with the *duff-duff* of the bass. As Blake approached him, Damo realized he'd shaved off the scruff, but there was a hint of five o'clock shadow.

"Hey!" Damo shouted way too loudly.

"You came!"

"Um, yep. Here I am in all my glory. And here you are in yours!" He cringed as the awkward words escaped. "Far out."

Blake's smile faltered. "Too much?"

"No! I didn't mean anything by it." His cheeks went hot. "I talk too much. Ignore me."

A furrow formed between Blake's brows. "I want to hear what you have to say."

"Careful what you wish for, mate. Hasn't Kat told you I'm a pork chop?"

A smile tugged at Blake's glossy lips. "I believe the word they used was 'knob.'"

"See?" He had to laugh, his shoulders relaxing a fraction. "Look, I think you're rockin' it. Honest."

Blake grinned. "Thanks. I like dressing up a bit when I go clubbing. Spend all day in a grubby uniform."

"Looks great." *Great?* Was that the right word? Was that a stupid thing to say? Probably. "Let me shout you that beer. Which kind?"

"Whatever you're drinking."

Damo pushed past a few people to get to the bartender. He pulled out a fifty from his pocket and realized his hands were sweating. He wiped them on his jeans, which was pointless since the bottles of Little Creatures pale ale were instantly damp in the humidity of all the bodies in the club. Impulsively, he ordered double shots of tequila as well.

He returned to Blake with two drinks in each hand. They downed the shots with grimaces and clinked the necks of their bottles.

Damo said, "Here's to saving me from being drowned by a mad Irishman."

Blake grinned, the lippy gleaming and dimples out. He said something Damo couldn't hear.

Damo chugged half his beer to chase the burn of cheap tequila. He shouted, "What?"

Blake nodded toward a corner of the club and reached out to circle Damo's wrist, his fingers warm as he tugged him through the crowd. They reached stairs to a rooftop patio where a few people in a corner vaped and others chatted and drank.

Blake let go of his wrist, and Damo's skin felt warm and damp in the cool evening air. The bass from downstairs thrummed through his feet.

"Don't have to yell up here," Blake said.

"Cool." Damo nodded, trying to keep his eyes off Blake's nipples. It was too dark on the roof to even see them, but his gaze kept dropping down over Blake's body. "Um… That makes sense."

Did it? What were they even talking about?

Blake laughed, a soft rumble. "I think so." He watched Damo with a little smile tugging at his shiny lips, and Damo stared at those lips and wondered…

Everything.

He wondered it all in such a chaotic mess that he couldn't even organize his thoughts. He felt jittery the way he did watching tourists ignore the warnings and swim in the rips, knowing it was only a matter of time before he'd have to paddle out and haul them back.

With Blake, it was only a matter of time until…what?

"So, um…" Blake said.

Damo shifted from foot to foot. He had to say something. Pretend Blake was just another bloke. He *was* just another bloke! Damo needed to talk to him like he would to anyone.

He blurted, "Were you a garbo in South Australia too? Are you from Adelaide? How old are you?" The silver light of the full moon peeked out from clouds, and now Damo could definitely make out Blake's nipples. His chest hair poked out in a few places. Damo had to fist his fingers to stop the insane urge to touch.

"I'm twenty-seven and from Blinman. Back of beyond in the Flinders Ranges. Old mining town, although the copper mine's been closed more than a hundred years, and calling it a 'town' is generous. Last I heard, there were forty-three people living there. My parents run the hotel and pub, and I worked for them doing dishes until I went to uni."

"Wow. Forty-three. How does the pub survive? Is it one of those classic outback hotels?"

"Yep. Heritage listed, and it's been in Mum's family for generations. Twelve rooms upstairs with shared bathrooms and covered balcony across the front. But it's the pub that keeps the lights on. Folks come in from the sheep stations, and there are a surprising number of tourists passing through and visiting the old mine. Blinman's biggest claim to fame before opening the mine for tours in 2011 was our historic slag heap."

Damo laughed, a little bit of nervous tension easing as he did. "I'm sure it's a spectacular heap."

"You've never seen slag quite like it." Blake swallowed a mouthful of beer, his Adam's apple bobbing above the neckline of the sheer shirt. Damo wondered if the material was as silky as it looked.

Blake said, "Kat mentioned they grew up with you here?"

"Yep, Barkers born and bred. Nowhere better. You've found the right spot, that's for sure."

"I think so. Always dreamed of living on the water. I wanted to come to Perth for uni, but I ended up in Melbourne with a scholarship."

"Great city." Why was he acting like he'd been anywhere near it? "So I hear."

"Oh, yeah. The cafes, the culture. I had a great time. It's just sadly lacking that oceanfront view."

"If you went to uni, how'd you end up a garbo?" Wait, what did he just say? "Not that there's anything wrong with it!"

Stop. Being. A. Dickhead.

"Nah, it's a fair question, although these days a degree doesn't guarantee a job, that's for sure. I studied English lit and art history. I knew going in that there're few jobs in the arts except for teaching, so that was my plan. Then I did a volunteer placement in a classroom and realized that even though I want kids, I do not want thirty of them at the same time."

Damo shuddered at the thought. "You made the right call on that one. Teachers should be paid millions like footy players." He wanted kids too, but one at a time. The whole idea of kids seemed very, very far into the future.

"Definitely. So, I changed my plan. I love reading, and I decided to write the next great Aussie novel."

"Wow. And?"

"Oh, I'm hard at work on it," he said seriously. "I'm about two chapters in, and I haven't written a word in seven years."

Damo laughed as the word "hard" echoed in his mind.

"Writing's not for me. Honestly, I didn't even really want to go to uni that much, but I had top marks and needed a reason to leave home."

Damo frowned. "Your folks expected you to stay in a town of

forty-three people?"

Blake's smile tightened. "Well, my older brothers and sister had already left. I'm the youngest."

"Did your sister and brothers need a reason to leave?"

Shifting and looking away, Blake said, "No."

Shit, Damo was stuffing this up. Why had he asked that? "Sorry, mate. I didn't mean to—family stuff's hard." Didn't he know it.

Blake gave him a smile. "It is."

The fact that Blake had his own family dramas was weirdly reassuring. Probably couldn't compete with Damo's. Not that it was a competition!

Change the bloody subject!

"But now you're here where you want to be."

A smile bloomed on Blake's handsome face, his cheeks dimpling. "I am. Getting my life back on track. Trying to take it one step at a time and not get too ahead of myself." He laughed. "Imagine thinking I could just write a novel and make a living at it."

Damo chuckled. "Easy as."

"Fortunately, I realized pretty quickly that I needed a better plan. I got my heavy truck licenses during uni and drove during school breaks. I was picking up contract work again in Adelaide, but there's a big shortage of drivers in WA the last few years. Couldn't believe my luck to get hired near Barking. I'm working inland in Armadale, but it's an easy commute, especially at four thirty in the morning."

"Long days, or do you get surfing time in the arvo?"

"Depends on the day. It can be ten or twelve hours, but I start early. Always try to get here for a few waves before sunset."

"Sweet."

"Yep. Barking's where I want to be." His eyes locked with Damo's. "Exactly where I want to be."

After gulping the rest of his beer, Damo squeaked out, "Good to have ya here, mate."

"In all my glory. I should've warned you."

"No! I'm not—I have no problem with—" He waved his hand. "This. I reckon it didn't go down too well in Blinman that you're…" Damo motioned to Blake's sheer shirt—his eyes catching again on the shadowy discs of Blake's nipples. "I mean that you wear…" He waved his hand around, higher up at the level of Blake's face where his mouth glistened and his eyes were lined. "That you wear lippy and stuff."

Blake's smile went stiff. "Oh, I don't wear this at home. My parents wouldn't like that. They know I'm gay, but…"

Shit, he was stuffing up *again*. Damo nodded and drank again from his bottle, finding it sadly empty. "Gotcha."

He thought of his own parents and wondered what they'd say if he was Blake. His dad was in so much pain every day that Damo wasn't even sure he'd comprehend it between the pills and the weed. Mum was so exhausted from working overtime that she'd probably nod absently and go back to the telly.

"How did you start dressing up? Like, in the day, you don't seem at all…" Damo peeled the damp label from his beer bottle. "Never mind. I don't know what I'm saying."

Blake raised a thick eyebrow. "I don't seem at all…girly?"

"Not that there's anything wrong with it! But when I met you at Barking, you seemed totally normal." He winced. "Shit, that's not what I meant. Of course you're normal. I just didn't think you were—" He snapped his jaw shut before he could jam his foot in it any farther.

Blake only laughed softly. "All good. I know what you're saying. At work and the beach, I'm not wearing lippy and see-through club wear. This is for going out. It's fun to get glammed up."

"Sorry to be a dickhead. I'm a bit out of my depth."

Blake smiled. "Swimming outside the flags?"

"Something like that. Just so you know, it suits you." Though he probably knew that or he wouldn't be wearing it.

Blake tipped his head, silent, as if he was assessing whether or not Damo meant it. Finally, he said, "Thanks. I guess it's like girls getting dressed up when they go out. It makes me feel good." He glanced around the patio. "And everyone's chill at this club. Not judgy like at some spots."

"Right. I mean, I'm straight, and it doesn't bother me at all."

"Right." Blake's gaze dragged down Damo's body and back up like he was actually using his hands. Damo struggled to take a breath as Blake said, "Let's dance."

"Oh, no." Damo laughed, shaking his head and backing up a step. "Trust me. I'm the actual worst."

"I've seen you surf. You can dance."

"They are not the same at all!" *How often have you seen me? When, exactly? Did I wipe out or catch some sweet rides?* "I cannot dance for shit."

"Will you try?"

How could he say no? He was here at a gay club on something that was feeling more and more like a date. What did he have to lose? Aside from his dignity.

Eyes on Blake's arse in those skintight jeans, Damo followed him back downstairs. The bass was alive in his bloodstream, and Blake's heavy gaze drew him onto the dance floor like a rip current—undeniable. A fog machine pumped dry air that snaked between the sweaty, writhing bodies. The silver glitter of the disco ball circled, the strobes almost blinding Damo.

Transporting him.

Blake moved with the beat, his hips surprisingly loose given how solidly built he was. A little smile tugged at his glossy lips as he watched Damo attempt to shuffle. But it wasn't cruel, and Damo found himself smiling back.

People flowed around them, the crowd surging and receding as songs changed, the beats all similar. They stopped to drink more beer and have another shot before dancing again. He spotted Kat grinning at them and he waved awkwardly.

There were only a few inches between them now, and Blake shouted, "Having fun?" His warm breath ghosted over Damo's cheek.

"Yeah, even though I can't dance. Now you see the proof for yourself."

"But you *are* dancing."

Damo scoffed, shifting his feet in an awkward shuffle. "Barely!"

"I'm really glad you came tonight."

His stomach swooped. "Me too. I mean, I owed you that beer."

Blake edged closer, their bodies brushing together in the crowd. He spoke loudly enough, but didn't shout, leaning down to angle his mouth closer to Damo's ear. "I don't usually ask out men unless I'm sure they're interested."

Adrenaline spiked in a shower of sparks, Damo's stomach doing a full backwards somersault like it was training for the Olympics. "This is a date?" he squeaked as someone bumped him from behind and he stumbled into Blake.

Blake steadied him, his hands heavy and hot on Damo's shoulders for a long moment before dropping. "If you want it to be? And if you don't, then I'd love another mate in Barking." They weren't dancing anymore, just standing really close as people jostled them, the smoke machine pumping again, Damo's heart about to explode.

"This is really weird." He quickly added, "Not that *you're* weird. I've just never... I'm not..." He swallowed hard. "I'm heaps nervous."

Blake's rimmed eyes were intense in the flashing colored lights. "Me too."

That was such a relief that Damo found himself grinning.

"We don't have to do anything," Blake said, taking a step back. He swayed as a dancer bumped into him. "Unless you want to."

Did Damo want to? What exactly did "anything" mean?

Who was he kidding?

He was bloody *dying* to.

Head light, he nodded, praying Blake would get it. Blake raised his eyebrows, and Damo nodded again. He tucked his hair behind his ear, sweat damp on the back of his neck.

The curiosity had sparked when Cody and Liam had gotten together, and it had built steadily for months. And months. Christ, it had been more than a year.

Blake traced the tip of his finger up and down Damo's arm, dipping under the edge of his short sleeve. It was barely a touch, but he might as well have been jerking Damo's cock. Then he leaned in, his lips brushing Damo's ear, breath gusting warm.

"I'll take care of you."

Shuddering with desire he couldn't deny even if he tried, Damo held on as Blake took his hand and swept him out into the night.

Chapter Five

DURING THE SHORT drive south to Barking, Damo rolled the window down, the heat of Blake's body close by on the back seat a massive distraction.

Blake had dropped his hand with a parting squeeze once they were outside the club to pull out his phone and order a ride. Damo's fingers still tingled, and since neither of them had sat in the front like Damo normally would if he was alone in a taxi, there was nothing stopping him from sliding his hand across the fabric seat and touching Blake's fingers…

But then they were in front of a two-story block of apartments in North Barking, and Damo was following Blake up the cement steps to the second level and a white door three down.

Did he really want this? How curious *was* he?

The effects of the drinks were wearing off, and without the flashing lights and thumping bass, he was crashing down to earth.

Standing in Blake's living room in his socked feet because Mum had always taught him to take off real shoes in the house, Damo fidgeted. Would it be weird to take off his socks too? He couldn't remember the last time he'd worn any.

Blake switched on a lamp with a soft click. In the yellow light, the navy fabric couch and big armchair looked comfy. The floor was battered wood that had seen better days, but the green oval rug seemed new and vacuumed. There was a TV opposite the couch, a gaming system on a shelf underneath with controllers lined up neatly. Beige curtains were drawn over windows and what Damo assumed was a sliding door to a balcony.

"Sorry for the mess." Blake grabbed a cola can and napkin from the low wooden coffee table and disappeared into the kitchen.

"Mess?" Puzzled, Damo glanced around. "No worries." He thought of the dishes piled up in the sink at home with an uncomfortable squirm and peeled off his socks, tucking them into his shoes by the door.

Stepping onto the soft rug, he craned his neck to see the title of the paperback on the coffee table. It was called *Woo Woo* by Ella Baxter, and there was some half-eaten fruit and birds of paradise on the cover. A bookmark poked out from about halfway.

Blake returned with a damp cloth and wiped the table, placing the book on the arm of the couch.

"Good book?" Damo asked—immediately regretting it in case Blake asked him what he was reading.

The answer would be either the surf report or instructions on how long to microwave a butter chicken ready meal from Woolies. Not that he needed to look—it was seven and a half minutes from frozen.

"Yeah, it's interesting. It's a satire on the art world and contemporary performance art in particular. Dark comedy sort of thing." Blake disappeared back into the kitchen.

"Cool," Damo said.

What was satire again? He reckoned it was making fun of something but in a smart way? Fucked if he knew.

The soft white walls were decorated with framed blue ocean and red-earth desert prints. The frames were fancy too—like it was real art and not from the Reject Shop. It was all so normal.

So *adult.*

Damo inhaled through a pang of jealousy, sharp and shocking. Blake had this space all to himself, and the bedroom Damo had grown up in was absolutely pathetic in comparison. The fact that he still slept in the same bed he'd had for more than a decade made him feel stupid and young and…

Scared.

The worn floor creaked under Damo as he shifted back and forth, shoving his hands in his pockets. Was he really going to do this?

It reminded him of the first time he'd jumped off the cliff south of Barking. He'd had to rescue a surfer trapped by the pounding swells, the white water too rough to take in the Jet Ski or rescue board and the coast guard helicopter still on its way.

He'd only had a rescue tube—little more than a floaty—when he'd leapt, flinging himself off the cliff with only a ragged heartbeat of hesitation. The surfer had needed him. There was no option.

Now, his lungs tightened and sweat prickled his neck, and he absolutely had a choice. Standing in Blake's clean, grown-up unit, he could creep back from the edge and run home to his bedroom with dirty laundry piled in the corner and tacked-up bikini-babe posters faded by the sun. He realized he'd never had anything on his walls that was actually framed.

Was that a painting or a photo over the TV? He took a step, peering intently at the gorgeous art. It was a close-up of a curling wave, the water different shades of bluey-green. White droplets sprayed into the blue sky from the wave's lip, white froth on the edge of the barrel over pale turquoise.

Blake said from behind him, "It's called 'Clean Swell.' Scott Christensen. I'm hoping one day I can afford an original oil of his instead of a canvas edition. It's signed and numbered, though."

"It's amazing." Damo honestly wasn't sure what was bad about canvas—it sure looked like a real painting to him. "Thought it was a pic at first."

"Isn't the detail incredible? The brushstrokes are so fine."

"Yeah." He didn't know shit about art. Damo motioned to the apartment, not knowing what else to say. "Great place."

"Thanks. It's not much, I know." For the first time, Blake seemed a little unsure as he scratched the back of his neck.

"It's sweet as. I mean, I still live at home. Want to move out, but I can't."

"I get it. So hard these days to afford it."

"It's not just the money, it's—" Damo shoved away thoughts of his dad wailing in agony and Tabby's helpless, silent tears, locking that box up tight. "I pay rent."

"Right, of course. I lived at home a few years after uni. Plenty of people do these days."

"You went back to Blinman?" He was surprised to hear it.

"Yeah, there was some family stuff." Blake waved a hand.

He was dying to ask but bit his tongue for once. "This place is awesome." He forced a smile, trying not to think about Tabby and whether Mum was home safely and if he should—

Exhaling, Damo closed that door, at least for tonight. He didn't want to go home. He didn't want to pull out his phone. He wanted to be right where he was.

"I'm jealous," he added. "This is a terrific spot. Trust me, even if it was a dive, I'm not judging."

"Neither am I."

Damo blinked, realizing he was staring at Blake's nipples through the sheer shirt. He forced his gaze upward. "Huh?"

Blake smiled softly in that kind way he had as he stepped closer. "It's okay. We don't have to do anything. We can just talk. Or watch TV or play the new *Elden Ring*. Whatever you want."

"You don't want to do…anything else?" It was mental, but that hurt.

"*Oh*, I do, but not if you don't? You look like you might spew."

Damo tried to laugh, smoothing down his hair. "No worries, I didn't have that much to drink."

"You want something now? I've got a goon bag. Sauv blanc, I think. Or Toohey's."

"Sure. Beer, thanks."

Blake disappeared into the little kitchen, his bare feet quiet. Damo could glimpse the corner of a white fridge opening and closing, the light briefly shining. Blake returned and handed him a bottle in a neoprene stubbie holder with the Freo Dockers' logo on the side.

After gulping half, Damo asked, "You don't support the Crows?"

Blake shrugged and motioned to the couch before sitting. He put the book back on the table. "Yeah, but when in Rome and all that. Hey, I guess you know Liam Fox? I vaguely remember him playing for Perth before he blew out his knee. Saw his coming-out interview last year. Well, me and probably every queer person in Australia."

Queer. The word made Damo's pulse race as he sat on the other end of the couch. The middle cushion was between them, but he immediately second-guessed whether he should have sat closer.

What were they talking about? Right.

Damo said, "Yeah, he's famous. I mean, he was before for footy, but now he's famous again."

"He seems to be doing well? I've seen him working at Barking, but I didn't want to hassle him."

Damo snorted. "It sure doesn't stop anyone else. At least most people are supportive."

"His boyfriend's on the service too, right? The guy who paddled out to help with those tourists the other day. American?"

"Canadian. And yeah, they're mad about each other, but they try not to let it show at work. Usually they're all business."

"Usually?" Blake sipped his beer. In the glow of the lamp, his eyeliner was smudged in the corners, and his lipstick was faded. His nipples were still visible through the sheer black shirt.

He was *gorgeous*. Had blokes always been this gorgeous?

Damo shrugged. His cheeks flamed hot, and he laughed awkwardly, crossing and uncrossing his ankles. How did he usually sit on a couch? What did he do with his feet?

"Oh, there's a story there. Come on. It's safe with me."

Safe.

Damo gulped his beer and launched into the story he'd never told anyone before he could talk himself out of it.

"One night, I forgot my phone in the tower. I went back up the stairs, and the door was still unlocked. Liam and Cody were inside finishing up. They were, um, kissing."

He couldn't believe he was actually saying it out loud, but once he got going, he'd never been good at shutting up. He quickly added, "They were off duty—the shutters were down, and it was night. It was just a little cuddle after a hard day. They weren't doing anything wrong."

Blake lifted his hands. "I won't report them, I promise."

"Nah, yeah. I know. Anyway, it was… Not that I *spied* on them. I wasn't perving." His face was boiling hot, and he hoped the low light hid it. "They're my mates."

"I get it," Blake said calmly. "You were curious." He took a swig of beer, his Adam's apple bobbing. "And seeing them being intimate made you even more curious?"

Damo shrugged and didn't answer, but his mind filled with remembered images—Cody sitting in Liam's lap by the shuttered windows, Liam's big hand spread over his lower back as they kissed with quiet little murmurs and nose rubs.

Damo was honestly pretty sure Cody was the one usually in charge in that relationship even though he was younger and half Liam's size. But there was something about seeing him in Liam's lap that had made Damo…

Interested.

He wasn't even sure why. Maybe just something about being with someone bigger and stronger. He seemed to attract petite girls, and while he liked that a lot on one hand—liked holding them and scooping them up, covering them with his body and feeling their soft tits squish against his chest—he wondered what it would be like with someone bigger and stronger than he was. Not that there weren't big and strong chicks out there.

Fine, he wondered what it would be like with a bloke.

That word Blake had used—*intimate*—rang in his head. He wanted that. He'd had it with girls, but the idea of getting that close to a guy excited him in a new way.

Damo swallowed a mouthful of beer, his fingers digging into the stubbie holder. He didn't tell Blake how he'd crept back out of the tower that night with a huge boner and waited in the dark under the Norfolk pines lining the boardwalk, half ashamed at being a perv and half dying to wank right there.

Doing multiplication in his head had gotten him back in control. He'd always been crap at maths, and figuring out seven times eighty-two took all his focus.

He'd waited until Cody and Liam came out, then ran up and pretended he'd just arrived. They'd walked back through the car park with him after he grabbed his phone, holding hands easily.

"I'm really proud of him," Damo said. "Liam, I mean. He was so deep in the closet for ages. None of us knew until we found out about him and Cody." In a *heaps* dramatic way, but he didn't go into that.

"You never suspected?"

"Nah. I mean, he's so…manly. You don't imagine footy players being on the other team."

"Speak for yourself." Blake's cheeks dimpled. "I imagine it often."

Now Damo was totally imagining it too, and his face went hot again. He drained the bottle and stood, needing to move or he'd fidget out of his skin. He was in a gay clubbie's living room talking about fancying footy players.

He walked back to the ocean painting over the TV. "This, um, this really is cool."

Silence stretched out, and Damo turned to find Blake stepping slowly toward him. "I understand how seeing Liam and Cody together piqued your interest. And are you still curious tonight?" Blake asked, his voice even lower.

Damo's belly tightened, his dick pulsing. "Maybe."

"You're a terrible liar, aren't you?" Blake put down his beer on the coffee table and held a hand out for Damo's empty bottle, depositing that too.

"Usually."

Though he *was* a liar. He'd never told anyone about what it was really like at home. On the beach, he cracked jokes and talked about hot chicks and kept a smile on his face. But that wasn't actually lying, was it?

Blake's smile was warm like honey in tea the way Mum made it when Damo was sick. "I like that."

"But you know I'm into girls, right? I've always liked girls. Tits are the best. Chicks get me off big time."

They really did—he wasn't bullshitting. He paced the living room, too much energy zipping through him.

"You can like both girls and guys. You can like anyone you want."

Damo bit his lip. "You wouldn't get aggro if I backed out?"

Blake pulled a face, and his voice lost that smooth rumble. "No. I want the men I fuck to be a hundred percent willing."

Fear and a deep, secret thrill spiraled through Damo. "Do you—are we going to actually—" He'd screwed his fair share of chicks, but not in the arse, and he'd definitely not had it done to him. Blood rushed in his ears.

At first, he thought the buzzing was from the panic—and excitement—filling him. But Blake dug his phone out of his pocket.

"Shit, sorry," he said, brow furrowing. "My Mum texted. She should be fast asleep."

"No dramas." Maybe an interruption was a good thing.

Damo peeked at his own phone to make sure he didn't have any messages. The lock screen was blissfully empty aside from his favorite pic of Barking at sunset, the sky painted orange and pink and red and reflected on the swells.

Blake sighed as he tapped out a text. "Sorry," he repeated. "She's fine. Just can't sleep. Putting this on silent now." He put the phone on the table face down. "So…"

"Um…"

They laughed awkwardly, and Blake's gaze flicked to his phone.

"Are you sure you don't need to talk to her?" Damo asked, shoving his hands in his pockets. Yeah, maybe it was a good idea to slow down.

"Let me just make sure that she's not…" Grabbing his phone, Blake trailed off and tapped out another message before waiting.

"She right?" Concern crept in around Damo's jangling nerves.

"Yeah. I…" Blake exhaled noisily, eyes on his screen. "She had a stroke a few years back. I had to go home to help. Dad didn't know which way was up."

"Shit."

Damo wasn't sure what he was feeling. Not that he was *happy* to hear it, but it was a weird relief somehow that Blake had to deal with something similar. Damo could probably tell him all about home—

The calming warmth that filled him curdled in a flood of acid. No. He didn't want to talk about home. Not tonight. Couldn't he have this night just for himself?

Still looking at his phone, Blake said, "Even though the stroke was relatively mild, they needed me."

For three years? "I get it." Eventually—if there was more than tonight—he'd tell Blake how much.

Breathing out, Blake's shoulders loosened. "Okay. She's not having any symptoms, and—" He smiled tenderly. "She says she hopes I'm having a good night out."

After putting his phone face down on the table again, Blake grimaced. "Really hot, huh? Nothing like a guy bringing you home and texting his mum."

All Damo could do was step toward him and press their lips together like his life depended on it.

Chapter Six

BLAKE TASTED LIKE beer and a trace of berry lippy, his stubble scratching. Damo's heart thumped like the music from the club was blaring around them. *Through* them.

He was kissing a bloke.

He was kissing a bloke and he liked it.

Shit, Damo loved it. Loved the strong, taller body shoving against him, both of them instantly hard in their tight jeans.

Everything was sensation and taste, Blake gripping Damo's face with one hand. The other grabbed Damo's arse and pulled their bodies together on a mutual moan.

The still air was full of their shared wet gasps, their lips searching. Needing to touch, Damo squeezed his hands between them, rubbing over the silky fabric covering Blake's torso, his chest hair rough underneath the softness.

Blake's tongue slid into Damo's mouth, stroking and leading the kiss. Damo leaned into him, loving the firm muscles against him. His head spun, and he gasped for a breath, words tumbling out.

"I've never done that before. Never done any of this. Not with a bloke."

"I know." Blake held his gaze, leaning back a fraction when Damo tried for another kiss. Slowly, slowly, Blake ran his palms down Damo's arms. They were rough and warm. Strong and steady. "I'm on PrEP. You?"

Damo shook his head. He knew what that was but had never thought about it since his mum had drummed always using condoms into his thick skull. "I'm careful, though."

Blake nodded. "I always use condoms for anal, and the risk of STI transmission during oral is low. For me, it's worth it."

"Right. So, we can…use our mouths if we don't do…" Damo swallowed hard. Was he really going to do any of this?

Stroking Damo's arms, Blake murmured, "We can take it nice and slow. Or not at all." He smiled, and this one had a hint of smirk. "I'll just have to jerk off when you leave."

Damo's laugh was high and breathy. "Would you think about me?"

Blake held Damo's wrists, and he circled his thumbs softly, his gaze raking down Damo's body and back up in a slow arc. "Oh, yeah."

When Damo licked his lips, Blake tilted his head, still watching closely. The smudged eyeliner made Blake's stare even more intense. It was sexy *as*.

Yes, sexy.

Blake asked, "You like that idea? Me touching myself while I think about you?"

"Heck, yeah." He couldn't deny it. Didn't want to. The water was surging, pushing up the tail of his surfboard, and he was ready to ride the wave.

Blake dropped one of Damo's wrists and reached down to rub himself through his tight jeans. Damo could see the thick bulge, and it sent every drop of blood in his body straight to his own dick. His mouth was dry as the desert.

"This makes you hard," Blake stated.

"Obviously." Damo was shivery all over, sweat gathering where Blake still held one wrist. He swayed forward, chasing more heat.

Blake was still rubbing himself through his jeans, the outline of his cock clear as day. "Do you want me to touch you? Or maybe you want to watch me jerk off?"

As surprisingly good as the last part sounded, Damo could only beg, "Please touch me." He spread his hands over Blake's chest. "So hot," he mumbled, finding Blake's nipples through the sheer fabric with his thumbs.

Blake moaned. "Glad you like it." He ran his hands up under Damo's shirt, but couldn't get past his ribs.

Damo pulled back enough to undo the top few buttons and rip the shirt over his head. He met Blake's grin with his own, and while he was at it, he unzipped his jeans and peeled them off with his briefs, hopping on one foot and then the other, cursing the tight fabric.

Then he was buck naked.

He'd been naked with plenty of guys before in locker rooms and whatever, but not like this. Not when he was so hard he thought he might explode just from the way Blake eyed his straining cock, his chest rising and falling. The last bit of lippy was smeared in the corner of Blake's mouth from their kisses.

Damo wanted to push Blake to the soft green rug and rut against him until he came, which would probably be in about five seconds. Another drop of fluid leaked from the tip of Damo's cock, his foreskin lowered and balls heavy and tight. His dick was long and rigid under Blake's heavy-lidded, smoky gaze.

Slowly, Blake lowered a fingertip and brushed the head of Damo's shaft, capturing the liquid. Damo whimpered at the touch, his hips thrusting into the air as Blake lifted the finger to his full lips and sucked it clean with a wet, gentle noise that sounded like a kiss.

"Please," Damo whispered. He had to know. Had to cross this bridge before he shattered into a million pieces.

Blake's smile was sly as he caressed Damo's wavy hair, wrapping a curl around his finger. Then he unzipped his own trousers. He wasn't wearing anything under them, and Damo groaned as Blake's dick sprang free from a trimmed thatch of dark hair.

Damo reached out eagerly, running his fingers through the coarse hair, Blake's cock thick and hot in his hands, the red, shiny head peeking out from the foreskin.

"Is this okay?" Damo asked. "I don't know what I'm doing."

"Mmm. Sure you do." Blake rolled his hips as Damo hesitantly stroked him. "You know what feels good."

Damo wrapped his hand around the shaft more tightly, spitting on it to ease the way. The angle was different, but it was true he'd wanked about a billion times. Blake throbbed in his hand, their foreheads close as they watched Damo stroke him.

Blake walked him backwards, and Damo plopped down on the armchair, breathing shallowly. Looming over him, Blake leaned on the armrests and licked at Damo's lips, teasing until they were taking turns kissing down each other's throats, tongues exploring. Damo gripped Blake's corded forearms, the scratch of hair and shift of muscle heating his blood.

With a gulp of air, Blake broke away and stood straight. He peeled off his jeans and dropped them to the floor. Then he teased his nipples through the sheer black shirt, making Damo's cock sing.

Damo could just make out the tattooed birds on Blake's left ribcage. Below the hem of the skin-tight shirt, Blake's dick jutted up flushed and thick. He sank down, grabbing a throw pillow from the sofa to shove under his knees.

Oh, holy shit.

Apparently, Damo had said it out loud, because Blake chuckled, rubbing Damo's knees with his palms and urging him to sit closer to the edge.

Damo slouched, his legs spread wide with Blake between them. The armchair was soft like a hug, and he was both comfy and as wound tight as he'd ever been in his entire freaking life.

He had a dusting of pale hair on his chest and limbs, and he kept his darker pubes neat. He was extremely glad of that considering he was on display, Blake still slowly caressing his knees while he looked his fill.

Then Blake leaned forward and circled Damo's bellybutton with a wet, textured swipe of his tongue, and Damo's hips bucked, a hand flying to Blake's head. Blake laughed against his fevered skin with a warm puff and licked again.

It felt good, but it was also knowing where that tongue and mouth were surely going to end up that strung Damo tighter than a bow. He'd been blown plenty of times and always loved it, but this was different.

He could feel the scrape of stubble on his inner thighs, and he curled his toes helplessly on the wood floor as Blake finally licked up and down his shaft.

Watching him under his lined lids, Blake sucked Damo into his mouth, his cheeks hollowing. Damo tried to keep still, biting his lip and crying out anyway. "Gonna blow already."

Blake pulled off, kissing the wet head and rubbing it over his mouth like the dirtiest lipstick ever. "You ever get fingered? Or do it yourself?"

"Sometimes."

Blake snagged his jeans and pulled out a flat little package of lube from a pocket. He ripped it open and squeezed the cool gel onto Damo's middle finger. "Show me."

Damo squirmed. "I'll do it wrong."

"There's no wrong way." Blake smiled gently, patient kindness shining in his hazel eyes that were so damn pretty.

So, Damo shoved his finger in his arse, slouching even lower so he could tilt his hips. A few girls had put in a fingertip and rubbed, and he'd experimented sometimes. It usually felt good, but with Blake watching, Damo was awkward and hesitant.

He pulled out his finger. "I'd really rather you go back to what you were doing."

Laughing, Blake went up on his knees and kissed Damo sweetly. "It's okay. I've got you."

Damo realized the salty-musk taste was from his own dick being in Blake's mouth, and his balls tingled. He was still hard, the edge taken off from the clumsy fingering, and Jesus, he wanted to come.

Blake apparently read his mind, dipping his head and sucking Damo again, fast and slow, hard and soft, his tongue pushing. His lips looked swollen now, and they felt amazing as he ducked lower to suck Damo's balls. Wet slurps echoed in the stillness.

Head rolling side-to-side, Damo's eyes flickered open and shut. His legs were splayed as wide as they could go, Blake's strong hands holding his thighs. Blake lapped at his balls, then across his taint, which felt incredible.

"Oh my *gaaawd*," Damo whined.

"I'm going to use my finger, okay?"

"Huh? Yeah. Whatever, I just need…" His body was tense and quivering, and he clutched at Blake's shoulders. He gasped as Blake's lubed finger entered him, Blake sucking his cock again as he probed.

He crooked his finger, rubbing against the perfect spot, and Damo groaned. "Don't. Stop."

Immediately, Blake lifted his head, Damo's shaft bobbing free of his mouth. His finger was frozen inside Damo's clenching arse. Forehead creased, Blake asked, "Did you say stop?"

"No! Opposite! Don't fucking stop, because I have definitely been doing it wrong and that feels incredible."

Grinning, Blake crooked his finger again, sending sparks everywhere, Damo's whole groin lit up like a Christmas tree. "Are you ready to come?" he asked.

"Been ready since I saw you in that shirt."

Finger still working its magic, Blake swallowed Damo completely, sucking hard and fast. The orgasm unleashed, and Damo closed his eyes, his whole body shaking as he spilled down Blake's throat.

It was wet and slurpy and completely amazing, and Damo was absolutely wrecked, his back arching and every nerve firing.

He'd just been blown by a dude.

A dude who licked him clean and mouthed his spent balls. Who kissed his inner thighs, stubble rasping perfectly as he caressed Damo's knees. Blake was bigger and stronger—yet he was kneeling and nuzzling. It made Damo feel protected in a way he'd never expected.

He tried to catch his breath as Blake ran his palm up his chest, resting his hand there like an anchor, his fingers brushing the purple cord at Damo's throat. He started working himself with his other hand.

"Can I see?" Damo asked hoarsely.

Blake stopped jacking himself mid-motion, eyes dark and intense, licking his parted lips. Pushing off Damo's sternum, he stood and leaned over him. One knee on the wide, padded armrest, he braced a hand on the back of the chair beside Damo's head.

A few strands of Damo's hair caught under Blake's palm, but he didn't mind the tug. He kind of liked it? Even if he didn't, he wasn't capable of saying a bloody thing—not with Blake's massive dick blotting out any other thoughts like an eclipse he couldn't tear his eyes away from.

It was in his face—purplish and veiny and clearly ready to blow. And Blake was so hard for *him*, panting and caressing his own balls, which hung low and heavy. Damo was on another wave, adrenaline surging as the water lifted him, excitement zipping to the tips of his toes.

Blake stroked himself, playing with his foreskin, the head of his cock leaking and shiny. "You like watching me?" he asked.

Damo nodded, his hair tugging and sending shivers over his scalp. He'd never been this close to another bloke's dick, and definitely not one that was hard.

That it was hard for *him* was also blowing his mind.

Yeah, he liked it *heaps*, but he wanted more. He'd already been sucked off by a bloke, so why not? He was going all in, riding through the wave's barrel even if he ended up getting smoked on the reef.

After a gulp of air, he jerked forward and sucked on the tip of Blake's cock. Blake shouted something that didn't really sound like a word, his hips stuttering and dick pushing farther into Damo's mouth. Damo licked like he would an icy pole, though this sure as hell wasn't a sweet fruit flavor.

No, Blake was hot and throbbing in Damo's mouth, a little salty and sweaty. It made him think of the locker room back in school, and instead of grossing him out, he moaned around the shaft stretching his lips. It was male and exciting in a way that felt wrong but bloody fucking right.

It felt…

The only word that came to mind was *naughty*, because he really was a complete boofhead. Like he was breaking the rules in the best way even though he knew there was nothing wrong with it.

He was probably crap at blow jobs, but he sucked and slurped, slumped down in the chair. Blake quivered above him, rigid, letting Damo do as much as he wanted. He only moved to pet Damo's head, murmuring, "That's it. That's so good."

It was music to Damo's ears, and he sucked harder, wanting to earn more praise, wanting to give Blake what he needed. Running his hands up Blake's muscular thighs, hair tickled his palms.

Blake's arse was solid, and Damo squeezed the flesh he'd admired on the beach. Spit dribbled down his chin. His mouth was so full. Full of cock, and it was like when the winning piece of Tetris was finally slotted into place. He moaned loudly.

"Oh! I'm—" Blake shuddered, his hips stuttering again as he exploded.

Coughing, Damo tried to swallow. Blake pulled out, splattering Damo's lips and chin with his warm spunk. Taking himself in hand, Blake milked his cock, mouth open on soft gasps, the last drops hitting Damo's cheeks.

It was unbelievably dirty.

Damo *loved* it.

Reaching up, he pushed a few drops of jizz into his mouth, licking his lips at the salty, earthy-bitter taste. Blake groaned and bent to take Damo's head in his hands, thumbs stroking his cheekbones. Then he licked up the drops from Damo's face, his tongue rough and hot.

Damo almost complained that he wanted to try more of it, but he didn't need to because Blake kissed him with his mouth tasting of jizz.

Damo gasped. Forget dirty—this was bloody *filthy*, and his spent balls twitched.

When Blake straightened up, Damo chased after him for more kisses. Instead, he slipped off the edge of the armchair, landing on his arse with his legs spread wide, Blake's limp cock slapping him in the forehead as he went.

Laughing, he muttered, "Graceful, hey?"

Blake was laughing too, but he stepped back and hooked his hands under Damo's arms, lifting him to his feet. It didn't seem to take much effort, and Damo *really* liked that Blake was so strong. He liked it even more when Blake wrapped his arms around him in a hug that went on and on.

They stood there naked except for the see-through shirt, which was silky and cool against Damo's chest. He leaned in, hugging Blake back and dropping his head on his shoulder. He'd done it.

After all his secret little thoughts, he'd gotten off with a bloke. A bloke named Blake. Blake the bloke.

He burst out laughing and slapped a hand over his mouth. He lifted his head to meet Blake's puzzled gaze.

Blake smiled tentatively. "What?"

"It's nothing bad! I was just thinking about how I finally hooked up with a bloke, and that your name is Blake. Bloke. Blake." He laughed again. "It's funny for some reason. Probably because I'm a total freak."

Blake grinned. "I like that about you." He brushed back Damo's hair in a slow, steady pattern that made Damo want to melt. "And did you like hooking up with a bloke named Blake?"

He was going to joke—make some cheeky remark about how he supposed it was okay. But all he could say was, "Yes."

Blake kissed his cheek softly and pulled Damo into a tight hug again. "I'll take care of you." As he caressed Damo's hair, the promise felt like it was about more than sex.

Chest tightening with a swell of want so powerful he was afraid his knees would give out, Damo hung on. Nothing else mattered right then—not what people might think, not the mess of home and his fucked-up life.

Safe in Blake's arms, the wave surged, lifting him up, up, up. Right now, the rest of the world could wait.

Chapter Seven

DAMO'S HAIR WAS stuck to Blake's sweaty neck, but he didn't brush it away. The surfer of his dreams was naked in his arms, and Blake wasn't letting go if he could help it. They stood on the rug, and he was keen to shuffle them into the bedroom. But he was afraid if he did, the spell would be broken and Damo would make a break for it.

Not that there was any indication at the moment that he wanted to run. He clung to Blake, his fingers stroking the sheer fabric of Blake's new shirt.

Blake hadn't been with someone inexperienced since uni—though he wasn't complaining. The satisfaction in giving Damo pleasure ran shockingly deep. It was so much more than orgasms—which had been spectacular.

Damo had *needed* him, and Blake was proud to be able to help. Making Damo feel good—showing him how much Blake wanted him, allaying his fear—had been such a turn-on.

At Barking, Damo came across as confident and supremely chill. But he'd been undeniably nervous earlier. Blake stroked his shoulder now, loving the way Damo leaned into his side. Forget the fantasy—this was so much better. Blake wanted to tuck him into bed and make him breakfast in the morning.

He murmured, "Thank you."

Damo lifted his head. "For what?"

"For showing up tonight." Blake ran his fingertip over the swell of Damo's bottom lip. "For being brave." The bedroom might be too much, so he urged Damo toward the couch and sat beside him, his arm tight around Damo's shoulders, their naked thighs pressed together.

Damo looked down, seemingly at their spent cocks. He laughed giddily. "Can't believe I just did that."

"And you did it so well." Blake grinned.

An adorable pink flushed Damo's face. "Did I?"

"Yes."

"How good's that." He *beamed*, and a wave of tenderness washed through Blake as Damo asked, "Did you... When you asked me out, how did you know I'd be into this?"

"I didn't. Not for sure. Kat was convinced you were into blokes—"

Damo stiffened. "What? Are they—how? They're not gonna tell anyone, right?"

That stung, but Blake forced a smile. "No. Of course not."

Damo's shoulders lowered. "It's not that I'm—I just... Thought I was hiding it better."

"Do you want to hide it?"

Brow furrowed, he said, "I don't know?"

"It's okay not to know right this minute." Blake stroked Damo's collarbone with his thumb. "But Kat suggested asking you to Rodeo, and I figured, nothing ventured..."

"So you seduced me with your guyliner and nipples."

Laughter warmed his chest. "Apparently. I decided if you did a runner because of how I looked, we weren't going to be friends after all. Glad you didn't sneer at me in disgust and call me a name. It would have sucked if my fantasy man had turned out to be a dickhead."

Damo scoffed incredulously. "I don't think I've ever been

anyone's *fantasy*. You're going to be disappointed when I let a juicy fart rip."

He laughed. "You've got quite a way with words."

"I try." Damo's grin faded. "Has that happened before? Blokes called you names and shit?"

"Not too often, but a few times. I usually only dress up to go dancing. One time, I met someone on an app when I was in the cab going home, and I got the driver to take me to the guy's place. He slammed the door in my face after a few…comments. There are those macho guys who hate anything slightly femme. 'Straight-acting' all the way."

Damo wrinkled his nose. "They sound like arseholes."

"Yup."

After a few moments of silence, Damo said, "It's weird that this doesn't feel weird. Not bad-weird. Good-weird. As curious as I was, I didn't imagine actually, you know." He flushed. "Putting a dick in my mouth. I mean, I tried with my own in year nine, but I wasn't flexible enough."

Blake shook with laughter. This was the most fun he'd had with a hookup in too long. Hopefully *not* just a hookup. Would Damo want to see him again? Or would he freak out in the light of day?

He's here now. One step at a time.

He nuzzled Damo's cheek. "And what did you think? In general. You don't need to wax poetic about my cock."

"There once was a bloke from Blinman…"

They laughed, and Blake said, "Limericks of course being the highest form of poetry."

"Except nothing rhymes with bloody Blinman." Damo spread his fingers over Blake's thigh. "I liked it. More than liked. It felt…right. Like, it made sense. Is that mental?"

"Nope. I knew I was gay long before I acted on it, and when I did, it came naturally. Like a hand in a glove."

"Yes!" Damo nodded excitedly. "I always knew I fancied chicks, but I wasn't sure about blokes. Now I'm sure." He frowned. "Does everyone else know already? Did you talk about me with other clubbies too?"

"No, never. Kat just liked to tease me about my crush on you. They insisted you were checking out my arse the other week."

"Oh, mate." He rubbed his face ruefully. "Guilty as charged. Can you blame me?"

Blake grinned. "You're only human."

"And it's not that I'm ashamed or anything. Honestly."

"It's okay. You get to take more than fifteen minutes to get your head around it."

"Right. Okay." His gaze dropped to Blake's mouth and back up. Then he leaned in and pressed their lips together.

They kissed for a minute, Damo rubbing his sweaty palm up and down Blake's thigh. He whispered, "I like how hairy you are."

"Yeah?" His balls were tingling again.

"Never imagined a garbo dressing up like you do. Granted, our bin guy is about sixty and looks like Alf from *Home and Away*."

Blake laughed. "Sounds like most of the blokes where I work in Armadale. You know, I wouldn't have pegged you for a soap fan."

Damo squirmed. "I'm not, but… Fine. I am."

"You really aren't very good at keeping secrets, are you?"

He looked away and squirmed again. "Wouldn't exactly call that a secret. I watched it with my nan growing up. It's bloody addictive!"

"I'm sure it is. Is she still around?"

"Nah. Died a few years back. Smoked like a chimney and drank like a fish and said she had zero regrets."

Blake smiled. "And you said you live at home? What's the rest of your family like?"

Damo shrugged, dropping his face. "Not much to tell. Mum and Dad and a little sister. Can't complain."

Blake nuzzled behind Damo's ear. He didn't seem keen to talk about his family, which was fair enough since they were sitting there with their cocks out.

"When did you first try the makeup?" Damo asked.

"Joined the theater club at uni. Played the emcee in *Cabaret*. Have you seen it?"

"Is that a musical? I saw *Wicked* when I was a kid. That's about it."

Blake grabbed his phone from the table and turned it on. An email notification bubble appeared at the top of the screen from an address he didn't recognize. He thumbed it away and searched for an image of the emcee and showed it to Damo.

"Whoa. Suspenders and short pants and lots of makeup." He raked his gaze over Blake. "I can picture it." He circled one of Blake's nipples through his sheer shirt.

Blake shivered. "Reckon you'd be a musical fan if you'd seen it?"

"Hundred percent, mate."

They kissed again, and Blake tossed his phone aside. When he pulled Damo over his lap, Damo moaned, his cock swelling. He pressed his hands against Blake's chest, caressing through the silky fabric.

"Still can't believe I'm doin' this," Damo whispered.

"We don't have to."

"I want to." He rolled his hips determinedly. "See?"

"Hmm. I feel a little something too."

"Mate!"

"Sorry! Not little. Huge! Enormous. Monstrous." Blake squeezed Damo's cock—which was a perfectly respectable size— then spread his hands over Damo's wiry, muscular back. He was slim but strong.

"All right, don't get carried away."

Through the sheer fabric of Blake's shirt, Damo played with his nipples. Blake sat back and enjoyed the tingles fluttering over his skin. The shirt was sweat-damp, and Blake wanted Damo's hands on his bare flesh, so he pulled the material over his head and tossed it.

"Mmm." Damo eyed Blake's chest avidly and ran his fingers through the swirls of hair, sending more electric ripples over Blake's skin right down to his balls. "Dunno why I like your nips so much." He licked his lips as he circled them again. "Obviously, I love tits."

"Obviously," Blake agreed, gasping softly as Damo pinched.

"Tits are so soft. They're awesome. But I dig that your nipples are smaller. Harder. Hairy." He leaned down and nipped with his teeth.

Blake arched his spine, his cock getting fully back in the game. "Lick them."

With a shaky breath, Damo did, ducking his head, his tongue wet and rough and perfect. Blake traced his spine with his fingers. "That's it."

Damo licked and sucked and made Blake gasp, both of them breathing hard, Blake twisting Damo's hair around his fingers. God, he wanted to push him over the table and fuck him until neither of them could walk. But not yet. This was Damo's first time with a man, and Blake hoped they had plenty of time to work up to that.

He couldn't deny that being Damo's first bloke was sexy as hell. That Damo had shown up at the club at all, then trusted Blake enough to go home with him and take the leap... It made his heart swell dangerously.

He pulled up Damo's head for a deep, wet kiss. It was like surfacing after getting smoked by a wave, the kiss as sweet as that first gulp of air. He reached between them and pumped their cocks together, swallowing Damo's little cries, then panting with him in hot gusts as they strained to come again. Damo was leaking, and Blake thumbed the fluid and used it to slick the way.

"You like this?" Blake asked, indulgently wanting to hear it aloud.

Damo leaned back, his face flushed and lips parted. "It's all right." He couldn't keep a straight face and burst out laughing, his hips still thrusting, their cocks hot and heavy in Blake's grip. He grimaced. "I need to come again."

"I've got you."

Blake's left fingers were still threaded through Damo's long hair, and he gave a playful tug. And *oh.* Oh, *fuck* yes, because Damo gasped and bucked and clutched Blake's shoulders as he muttered, "That's it."

Blake twisted the curls around his fingers tighter. "You gonna come all over my hairy chest?"

"Yes!" Damo strained, the muscles in his neck standing out beneath the simple purple cord necklace, sweat glistening on his forehead.

Blake loosened his grip on their shafts. "You really want to?"

Huffing, Damo dug his fingers into Blake's shoulders. "Don't make me beg."

"Maybe that's my goal." He grinned, twisting and untwisting Damo's thick hair on his fingers. He couldn't remember the last time he'd laughed so much during sex. Usually it was getting off, some small talk and a coldie, a thanks and see ya. The order wasn't always the same, but that was most of his hookups in a nutshell.

With Damo, he wanted to tease and play and make it last.

"Please let me come all over your big hairy chest," Damo begged, laughing.

Their thighs were slick with sweat where their bodies pressed, and Blake caressed Damo's spine. With his other hand, he gathered a bigger bunch of Damo's hair and spun it around his hand slowly, tightly, watching pleasure flicker through Damo, his blue eyes intent with lust.

Now Damo wasn't smiling.

Now he was breathing hard, rutting against Blake. "Please. Make me come." He gripped Blake's face and kissed him roughly. "Want this. Want you. Love being naked with you." He laughed again, disbelieving. "I'm *naked* with you."

The wonder and trust shining from Damo's lust-dark eyes made Blake's heart clench. He wanted to keep Damo safe in his arms, the protective urge knocking the breath out of him like being dumped on the sand by a shore break.

He gripped Damo's hair and jerked him fast until he exploded in a shout, spraying Blake's chest with jizz, shaking and clinging to him. As Damo heaved great gasps, Blake stroked himself, imagining what it would be like to fuck Damo's arse, to see him split open on his dick...

Blake's orgasm ripped out of him almost painfully, but then the beautiful rush of warmth flowed to the tips of his toes and fingers, which were still tight in Damo's hair.

Sweaty and sticky, they caught their breath. "Wow," Damo murmured.

"Uh-huh."

"That was... Thanks, mate."

"Anytime." Before he could play it cool, Blake asked, "Like, tomorrow, for instance? If you're not busy?"

Damo stiffened. Not a lot, but enough. He lifted his head. "I can't. Working, and then I've got...uh, stuff."

"Oh. Okay." Blake tried to sound casual. "No worries." Suddenly, Damo felt heavy on his lap, the sweat and jizz sticky and unpleasant as he fought his disappointment. Maybe this was a one-night thing? He took Damo's waist to shift him off.

"I really do have plans." Damo tightened his thighs around Blake's hips and gripped his shoulders. "I'm not blowin' ya off.

Surf report for Sunday arvo looks sweet, though. You free then?"

Blake exhaled. "Yeah. Sounds good."

"Cool. Because I… I liked this. A lot."

"Same."

Damo smiled. His slightly crooked canine was damn adorable. "Cool," he repeated. "Are you volunteering tomorrow?"

"Normally I would, but my mate Rocky from work needs a hand building a new sunshade in his yard. I'll be there Sunday morning. Then we'll meet up?"

"Sweet." Grinning, Damo looked down at himself and grimaced. "I'm a mess. I've got to be at work at nine. Can I use the toilet? Better get going."

Blake pointed him to it and sat sprawled on the couch with jizz drying in his chest hair. He couldn't get ahead of himself, but Damo wanted to see him again! He realized he was grinning and released a giddy little secret laugh.

Life was good.

He grabbed his phone to check that Sunday surf report, excitement building already. They could catch some waves, have dinner, then more orgasms. It sounded like paradise. He reminded himself again that this was only the first date.

The red number on the email app that Blake obsessively kept at zero was up to five. He tapped it open and listened to the water running in the bathroom, smiling at the thought of Damo scrubbing himself. Blake should have offered to help…

The unfamiliar email address was there at the top: *t.rutledge@nsw.mail.com.au.* The subject line read: *"Important message for Blake Holbrook."*

Frowning, Blake opened it. Probably some scammer Nigerian prince or spam. He scanned the message, his eyes taking in key words.

A giant invisible fist squeezed his chest.

All the oxygen in the room was sucked out in a giant whoosh.

Mouth dry, his head spun.

He wasn't actually reading this email. He *couldn't* be reading this. It wasn't possible. Was it a joke? He'd been waiting for a prank from the clubbies, but no. It couldn't be.

Damo appeared, dressed. "I'd better get going. Do—" He was suddenly standing at Blake's feet. "You right? You look pale *as*." He bent and took Blake's shoulder. "Gonna spew? Come on. Up."

Damo had snapped into first aid mode, all commanding and bossy, and under other circumstances, Blake would have enjoyed it immensely. He shook his head. "I'm okay. Thirsty." He dropped the phone face down, as if he could block out the contents of that email.

But if it were true…

Along with the shock, joy bloomed like a tiny spring wildflower in the sunshine.

Then Damo was pressing a glass into his hand. "You sure that's all? Look like you've seen a ghost." He sat beside Blake and watched him drink.

Blake gulped gratefully. "I'm good." Was he? Maybe? For a moment, he almost showed Damo the email, but what kind of end was *that* to a first date? Way too heavy, and Blake needed to process. Besides, Damo had to get some sleep. It was the middle of the night. "You've got lives to save in the morning."

Damo frowned. "Your heart's not racing?" He took Blake's wrist to feel his pulse.

"I'm okay. Honestly." Blake's head was still spinning, but he was breathing again. "I'll see you Sunday. Can I get your number?"

"Had your dick in my mouth, so I guess so." Damo laughed, blushing and pulling out his phone. "What's yours? I'll text you now."

Blake rattled off his number in a fog, his mind racing. His phone pinged on cue, but he left the screen face down on the cushion.

How is this possible? This isn't… How?? Could it really be true?

He realized Damo was saying something, a frown creasing his face. Blake said, "I'm good. Too many orgasms." He gave his head a shake. "This was an amazing night. Can't wait for Sunday."

"Me too," Damo said. He bit his lip, then kissed Blake softly. "See you then." He glanced down. "Better clean up or that'll be murder to get out of your chest hair." He giggled, and Blake was grateful to smile back.

In the shower after he'd kissed Damo goodbye again at the door, Blake's mind whirled. He needed to read the email again. He needed to respond. Just when he thought his life was officially back on track, *t.rutledge@nsw.mail.com.au* had blown up his plan.

Chapter Eight

As his phone chimed, Damo blinked awake and thought of jizz in chest hair.

A thrill whipped through him, his morning wood throbbing as he fumbled to turn off the alarm. The night before replayed through his head, and he laughed to himself. He'd actually *done it.* There was no going back to his previous status as Officially Curious. He hadn't done anything this exciting in…possibly ever?

Which was scary, but also such a bloody relief. He couldn't take it back—and he didn't want to.

His belly fluttered as he remembered getting off with Blake. Big hands on his back. Blake sucking his cock. Blake looming over him and coming in his mouth. Blake lifting him up into his strong arms…

"I'll take care of you."

Jesus, it had been so *sexy.*

Damo fumbled for the lotion and tugged himself, spreading his legs. He closed his eyes to the faded posters—surfers and beach babes. He was waking up in the same old room, but he'd finally gone outside his comfort zone.

Outside his open window, ravens cawed loudly. Even though he'd blown his load twice the night before, Damo's balls tightened, and he bent his knees, breathing hard, digging his heels into the saggy single mattress. Fucking up into his fist, he was so close already—

The *thud* echoed through the single-story house, followed by Tabby's curse. Damo cursed too, rolling out of bed and yanking on his board shorts. He wiped his hand on the pile of dirty laundry in the corner as he crashed back down to earth. Nothing killed a boner quite like his baby sister needing help.

Their parents' room was at the end of the hall, and Damo was there in a flash. As he suspected, Dad was on the floor, sprawled face down on the faded blue rug beside the bed. His walker stood by uselessly. Tabby stood over him, red-faced in the gloom, the blinds drawn as always.

"I told him to wait until I had it steady!" Her golden hair was pulled back in her usual ponytail, and she stood with hands on her skinny hips, wearing her green footy kit. To their dad, she pleaded, "Why couldn't you wait?"

"I need to piss!" Dad barked, then muttered, "Stupid girl."

"Oi!" Damo closed the door quietly and marched over. "None of that." He bent at his knees and heaved his father onto his back as gently as he could. Dad grimaced, his drawn, craggy face turning from the usual grayish-yellow pallor to red.

Hoisting his father onto his feet was no easy task. Dad was a head taller than Damo, and though his weight went up and down depending on what drugs he was taking, he was a big man even at his thinnest. More than that, he was dead weight, no matter how often Damo asked him to push with his legs.

Dad just gritted his teeth and groaned as Damo hauled him up like he was a drowned patient he needed to get on his board. Tabby was ready with the walker, and they hovered nearby as Dad grumbled and moved by centimeters to the adjoining toilet.

Over his usual pajama bottoms, his bare back was sweaty and pale. Jagged, shiny scars where the doctors had put in pins to try and fix his broken bones were stark even in the murky light. Once he was inside on the crapper, Damo shut the door.

The ceiling fan thumped overhead in the bedroom. It stank of cigarettes, pot, sweat, and something that had to be complete fucking misery. Lips pressed in a line, Tabby crossed her arms. Damo slung an arm around her rigid shoulders.

"You'd better get to practice, hey? I'll get him settled back down. Careful not to wake Mum on your way out."

"Dunno how she slept through that," Tabby muttered.

"Mum's exhausted."

"She always sleeps on the couch now. Never in here."

Can't say I blame her. "You better get a wriggle on. I'll make dinner, okay?"

Tabby's narrow shoulders loosened. "Okay." She glanced at the bathroom door, sadness and resentment souring her freckled face.

"Sorry I didn't get up earlier to check on him," Damo said. "It's hectic when he gets like that."

When he wasn't at work, he always tried to be the one looking in on him. Dad usually slept late, so Damo could go for a dawn surf if he wasn't on the opening shift and still make it back in plenty of time.

When he wasn't out with a bloke, that was. He cursed himself for not setting his alarm for earlier.

Tabby shrugged, and he hated that she had to deal with any of this. She shouldn't have had to handle anything more than homework and playing footy and her first crush.

"You were home late," she said, eyeing him curiously.

Guilt nipped with sharp teeth, and he kissed Tabby's head and gave her a little shove. "On yer bike!"

While he waited for his father to finish shitting, Damo picked up the dirty plate left on the one bit of the side table not lined with pill bottles. A chip packet had floated to the carpet, and he grabbed that on the way to the kitchen.

From the hall, he could peek into the living room. Mum's light hair was messy on a pillow on the couch, and she didn't move. He left the plate on the kitchen benchtop and padded back to the bedroom.

Dad was shuffling across the carpet with the walker. At least once he got up, he was usually okay to go to the toilet and back alone. Damo hovered nearby, prepared to steady him but not getting too close.

He couldn't resist saying, "You shouldn't talk to Tabs like that. You know—"

"Don't fuckin' tell me what I know!" Dad cringed as he lowered himself to the bed, holding on to the side rail they'd installed years back. He sucked in a gasp. "Feet."

Damo hefted his father's swollen feet and legs up and helped pivot him onto his back. Once he was settled, Damo asked flatly, "What do you want for brekkie?"

"Whaddya think I want?"

Turning away, Damo went to fetch the coffee, toast, and a Cherry Ripe. A horrible little cry made him jolt around.

Tears shone in Dad's red-rimmed eyes. "Sorry," he whispered, a hoarse—and increasingly rare—confession. For a second, he was like himself again. The dad he'd been before the accident and the personality changes that came with it.

Just for a second.

"I know." Damo tried to smile and escaped to the kitchen.

He scraped the thin layer of Vegemite on the buttered toast just like Dad liked, struck by a memory of when he was Tabby's age and Dad was home early from a job, still in his high-vis tradie gear. Damo had helped him make brekkie in bed for Mum's birthday while Tabby had gotten underfoot.

Dad had swung her up onto his back, shushing her as she laughed. She'd clung to him while he'd scrambled the eggs, and Damo had buttered and Vegemite-d the toast. They'd all climbed into bed with Mum. She was groggy after her hospital shift but beaming, snuggling them close while they got crumbs all over the doona.

He blinked up at the water stains on the ceiling, a remnant of a summer storm and faulty roof tiles they couldn't afford to fix. He wasn't sure what would be worse—allowing Dad to see tears in his eyes or letting the toast get cold.

"SWIMMERS IN FRONT of us! Come straight back to shore. This is not a safe swimming area!"

Damo sat beside Liam Fox in the buggy at the north end of Barking, watching as the people completely ignored him. Still holding the smooth plastic of the transmitter attached to the megaphone on the buggy's roof, Damo shook his head.

"Foxy, ya reckon they think I'm talking to you?"

Liam chuckled and adjusted his mirrored Aviators. "Apparently."

Damo pressed the microphone button, blowing into the transmitter to make a static noise to attract attention before saying, "Did you know that this area of the beach is not for swimming? There are big yellow warning signs and everything. And lifeguards going hoarse."

"In fact, I did know that," Liam said, scanning the water back and forth.

"Glad the message is getting through to someone. It'll be gnarly soon."

Damo propped his bare foot on the dashboard. It was clouding over, but the sun still broke through to glimmer on the waves. The tide was turning low, and the Croc would start biting, and the people who ignored the warnings and refused to swim between the flags would be caught in the rip.

Kids playing on the sand shrieked and laughed, and Damo breathed in the fresh, briny scent of the beach—salt, seaweed, and the sweet slap of sunscreen and surfboard wax. Someone nearby was using Mr. Zogs Sex Wax with a coconut scent he'd know anywhere.

Annnd now he was thinking about sex, which meant thinking about Blake. About his cock and foreskin and those nipples surrounded by hair. About said cock stretching Damo's lips, tasting like skin and *man*.

He'd finally done it. Tomorrow, he'd do it again, which gave him a secret shiver. He was wishing like hell he'd told Blake he'd see him tonight, but he couldn't leave Tabby alone two nights in a row.

Damo's phone was locked up in the staffroom in the lifeguard tower, so he couldn't check to see if Blake had texted. He should've sent a message himself before his shift, but after dealing with Dad and tiptoeing around while Mum slept, he'd had to jog the few blocks to the beach to make it on time. At least their house was in a prime spot in Barking.

As a kid, Damo hadn't wondered if it was weird for his dad to live in his childhood home as an adult, and now it was too late to ask. If he tried to bring it up, Dad would probably call him names in one of the surges of fury that simmered under the surface, ready to explode.

Damo forced away thoughts of home. The beach was *his* place. His freedom. Also his job, and he sternly reminded himself to be vigilant. He watched a young couple having a play on a sandbank. Any minute now, they'd get lifted off it, not be able to touch the bottom, and full-on panic. You could set your bloody watch by it.

His gaze drifted over to the surfers out the back. The waves were only okay, and he could tell there were a lot of beginners in the lineup. It occurred to him that Blake had to be a relative newbie if he'd grown up in the Flinders Ranges.

He looked for Blake, his pulse fluttering just at the thought of seeing him again. Which was mental, right? First off, Blake had said he was helping out a mate. Second, he'd only just met him. Fair enough, they'd shared spit and jizz, which was a pretty big deal—at least to Damo.

Even with chicks, he'd never had many hookups. Or any, now that he thought about it. Aside from Shaz, there'd been a couple of girls who hadn't lasted long, but they were more than just a one-nighter.

But was it different with guys?

He chewed that over as he watched a new group of swimmers leave their towels right by the DANGEROUS CURRENT warning sign.

When Damo had left the toilet, Blake had seemed…distracted? Before, his attention had been intense, and it wasn't only the guyliner making his eyes more dramatic.

Yet when Damo had left his apartment, Blake had seemed preoccupied. Not quite as present. Damo couldn't help but wonder if it was because they'd gotten off. Maybe the excitement was gone? The mission was accomplished, so Damo wouldn't be interesting anymore?

He scoffed at himself. As if he was some man of *mystery*. Still, it wouldn't be the first time a bloke lost interest after orgasms, would it? Chicks complained about that all the time— understandably. And if Blake wasn't fussed with him anymore, Damo had to admit the disappointment would be…

"You right?" Liam asked.

"Huh?" Damo glanced away from the water to find Liam frowning at him.

"Got ants in your pants and you're sighing every five seconds."

"Sorry, mate."

Eyes on the water, Liam shrugged. "No worries. Everything good?"

"Yep," he answered too quickly. "I'm sweet."

And everything *was* good. Blake had clearly wanted to see him again, so why was he worrying about being brushed?

Because thinking of Blake had him hot and nervous and excited, and he tapped his foot against the dash.

"Excuse me?" a teenage girl asked.

Damo jolted guiltily, and he and Liam turned as she tentatively approached the buggy on the left where Liam sat. Liam said, "G'day."

She brushed a dark, frizzy curl from her face. "You're Liam Fox, right?"

Damo could feel the tension ripple through Liam's big body even though they weren't touching. Liam nodded, waiting. The girl couldn't be more than fourteen and fiddled with the strap of her striped bathers.

Damo said, "This is the legend in the flesh." He was pretty sure the girl wasn't about to tell Liam he was a pervert going to hell since she was practically vibrating from nerves. He hoped not, at least.

"Um, I…" She shifted on the sand. "I just wanted to say thanks. For coming out. I'm bi, and when I told my dad, he didn't even get mad. You helped him understand."

Liam exhaled. "I'm glad. What's your name?"

Smiling, Damo looked back at the water—and jumped to his feet. He pulled off his long-sleeved blue uniform shirt. Sure enough, the couple had been lifted off the sandbank by the swells, and they couldn't swim a stroke. At times, lifeguards waited to see if people could get themselves out of trouble, but Damo knew instantly he was in.

"There they go. I'm gettin' wet!"

He could hear Liam on the radio calling the tower, where other lifeguards would be watching with binoculars. Rescue board in hand, Damo raced in, punching past the impact zone and paddling hard to where the couple flailed and grabbed at each other in their terror, pulling each other under.

"I told ya not to swim here!" he couldn't resist shouting as he grasped their arms. "Especially if you can't actually swim!"

They couldn't speak English, which was common on Barking. They were close enough to shore that he was able to drag them back to the sandbank and walk them out of the water.

He pointed to the danger signs, and then down towards the safe swimming area. They nodded and thanked him, the woman gripping his hands gratefully.

Damo's frustration ebbed as he returned to the buggy. He knew no one wanted to get into trouble in the waves, but he wished they'd give the ocean the respect it demanded.

Liam shook his head. "Couldn't swim a stroke."

"Nope." Damo rubbed a towel over his arms. "That was nice of that girl, hey?"

"Yeah. Took a selfie with her." Liam looked vaguely embarrassed.

"You should be used to it by now, Foxy." Damo shoved his shoulder playfully.

Liam huffed, but he smiled too. "I can't imagine coming out at her age. Maybe things really are changing."

"Hope so, mate."

They went back to patrolling in comfortable silence when they weren't hopping on the megaphone to tell people to move to the safe part of the beach—to little effect, as usual. Damo pulled his shirt back on and swatted a persistent fly, and the girl's voice echoed in his head.

"I'm bi."

Was he bi too? He rolled the word around in his head. *Bi. Bisexual. Biiiiiiiii.*

Yeah, he'd been curious for a while—probably longer than he'd admitted to himself—but putting words on it made his palms sweat. Which was bloody stupid given he and Blake had gotten naked together.

Crap, now he was thinking about jizz in chest hair again, and Blake's big hands, and his stubbly, heart-stopping kisses—

"What's got you all tied up in knots?" Liam asked.

His cheeks went hot. "Nothing!"

"You can…" Liam waved a hand. "I can listen."

Damo had to smile. Before Cody, Liam would have rather pulled out his fingernails than have a deep and meaningful.

"Yeah, nah. Just have a lot on my mind."

"Hot chicks and the next party?"

And shit, that shouldn't have hurt, but it *did*. Damo put on a grin. "You know me, Foxy."

It wasn't Liam's fault. Damo had created an image for himself on the lifeguard service. Always keen for a joke and a comment about bikinis. It hadn't been intentional, but since he never talked about home, the boys had no clue. Damo rocked up to work with a smile no matter what else was happening.

There was no reason Liam's offhand comment should sting. Yet Damo sat there feeling like a dickhead. And it was ironic that Liam of all people was the one buying into the act when Liam had pretended to be straight for years.

Though Damo *did* like hot chicks in bikinis, and he did like a joke. He'd wanted to keep the beach his sanctuary. It wasn't like he was pretending to be someone he wasn't.

Jesus, he didn't know which end was up.

As he scanned the waves with his foot on the dash, Damo asked as casually as possible, "How's it been lately? Being out and everything."

Liam was quiet for a few seconds. "Good. Mostly good."

"No regrets?"

"Not one," he said right away. "Well, aside from regretting that my parents still won't talk to me. I can't control that, though.

I can only control how I respond."

It was clear Liam had been going to therapy. Damo nodded.

"Now that Cody and I are getting—" he stopped.

Leaning forward, Damo examined the water. "See something?"

"No, it's fine," Liam said quickly. A flush rose over his bearded cheeks.

Narrowing his gaze, Damo asked, "Now that you and Cody are what?" His Spidey senses were tingling.

"Nothing!" Liam pushed to his feet, moving faster than you'd expect given his size. "I'm going to—"

"You're going to cough up what you were gonna say!" Damo tugged on Liam's sleeve. "You and Cody are... Let's see. You already live together. You have a dog." He half-joked, "Are you getting hitched?"

"Shh!" Liam hissed, jumping back in the buggy.

"Are you?" Damo drummed his hands on the dash. "You are!"

With a hilarious scowl, Liam shook his head but didn't deny it.

"Far out!" Ignoring Liam's head shaking, Damo grinned. "I won't tell, Foxy. It'll be our little secret."

With a heavy sigh, Liam shot him a skeptical look.

"I swear. My lips are sealed." He dropped the smile. "Look, I know people think I'm a total boofhead, but I can keep a secret. Maybe better than you think."

Brow furrowed, Liam nodded. "Thanks."

"Right, now tell me all about the proposal."

Liam flushed an even darker shade of red, and Damo whistled. "There's an adults only story there, hey?" And he was not allowed to think about it because Cody and Liam were his mates.

"No more questions," Liam muttered.

"Whoa!" Damo exclaimed. "That chick got smoked." He watched as the young woman's surfboard popped up in the shallows. She'd disappeared in the white froth of the worsening impact zone, nosediving on her way back to shore on a breaking swell that dumped her in a meter of water. Damo and Liam sat bolt upright, watching and waiting, all joking and talk of weddings forgotten.

The woman did appear, staggering to her feet unsteadily. Damo said, "Gonna make sure she's okay." He hopped out of the buggy and jogged over to her. Dark-skinned and gorgeous, she was about thirty, her long legs shaky under her half wetsuit.

"How ya goin'?" he asked.

"Been better," she replied in a Brit accent.

"Copped it hard, hey?" He reached out and touched her shoulder. "Did you hit your head at all?"

"No. But my back feels sore."

Damo led her to dry sand. "Sit for a minute. You probably just tensed up and strained the muscles a bit, but let's make sure."

He went through the questions they asked to rule out a spinal injury. If there was any doubt, he'd call for a spinal board to be brought down and tell the tower to ring an ambulance. But after a few minutes, he was satisfied she was okay.

The woman—Ella—put her warm hand on his knee where he crouched beside her. Smiling, she said, "It's nice to know there are lifeguards like you to take such good care of us."

Last week, Damo probably would have smiled back and chatted her up for a minute if it wasn't busy. But now, he leapt up and smiled too wide. "No worries! Just doin' our job, hey? Later!"

What was that? He was still allowed to enjoy a moment's flirt with a gorgeous chick, wasn't he? It wasn't cheating. He and Blake had only had one date! And he still liked women. He was allowed to like boys and girls—Blake had said so himself.

Wiping his sunnies on his shirt, Damo cursed himself. He was strung so tightly he was going to snap. He never picked up chicks while on shift, but there was no harm in being friendly. So why did he feel so guilty and weird?

It had been less than twenty-four hours since he'd finally hooked up with a bloke, and he needed to tell someone or he'd explode. There was already so much he didn't talk about. There was no room inside for this too. If only Blake was there to give him another one of those long hugs and whisper in his ear.

"I'll take care of you."

Back in the buggy, Liam said, "That surfer gave herself a fright?"

"Yeah, I think she's done with learning to surf for today." Damo glanced at Liam's familiar profile. Liam would understand. He didn't talk much, but he'd listen. Damo could just…tell him. Open his mouth and say, *"I got off with a bloke last night."*

Not that this was a good time for it. Not for bisexual confessions or teasing Liam more about apparently getting engaged to Cody.

Indeed, Liam said, "Croc's going to be full on any minute."

It sure was—all the lifeguards in and out of the water bringing back patients who got in over their heads. It was a strange relief since Damo could only think about patients and paddling, all his energy zeroed in on rescues.

It clouded over fully around four and rain started sprinkling. Fortunately, most people packed up, and he breathed easier without thousands in the water to monitor.

In the two-story tower, Damo cleaned up the first aid area by the back ramp that zigzagged up to the second level, forcing himself to stay away from the locker room beyond the kitchenette.

He ate a chicken schnitty from the cafe and watched the gray waves, half listening to a few of the guys on shift and thinking about what he'd make Tabby for dinner.

He'd been paid that week and stocked up on groceries, so at least he knew there was dried pasta and a can of sauce. He'd grabbed a pack of mince at thirty percent off since it was due to expire. He'd text Tabby and tell her to take it out of the freezer.

The thought of texting made him fidget in his office chair, wondering if Blake had been in touch. Rain splattered the large curving windows of the viewing area, and he tapped on the benchtop that ran under the windows.

A few feet away, Bickie toweled off his floppy brown hair— now going gray at the temples—and answered one of the office phones that sat on the bench.

Damo tucked one foot up under him. Then switched it to the other, the chair creaking as he spun in little half circles. If Blake—

Stop thinking about Blake!

"Good work today," Teddy said as he hopped up the three steps to the main viewing area. Damo jolted guiltily before forcing a smile.

"Thanks, boss," Bickie said, crunching on one of the biscuits that gave him his nickname. He looked through binos toward the north end, where surfers ignored the drizzle.

Teddy—also known as Cyclone—ran a hand over his buzzed hair. His tanned face was etched with laugh lines, and he was going gray too. "Tomorrow's going to be chockers. Twenty thousand at least with the heat."

"Glad I'll be catching waves," Damo said. His belly fluttered as he imagined paddling out with Blake. Would it be considered their second date? Was he going to have a *boyfriend?*

"Same," Cody said and gave Damo a fist bump. "I'm outta here." He'd already changed into his street clothes.

"Not before you scrub the toilet and shower," Teddy called.

By the back tower door behind the small first aid area, Cody groaned. "Come on. You're not really going to make me, are you?" He looked up the few steps at Teddy with big puppy eyes. "Liam's already at the cafe. I'm starving."

"Uh-uh, Chook—you lost that bet fair and square," Bickie insisted. Bare feet up on the long, curved bench under the windows, he popped one of his trademark biscuits in his mouth, this one a mint choc Tim Tam.

Cody grumbled. "Don't call me that. I'm Tassie, remember?"

Bickie laughed. "You're not gonna ditch the original nickname if you whinge about losing bets. Get scrubbin', mate."

Cody groaned dramatically, smiling as he disappeared into the locker room. Damo was dying to ask him about getting secretly engaged, but no, he'd promised Liam. And while earlier he'd merely considered telling Liam about Blake, now the need to talk *burned*.

Damo handed Teddy his binos. "Hardly anything happening. I'll give him a hand." He realized Teddy and Bickie were staring in disbelief. "What? I'm a kind and generous pal."

"More than we knew, apparently," Bickie said through a mouthful of chocolate crumbs.

Heart thumping, Damo hopped down the steps and hurried along the short passage, the tile cool under his bare feet. He pushed open the door to the small locker room ringed by battered yellow lockers. He could hear running water in the adjoining toilet. What should he say to Cody?

To start, he could tell him about Blake—

With a giddy rush, Damo had to stop and get a grip. Just thinking Blake's name was enough for a flood of memories— *dancing, touching, kissing, sucking, talking, laughing*. Standing in the locker room, his fingers twitched to get out his phone. What if Blake hadn't texted?

"What if the pope grows a set of wings and flies away?" he muttered to himself. "Check the bloody thing, ya pork chop."

He fumbled with the lock, and it took three tries to get the right combination. His heart was ready to explode by the time he looked at the messages appearing on the screen. There were a couple from Mum and Tabby and—*there*. There!

Hey. I had an amazing time last night. Looking forward to to-

morrow. I hope—

Damo lifted the phone to his face to unlock it. "Come on, come on…" He continued reading the message, holding his breath like he was under crashing swells.

—you are too. If you're freaking out or anything, you can tell me.

He reread those four words: *You can tell me.*

Relief washed through him. Blake somehow understood. Now he needed to respond. Shit. Damo typed and retyped before going with a simple white lie:

Not freaking. See u tomorrow :)

He hit send before he could second-guess the smiley face. Then he stared at the text for a good solid minute, praying the reply bubbles would appear.

It was fine. He wasn't freaking out. He was going to put away his phone and continue definitely, positively, a hundred percent not freaking out. He locked his phone with determination.

Leaning in the doorway to the toilet, he said to Cody, who was bent over the bowl with the seat up, holding a stained scrubber, "I'll give you a hand."

"Yeah? Sweet, thanks." Cody grimaced. "Council needs to pay cleaners for this shit. Literally." He motioned to the open door next to the toilet, a small white-tiled room that held a single shower stall. "And if everyone would squeegee the shower after like they're supposed to, it wouldn't build up like this."

"Mm."

"The tile cleaner's there by the bucket."

"Uh-huh."

Maybe he should have left off the smiley? He wouldn't have thought twice with a chick, so maybe he was being sexist or something? Tabby would probably have an opinion—not that he was going to tell her about Blake. Not yet. Not until he knew for sure there was something to tell.

He twisted his hair around his index finger, going to the root then back down to repeat.

"So, by giving me a hand, you mean you're going to watch me clean?" Cody asked.

"Huh? Yep."

Cody snorted. "You're all heart." The yellow cleaning gloves went almost to his elbows below his faded Billabong T-shirt. He scratched his nose with his upper arm. "Had enough cleaning toilets lately. Did I tell you there was a flood in the new pod we bought for guests?"

"The what?"

"The steel pod we put in the backyard after all the council paperwork. One bedroom and bathroom, but the bloody plumber didn't hook up the water properly. Good thing no one'd actually used the toilet. Liam flushed it to make sure it was working."

"Good thing you found out sooner rather than later."

Cody grimaced. "You're telling me. One of my sisters is visiting later this year for a month, so we decided to invest in it since Liam's house isn't that big."

"Isn't it your house now too?"

"I guess so, yeah." He smiled softly. "Moved in over a year ago, and sometimes, it still feels like a dream. In the best way."

Heart thumping, Damo looked behind to make sure they were still alone and that the locker room door was shut. He cleared his throat, breathing through the rush of nerves. "Remember that clubbie who helped with those Irish tourists panicking in the Croc?"

"Uh, I think so? The surfer? You know, I thought he looked familiar." Cody cringed as he got the scrubber up under the rim. "Good thing he was there. That was hectic."

"Yeah. I saw him last night. At, um, Rodeo, that new club in Freo."

"Cool. Who'd you go with? I wish Liam would give it a try. It'd be fun to go dancing for a change. Not that Liam would dance in public, but if we went with a group, it could be fun."

"It is, yeah. Blake and I were dancing. That's his name—Blake. Blake the bloke." Damo laughed, his breath high and tight, fingers twitching. "That's who I went with."

Cody glanced up from the toilet. "Cool. I didn't realize you were mates."

"It was kinda like, you know." He glanced behind him and lowered his voice. "Like a date."

Of course, Cody had flushed the toilet at the same moment. "Sorry, what?" He dropped the scrubber back in its holder with a grimace. "You went on a date? Do I know her?"

Damo fidgeted. "*Maaate*, don't make me say it again."

Forehead creased, Cody said, "Sorry, I'm confused."

"Forget it." Damo backed up and thumped into the doorframe. "I should get back."

"Wait. You're upset." Cody reached out, and Damo dodged the yellow glove with a yelp. "Ugh, hold on." Cody stripped off the gloves, dropping them on the sink ledge with a *thwap*. "What did you want to tell me?"

"Nothing! Everything. Dunno." Damo crossed his arms, then fiddled with the cord necklace.

"It's okay. I'm listening." Cody waited patiently. This was why Cody was the perfect person to tell. Not only because he was gay, but of Damo's mates, he was by far the most in touch with feelings and all that shit.

"I'm bloody tryin' but…" He exhaled a long breath.

"So, you went on a date? What does it have to do with the clubbie?"

"Everything! I met up with Blake the clubbie at the new gay place. There were no chicks. I mean, of course there were chicks there, but I wasn't—we were—I was with *him*."

Cody's eyebrows shot up. "Oh! I didn't think you—" He nodded. "Huh. Okay, cool." He blinked a few times, then grinned. "Liam was right."

"Wait, what? Liam thinks that I'm—" Damo waved his hand.

"It occurred to him. Don't worry, we don't regularly sit around talking about your sexuality. But you're…exploring? That's awesome. Right?"

"Kind of? Yes?" He glanced at the door again, but they were still alone.

"It's okay. Breathe." Cody kept his voice low and steady. "This disgusting bathroom is a safe space."

Damo nodded. After breathing in and out, the humid air smelling like fake lemons, he whispered, "I've never been with a bloke before. But after the rescue, he kind of asked me out. I don't know why I went."

"Yes, you do," Cody said calmly.

"I mean, I guess I was curious?" He shifted restlessly. "No, I definitely was."

"Was this the first time you've been curious?"

He thought of getting hard watching Cody and Liam kissing in the tower. His face went so hot he must've looked like a lobster. He shook his head. "But it's the first time I've done something about it."

"And you did some…" Cody made a rolling motion with his hand. "Things?"

"I had a dick in my mouth!" he whisper-shouted. "*His* dick!"

Cody laughed. "You'd be pretty flexible if it was your own. And did you like it?"

"Heck yeah." Damo giggled, his body flushing to talk about it out loud. "I liked it. We kissed and got naked and rubbed off. Nothing else. Like, we didn't…you know."

"Right. Take it slow."

Damo nodded. Then burst out with, "I don't want to! I'm dying to do it again. Do everything." He ran his bare toe along the grouted tile floor, tracing a square. "I'm nervous but excited at the same time."

"I know that feeling." Cody smiled, his gaze going fond and distant. "Experimenting can be awesome. Do you want to go back to the club and meet more guys? I could be your wingman."

It hadn't even occurred to him, and Damo fidgeted as he imagined hooking up with other faceless blokes. "But they wouldn't be Blake."

"I'll take care of you."

Cody's smile brightened. "Oh, so you like him! It wasn't just a hookup."

"I don't really do that."

"Okay. I guess I assumed you did since I don't think you've had a steady girlfriend since I've known you?"

Damo shrugged. "I haven't."

Memories of Shaz filled his mind, dominated by the first and only night she'd spent at the house. He cringed to think of it. They'd been nineteen, and Mum had said of course his girlfriend could stay over.

Crammed onto his twin bed with the saggy mattress and creaky springs. Not that they'd been up to anything aside from trying to sleep before everything went wrong…

"Hey, it's okay." Cody was frowning at him. "You don't have to have a bunch of hookups. Do you want to see Blake again?"

He nodded. "I like him. We just met, but… I feel like I can trust him." Damo thought of Blake's strong arms around him, his offer to play video games, texting his mum to make sure she was right. "Is that weird?"

"Nope. That's how you know you're a grownup. Responsibility becomes super hot." Cody shuddered. "I did the bad boy thing once upon a time, and yeah, nah."

"I just met him, so it's not like we even know each other."

"Yeah, but you know when there's a spark."

Damo nodded. "Kissing was like…New Year's Eve. Fireworks,

I mean—not bogans puking on the beach."

"Duly noted."

"What if it's just because I haven't gotten off with anyone in an embarrassingly long time?"

"Hey, it's nothing to be embarrassed about," Cody said seriously. "Nothing wrong with being celibate."

Damo cringed. "I'm not a bloody priest."

"I know, but—okay, what's your concern? That you're having these feelings for Blake because of the good sex?" At Damo's nod, Cody said, "Sure, pheromones and stuff like that can be part of it. There's only one way to find out, and that's to spend more time with Blake. See where it goes."

Damo shivered with eagerness. "Hate waiting until tomorrow to see him again. Haven't liked someone this much in a while." He thought of Shaz again with a mix of fondness and regret.

"When was the last time?" Cody asked. "A few years ago?"

Damo hesitated. His stomach gurgled with acid thinking about it. It wasn't like it had ended with a big fight or anything. Shaz was a great chick. But Damo had ruined it. Why had he ever thought her staying over was a good idea?

He wouldn't make that mistake again.

"Yeah. Shaz Warner. She lives in the valley past Barking. She went to uni in Perth." He shrugged. "Just fizzled out." It was mostly true. The awkwardness had been too much to get past. "Got busy with work and surfing. Thought maybe there could be something with Mia at first, but we're much better as mates."

He'd realized he'd dodged a bullet anyway. The beach was separate from home, and it was better that way. Sure, Blake was a clubbie, but they didn't work together. It would just get too messy otherwise.

"Bet Blake made a good first impression helping you with that rescue." Cody waggled his eyebrows. "Pretty hot that he backed up."

Damo couldn't hide a grin. "Yeah. I told him I'd shout him a beer, and he invited me to Rodeo."

"Were you nervous? Good on ya for going. That took guts."

Damo flushed with pleasure. "Thanks. Yeah, I was heaps nervous, but I guess I couldn't resist." He added, "I still like chicks. I'm not, like, suddenly gay."

Cody squeezed his shoulder. "Whatever and whoever you are is a hundred percent okay. You don't have to figure it out today."

"Right." Damo took a deep breath and huffed it out. "Thanks, mate. You're good to talk to about this."

"Anytime. I mean it."

"You won't tell anyone, though?" He shook his head quickly. "No. I know you won't. Sorry."

"S'okay." Cody grimaced. "After what happened with Liam…"

"Nah. You were off your head. Doesn't count. Speaking of Liam—" *God*, he was so curious, but he had to wait for Cody to spill about this possible engagement. "If you want to tell him, that's cool."

"Trust me, he can keep a secret." Cody hesitated. "You know Liam had a really tough time coming out. It's still hard sometimes, especially with his asshole parents, but he's so much happier now. Everyone has their own situation and journey, but anytime you want to talk, we're here for you."

"Thanks, mate. I'm here for you guys too. For anything you might want to tell me. Or not! Whatever. I'm here. Anything. Big or small. Something pretty big, maybe?"

With a deep sigh, Cody rolled his eyes. "Don't tell me Liam spilled it. After I just said he was the best at keeping secrets!"

"Not his fault! I'm an ace detective. It's true, though?" Damo glanced at the empty locker room and made a motion with his hands.

"That I'm jerking him off?" A smile tugged on Cody's lips.

Damo looked down at his hands. "This is putting a ring on!"

"Then why are you going up and down? Just put it on once. And yes," he whispered, clearly trying to fight a grin. "We're going to get married. Not sure when yet."

"And I'll be your best man? Sounds great."

Cody laughed. "I was thinking flower girl."

"Ohhh. I can braid some in my hair." He twirled, full of nerves and excitement. He needed a good paddle out to burn off the energy. "Don't worry, I won't say a word until you guys announce it to the world. And thanks, mate. I feel better. Feeling a million things."

"It's been, what, a day? Feel all the feels. Be excited about this guy. You deserve it."

Damo scoffed. "Dunno about that." He thought of that morning and how he should've set an alarm so Tabby didn't have to deal with Dad.

Cody frowned. "Of course you deserve it. All work and no play, right? See what happens with Blake." He pulled Damo into a tight hug, and Damo held on gratefully.

Cody stepped back and grinned. "Have fun. Now get out of here before I make you help for real." He looked down at the shower stall floor. "How is there so much hair in that drain?"

Damo backed away, hands up. "Later!"

Back by the tower windows, he scanned the gray waves and the handful of swimmers back in the water now that the drizzle had let up.

Bickie asked, "What are you grinning about?"

Damo shrugged, spinning on his chair. "Dunno."

He decided he was glad he'd sent Blake the smiley face, and almost wished it had been a heart.

Chapter Nine

"**B**LAKE!"

He turned, wincing as Kat marched toward him in their uniform. He'd just changed out of his into his half wetsuit after his morning shift. Blake planted his board in the sand.

Frowning, Kat asked, "You right?"

"Yeah, I'm good. You?"

"Then why are you ignoring my texts?"

He winced. Had he not responded at all? "Sorry. Thought I replied. Yesterday was really busy."

Pursing their lips, Kat pulled out their phone. "When I asked how Friday night went, you replied, and I quote, 'It was great!' and didn't answer any follow-up questions."

"Oops. I was distracted yesterday. Helped my mate Rocky from work, and then he had a barbecue and insisted I stay. And I…had a lot on my mind."

Kat stepped closer on the hot sand, shielding their eyes from the sun. "And did that include a certain spunky lifeguard you left the club with?"

He couldn't hide a grin. "It did." Among other things.

Kat lifted their hand for a high five. "So, it really was great? Didn't know whether to believe you or let you lick your wounds in peace."

"How many follow-up texts did you send?" Aside from texting Damo, he'd ignored his other texts since he'd been too busy hitting refresh on his email.

"I definitely didn't leave you in peace. So?" They smacked his arm. "Spill!"

"I can't!" Blake glanced around. "I'm meeting him here any minute. And aren't you on patrol?"

Kat groaned. "Fine." Their eyes lit up. "Here he comes." They waved. "Hiya, Damo!"

"Hey, mate." Longboard the color of the sky under one arm, blond hair flowing, and his wetsuit unzipped to his navel, Damo slapped Kat's hand and gave them a half-hug. "How ya goin'?"

God, he was *gorgeous*. Seeing him again had Blake tingling all over.

"Not as good as you two." Kat grinned, then made a lip-zipping motion and disappeared into the crowd.

"I didn't tell them anything!" Blake said, exhaling when Damo just laughed.

"It's okay."

"You sure?"

"Yeah. I think so? They're not going to tell anyone, right?"

"No, don't worry." He hadn't known Kat long, but Blake trusted them.

"Cool." Biting his lip, Damo said, "Um, hi."

"Hi." The urge to pull him close for a kiss was overwhelming, and Blake picked up his board for something to do with his hands. "You're doing okay with…everything?"

"Yeah." Damo was jostled by a pack of kids racing by. "Is that weird?"

"No! That's awesome. I'm really glad to hear it. Relieved. First times can be…confronting. Not in a bad way, but. Well, sometimes in a bad way, I suppose."

"Right." Damo's gaze dipped down Blake's body and back up.

"Feelin' pretty good about it, to be honest." He ducked his head.

"Glad to hear it." He'd worried about it a bit but Tasha's email had taken up most of his mental energy. Maybe that was a blessing in disguise.

They grinned at each other until Damo said, "Should we get in?"

Ahh.

The first wash of cool water over his feet and shins as his toes sank into the wet sand was a moment Blake savored every single time he walked into the ocean. For that moment, the noise and bustle of Barking faded.

"Feels good, hey?" Damo grinned, and Blake realized he'd *ahhhed* aloud.

"Like the sea's giving me a kiss in welcome. Or benediction, maybe."

Damo whistled, adjusting his board under his arm. "That's a ten-dollar word. Bloody poetic. Can tell you were artsy-fartsy at uni."

Blake laughed. "Guilty."

"Like a kiss," Damo murmured, pausing with the water around his shins, the leash around his ankle floating up. They both wore summer wetsuits that came to their knees with sleeves cut just above the elbows. "Know what I love? When you stand here, and the tide steals the sand from under your feet. Like the sea's grabbin' hold. Sucking you out."

"Into its oft-deadly embrace like a siren's song?"

Damo laughed. "Sure. We'll go with that." He marched on, bracing as the shore break crashed and foamed around his slim thighs, the black neoprene showing off lean muscles. His sun-touched blond curls brushed the tops of his shoulder blades. He really was a stereotypical surfer fantasy brought to life.

Blake's belly tightened as he remembered those lean thighs spread and trembling under his mouth and hands. Damo vulnerable and trusting and beautiful. Blake practically had to pinch himself that he was seeing him again. With everything going on—

No.

He wasn't going to worry about that while he was with Damo. He couldn't check his email while surfing. For now, he had to be in the moment.

Flat on their boards on their stomachs, they paddled out, punching through the swells. Gripping the sides of his board on the rails, Blake duck-dived under a curling wave, straightening his arms and pushing the nose of his board down as hard as he could while lifting his hips and shoving down with his knee.

He just made it out of the impact zone, holding on to the rails as hard as he could, fighting the water's force that wanted to rip the board from his hands.

When he popped up safely on the other side, he licked happily at the salt on his lips, blinking in the sunlight warm on his skin. As usual on a sunny Sunday, Barking Beach thronged with people, and they were careful to stay out of the way of the incoming surfers while avoiding the swimmers who ignored the signs not to swim at the north end of the beach.

They joined the lineup out the back of the breakers where other surfers waited for good sets to roll in, staying out of the Croc's jaws. They sat up, straddling their boards, feet dangling in the clear blue water. There wasn't much at the moment, the sea flattening out.

"Do the garbos appreciate your poetry?"

"Oh yeah," Blake said very seriously. "I started a book club. We're discussing pathetic fallacy in twentieth century Depression-era fiction."

"Bet my garbo Alf would have some keen insights."

"Undoubtedly." Blake chuckled. "They're good blokes. Maybe not the most poetically minded, but solid. They remind me of the stockmen who looked after the sheep and cattle where I grew up. What you see is what you get."

"It's the only way to be." Damo gazed out at the flattening surf. "Looks like we'll have to wait a bit. Unless you want to go in and grab one of the smaller breaks?"

"Nah. Happy to wait." Blake smoothed his palm over the waxy fiberglass of his board, the red-tinged orange bright against his tanned skin. The salty breeze was perfect under the powerful sun. A world away from Blinman.

Damo asked, "So, were you one of those outback kids with posters of Mick Fanning in your room, choking on red dust and dreaming of the ocean?"

He laughed. "Yep. Had a few of Mick and Luke Steadman. I didn't mind the bush, but the coast drew me like a magnet. I always knew I wanted to move away for uni. Country life isn't for me."

"You don't sound like you're from the bush."

He laughed. "Let's just say my vocab improved when I moved to Melbourne."

"Did you always have your nose in books?"

"Definitely." Blake ran his fingers through the water. "Good thing I didn't get sick reading on the bus since it was almost an hour and a half each way to school."

Damo whistled. "Puts my fifteen-minute walk to shame!" He squinted behind them. "Swells should pick up soon." Turning his blue eyes to Blake, he said, "What hooked you on the water?"

He thought of school holidays and begging his parents to take him to the Gold Coast. "It was so far from home. From my little world. Then I tried surfing during uni. A mate was going for a weekend beginners' lesson in Torquay, and she didn't want to go alone."

"Don't tell me you learned at Bells? You legend!"

Blake laughed. "That would be intense. We learned close to it, though. Went down to watch the experts on Rincon and the Bowl. Those breaks are epic."

"I've got to make the trip one day."

"The pilgrimage is definitely worth it." Blake hadn't thought about Bells Beach or surfing in Torquay for ages. Melbourne and uni seemed so long ago even though it'd only been a few years.

Returning to Blinman and the endless dirt and dry, rocky ranges had made it seem like a dream. But now, he was here in Barking. He'd made it happen.

"How're you likin' being a clubbie?"

"I love it. Kat and the others are great. Really made me feel welcome. I'm spending my free time here anyway, *and* I get to help people. Best of both worlds."

"I know what ya mean. I admit, I do like gettin' paid for it. You could always take the lifeguard test and come on as a casual worker. Some of the boys have other full-time jobs."

"Hmm. I'm probably more needed as a volunteer, though. There's so much I can do to help."

Damo watched him, a little smile tugging at his full lips. "Clubbies are lucky to have ya. So's Barkers."

Secretly pleased, Blake shrugged.

Damo closed his eyes and tipped his head back, the sun bright on his tanned face, the freckles on his nose adorable—and sexy. "How good's this?" he asked, eyes still shut as a small swell lifted their boards like they were being rocked gently in a cradle.

"Damn good."

It was everything Blake had fantasized about when he'd bobbed out there alone, letting quality waves pass by if Damo was out doing a rescue. Watching from afar and indulging his little crush on a cute lifeguard with red sunnies and blond hair and a crooked smile…

Now here they were. It was too good to be true.

The nagging worry about the email and everything it meant

was eclipsed by sudden fear that he was getting ahead of himself. Yes, Damo had wanted to see him again today, but what if it fizzled out tomorrow?

It had been Damo's first time with a man, and Blake couldn't let himself get carried away. He'd already had a little daydream earlier about what it would be like to actually have a partner and a family…

He blurted, "Do you really like me?" and his stomach dropped into the ocean depths. He was usually so much better at biting his tongue.

Damo lifted his head and blinked at him. "Uh, yeah, mate." He glanced around, perhaps seeing if the other surfers were in earshot, and lowered his voice. "Would've brushed you if I didn't like you."

"Right, of course. Forget I asked. Please."

Damo was frowning now, though. "You like me too, right?"

"Yes!" He wanted to reach out and take Damo's hand but it might make him uncomfortable. "I just had the thought that this was way too good to be true."

"Like, *I* am?" Damo looked incredulous as he jabbed a thumb at his chest.

"Yes, you." Blake stroked his hands through the clear water and kicked closer, just out of reach, keeping his voice low. "I know you had a good time Friday night. But it was also your first time. What if you're just caught up in that, and it's not really *me*?"

"Like, it's hormones or something?" Damo bit his lip. "Look, I'm not sayin' sex isn't on my mind." He lifted his eyebrows. "It *is*. Like, a *lot*. But I wouldn't want to surf with ya if that's all it was."

Blake found himself grinning. "So, it's on your mind?"

Damo rolled his eyes with a laugh. "You haven't thought about it?"

"Oh, I've thought about it. This is good too, though. Surfing. Talking."

"Yeah."

"And I know you're still acclimating. I'm not expecting anything."

Damo's brows met. "I'm what?"

"Getting used to this. New feelings and experiences. I'll keep my distance in public."

"Right, that." He glanced around. "Yeah, I think I want to get used to it more before everyone knows." He quickly added, "I'm not ashamed. I don't think it's that? If I'm bi or whatever, that's cool. I just... I want this to be for me right now. It's mine."

Blake smiled softly. "I'll be yours as long as you want me." He raised his hands. "No pressure. That sounded way too intense. Sorry. I tend to go all in when I want something." He grimaced. "Just ask my ex."

And why hadn't Tasha responded to his reply to her email yet? Had he come on too strong?

Damo's eyes widened as a bigger swell lifted them. "What happened?"

Blake sighed. "I met Lance in my last year of uni. Everything was great at first. He wasn't interested in surfing or swimming, but he was kind and sweet. I really wanted a steady boyfriend. A partner. We had fun together, but I rushed us into moving in together. I suppose it was good in a way because we realized we were *not* compatible. God, he was so messy."

Damo winced. "Uh-oh. I have bad news about my tidiness."

Blake laughed. "Don't worry, I know not everyone is a neat freak like me. The issue with Lance was he didn't want me doing his dishes or picking up his socks. He'd get mad, but he wouldn't do it himself."

Laughing, Damo waved a dismissive hand. "No worries, mate. You're free to clean up after me all ya like. Encouraged, even."

"Yeah? Lance found it 'overbearing,' even though I was only trying to help. Also, yeah, nah—I can't have smelly socks just lying around when there's a perfectly good hamper."

"Reckon most people aren't keen on it. Can't say it bothers me." Damo frowned. "Dunno. That might not be true. It's just lower down the list of shit to do."

"Honestly, his not letting me clean up after him was a metaphor for our relationship. I was too much, and he was too stubborn. He hated taking help. He'd say he didn't need handouts—as if that even made sense with a sink of dirty dishes. His dad did a real number on him, I think."

"So, that's what did ya in?"

"For the most part. We were fundamentally incompatible. We graduated, and then I had to go home to help Mum and Dad. After a few weeks, Lance didn't understand why I was still there, and there was no point in trying long distance. It wasn't that I didn't love him. I did. He's a great person. We still text once in a while. But to go from living together and quarreling most of the time to long distance didn't make sense. It felt like going backward."

Damo nodded seriously. "I know exactly what you mean. You can't go from all in to halfway."

"Exactly!" Damo got it—which of course only made Blake like him more. He forced himself to be logical. "So, we're agreed we should take things slowly. Not get ahead of ourselves."

Damo leaned sideways and held out his fist to be bumped. "Deal."

The fleeting touch of Damo's warm knuckles sent a bolt of desire through Blake. They shared a long, silent look as they rose up on a growing swell.

Damo said, "But that doesn't mean we're not gonna, you know."

"Definitely not. We're going to. ASAP, really."

They laughed, and he gazed out at the horizon and the faint pink that sometimes appeared where the blue sky met the ocean.

"I love this. With Lance, we didn't want to do the same things on the weekend. Not that the guy I'm dating has to share all my interests, but surfing's…"

"More than an interest, mate. It's life."

Blake's heart skipped. "Yes."

Go. Slowly. Stop thinking about how perfect he is.

Unfortunately, his brain instead called up the anxiety about not hearing back from Tasha yet. He had to be patient. He'd taken his time that night to think before replying to her as the sun came up. He'd crashed for a few hours of sleep before going to Rocky's, hoping she'd have replied that morning.

Now it was Sunday afternoon, and nothing. He reminded himself again it was the weekend and she was surely busy.

"You right?"

Blake jerked his gaze from the rippled surface of the water to Damo. "Sorry." He forced a smile. "I was… Uh, thinking poetic thoughts about the cerulean blue of the sea. Or maybe it's azure."

Damo's furrowed brow smoothed. "Or…navy?" He laughed. "I think 'turquoise' is the fanciest word for blue I know."

"Sapphire? Like your eyes."

Damo laughed again, but this time he ducked his head, golden hair falling to obscure the pink flushing his cheeks. There were some shouts from nearby, and they turned.

"Go the groms!" Damo cheered for the group of preteen boys paddling for the small set coming through. "Get it!"

Blake watched them, and another bolt of tension returned. He tried to shove it aside again. He asked Damo, "Guess you were a grommet here too?"

"Yep." Damo tucked his hair behind his ear as the sea surged beneath them. "I was here every day, all day, until Mum told me it was time to come home. Back then, you could see the corner of our front porch if you stood on the concrete wall along the back of the sand. She'd put out a ratty old yellow towel when it was time for me to come in. I'd hop up on the wall holding my breath, hoping to just see the faded blue wood and no yellow."

Blake glanced toward shore, squinting at the roofs of the houses that fanned out on quiet little twisty streets. "Wow, you live close."

Damo hesitated, then said, "Yeah, stone's throw."

"Cool." He wasn't sure what had caused the hesitation.

It was back now, Damo looking toward shore with a little frown. He pointed. "You see the big brick and glass monstrosity back there to the left of the tower? We're behind it. Used to be a single-story cottage in front of us. The new house barely fits on the property. Wankers. Council should never have approved it."

"Definitely not."

Blake watched another boy paddle madly for a small wave, trying to time it right. Something brushed his foot, and he jerked, heart in his throat, sending up a splash as he spun and searched for a killer fin, even though a shark would chomp his foot off, not stroke it gently.

Damo laughed. "Chill! It was me." He leaned forward, whispering, "Was just trying to get your attention." He glanced around. The closest surfers were at least five meters away—and apparently Damo deemed that far enough because he gave him a flirty little grin.

"Sorry. I'm slightly paranoid about sharks. Footsy wouldn't normally freak me out that much."

"It's cool." The crease reappeared between Damo's brows. "You seem distracted, though. Sure you're okay?"

"Yeah." He rubbed his face, saltwater stinging his eye thanks to his wet hand. "Look, it's not you. God, we literally just agreed to go slowly, but I have to tell you—I just went all in on something else. Something big. Huge."

Damo tilted his head. "You're not, like, seeing someone else?"

"No, no! Nothing like that. You're the only person I'm seeing.

The only guy I want to see!"

Slow. Down.

His throat was dry. He hadn't planned on talking about it to Damo, and he hadn't spoken of it to anyone yet. The words didn't want to budge.

"You can tell me," Damo said, his tone so serious and sweet, his expression open again.

Damo had trusted Blake the other night. He deserved the same in return, and even if they were going to take things slowly, this was too big to keep under wraps. If it scared off Damo, Blake would have to accept that.

He took a deep breath. "It's a game changer. A *life* changer. It's heavy for a second date."

Damo looked at him with concern, those sapphire eyes soft. "You can tell me. What happened?"

Blake swung his feet restlessly in the water. The lifeguard Jet Ski roared in the distance, on an endless loop of picking up swimmers in over their heads.

"I got an email. Didn't recognize the name, and then I realized it was from Tasha Rutledge, the cousin of one of my old mates from home. I only met her once, and it was years ago. Almost nine years ago, as a matter of fact. Tasha visited Blinman one summer, just for a week. A bunch of us went bush camping. Lazed around the swimming hole during the day, then drank beer by the fire. You know."

"Talkin' shit, looking at the stars."

"Yep. And hooking up. I hadn't been with a bloke yet, and there were zero local prospects. I was horny as hell. Tash was keen, so I thought, Why not? Everyone was pairing off, and I reckoned it was my chance to experiment. She said she was on the pill, so there was nothing to worry about."

Damo's eyes widened. "Those words just struck fear in my soul."

Blake sucked in a breath and blew it out shakily. "Turns out I have a son." A shiver raced down his spine to hear himself say it.

I have a son.

It still didn't sound true. "I have a *son*," he repeated. "He's eight. He lives in Sydney with Tash and her husband."

Damo's cheeks puffed out. "Whoa."

"Yeah."

"Far out," Damo murmured, tucking a damp curl behind his ear. "I'm sorry? No, that doesn't feel like the right thing to say."

"I didn't know how to feel." The breeze misted salt over Blake's face. He closed his eyes briefly and breathed, the sun bright behind his eyes.

"And you just found out?"

"Got the email Friday night. It was when you went to the toilet, actually. I was in shock. Felt like all the air had been sucked out of my flat with a giant vacuum."

"Ohhh. Yeah, you seemed distracted. I was afraid you were going to ghost me since you'd gotten what you wanted." Damo fiddled with his hair, looking away.

Blake waited until Damo's skittish gaze met his. "Trust me, I haven't even come close to getting what I want from you. *With* you. Barely scratched the surface."

Damo laughed, nervous and breathy. "Cool." A bigger swell rolled through, the wind spraying them with foam. A drop hung on his chin, and Blake wanted to lick it away.

Damo said, "It must've blown your mind, dude. The email, I mean."

"Yeah. Lots of mind-blowing activities lately."

There was that pretty blush again. "So, what did she say? Why tell you now after so long?"

"Said she realized it had been unfair not to tell me. She wanted to make it right for me and Cooper. That's his name. God, it's bizarre to be saying this. I still can't believe it's real."

"I can imagine. My email's lifeguard scheduling, daft forwards from my Auntie Shirl down in Tassie—that woman's never met a conspiracy theory she didn't believe—and spam from Optus trying to get me to increase my mobile coverage. Haven't had any 'Long time no see, P.S., you're a dad. Good on ya.'"

Bobbing on the waves, Blake laughed, and it felt *amazing*. He'd been joking and smiling with Damo earlier, and he hadn't fully clocked how tense he'd been underneath. The lump of stress lodged in his chest was loosening. "It's a first for me too. That was the only time I've had sex with a woman, and there are no plans for an encore."

"If she was your first and only, doesn't sound like she made a great impression in the bedroom," Damo joked. "Or I guess it was in a swag or tent."

"Just the swag, off in the bushes away from everyone else."

"You're lucky a snake didn't chomp yer balls! You outback kids."

"You're telling me you've never gotten up to mischief in those beach dunes? There are snakes in there too."

"Yeah, fair cop." Damo grimaced. "My old girlfriend Mel lost her sparkly new thongs in the dunes in year ten." He pointed to the north of Barking, where a rocky spit of land jutted out. "Around the bend over there. Made me go back and look for them. I admit I didn't look too hard. I'm not sticking my hand in a dugite nest or whatever they call their little snake houses. Then I had to piggyback her all the way home because she said the pavement hurt her feet."

Blake frowned. "What kind of Aussie girl can't walk in bare feet?"

"Thank you! That's what I said. She didn't appreciate it. At all."

"Can't blame her for wanting to climb on you. And in Tash's defense, it really was me and not her. She was beautiful. Older, so she knew what she was doing, which was part of the appeal. I'd planned to have sex for the first time when I went to uni, but I decided it was a good opportunity to gain some experience."

"Like a science experiment."

He laughed. "I suppose so. I had fun that night, though. First orgasm with another person. Friction is a wonderful thing."

"Mate!" Damo grinned, shaking his head. "You never got off with another boy?"

"I wish. My options were extremely limited. Even at school. There was a bit of experimenting when I was twelve or thirteen with one of my mates. It never really went anywhere."

"So, you enjoyed your experiment, but not enough to get with a chick again?"

"Nah. The spark's missing. I don't feel the way I do with men. Don't feel that…hunger."

Damo shifted on his board, his fingers opening and closing where his hand rested on his thigh. "Right."

Blake watched the motion of Damo's fingers, a curl of lust rippling through his belly. "Anyway, Tash was finishing uni back then. She's about four years older."

Damo frowned. "Pretty big difference. I can't imagine getting with a teenager now."

"I hear you. It didn't seem strange at the time. It's different in the country. Did I mention my town has a population of less than fifty and a lot of them are either related to me or old?"

"Fair enough, hey." Damo chuckled.

"She said in the email that her husband's been a great father. They've got another kid as well. But I guess Cooper's been asking about who I am."

"Why didn't she tell you at the time?"

"She figured it was her problem. That's how she put it. I was seventeen, and she lived in Sydney a few thousand kilometers away. She didn't say much else. Not yet, anyway." The sun was hot on the back of his neck, the neoprene leaving a few bare centimeters. "She also said there's no pressure. If I don't want anything to do with Cooper, that would be that."

Damo didn't hesitate. "Nah. Not an option."

"Nope." Blake's lungs expanded more freely, sucking in the fresh salty air. "He's my son. I have to know him. I've always wanted kids, but being gay, I knew it wouldn't be easy. But I have a *child.* He's already out there in the world. Right now, he's breathing and thinking and talking and doing whatever kids do on summer Sundays."

"Maybe he's at the beach in Sydney."

Blake grinned. "Maybe." His smile faded. "I'm still waiting for Tasha to reply to me. I told her I absolutely want to be a father to Cooper. I'm all in. Maybe she wasn't expecting that? I don't know. I need to be patient. I'm sure she didn't know if I'd even reply. If it was even the right email address."

"Right. Give her time." Damo whistled. "Bro, that *is* heavy. But I'm glad you told me."

"Me too. I didn't want to dump it on you, but it feels good to say it out loud."

"Don't want to open up to the garbos after book club?"

Blake laughed, his shoulders shaking and head back in the bright sun. "Most of those blokes have kids, so maybe I should. I almost told my mate Rocky yesterday, but I was still processing."

He watched a big set roll in, lifting them on a powerful surge, powering toward the break, where surfers paddled hard to catch it. "*I* have a kid. Don't even know where to start."

"Sure ya do. First, we're going for this next set, because it's going to be roarin'. We'll carve it up and try not to nosedive, then paddle back out and do it again. And again. Then we'll grab a feed, and hopefully by tonight, she'll have emailed back."

"That's a good plan. I like having a plan."

"Fair warning: I'm gonna touch your foot with mine. I'm not a shark."

"I appreciate the heads-up." Blake rubbed his foot against Damo's under the water. "You make me believe everything'll be okay."

"It will, mate." Damo looked out into the endless blue. "This is where you don't have to worry. Where you can just be. You can catch this wave and not think about anything but the ride. Get this one. Now paddle!"

Blake flopped down and paddled toward the break where the wave met the reef and carried them up and away.

"Go, you good thing!" Damo shouted.

Blake barely made it to his feet as the water surged up beneath him, the power still shocking no matter how many countless hours he'd practiced. He only held his crouch for two seconds before the wall of water closed in around him in an explosion of foam.

Holding his breath, he counted the seconds as he was tossed back and forth under the churning surface, powerless to do anything but wait until the wave chewed him up and spit him out.

It was six seconds before he came up, his board rebounding on the leash around his ankle and thunking into his side. Kicking hard, he swam out of the impact zone and back into the rip, climbing on his board and letting the Croc take him out the back.

He blinked in surprise to see Damo waiting. "You didn't get the next one?" he called as Damo paddled over to him.

"Bailed at the last second. You right?" Damo peered at Blake seriously.

"Aside from getting smoked? I'm great." He sat up, straddling his board and wiping water from his face.

"Did you swallow much water?" Damo sat up too, his knee bumping Blake's as he peered at him seriously.

"Nah. I'm good. You're hot when you're in lifeguard mode, you know that?"

"What?" Damo fought a smile. "Shut up." He grew serious again. "Want to head in?"

"Are you kidding? Wiping out is part of the fun. I can handle it. I'm not a kook."

Damo laughed beside him. "Didn't say ya were, but just because you're not brand new with shit technique doesn't mean you're an expert. These sets have really picked up. Guess we were distracted." He glanced over his shoulder. "Ready?"

Blake grinned. "Ready."

Later, after he managed to stand up on a few waves, Blake watched as Damo unzipped his wetsuit on the beach and let it hang from his waist, his tanned chest glistening, dusted with hair the color of his darker roots beneath the sun-bleached gold. Sand clung to the two ridges in his abdominals, and Blake could imagine the flesh rippling under his touch. How ticklish was he?

Blake breathed through the surge of desire as Damo greeted someone he knew. He wanted to topple Damo into the sand and claim his mouth until the sun disappeared and it was only them left with the moon and the tide and hungry kisses.

"You up for grabbing a takeaway?" Damo asked, making Blake grin.

"Yeah. I'm starving. Want to drop off your board at home?"

Damo's head was down, his voice muffled as he unstrapped his leash from his ankle. "Nah. Come on, I'll show you the lifeguards' secret spot. My stuff's there."

Blake grabbed the reusable Woolies bag holding his towel, uniform, and fresh clothes, unzipping his wetsuit as well and letting the saltwater dry on his skin. Boards tucked under their arms, they crossed the hot sand, laughing at a girl bunny-hopping across it while complaining loudly to her mum, who ignored her.

Damo led the way into the garage under the lifeguard tower, and Blake leaned his board against the wall temporarily. Since the buggies and Jet Ski were in service, the bulk of the space was empty.

The metal trailer with racks where they'd stack the flags and warning signs at the end of the day sat waiting to be hooked up to one of the buggies. Various equipment lined the walls and was stacked in dank corners, and a hose hung on a hook.

In the back, Damo squeezed past a bike into a small storage room where a few sandy surfboards sat against the wall and another bike leaned on a kickstand.

He said, "Keep my board here sometimes, especially if I know I'm coming back early to catch a few sets before work. We can use the hose too." He grabbed his phone from a little hidden nook and frowned at it. "Sorry, hold on a sec."

"No worries." Blake itched to check his email, but his phone was safely locked in his glovebox. He knew some people buried their valuables in the sand before going in the water, but there were far too many thieves about.

As much as he wanted to check for Tasha's reply, his anxiety had calmed after talking to Damo. He waited while Damo tapped out a text, his brow furrowed deeply.

"Everything all right?" Blake asked after a few moments of Damo staring wordlessly at the screen.

"Yeah, 'course!" He tucked his phone in his bag.

Blake didn't quite believe him but didn't press. They were going slowly, after all.

He hadn't figured out Damo's family situation yet. Whatever it was, it stressed out Damo, although the text could have been about anything. Still, he wished he could help fix whatever it was that put the tension in Damo's shoulders and dropped the smile from his face.

In the main garage area, the concrete was damp and sandy and refreshingly cool after the scorched sand. The shade was a relief and the reliable afternoon breeze locals called the Doctor coming in off the ocean was bliss.

Beyond the garage's dimness, the sun and sand were blinding, the glare too strong to really even see the blue of the water. The noise of the beach—laughter and joyful shrieks, someone's obnoxious music on a boombox, gulls fighting over crumbs—fell away.

Damo turned on the hose and playfully sprayed it at Blake. Blake opened his arms wide and tipped back his head. "Have at it." He sighed contentedly as Damo cleaned him with the cool water, turning a full circle in the spray.

When Blake lifted his head, Damo was staring at his chest. Blake leered, and Damo blushed prettily before hosing himself down.

Damo's boardies and T-shirt were crumpled on a shelf in the little back storage room, and they returned there to change. Wetsuit still hanging from around his waist, Blake watched as Damo got naked—and realized he had an audience. The blush traveled down Damo's neck, and his Adam's apple bobbed.

"We can't," he whispered, craning his neck to peek into the garage. "Not here."

"Of course not." Still, Blake let his gaze travel slowly down and up Damo's bare body. He was still surprised he didn't see any tattoos. The tan line was just under Damo's waist where his boardies would sit. The upper half of his body and his feet and calves were bronzed and freckled, but his upper thighs and hips were pale as winter. His arse too.

Watching Damo's cock swell before his eyes was absolutely glorious. Blake murmured, "I'd never drop to my knees here and suck you off. Even though I bet I could have you coming down my throat in less than a minute."

"*Mate!*" Damo shout-whispered, sounding adorably scandalized, his eyes wide.

Blake could barely take his eyes off the pale, vulnerable skin of Damo's slim thighs. There was something so beautiful about it, the contrast to his tanned skin making it even more enticing. Like a secret to uncover. "Or I could eat your arse. Anyone ever rimmed you? I think you'll like it."

Those blue eyes grew even wider. "You mean, like…"

"I mean spreading you open and licking your hole. If I do it now—which I won't, of course since I wouldn't dream of it—it'll be salty, even a bit sandy. You'll taste like the beach, and I'll fuck you with my tongue and my fingers until you can barely stand."

He smiled slowly, looking down pointedly at Damo's flushed and straining cock, now fully hard. "Yeah, I think you'll like it." He rubbed his own hardening erection with the heel of his hand through his wetsuit. "We both will."

Damo licked his lips, his chest rising and falling as he stood frozen.

"Anyway, we'd better get going. I'm dying for a taco." Blake stripped off and changed into his boardies and white singlet as if they'd been talking about the weather. He kept his gaze anywhere but on Damo, who finally made a high-pitched sound of outrage.

"You're—you're…diabolical!"

"Now there's a ten-dollar word."

"You can't just, just—" Damo waved a hand.

Struggling to keep from grinning, Blake said, "Hmm?" A moment later, he got a wetsuit in the face, and they laughed as Damo hurried to dress, muttering and trying to adjust himself.

They were almost out of the garage before Blake said, "Hold on. I just need to…" He hurried back to the storage area, hoping Damo would follow. He did, opening his mouth to likely ask what Blake had forgotten.

Blake took Damo's face in his hands and kissed him. For a heartbeat, their chapped lips pressed together perfectly, and then Damo gasped. Blake chased the breathy little sound with his tongue, going deep as their tongues met. Damo swayed against him.

It was salty and sweet, the hint of an orange lolly lingering in Damo's mouth. They were both hard, but Blake pulled back, still holding Damo's flushed, stubbly face.

"Just needed to kiss you," Blake whispered. "Couldn't wait another second."

And Damo beamed with that crooked grin, his fingers gripping at the cotton of Blake's singlet. "Yeah?"

"Yeah."

"And that arse business?"

Blake shrugged, fighting to keep a straight face. "Something to think about until next time."

"What? 'Next time'?" Damo almost squeaked in outrage. "*Diabolical.*"

Blake kissed him until they were breathless. He nuzzled Damo's cheek. "Will you let me do that?"

"Let you? Is that a trick question?"

"What are you doing later?" Blake had to be up in the middle of the night to head into work, but missing the sleep would be worth it.

Damo's breathless smile faded. "Can't tonight."

"No worries." Blake tamped down the disappointment and leaned close to Damo's ear, skimming his fingers under his T-shirt. "Will you think about it until we can?"

Shivering, Damo nodded. "I want you to show me. I'll let you do anything. *Everything.*"

Blake lifted Damo off his feet and kissed him fiercely. After he spoke to Tasha, he'd finalize a new plan, and there would definitely be a subsection on all the things—*everything*—he and Damo would do together.

Chapter Ten

MONDAY EVENING, BLAKE paced his apartment and checked the time again. Three more minutes until he was due to call Tasha.

Snippets of her initial email scrolled through his mind. He'd read it so many times now he could have performed it like a Shakespeare soliloquy.

You probably don't remember me

I'm not asking for anything

We don't want money

I made the choice that was right for me

I should have told you back then

Please let me know if you even get this email

If you want to walk away, just tell me and that'll be it

He couldn't get the last words out of his head. *That'll be it.* He could have replied to the email and said, "Thanks but no thanks" about being part of his child's life. Simple as that.

As Damo had said—nope. Not an option.

The reply from Tasha had been waiting when he woke early that morning, the red number one on his email app like a beacon.

She'd said she was glad he was interested, and they'd set up the time for the call.

He did another loop of his apartment, the stir fry he'd eaten sitting in his gut like lead.

Blake checked the time again. Another minute. His phone buzzed in his hand, and he fumbled it, his heart thudding. It was Mum's face on the screen, and he groaned.

No, he couldn't talk to her right now. As thrilled as she'd be to hear about Cooper…no. Blake thought of what Damo had said—that for now, he just wanted the nascent relationship with Blake to be *his*. There was nothing wrong with that, and there was nothing wrong with Blake not sharing this news with his family yet.

He declined the call and quickly tapped out an apology text asking if everything was okay. The seconds ticked by agonizingly, but thankfully, Mum replied that they were fine and not to worry.

Seven o'clock appeared on his screen, and he punched in the number he'd memorized from reading and rereading Tasha's email response. A female voice answered, and Blake cleared his throat.

"Uh, is that Tasha?" He hadn't even known her well enough to hope to recognize her voice, yet they'd created an entire human being together. How weird was that?

"It is. Hi."

"Hi."

Silence, then: "This must be Blake."

"It is. Um, good to talk to you?" He had his mobile pressed too hard to his ear and forced himself to breathe. Why had he made that a question?

Tasha laughed softly. "Is it? I hope so."

"Yes." There was more silence, and he added, "I mean it's good to talk to you. It was a shock getting your email, but I'm grateful you got in touch."

She was quiet a few moments. "Okay. Because the offer still

stands—you can walk away, and if Coop wants to find you when he's eighteen, we'll give him your name and he can go from there."

Blake paced his living room, the wood floor creaking under his bare feet, the rug soft. He had to say something, and he grasped for the right words in his spinning mind. "Is that what you and your husband would prefer?"

Silence for a heartbeat. Another. Another. Then she said, "Honestly, I don't know. Part of me does, yeah. It was Tony who made the case that you had a right to know. That it wasn't fair to you or Coop. It isn't, I agree. But if you're not ready to really take this on, I'd rather you own it now and we can call it a day."

Blake stared at the surfer over his TV. "I'm ready. I admit I have no idea what I'm doing, but I'm in. He's my son. I want to know him. Walking away isn't an option."

She exhaled noisily. "Right. Okay. We're doing this, then. I'm not sure where to start."

He laughed uneasily. "Me either. I haven't thought about you in years, and now we have a kid. Uh, no offense with the not thinking about you."

"None taken, mate. I didn't think of you beyond being a sperm donor. Not that the pregnancy was planned, I assure you. Must have accidentally skipped a pill or mistimed it. I was stupid."

Blake's stomach roiled with a surge of acid. "There's something else you should know before we go any further."

"Okay," she said warily.

"I'm gay."

Tasha chuckled. "Oh, cool. No worries."

"You knew?"

"I didn't *know*, not back then, but in hindsight, it all fits. You couldn't keep your eyes off my cousin's arse that whole weekend. But you were sweet and cute, and I wanted to fuck." Blake could hear the shrug in her no-nonsense voice. "Honestly, it was all so long ago. I think you seemed keen and a little confused, and I figured there was no harm in it."

"Except for getting you pregnant, apparently."

"Oh right, *that*." She laughed, before her tone got serious. "But Coop's the greatest. No regrets. It wasn't easy by a long shot, but I wouldn't change it. If Tony was his bio dad, Coop wouldn't be the same weird, amazing kid he is. I can't regret it. Although you need to understand that Tony *is* Coop's father. He's raised him since he was two. Coop calls him 'dad,' and that's not going to change no matter what kind of relationship he builds with you."

"I understand. I… Well, I don't know the first thing about parenting, and you live on the other side of the country. I won't try to take anyone's place. Just try to find one for myself." Was he making sense? Sounding responsible and reasonable? He'd made a list of talking points, and he quickly scanned the paper. The silence stretched out, and he said, "Hello?"

"Yeah, I'm here. I'm…" She laughed softly. "I guess I'm pleasantly surprised by how reasonable you're being about all of this."

Success! He laughed too. "I don't think it'll help anyone to be a giant dickhead."

"I appreciate that. I should have told you when I found out. But it was a few months later and you weren't even in uni yet. Blinman felt like a billion miles from Sydney, and I didn't know you. But I still should have told you. I'm sorry."

"Apology accepted. At this point all we can do is move forward."

"Speaking of which, we're actually coming to Perth for a wedding."

"Oh! When?"

"Next week. That's one of the reasons I got in touch. Squid mentioned you were living out there."

"Oh!" he repeated. "Next week. That's really soon." Holy shit.

His son—he had a *son!*—was visiting. Blake could actually meet him. *Next week.* His heart hammered. "Great!"

"Yeah?" Tash sounded decidedly skeptical. "It's probably too soon. Isn't it?"

"It's been eight years, so not really that soon when you think about it."

"Good point." She paused. "Hey, can we do a video call?"

His pulse raced faster. "Sure. Do you want to… I'll just… You can call me back." He tapped the button to hang up, then sprinted to the bathroom to look in the mirror.

His short hair looked neat, but he wet his hand and ran it over his skull anyway. No traces of makeup since it had been days. His stomach tightened. What would Tash think about that?

She was cool with him being gay—would she be equally as cool about him wearing eyeliner and lippy when he clubbed? What would this Tony think? What was he like? How would Blake compare to him?

Will Cooper even like me?

The phone in his hand buzzed, and he realized he needed a better backdrop than the toilet. He sprinted back to the living room and sat on the couch before answering. On the screen, Tasha waved. Blake waved back, holding up his phone for a better angle on his round face.

"G'day again. Long time no see," he said, which was likely a ridiculous thing to say.

But Tash smiled and said, "Indeed." She was just as pretty as he remembered, with pale skin, freckles, thick, brown hair that was now bobbed around her chin, wide-set brown eyes, and a thin nose. Her lips were glossy in a neutral tone, and he almost asked her which brand she was wearing.

She said, "This is weird, hey? We're all grown-up."

"Suppose we are."

"Have you told your parents about this?"

"Not yet. I will, but I want to see how things go."

There was no sense in telling them he had a son if it all went pear-shaped. He wasn't telling them about Damo either. There was hardly anything to tell. Not yet. He'd been tempted to text his sibling group chat for advice, but they were all so busy with their own kids. And it felt like jinxing it before actually meeting Cooper.

He added, "Cooper will have loads of cousins. My sis has a baby, my oldest brother's wife just had their second, and my other brother's wife just announced she's pregnant with their third."

"Busy, busy. Are they still in Blinman?"

"God, no. My brothers are in Queensland, and Ella's in Adelaide. Squid moved there too, didn't he?"

Everyone had called Tasha's cousin, Callum, "Squid," since it was shorter than "calamari." And Blake really must have been hard up if he'd been checking out Squid's arse that weekend.

"Yep. It was a tricky business getting your email off him. He wanted to know why I wanted to contact Blake the Snake, so I made up some bullshit about wanting to reconnect with old friends. He told me to message you on Insta, but I thought email would be better. He had to ask your brother for your address, apparently. He texted back an FYI that I 'turned you.' Which of course he would since he's a bloody knobhead."

"He is," Blake agreed with a grin. "Means well, though."

"He does, bless him." She tucked her hair behind her ear.

"And shit, haven't heard 'Blake the Snake' in forever."

She laughed. "Surprised you've managed to shake it."

"Same, to be honest. The other garbos do call me 'Moose,' though."

"How'd they get that one?"

"My training supervisor is Rocky, so they started calling me 'Bullwinkle' since we were always together. After that old cartoon? Then eventually it became Moose." He shrugged. "You know how it is."

Tasha grinned. "Yep. I got off easy." Her smile faded. "I haven't told my parents about you either. When I rocked up pregnant, it wasn't the best day. But they adjusted, and they've been awesome with Coop and love Tony. I'll talk to them once we know where all this is…going."

"Makes sense."

"Anyway, about our visit. Tony's brother's marrying a Freo girl, so we decided to make a holiday of it. Had to wrangle with Coop's school to get him the time off, but he can handle it. He's smart *as*." She beamed. "His grades are top of the class, and he's so curious about the world. He always has been. When he started crawling, it was game on."

For an awful moment, Blake couldn't breathe through a swell of regret and longing that choked him like grief. He'd missed out on so much. He'd never get to see his son as a newborn. Or rolling over, crawling, taking his first steps…

What if his son had needed his help and he hadn't been there? Of course Cooper had needed him. Thank God he'd had Tasha and Tony, but there were so many things Blake could've helped with.

"What was his first word?" he asked, his voice gone hoarse.

Tasha's smile faded as her face softened into a sad, sympathetic expression. "It was 'meow.' He loved talking to our cat, Gorgonzola. It took him a while to be able to say her actual name. She was just 'Meow' to him."

Blake laughed, blinking away sudden tears. "Sorry I missed that."

Tasha's eyes glistened. "I am too. I really am."

"I understand why you didn't tell me. I'm just starting to really think about what I missed."

"I can send you all the pictures and videos we have. Well, maybe not all of them since it would take you months to get through."

"I'll take everything. Please."

"Of course. I wish—I wish I could turn back time."

Blake smiled sadly. "I do too. But all we can do is move forward. What about child support?"

Tasha shook her head. "Not necessary. We're good."

"It's absolutely necessary. I owe you backpay and of course going forward. What about uni? An education fund."

"Already covered. Honestly, this isn't about money. I really want to make that clear. We don't need or want your money."

Blake took a deep breath, trying to calm his agitation. "I understand that. Regardless, Cooper is my son, and I need to help him financially. *Please*."

Tasha smiled softly. "All right. I'll discuss with Tony, and the three of us can come up with a plan."

He exhaled slowly. "A plan sounds good." Even if Cooper wasn't keen on having a relationship with him—something Blake really didn't want to ponder—he would help him financially.

"Right. Speaking of plans, we'll be out there a week—arriving Friday, wedding Saturday. Meet you Sunday? We can see how it goes. It's short notice, I realize. Not sure what your schedule's like."

"Whatever works best for you. I can have a chat to my boss about taking a few days off. I've got some time accrued."

She smiled, looking relieved. "All right. We're heading down to Bremer Bay for two nights to see the killer whales. Coop's obsessed. Depending on how you and he feel, maybe you could come with?"

"Absolutely! I'd love it." He wasn't sure exactly where Bremer Bay was, but it didn't matter. He'd be there.

"Okay. We'll see how things go, yeah?"

He nodded again, trying not to think about the possibility of things going badly. "Have you—he doesn't know anything about this yet? Meeting me, I mean."

"Not yet. That'll be for tomorrow after school." She lifted her shoulders in an exaggerated shrug, her thick, sculpted eyebrows rising in tandem. "Suppose we'll see how he reacts. It'll be up to him in the end if he's keen to meet you so soon or not."

"Of course." Blake tried to keep an even expression on his face while his mind pleaded, *Please like me!* "If he doesn't want to meet me for whatever reason, I'll respect that." Even though the idea of it made him want to spew.

Tash tilted her head, gazing at him, assessing. Behind her, shadows from a lamp painted a beige wall and ceiling, the corner of a painting in view, though Blake couldn't make out more than a green shape. "You really do seem grown-up."

"You too."

"Yeah, I guess we're proper adults or something. Rumor has it, anyway. I have two brilliant kids, so I suppose I'm doing all right. Did I tell you about Rosie?"

After Tasha spoke about her daughter, he said, "They both sound amazing. Cooper's brilliant, huh?"

Tasha beamed again. "He is. I realize I'm extremely biased, but yes."

"He must get the brains from you."

"Didn't you have a scholarship to uni, or am I remembering wrong?"

"Yeah, but I'm a garbo now."

"Council job with benefits, right? That's smart, mate. Not that I don't love working for a nonprofit, but sometimes I think I should've become a tradie."

"What kind of nonprofit?"

Tasha told him about the food bank she worked for before saying, "By the way, do you have a boyfriend?"

He actually almost said yes, which was crazy. "I just started seeing someone, actually. It's still new, but..." He shrugged.

Tash laughed, the most loudly and genuinely since they'd been speaking. "But you fancy him quite a lot." She grinned. "Nah, don't deny it. Your whole face lit up."

"Did it?" He realized he was grinning too, and his face flushed warm all the way down to his chest. "Yeah, I... I like him. Still early days, though."

She sat her chin on her hand and said in a teasing tone, "Come on, tell me everything." She straightened. "You don't have to tell me anything, though. I didn't mean to overstep."

"All good. I..." He inhaled and breathed out slowly. "This has been quite a week. I'm a clubbie here at Barking Beach, and I've had this crush on a lifeguard. And he actually likes me back. Then I became a father overnight. Haven't had this much excitement since... I think this is probably the most exciting week of my life, actually."

She smiled sympathetically. "Exciting and terrifying?"

"Definitely." He laughed. "I didn't plan for any of this, and I usually have multiple contingencies in place. Didn't see this coming. Not that going on a couple of dates with a guy compares to having a son."

I have a son.

"No, but tell me more about this hot lifeguard." She waggled her eyebrows. "If I can't live vicariously through my gay secret baby daddy's love life, where can I?"

Blake grinned. "His name's Damo. Like I said, he's a lifeguard at Barking."

"The new Bondi, right? It's on our to-do list, actually. Living in Parramatta, we don't get to the beaches too often, and Coop wants to see it even though it'll be crowded as hell."

"Maybe Damo can give you a tour or something. Show Cooper the lifeguard tower and all that. If Coop wants to. If he even wants to meet me. And if Damo's able. I shouldn't be making any promises for him."

"It's all right, you're not. Actually, if everything goes well, maybe you could bring him to Bremer? Or another friend? Might help take the pressure off. So it's not just you feeling awkward with us. Our daughter Rosie will be staying in Perth with her grandparents. She's too young for the whale watching."

"That would be amazing." He could ask Kat, but the idea of going to Bremer Bay with Damo to whale watch made him feel like the sun was shining. Damo would love it.

"You met at the beach?"

"Yeah. Kind of a funny story, actually. Could have been tragic, but it wasn't."

She leaned back on her leather couch and sipped from a glass of red. "I'm all ears."

So, Blake told the mother of his child how he'd helped Damo with the panicking tourists, and she laughed and smiled in all the right parts, and hope filled him like a balloon.

It was all new with Damo and Cooper, but Blake's confidence swelled. Look how well this talk with Tasha had gone. The new plan was in motion.

Chapter Eleven

"I MIGHT BE in here," Baz said over the radio, his usual low drawl sharp.

"Yeah, you're in for sure," Damo replied, keeping his binoculars trained on the head out the back.

From the tower, Damo watched Baz going flat stick in the buggy across the sand to reach the south end. It was a safer place to swim, but the patient had drifted way too far out and was tiring fast.

There was fresh chatter behind him in the tower, but Damo stayed focused on the man who was about to be rescued. Mid-morning, the crowd wasn't hectic yet, but there were enough on the sand that it was eating into precious seconds before Baz finally made it.

He hopped out, taking off his blue uniform shirt and picking up the rescue board in one smooth movement that came from years of experience.

"Come on," Ryan muttered, standing beside Damo and watching through another pair of binos, the chatter falling silent as they watched Baz punch through waves with powerful strokes. Water shone on his bald head and brown skin before he disappeared beyond a swell.

Damo's heart thumped as the patient disappeared as well—

before popping up again. A few moments later, Baz reached him, and everyone in the tower exhaled. Damo kept watch until Baz and the patient were back on shore, listening to Ryan talk to—

"Hang on!" Damo spun his chair to find Lachlan Yang with another lifeguard they all called Ronnie thanks to his horsey grin and ginger hair like Ronald McDonald. "The Shark returns! Shouldn't you be in an office tower? Where's your suit and Rolex?" He stood and held up a hand for a slap-shake.

Lachlan shook Damo's hand with a smile that didn't seem as big as usual. "Left them in the Bentley."

Ryan threw an arm around Lachlan, his grin showing off the little gap between his front teeth. His brown hair was short and messy and his white skin was rosy where he'd gotten too much sun on his nose. He had another fresh tattoo inked on his lean torso. This one looked like a horse, which struck Damo as ironic since Ryan's surname was Bullock.

He'd initially been called "Bull Jr." when he'd joined the service by the older guys who'd known his father, but he'd genuinely hated it so much that they'd relented.

Ryan said, "He doesn't need them anymore. He's back in action."

Ronnie shared a surprised glance with Damo before saying, "Wait. Sharky, you're coming back to the service?"

Lachlan shrugged, but it was anything but relaxed. "Yep. Missed all your ugly mugs too much." He was tall with light brown skin and dark hair, his white teeth straight and even. But his smile was *definitely* not the usual wattage. He was still gorgeous, and—

Don't think about Lachie being gorgeous!

Wait, why not? I'm allowed to.

No, you're not! You have a boy—you have Blake. Who could maybe be your boyfriend. You have a boy Blake.

He was definitely allowed to think about Blake. Which was

good, because he did almost every second he wasn't concentrating on his job. Apparently, Damo was more vanilla than he thought. He'd never considered himself a prude or uneducated about sex, but bloody hell!

What Blake had said down in the garage under the tower was living in Damo's head rent-free. None of his girlfriends had licked his arsehole, and it had never occurred to him to lick theirs.

After how far he'd gone with Blake that first night, he didn't mind that they'd slowed down a bit. While part of him was dying to suck Blake's cock again and have his own sucked—and try that arse business, definitely—he didn't mind catching his breath.

For now.

God, he wanted to kiss him now and—

The radio in Damo's hand squawked to life, and he dropped it with a yelp. It clattered onto the floor and he scooped it up as his face burned. He answered Baz, who cleared the patient he'd brought in to the beach, and Damo ordered himself to focus on work. He'd be seeing Blake in a few hours.

Six hours and forty-two minutes. Er, approximately.

He tuned back in to the conversation going on a few feet away as Ronnie asked, "Coming back as casual on weekends?"

"Nah," Ryan answered for Lachlan. "We're both full-timers again. I tried that job out at the mine, but all that money wasn't enough. I need to be by the water." He tightened his arm around Lachlan's neck. "Lachie couldn't stay away either."

"Far out. It'll be like old times," Ronnie said as Teddy entered the tower. "Right, boss?"

Teddy said to Ryan, "Next, I'll grow my hair back and your old man'll waltz through the door again."

Ryan's face soured. "Yeah, nah. That arsehole can stay in Queensland."

Teddy frowned, but didn't say anything.

Damo asked Lachlan, "You're not a lawyer anymore?" in the

sudden silence, opening his mouth and jamming in his foot. Ryan glared daggers.

Lachlan flushed. "Well, I am, but, uh, I'm taking a break."

"Don't blame ya!" Ronnie quickly said. "No better place than Barkers."

They all nodded and agreed, trying to smooth over the awkwardness as Teddy gave Lachlan his uniform, and Damo felt like the world's biggest pork chop since clearly something had happened.

Lachlan had been a lifeguard all the way through law school before leaving for a fancy job in one of the posh office buildings in the CBD. He'd left shortly before Cody and Mia had joined, and it had barely been a couple of years.

Ryan clapped a hand on Lachlan's back. "Come on, bruv. Let's get you back in uniform and hit the beach."

Damo scanned the water with the binoculars—and his mind started randomly turning over the word. *Binoculars. Binos. Bi. Bisexual binos. Biiiiiiii.* Did it fit him? What was the other word people used? As he watched swimmers playing at the south end, he rolled that word around on his tongue.

Then he was thinking about *Blake's* tongue, and he was going to cop it if he got a hard-on in the tower. Jesus, he'd never live that down if he still had a job.

As Teddy checked medical equipment in the first aid area, Ronnie sat and wheeled close to Damo, keeping his voice low. "Whaddya reckon happened with the Shark? Never thought we'd see him back in blue."

"Dunno. It's definitely weird."

Lachlan had gotten that nickname—the Shark—when he'd gone to law school, and they'd all joked about how they'd hire him to defend them when they got in trouble.

Had he always been gorgeous?

Duh, obviously. Damo remembered Lachlan's sister had been

a babe. Their dad had been Asian and mum white, and they were both beautiful. What he wasn't clear on was if he'd really noticed Lachlan's looks or if he was viewing everyone differently now. He'd been curious for a while, but had he always subconsciously noticed blokes like he noticed chicks?

He wasn't sure, and it probably didn't matter anyway, but as Damo watched the beach, he wished he had a perfect, easy answer.

Later, Lachlan was in the tower for his break as Damo got ready to hand off control of the tower to Ronnie. Lachlan grimaced. "I see the microwave isn't any cleaner."

Damo laughed. "No, but it's the new guy's duty to give her a good scrub."

"Too right," agreed Ronnie. He watched the surf with the binoculars.

"I'm not new," Lachlan grumbled, and he was definitely gorgeous, Damo decided. Not that it mattered—he had Blake, who was also gorgeous.

Did he have Blake? It had been less than a week, and it wasn't like they needed to declare they were boyfriends. Why was Damo getting so hung up on labels? Bi, boyfriends—he needed to chill and go with the flow. He was at work. He was supposed to be laid-back except when someone was drowning.

Now he was thinking about home, and he tensed as he did another scan, fingering the purple cord around his neck. Mum was working a double, and he hadn't actually seen her in a week. What would she think about Blake? Tabby would like him. Wouldn't she?

"It was worth a try, mate," Ronnie said to Lachlan before falling silent. He watched something on the beach intently before sitting back. "Hey, what's the deal with Ry's old man? He was pretty aggro about him."

Lachlan sighed. "Yeah. Ry moved to Queensland with his parents when we were about fifteen. He moved back after high school—he'd never wanted to leave Barkers, and he and his dad had a falling out. His parents split a few years back, and he blamed his father."

Ronnie asked, "His old man was a lifeguard here?"

"Yeah. Taught us to surf. He's still a lifeguard out on the Gold Coast."

"Guess he's a real dickhead?" Damo asked as he watched a group of kids splashing in the shore break north of the flags. *Close to the flags, but still outside the safe zone.*

"No!" Lachlan cleared his throat. "He made a mistake, but Mr. Bullock wasn't a bad bloke. He was cool."

"Cool," Damo echoed as he scanned the water.

"Anyway. Ry's my best friend, and he has every reason to be aggro. Guess I just have a soft spot for his dad. We were both lifeguards because of him." His face clouded. "*Are*, I should say." He fiddled with the wrapper of the frozen burrito he was going to microwave.

"Bloody brilliant to have you here, mate." Damo stood and slapped Lachlan's back.

He gave Damo a small smile. "Thanks. Good to be back. Filthy microwave and all. It's like I never left."

Despite his curiosity about why the hell Lachlan had apparently given up his job as a lawyer, Damo bit his tongue for once. "I'm going out in the pink buggy. Ronnie, you and Sharky have fun."

"Just Lachie," he said. "I'm not a shark. Never was."

"Exactly what a shark would say," Ronnie replied, and they all laughed, though Damo wasn't sure Lachlan's heart was in it.

〜〜〜

AFTER HIS SHIFT ended late afternoon, Damo was happy to change into street clothes, pulling on board shorts and a tee. Feet still bare, he said bye to the guys on the pack-up shift and hopped down the sun-warm wooden stairs.

The grass in the park behind the beach was springy underfoot, and he was practically skipping, his backpack slung over a shoulder. Scanning the long, narrow car park, he realized he had no idea what Blake drove.

Huh. This thing with Blake really was brand new, wasn't it?

Beachgoers were drifting away, but the after-work crowd were stalking, creeping up and down, waiting to pounce as a spot opened. There were only spots on either side making two long rows, the car park built years ago before Barking became so crowded. Overflow parking was desperately needed, but there really wasn't room unless they bulldozed the park, and residents had fought it for years.

Damo stopped in front of the cafe and took off his sunnies as if that would help.

"Oi!"

His heart skipped, and he spotted Blake down the end of the car park with his hazards on, standing half out of a small SUV waving. Knowing he was grinning like a fool, Damo practically sprinted down the footpath before forcing himself to slow.

The car was running, and it was blissfully cool inside. "G'day," Blake said from behind the wheel as Damo climbed in.

Damo lurched forward and yanked him into a kiss. Blake tasted like coffee and kissed him back hard, their tongues meeting. He slid his hand into Damo's hair, which was tangled from the dried salt water that Damo should have rinsed off. It tugged, the nerves flaring on his scalp, but Damo didn't mind.

Blake broke the kiss. "Sorry."

"No worries." He ran his hand through his hair awkwardly. He'd been too eager to rush out. Why hadn't he taken five more minutes? "Bit of a mess."

"I like it." Blake murmured. "You're like a selkie."

"A what?"

"Mythical creature that lives in the sea and shifts to human form."

"Like a merman?"

"Kind of. A cousin." He brushed back Damo's hair. "You're definitely a saltwater creature." His gaze dropped. "Do you ever wear shoes?"

"Got my thongs in my bag. Besides, I wore shoes to the club on Friday, remember?"

"That's true." Blake's gaze darkened. "I remember."

They met over the gearshift for another rough kiss, and Damo was ready to crawl right onto Blake's lap. He pushed his hand up under Blake's tee to rub his chest hair, and—

The *beep* had Damo jerking back against the passenger seat door, nearly hitting his head on the window. Shit. Shit! He whipped his head around, realizing they were blocking someone from leaving, and that another car was waiting to park.

Laughing, Blake gave an apologetic wave and shifted into drive, but Damo's mouth had gone dry. Did he know them? Had they seen him? He slumped low in his seat, face flaming. As Blake slowly drove along the car park toward the one exit, the seatbelt alarm started dinging.

"Sorry," Damo mumbled as he sat up straighter to yank it on.

Blake smiled uncertainly. "You right?"

"Yep!" he exclaimed too loudly and forcefully before wincing. "I'm just…" He shook his head.

Blake softened and reached over to squeeze Damo's knobby knee. "It's okay." He turned left and headed north. "You don't have to leap out of the closet overnight."

The closet. He hadn't really thought about it like that. Liam had been miserably closeted for years, going *really* far out of his way to keep being gay a secret. Damo was still rolling around *bisexual* in his head, but it hadn't been long. "Yeah. It's new. Just couldn't resist kissing ya. Didn't think about who might be watching."

Smiling, Blake rubbed his thumb across Damo's thigh before putting both hands on the wheel. "I'm hard to resist. But seriously, I can't expect you to be telling people already."

"I did, though. One person, at least. Cody. He was great."

Blake grinned. "Glad to hear it."

"Where are we going?" Traffic slowed on the coast road as they left Barking.

"Thought we could have dinner in Freo."

"Cool. What'dya feel like?"

"Oh, I made a reservation at an Asian fusion place. It's a great little spot." He frowned. "Unless you don't like Asian? I should've asked. We can go anywhere you like."

"Nah, I love Asian food. All kinds of food. Easy." He wasn't sure he'd ever made a restaurant reservation in his life. He eyed Blake's outfit of long navy shorts and a fitted white T-shirt. Not fancy, but neat. "Should I change, though?"

"Just put on your thongs, and we'll be sweet as."

"Suppose I can manage that." He worked his fingers through his tangled hair, wishing again he'd stopped to shower. "How're you feeling today? About the whole baby thing. Kid thing."

"Pretty good." Blake inhaled deeply and breathed out, nodding. "Moments of panic, but we've got a plan now."

"How long until you meet him?"

"Eleven days."

Damo teased, "And how many hours?"

Blake smiled. "Shut up."

"It's good that you're excited. If you didn't want anything to do with your own kid…" He grimaced. "That would be a huge red flag, mate. You don't even seem aggro that she kept it from you for so long."

Blake frowned as he slowed for a red light. "Of course not. It was her choice. We were strangers."

"Some blokes would be." Or they'd blow it off and not take

responsibility. Blake wasn't like that, and it made Damo want to kiss him again.

"Where would that get us, though? I'm not angry. Just sad about everything I've missed. I've daydreamed about maybe having a baby one day, and I missed those years with Cooper. Might be the only chance I have."

"Shit, yeah. I'm sorry." Damo reached over and gently squeezed Blake's thigh. In what he hoped was a comforting way. Was he doing it right? Why was he overthinking everything?

"Tash sent me hundreds of videos and pictures. Maybe we could watch some later?" Blake winced. "Because nothing says fun date like watching videos of someone's kid."

"No, I want to! Honest."

"It's not too much? I know we just met, and this is still new for you." He shook his head with a smile and turned right at a roundabout, heading inland. "I really wasn't expecting this when I asked you out."

"Expecting to have a secret baby? Who does?"

Blake's dimple appeared. "That, and also…you." He motioned between them. "This. I mean, am I being absurd, or do we have something here? Wait, you don't have to answer that."

"Yeah, nah." Heart racing, Damo stroked Blake's thigh with his thumb, brushing his skin just past the hem of his shorts. "You're not being absurd. Or…preposterous, even."

"Ohh, that's a fifteen-dollar word."

"Twelve at least, hey." They laughed, and Damo added, "Not sure where I dug that one up. Guess I learned a few things in school after all." He bit his lip. "But, yeah, this is good. I wasn't looking for it at all, but…it's good."

He buzzed with it—the thrill and…what? Hope? He'd gotten so set in his routine of work, surf, and home. Especially home, which was feeling more like a prison as time passed.

Now, out of nowhere, he had this new, exciting person to go

to dinner with and talk to and *kiss*. And he was all Damo's. His secret. His escape.

With a giddy rush like he'd just caught a wave, Damo leaned over and kissed Blake, who laughed and said, "You're going to get me ticketed!"

Damo raised his hands. "Sorry. I'll behave. Mostly. Can't get enough."

As he slowed for a light, Blake said, "Actually, I wanted to ask you something."

Damo was going to make a joke, but Blake had gone too serious. "Okay." His stomach flip-flopped.

"What do you think about coming with me, Cooper, Tasha and Tony down to Bremer Bay to see the killer whales? It'll be two nights."

The nerves evaporated into a burst of joy. "I'd be stoked!"

"Yeah?" Blake's face lit up.

"Totally."

Reality slapped Damo upside the head, and familiar dread sank through him. What was he saying? Go away for *two nights*? He hadn't slept away from home since the accident. Not even once. He'd been late after the night with Blake at the club, but he'd still gone home.

It'd been a bone of contention with Shaz, which was why she'd spent that one disastrous night at his place. *Ugh*. He cringed to remember it, fidgeting in his seat and tucking his foot under him.

"What is it?" Blake asked. "Look, no pressure at all. If it's too soon, or you can't get off work, or..."

"No, no! Like I said, I'm stoked."

And he was! It would be okay, wouldn't it? He was twenty-two, and he couldn't stay home for the next however many years. *Years*. He felt like he'd spew just thinking about the endless nights stretching out in front of him.

"I'll ask Teddy to be rostered off those days, and if it's too late, I can switch shifts. A few guys owe me." His heart thumped. He was going to do this.

"You sure?" Blake frowned.

Damo could just tell him it would be the first time sleeping away from home in seven years. But how would that sound? Like he was a *kid.* He'd tell him eventually, but not now. Not after a week.

Yeah, Blake had told him about his secret baby, but… Damo just wasn't ready. Not yet.

"Okay," Blake said, smiling. "And we might not go—it'll depend on how it is when I meet Cooper. We're going to play it by ear."

"All good. If we both have the days off, we can surf. And if it goes well, we'll check out Bremer Bay. Seeing killer whales would be sick."

"Have you ever been out there?"

"Nah. Only gone as far southwest as Walpole to see the tall trees when I was a kid. Went down to Augusta on a class trip to see where the Indian and Southern oceans meet, and I've been to Margs to surf a bunch of times."

"When I was a kid, I never understood how there was surfing at Margaret River."

Damo laughed. "I mean, there *is* a river! It ends at the ocean. The break's epic. We should go." He hadn't even stayed away for a single night yet, and he was already making plans.

But for once, Damo didn't want to rein himself in. It was bloody exciting to think about going away with Blake. Seeing new places and doing new things and spending the night together in the same bed…

The thrill that ran through him was followed by a wave of guilt. Damo realized with a sinking sensation that Tabby was expecting him home soon. Shit. Was there enough in the fridge?

He quickly thumbed a text, telling her he was going out to eat. At least he'd picked up some frozen meals on sale so she could toss one in the microwave.

"Semi-nervous about it?" he asked Blake. "Or heaps? Meeting Cooper, I mean."

"The latter." Blake shook his head as he slowed for a roundabout. "I wanted time to process, but now I'm dying to meet him."

"You've, like, processed having a kid?"

He laughed sharply. "No. But at least I feel like I can breathe. It's…not what I planned. Not when I planned it, at least."

"Guess there's no good time to find out you have a secret baby."

"Especially when the baby's eight."

"I'd be shitting myself."

"Oh, I am, trust me."

"This is you freaking out?"

"I guess so? It's not really my style. I usually have everything under control. Organized."

Damo ran his finger over the dash and fiddled with a vent. The car wasn't flashy, and the seats were fabric, but there wasn't a crumb or coffee spill in sight. Compared to his mum's mess of an SUV, Blake's seemed very grown-up. Which made no sense since Mum was twice his age.

It was certainly more grown-up than Damo's skateboard. He drove his dad's old ute to the grocery store and if Tabby needed a ride somewhere, but most of his life was walking distance.

"Everything okay?" Blake asked.

Damo blinked. "Yeah, why?"

Smiling, Blake nodded toward Damo's jiggling foot. He'd crossed his ankle over his knee and hadn't realized he'd been moving. He put his feet flat on the mat. "Sorry. I'm a fidgeter. Used to drive my dad mental."

"Not anymore?"

Here was a chance to tell Blake about his dad's accident and what it was like now. But Blake had enough on his mind with his secret-baby-who-wasn't-a-baby. He simply said, "Nah."

Blake tapped at the screen on the console, and a moment later, a song played. It sounded old and folky, and Damo leaned forward to read the title: "Ventura Highway."

"Cool tune," he said.

"Yeah?" Blake looked pleased. "I grew up listening to my parents' seventies stuff. Suppose it was my grandad's mostly. Cold Chisel and AC/DC. The Eagles and America. Makes me think of home and long drives."

"I bet. Was it hours to everywhere?"

"Oh, you'd better believe it. At least it was only two and a half to Port Augusta to get a taste of the sea. Well, technically Spencer Gulf, but I'd take it."

"Could you surf it?"

"Not even a little. It's the top end of the gulf, so it's more like a river. But I still loved getting the salt on my skin. There's just something about the water, you know?"

Damo had to lean over and kiss him quickly as they came to a stoplight. "I know." Leaning back, he couldn't stop smiling. "Can you play that again?"

Smiling too, Blake tapped the screen, and Damo opened his window, letting in the sunshine and breeze as they drove up the coast, the ocean glittering over the dunes.

Chapter Twelve

Parking in Fremantle was always a headache, but Blake found a spot and parallel parked so smoothly that Damo had to whistle. "Got it in one."

Blake waggled his eyebrows. "Sexy?"

"Sexy *as*." Damo pulled him in for a quick kiss—which turned into a full make-out sesh with Blake's tongue in his mouth and the gearshift in his ribs. The sun was still up, but Damo really, really wanted to shove his hand down Blake's shorts and—

Giggles rang out, and Damo pulled away as the group of girls Tabby's age laughed from the footpath. One of the girls called, "Good on ya!" as they walked on. There didn't seem to be anything hateful in their laughter, and Blake gave them a bow as they waved.

Still, Damo's face flamed, and he hid behind his hair. "We need to get a room."

Laughing, Blake kissed his cheek. "After dinner, you can come back to mine. Spend the night?"

Yes!

Of course he couldn't. He pulled his phone from his pocket, frowning to see that Tabby hadn't replied. "Can't tonight." He quickly tapped out another message. "Mum's working, and it's a school night. I need to get home after dinner to check on my little sis."

"Okay. Let's get inside or we'll be late. How old is she?"

Damo told Blake all about Tabby as they ate, sidestepping questions about their parents. She'd finally replied to his messages—a simple "*K*" that probably meant she was busy playing video games with her friends.

The restaurant was small and narrow and totally casual, but packed to the gills. The food was incredible, and Damo wished it was in Barking instead of Freo. His char sui pork shoulder with cucumber, mint, coriander, and lime was the best thing he'd eaten in ages.

After they ate, they sipped beer and flipped through pictures of Cooper on Blake's phone, both turning their heads and leaning close over the table. He looked like an average kid, and Damo spent more time looking at Blake's rapt expression—his brown eyes bright with excitement, the dimple appearing in his cheek as they watched a video of Cooper making faces.

Sure, maybe a surprise kid was a lot for their first week of dating, but Damo didn't mind. It was a weird relief that Blake had a big family situation to deal with. And the way he was dealing made Damo feel…good. Just…good.

"I really want to kiss you again, but I'm too full," Damo moaned on the drive back to Barkers in the dark.

Blake laughed. "Same. And I think I'll need to brush my teeth three times before my breath doesn't smell of garlic."

Damo sat up straighter as they approached the familiar shadows of the beach, the tower's outdoor light shining in the darkness. "You can just let me out here on your way."

"What? No, I'll drive you home."

"It's just around the corner."

"I know. I still want to drop you off."

"A gentleman, hey?"

"You deserve nothing less."

Damo laughed, but tension filled him. "Appreciate it, but really, I'll hop out at the corner."

Blake's smile faded. "You don't want me to take you home?"

"No, it's just easier to get out here. Then you can just carry on."

"We passed my place ten minutes ago. I'm in North Barking, remember?"

Shit. He'd been so buzzed and content he hadn't even clocked it. He snatched up his backpack from the floor. "Just here's great. Right here." He grabbed the door handle.

Blake had slowed, but now he braked. "Are you about to jump out of a moving vehicle rather than let me take you home?"

"No! But you've gone too far out of your way already." His pulse raced.

It would just be the outside of the house. It wasn't like Blake would be sleeping over like Shaz had, waking up in the middle of the night to Dad shouting and shouting, and then trying to help clean up the mess and Dad screaming awful things at her. The shame and anger Damo had felt even though he knew it wasn't Dad's fault.

The awkward, uncomfortable silence between them when he'd given Shaz a lift home in the morning knowing things had changed and neither of them could handle it.

Damo knew it could be different with Blake. Blake wasn't nineteen for starters. He'd helped his mum after a stroke. He was a *grown-up.* Why was Damo so afraid? His palms sweated, his full stomach churning.

Blake nodded and shifted into park. It was only nine, but the streets of Barking were already empty on a weeknight. "Okay. Here you go." His gaze was on the road.

"Sorry. I didn't—it's not—" Damo squirmed, not sure what to say. "Dinner was amazing. Thank you." Blake had insisted on paying, and now Damo felt like he hadn't held up his end.

After a few seconds, Blake gave him a genuine smile. "You're welcome. I'll see you tomorrow after work for a surf?"

"Yeah." Damo could breathe again. "I'm on opening, so I'll meet you at north end late arvo?"

"Perfect."

He was about to open the door, but he stopped. "Can I kiss you, or…?" *Or did I stuff up everything?*

In reply, Blake reached for him, threading his hand through Damo's hair and kissing him softly. When he pulled back, Damo wanted to follow. Wanted to crawl over the gearshift and sit on his lap and kiss him for days.

Instead, he said, "See what you mean about the garlic," and they laughed hard for such a silly joke.

He was still smiling as he jogged up to his street, thongs slapping. He turned around at the corner and of course Blake was still there. He waved, waiting until Blake flashed his lights and drove away.

Regret sank through Damo. He wanted to text Blake to come back so they could kiss more and talk more and get off. He wanted to tell Blake he was sorry and bring him inside, even though that thought put a chill down his spine.

Though if he did, Damo really did believe Blake wouldn't run the other way. He'd moved back home to help his parents. He'd understand. He was stepping up to take responsibility for his son. He wasn't a scared teenager. It was incredibly comforting.

Like they'd said, they had something here. The mess of Damo's family could wait. It sure as shit wasn't going anywhere.

As he walked across the front porch, he remembered again that the motion detector light needed a new bulb. Inside, he kicked off his thongs. To the right, the living room with its saggy couch and old rug was empty, the TV off. Mum's pillow and blanket were pushed to one side.

He turned left and passed the kitchen, making a note to come back and clean the sink full of dishes, annoyance flaring at how bloody loud Dad's TV was playing behind his closed door at the end of the hall. How was Tabby supposed to sleep? Heck, how was Damo?

He pushed open Dad's door, knowing that the odds of waking him were slim to bloody none. Indeed, Dad was snoring, flat on his back, pillows around him, pills in arm's reach. His CPAP machine sat gathering dust on the bedside table.

Damo turned the volume way down on home shopping and some Botoxed old presenter from channel nine selling face cream at a bargain. If Dad woke and the TV was switched off, he might fly into a rage, so Damo was careful to only turn it down. He left him in the flickering blue light, closing the door tightly behind him and turning to Tabby's room. He eased the door open a few centimeters.

Boom!

Adrenaline spiked at the sight of the empty bed. It was un-made, which was normal, but Tabby should have been under the covers playing on her phone instead of trying to sleep like usual. He retraced his steps, ducking fully into the living room. Empty.

He checked his room just in case, then raced on bare feet out past the laundry room, pushing open the screen door to the alfresco in the backyard. His breath whooshed out, relief flooding his veins.

"What are you doin' out here? Don't you have netball in the morning?"

Sitting on the couch under the alfresco roof and staring into the overgrown garden, Tabby shrugged.

"Hey, what's up? Did you and Hailey have a row about that dickhead boy you're both keen on? He's not worth it, trust me." Damo propped a hip on the back of the couch and gave her shoulder a squeeze.

She squirmed away from his touch and muttered, "It's not

about Ollie."

"Okay. What's it about?"

She shrugged, barely lifting her shoulders. Her phone sat face down on the cushion beside her, which was how he knew she was really upset. At least if she'd been scrolling or messaging her friends, he wouldn't have a growing knot of worry tightening in his full stomach. He flopped down beside her, trying to play it casual.

Tabby sighed dramatically. "I'm fine."

"Then why aren't you in bed? Or at least in your room scrolling your phone even though it's a school night?"

"Can't sleep." She wore her usual PJs: trackies and an old Dockers T-shirt. She crossed her arms, shivering as the wind picked up.

Damo slung an arm around her shoulders. One of the things he loved about the Perth area was the dry climate and cooler nights. He'd nearly carked it from the humidity in Queensland.

But in Barking, he could get cozy under the blankets even in summer. Snuggle up, think about Blake…

First, he had to figure out what was up with his sister.

She curled her bare feet under her and leaned into him, repeating, "I'm fine."

Under his arm, Tabby was slight, her shoulders bony like his had been—and probably still were despite all his paddling. "Did Dad do something?"

Her silence was the answer, and Damo sighed. "Did he have all his pills?"

She snorted. "As if he'd go without. He had 'em all, then accused me of stealing some."

"Shit." He could just imagine their dad hollering—or worse, hissing awful things. *Mean* things. He'd never been mean before. Not ever. "How bad?"

Tabby shrugged under his arm. "I told him to go fuck himself and walked out."

"Legend!" He held up a hand for a high five. It wasn't the way Mum would have handled it, but he'd told Tabby not to take any abuse. She shouldn't have had to deal with it at all. "Sorry I wasn't here, Tabs." Guilt made him ready to spew.

She shrugged again. "You're allowed to go out sometimes. I'm not a little kid anymore."

That just made him feel worse, because she *was* a little kid. "Next time, text me right away if he's acting up."

Another shrug, which was not reassuring. Then she asked, "What's her name?"

Tension zipped through him. "Huh? Who?"

"*Who?*" she parroted, her voice high and thin. "The girl you obviously met at the club on Friday."

"Didn't meet a girl on Friday." It was the truth, at least.

Tabby rolled her eyes. "Suuuurre."

"Not seeing a girl." He could just tell her, but… What if it didn't work out with Blake? It had been less than a week. Was he being a coward by not wanting to rush into announcing it? If Blake was a chick, would he keep her secret for the moment?

Maybe? Probably? He didn't have a bloody clue.

"Well, you definitely aren't dressed for a date." She eyed him with a frown.

In reply, he let out an epic burp and tugged on her ponytail. Laughing, Tabby shoved at him. "You're so gross!"

They were wrestling when their mum stepped out of the house. Tabby straightened, and Damo said, "Hey, Mum. We were just—"

"Did he eat? Tramadol PNR?"

Damo nodded. He didn't have to ask his sister. "PNR" was a medical term for "as needed," and he knew their father *always* needed his pills.

Still wearing her scrubs, Mum rubbed her face. "Great.

Thanks." Her hair had once been golden like Damo's and Tabby's, but now it was a mix of fake blonde and dull, gray-brown roots.

"I kept Tabs up," Damo said, waiting for Mum to notice.

She turned back. "Hmm?"

"Nothing," Tabby said. "Did you have a good day?"

Mum smiled weakly. "Busy. The ICU is full again. How about you, sweetheart?"

"Yeah," Tabby replied. "Busy."

"How was work?" Mum asked Damo, coming over to smooth a hand over his hair like he was a kid.

"Same old. Pulled tourists out of the rips."

"That's good." She frowned and looked at her watch. "Tabby, you should be in bed. Damo, are you on an early shift tomorrow?"

He would've argued that he was an adult and didn't have a bedtime anymore—certainly not before ten—but he was just glad for the attention. Tabby kissed their mum's cheek and disappeared.

Damo motioned to the couch. "Sit. I'll heat up your dinner."

Mum had been gazing into the distance and refocused on him. "I need to have a shower. It's okay. You get to bed."

"Go have your shower, and I'll fix you a plate."

She smiled tenderly. "Thanks, darling. What would I do without you?"

In the kitchen, Damo was relieved to see Tabby had apparently made a stir fry. He nuked it and grabbed one of the microwave rice packets from the cupboard while trying not to feel too shitty that she'd had to make her own dinner while he had delicious restaurant food. He had to make sure he was home tomorrow night to cook and deal with Dad.

As he poured a glass of white from the goon sack in the fridge, a shout almost had him dropping the glass. He let go of the plastic spout in the bag and froze, listening. After a few moments of silence, Dad's voice boomed again.

Still holding the glass, Damo crept down the hall. He always felt like a kid when his parents fought. It took him right back to those months after the accident when his dad became a stranger.

No more barbecuing in the yard. No more sweeping Tabby into his arms and spinning her around while she shrieked with laughter. No more watching the footy with his brickie mates, shouting at the TV and dancing with joy.

No more giving Mum a big kiss when he came home and calling her "Mrs. Claus." No one ever called her Christine, but since Chrissie made everyone think of Christmas, Dad had given her the Mrs. Claus nickname years before. It had been their special thing, with Mum calling him "Mr. Claus" in return.

"Give it here, you bitch!"

In the hall, Damo winced at the hate in his father's voice. Mum's reply was too soft for him to make out, though soon her voice rose.

"You've had *enough!*" Mum wrenched open the bedroom door, jolting when she spotted Damo.

"Sorry!" He thrust out the glass, wine sloshing over the side.

In her cotton nightie covered in little pastel ice cream cones, hair wet and face grim, Mum shut the door behind her and tried to smile—failing miserably. She took the wine and started down the hall. "Thanks, darling."

"He's worse." Damo hadn't planned on saying it, but there it was.

Mum glanced at Tabby's closed door—the old pink nameplate Dad had nailed on it when she was little still hanging there—and nodded toward the living room. Damo picked up her dinner and a fork on the way.

Before she could sink onto the couch where she'd spend the night, he said, "Let's go out. Fresh air's good for you."

Her slippers scuffed the floor rhythmically, and a ghost of a smile lifted her lips as she followed him outside. "Never had to tell you that. It was all I could do to get you back into the house at the end of the day."

"And look how good I turned out."

"You did." She put a hand to his cheek. "You really did."

Not sure what to do with the rush of emotion, he ducked his head and cracked a joke. "Not too late for me to start a life of crime."

With a faint chuckle, Mum took the plate and sat at the round table. There was enough light through the sliding door without turning on the overhead.

Damo pulled out a chair, the iron leg scraping on the concrete. The clothes horse that was never folded away anymore was full of dry laundry he'd have to take in before bed. The square of grass was dry and yellow, though the desert plants that circled the yard in long brick planters Dad had built were still going strong. They hadn't gotten attention in years but were apparently too prickly and tough to kill.

Like Dad.

The rush of guilt this time hit like a surfboard in the sternum. Still, Damo managed to say, "When's the next appointment?"

Eyes on her plate in the moonlight, Mum finished chewing. "A fortnight."

"Are you gonna tell the doc?"

"Tell her what?"

He bit back a surge of frustration. "That Dad's worse than ever. Forget about doing his exercises—he barely gets out of bed."

"Because he's in pain."

Damo muttered, "Don't see how he feels anything with all the pills."

Still not looking at him, Mum toyed with a mini corncob, stabbing it with her fork. "It's a problem. I know."

"Do you? You're hardly here." He winced, wishing he'd bitten his tongue.

She glanced up sharply. "I'm very aware. You think I like working double shifts at the hospital so we can keep this house?"

"No. I know. I'm sorry." Shame heated his cheeks. "I'm sorry," he repeated.

"Oh, bub." She grasped his forearm with her small, warm hand. "I'm the one who should be sorry. I know it's not fair on you and your sister. You do so much around here. You both do. You should be out with your mates, not home cooking dinner and taking care of your father."

Of course, he hadn't tonight, which made him feel even worse. He'd left it all to Tabby. He shrugged. "It's fine."

"It's not." Mum took a big swig of wine. "Seven years now, and it's only getting worse."

"He's addicted to those pills," Damo whispered.

"Yes."

Pills are all he cares about now.

Damo couldn't say that part out loud. "He's just never been the same, and now—" he motioned with his free hand.

Mum nodded. "I wish I had the answer."

"It's not your fault."

She gazed at him seriously. "It's not yours either. Or Tabby's. Or your dad's."

Eyes burning, he nodded, thinking about who his dad used to be and how much he'd fucking loved that man.

"Get to bed. Thanks for dinner."

He kissed her cheek and escaped, shutting himself in his room. He'd grab the laundry tomorrow. He got out his last fresh uniform for the morning and checked the surf report.

Damo wished he could remember the last time he and his dad had gone surfing. It had to have been that week of the accident. It might have been the day before, but he couldn't be sure.

At the time, it had just been another awesome day at Barking, paddling out with his old man in the sunshine. Nothing special. The way it'd always been and always would. He hadn't known it would be the last time—how could he?

But he wished so fucking hard that he had. That he'd appreciated it. That he'd known it was the end, and that life would change to Before and After.

Damo flopped on his stupid twin bed, the springs squeaking. His phone pinged, and his heart lifted as he read the message from Blake. It was just a simple good night and:

Thinking about you.

Damo replied with a "ditto," and then let himself think about Blake, locking up everything else into its little box that was fuller than ever.

He didn't want to take Blake for granted. Didn't want to forget any of the moments they'd shared.

Part of him wanted to race back outside and tell his mum all about Blake and being bi. Because it seemed like, yeah, he was bi. But it wasn't the right time. For now, Blake was just *his.*

With his headphones on in the darkness, Damo opened his music app and found the song from Blake's car.

Closing his eyes, he imagined the wind in his hair and salt on his skin as he and Blake paddled out beyond the breakers. In his head, he kissed Blake as the ocean swelled under them, not giving a shit who was looking.

One day, he'd do it for real—and he'd remember every second.

Chapter Thirteen

AS HE SIDESTEPPED a rogue cricket ball in the park behind the beach, Blake waved to acknowledge the shouted apology from the batter. It was too crowded to play a proper match, but the kids of the family were clearly practicing their bowling under the sun's glare.

The knot in Blake's stomach tightened as he adjusted his backpack on his shoulder and scanned the area again for any sign of Tasha and her family.

And my son, he thought. *My son!*

It still wasn't quite real. He checked his phone again—no new messages or calls—then opened one of the photos of Cooper that Tash had sent. Cooper looked like an average eight-year-old. Light brown hair, freckles on tanned skin, wiry build. He stood in shorts and a Sydney Roosters T-shirt in front of a golden Christmas tree. His nose was red from the sun, and he looked like any kid in the middle of school holidays who'd been living outside.

Any kid who happened to be Blake's son.

"Blake!" a woman called.

Heart in his throat, he spotted Tasha waving. Leggy and tall and wearing a flowy floral sundress, she carried a folded beach chair under her other arm and walked with a tall Black man and two children.

The little girl, Rosie, was curly haired and playing some sort of hopping game, holding the hand of her dad, Tony. He pulled a wagon loaded with beach supplies.

Cooper walked between his parents, carrying another chair. His face was…neutral? Not scowling or smiling. Wary, which was fair enough.

Blake made sure to smile widely despite suddenly feeling like he might spew. He jogged toward them, the grass springy under his bare feet. He'd made a list of things to say, including a plan with alternatives depending on how the interaction went.

Now that it was happening—and his son stood in front of him—all Blake could say was, "Hey."

Tasha put down the chair and opened her arms for a hug. Blake gratefully embraced her, inhaling coconut sunscreen and hibiscus. "Good to see you," he said. That hadn't been on his list, but it would do.

Smiling, Tony extended his hand, and they shook. Blake said hi to Rosie, who twirled her polka dot sundress. Her arm around Cooper's shoulders, Tasha said, "Coop, this is Blake."

This was it. It was happening. And somehow in all his preparation, Blake hadn't quite been able to imagine this moment. Hugging seemed too much. Handshake? Too formal. He gave an awkward little wave.

"Hey," Cooper said.

Blake smiled, remembering one of the phrases he'd written down. "I'm so glad you're here."

"Yeah." Cooper shrugged. "Cool." He tugged at the collar of his T-shirt and looked down at his thongs.

"We all are!" Tasha exclaimed. "Sorry we're late. Had to park blocks away."

"No worries. Here, let me help." Blake picked up her chair. "Let's find a spot. How was the wedding?"

After weaving around clumps of people in the park and on the boardwalk, they picked their way across the crowded sand. Tasha told him about the wedding, the words tumbling out a little quickly. They all seemed nervous aside from Rosie, who squealed and hopped with abandon.

They found a spot just north of the flags, and Blake was relieved to see Damo and his friend Cody stationed nearby in one of the buggies. Damo stood on the back, the wind catching his hair as he scanned the water.

He looked fantastic in his blue shirt and black boardies with *Lifeguard* written across his tight arse. It was somehow comforting that he was close by.

"Anyway, it was a fun wedding despite that little hiccup."

Blake realized he had no idea what Tasha'd been saying, but he nodded and said, "Glad to hear it."

Then there was silence aside from Rosie singing to herself and the chatter and playful shrieks around them on the beach. "Uh…" Blake cursed himself. He'd made a list of conversation topics, but his mind was a whistling blank as he watched his son.

He'd examined the photo again and again, searching for himself in Cooper's smiling face. He hadn't been sure, but now in person, he could spot that Cooper definitely had his slightly wide nose.

This was his *child*.

Blake wanted to drop to his knees and yank him into a fierce hug. Instead, he blurted, "School good?"

Cooper shrugged.

"Tell Blake about your science project," Tony said.

He rolled his eyes. "*Dad.*"

"What? We're proud of you!" Tony unfolded a sun shelter, the little tent popping up and almost blowing away in a gust of wind. He quickly jammed a peg into the sand, and Blake circled around the other side to help, not sure how he felt about hearing his son call another man "dad."

He'd known Tony was Cooper's father in every way except biological, but… It still hurt, which surprised him. Blake tamped the feeling down. He had to stay rational. He'd have to build his own relationship with Cooper over time.

It's been five minutes. Breathe.

"I'd love to hear about your project," Blake said.

Cooper eyed him. Not hostilely, but cautiously. "It was cool, I guess. Did you know temperature affects the size of crystals? If you're growing them."

"I had no idea. How does it work?"

Blake sat on the blanket Tasha spread out and nodded as Cooper explained, his voice getting livelier as he went on. Blake ohhed and ahhed in all the right places, or so it seemed. His pulse raced for no reason—other than meeting his son for the first time, which he supposed was reason enough.

When he was finished, Cooper abruptly said, "I'm hungry."

"You had a huge breakfast," Tony said.

Cooper shrugged. "But I'm *hungry*."

Tasha sighed. "Okay, you can have a snack—but you'll have to wait a little bit before you swim."

Blake said, "How about an ice cream?" He looked to Tasha and Tony. "Sorry, is it too early for sugar?"

"Never!" Cooper and Rosie responded in perfect unison.

They all laughed, and Blake added, "The cafe's just there. Do you fancy anything?"

"Oh, a flat white would be beautiful," Tasha said.

Tony nodded. "Make that two. And I have a sneaking suspicion Rosie-posie might want a mint choc chip. And the only reason both of you are getting ice cream this early is because we're on holiday."

She squealed and clapped. "Yes, yes, yes! Can I come?"

Blake looked to Tash and Tony, and they nodded. Tasha reached for her purse, but Blake shook his head. "My shout."

Rosie kept up a nonstop patter of talk, which Blake didn't mind one bit since it saved him and Cooper from having to think of things to say.

After they ordered at the counter, they got their ice cream cones and moved to the side of the building to wait for the coffee by a large open window. Inside, dishes clattered and voices murmured.

Licking her green ice cream, Rosie was momentarily distracted by a column of ants on the ground, and she crouched, watching them with incredible focus.

"Is it weird?" Cooper blurted.

Blake's heart skipped. "Is what weird?"

"This." He motioned between them before licking his hokey pokey ice cream.

"Is it weird for you?"

Cooper shrugged. "Yeah."

Blake had to smile. "Yeah, it is a bit, hey? It's also amazing. I'm really, really happy to meet you."

Cooper seemed to be assessing the veracity of that statement. Finally, he nodded seriously. "Okay."

"Thanks, Blake!" the girl behind the counter called, and he squeezed past a family for the tray of coffees as she picked up another bag and shouted, "Thanks, Siobhan!"

Rosie chattered again as they made their way back across the sand, only taking breaks to lick her ice cream cone. Cooper licked his own and Blake gulped his too-hot coffee. The caffeine wouldn't help his nerves in the end, but short term, it was soothing.

Back at the blanket in the partial shade of the pop-up tent, the kids finished their ice creams and the adults discussed rising real estate prices until Cooper said, "So many people here. Dunno how the lifeguards can see people drowning."

"They're like superheroes," Blake said. "Eyes in the back of their heads. We clubbies help out on weekends and holidays, but the pros are next level."

"You don't get paid, right?"

"Nope, we're volunteers. Helping people is way more important than money."

Cooper seemed to ponder this before nodding. "That's cool."

He was *cool*! Or being a clubbie was, which was close enough. And maybe he'd just helped give a life lesson about money not being everything? Had he just *parented*?

"Do you still rescue people?"

"Sometimes, especially if the lifeguards are flat out. I haven't yet, but I've done all the training. I'll be ready to jump right in."

"Isn't it kind of scary? Guess not since you surf too." Cooper squinted out at the swells.

"Oh, it can definitely be scary sometimes. But if someone needs help, that's the only thing that matters."

"Cool," Cooper repeated.

He was *cool*. Grinning, Blake said, "We can say hi to the lifeguards if you like." He nodded toward the buggy. "That's my friend, Damo, up there."

Tash looked up from under the brim of a floppy beige hat she'd just put on. "Oh, that's him?" She grinned. "Let's say hello. Tones, you and Rosie want to hold down the fort? Also, hats, hats, hats." She pulled the sun hats from her bag and passed them. Blake got his own cap from his backpack. He needed to be a good example.

As they approached the buggy, his nerves dialed up another few notches. A few weeks ago, he hadn't even known Damo or Cooper, and now it was vitally important that they liked each other. Not to mention vitally important that Cooper liked *Blake*, but Damo was so wonderful that it was sure to help.

He cleared his throat and called out a hello—and Damo's beautiful blue eyes lit up as he took off his red sunnies and hopped onto the sand from the back of the buggy while behind the wheel, Cody kept his eyes on the water.

"Hiya!" Damo's gaze traveled to Tasha and Cooper, his smile bright as Blake made introductions.

"How long have you worked here?" Cooper asked.

"Since I was eighteen, so four years. But I grew up at Barkers, so this is like my backyard."

Blake said, "Cooper was wondering how you spot swimmers in trouble when there are so many people."

"Look, it's not easy," Damo replied. "It's chockers, hey? But after a while, you can see the signs. We get a lot of tourists here who can't swim at all, and they're easy to spot. People caught in the rips are easy too. There are others who get real still and quiet like. Hair over their faces. Sometimes, it's a gut feeling."

"Like Spidey senses?" Cooper asked. He squinted, his freckled face screwed up, and Blake couldn't stop smiling at how adorable he was. His son!

"*Exactly* like that!" Damo said. "You reckon, Cody?" he asked over his shoulder.

Leaning forward across the passenger seat in the buggy, Cody said, "Absolutely." His gaze met Blake's, and recognition set in. Grinning, Cody said, "Good to see you again. Blake, is it?"

Blake hoped the sun's glare would hide the heat flushing his face. He and Cody shook hands, and Tasha asked, "Are you Liam Fox's boyfriend?"

"That's me."

"Cooper, you want to sit in the buggy?" Damo asked.

His little face lit up like a Christmas tree. "Can I?"

Cody patted the seat beside him. "Hop up, buddy."

"Thanks for this," Tash said to Damo as Cooper asked Cody questions.

"Anytime." Damo smiled, scanning the water. "We'd take ya for a spin if it wasn't so busy. There's a little flashy in the north, but otherwise conditions are good at the moment."

"No worries. It's great to meet you." She squeezed Blake's arm. "And to see you again. I think it's a little weird for all of us, but it's good. Yeah?"

"Yeah," Blake said, giving her a smile. "Thank you. You didn't have to do any of this."

"I did, though. Should've done it before."

He'd missed eight whole years of his son's life, and part of Blake wanted to say, *Yeah, you really should've.* But what was the point? It would just spoil the mood, and they couldn't turn back time. "We're here now. That's what matters."

Damo climbed up on the back of the buggy, peering into the distance. "Codes, you see just in front of third ramp?"

Tasha motioned for Cooper to climb out of the buggy as Cody and Damo stared intently. Then they both relaxed in unison. "False alarm," Damo said, smiling down at Cooper. "You gettin' wet, mate?"

"Yes!" Cooper answered.

"Where're ya gonna swim?"

"Between the red and yellow flags."

Damo's grin widened as he bent to give Cooper a high five. "That's exactly the right answer!"

"Hey, Damo…" Cody leaned forward, his tone suddenly serious. "Just in front of that sandcastle to the right… Go!"

In a blink, Damo had stripped off his shirt and was gone. Cody was on the radio, and Blake, Tash, and Cooper watched as Damo splashed into the water to help a man maneuver a staggering older woman onto the sand.

"Wow," Cooper breathed.

The woman seemed dazed, and Damo powered her to the dry part of the sand as people scurried out of the way. He called to Cody, "Defib and ambo!"

Everyone stood back as another buggy arrived a minute later, and Blake overheard snatches of conversation about a possible seizure. He watched Damo administer oxygen to the woman and comfort the older man with her. His heart swelled, and he was so damn *proud.*

He wanted to run over and kiss Damo once the paramedics arrived and took over, but of course he only watched.

"Superheroes indeed," Tasha said, giving Blake a wink. "He's lovely."

Blake couldn't stop grinning. "He is." Tearing his gaze away, Blake focused on Cooper. "Should we go for a swim?"

And Cooper *smiled* and said, "Okay," and it felt like the greatest victory.

〜〜〜

"AND DID I tell you he's a forward on the school's footy team?"

Damo smiled indulgently. "You did."

"God, sorry." Blake winced. "I'm repeating myself, aren't I?"

"Yeah, but don't be sorry, mate. He's your son. It's pretty freakin' cool."

Blake turned into the parking for his building. "It *is*. Did I tell you I'm meeting them for brekkie tomorrow? I did. Sorry."

"S'okay." Damo leaned across the gear shift and kissed Blake's cheek. "I reckon we're on for Bremer Bay too, hey?"

"I think so. Unless Cooper secretly hated me and never wants to see me again."

"Not a chance. Seems like a great kid."

Blake parked and blew out a long breath. "He does, doesn't he?"

His mind was still spinning. He'd met his son, and it had gone well as far as he could tell? Cooper hadn't said a lot, but that was understandable. He'd been shy and sweet and it was still hard to believe he even existed.

Blake was jittery and keyed up. It was exhausting trying to be his best self all day. He asked, "You sure you can't stay for dinner? Not that I'm cooking, but I'll order takeaway. We can watch telly and decompress."

Damo's face clouded. "Not today. Sorry. I just wanted to come up for a little bit. Make sure you're good. Reckon meeting your kid could be a lot to handle. Not in a bad way, but…"

"Yeah. It was a lot. Did I mention—yes, I've already told you everything in excruciating detail."

Damo grinned. "All good. I like listening to you talk."

"I don't even know what I'm saying anymore." He rolled his neck. "Didn't realize how stressed I was."

"I could help with that."

Breath hitching, Blake smiled. "Yeah? Anything particular in mind?"

Damo hopped out of the car, and Blake followed with a laugh. The key was still in the door of his apartment when Damo pressed against him tightly.

"Can I suck your dick?"

With a laugh, Blake shuffled inside with Damo attached to him like a barnacle. He closed the door behind them. "I thought you'd never a—"

The words were barely out before Damo spun them and lunged in for a kiss, shoving Blake against the closed door. He writhed against Blake as if trying to climb into his skin, and Blake was instantly hard.

They gasped for air, and Blake ran a thumb over Damo's wet lips. "You want me?" It was needy, but he still ached to hear it.

Damo nodded, shoving his warm hands under Blake's T-shirt and pulling it over his head. "Been thinking about this for days. Weeks? Since that first night." He hesitated. "Unless… Do you still wanna talk more and stuff? I can listen."

How was Blake not supposed to fall head over heels for this man?

"I think I've said enough." Blake inhaled sharply as Damo bent to suck his nipple. Fingers roaming through Damo's golden, wavy hair, he murmured, "Your mouth is incredible."

"It's all the talkin' I do," Damo mumbled against Blake's chest before licking his other nipple. He grasped for Blake's waist, opening the Velcro fastening of his boardies with a loud *riiiip*.

Blake kicked off his thongs, but before he could help with his shorts, Damo sank to his knees, pulling them down with him. He gazed up at Blake with such earnest openness that Blake struggled to breath through a surge of affection.

From a distance on Barking, he'd admired Damo's skills in the water and his easy, crooked smile. Now that he knew him, he was amazed by how guileless he was. Blake had hooked up with men who'd worked their arses off to come across as sexy, but Damo blew them out of the water without even trying.

Blake cupped his cheek. "Is this how you've been thinking about it? On your knees for me?"

"Yes." It was a breathless whisper, his eyes locked on Blake's. "Is it okay?"

"Are you kidding? You're so hot."

Damo's breath stuttered, and he swallowed hard before pulling down Blake's shorts the rest of the way. Blake lifted his feet, and Damo tossed the boardies aside. Running his damp palms over Blake's hairy thighs, Damo leaned in and rubbed his face in Blake's crotch.

"I'm all yours," Blake groaned.

Sitting back on his heels, Damo peered up at him before tentatively licking the head. He clutched at Blake's thighs and hips, his hands making nervous movements while he went in for slow, hesitant sucks and exploration with his beautiful mouth.

"Feels amazing." Blake stroked Damo's soft hair gently.

He'd wondered what more sex with Damo would be like, and this eager, sweet lust was better than anything he'd imagined. The way Damo moaned when he filled his mouth with Blake's cock, his eyes fluttering shut as he sucked, had Blake's toes curling on the wood floor.

"Fuck, *yes*," Blake muttered.

He let Damo take the lead, holding his head loosely, just needing to touch. His balls were tight already, the sight of Damo's lips stretched around him and the wet, slurping noises turning him on fiercely. Against the door, standing naked with Damo kneeling at his feet, Blake's whole body was taut with desire.

"You make me so hard."

Damo pulled off with an absolutely filthy wet suck, his swollen lips glistening. "I hadn't noticed. Do ya like it?"

Tightening his grip in Damo's hair, Blake laughed. He loved that they laughed so much together. Lance had typically been serious during sex, and it wasn't that it'd been bad—they'd had some great times.

But Damo's openness lit a fire in Blake's blood. "I love it. You were born for this."

Adam's apple bobbing, Damo breathed hard. "Will you come in my mouth?" Such an earnest, innocent way to ask such a question.

Blake could only nod, groaning as Damo swallowed him again. Now, Damo circled the base with his hand, trying to go deeper and choking. Blake wanted to thrust and fuck his mouth, the pressure to come almost unbearable in the best way.

But he kept his arse pinned to the door, giving Damo the freedom to experiment, holding his head loosely as Damo got back into a rhythm. It only took a few more long pulls and Damo's free hand fumbling for his balls before Blake tipped over the edge.

He tried to warn Damo, but instead of words, it was a jumble of moans and grunts as he came into his mouth. White-hot pleasure roared through him, his back arching.

But Blake quickly opened his eyes, needing to see Damo swallowing around him. Needing to see his jizz dripping out of swollen lips as Damo coughed, then grinned and swallowed Blake's cock again, licking and milking him until Blake had to ease him off.

"C'mere." He pulled Damo to his feet and kissed him deeply, tasting himself and reaching into Damo's shorts to work his hard dick.

Damo had to be aching, his cock straining and leaking in Blake's hand. With a few hard tugs, he came, moaning and jerking, splashing Blake's bare stomach. He wrapped Damo in his arms, taking his weight and stroking his spine, murmuring praise.

"Was it really good?" Damo mumbled hotly against Blake's neck.

"I couldn't fake that. Was it good for you?"

Damo nodded against him. "I was pretty sure, but that seals the deal. Sucking cock is awesome, hey?"

"Hell yes."

After an easy silence as they caught their breath, Damo asked, "Have you dated a bi bloke before?"

Was that the first time Damo had referred to himself as bi? Blake smiled at the thought.

Damo's brows met. "We are, right? Dating?"

"Yes! Sorry, got distracted. We definitely are. And I hooked up with a bi guy in uni before I met Lance but haven't properly dated anyone bi or pan."

Damo lifted his head from Blake's shoulder, his blue eyes serious. "'Till now?"

"'Till now."

They kissed and kissed until Damo reluctantly left. At least, it had seemed reluctant? Yeah, course it was. Damo wasn't *pretending* to not be able to stay. As eager as Blake was to understand what was going on with Damo's family, he had to be patient.

Still, as he tried to relax on the couch and watch mindless TV, he kept thinking about the way Damo tensed and frowned and took on a…heaviness when he had to go home.

Blake was dying to help. Surely there was something he could do? If he could lend a hand, he could smooth away that strain and ease the pressure. What good was he if he couldn't do that?

His phone pinged, and his heart leapt to see a text from Cooper:

Do you play Mortal Chronicles?

Blake looked it up, downloaded it, and replied: *Yep! Want to play sometime?*

Well, at least learning the game as fast as possible would keep him busy for the rest of the evening. He read and reread Cooper's single letter response—the letter K—and grinned like a fool.

He had a *son*.

And before he could talk himself out of it, he was ringing his mum. How could he wait any longer before telling his parents they had another grandchild? They'd be thrilled, and he had to share his joy with them.

He paced eagerly, imagining their delighted smiles. When Mum picked up the video call, her brow was furrowed.

"Blakey? You right?"

He laughed. "Yes! Everything's good. Fantastic, even. Magnificent. Tremendous." He heard Damo's voice saying those were ten-dollar words and grinned.

Mum was sitting on the brown leather couch in their apartment behind the pub. It was after closing time, and she was in one of her floral short-sleeved nighties.

The camera angle was low, but at least her face was visible. Behind her, the framed print Blake had bought them at the Pro Hart gallery in Broken Hill hung on the beige wall.

It was called "Mining Town Sunday," painted in earth tones depicting squat wooden buildings and tall, dry trees with spindly-legged townspeople playing and talking. It always made Blake feel good to see his gift hung proudly.

The murmur of the TV was silenced, and Dad squeezed into frame. He wore a white singlet. "Are you on drugs?"

Blake's smile stiffened. "When have you known me to ever do drugs?"

"Ya haven't, but you're going out to those nightclubs. We know what happens there. All sorts."

He didn't ask whether Dad meant nightclubs in general or queer ones specifically and forced a laugh. "Not sure the last time you two went clubbing, but again, I don't do drugs. I wanted to tell you some good news."

Mum's lined face lit up. "You're moving back home!"

Blake was stunned into silence. She couldn't *really* think that? They'd gone over it so many times. He blinked. "I… What? Why would you think that?"

Mum still beamed. "We need you here, Blakey." She wasn't joking. He could tell when she was.

His stomach dropped. "Why? Are you sick?"

"You know we have our aches and pains, and your father won't listen to the doctor even—"

"But you're not having any stroke symptoms?" He exhaled.

"No, love." Mum's smile was strained. "You know that wasn't the only reason we needed you home."

"I know," he said automatically. "But you're doing great without me." The last thing he wanted was to be drawn into that debate again. "No, I'm not moving home."

Their faces fell, and while part of Blake felt guilty—a bigger part had him clenching his fists, his phone in a death grip. How many times did he need to say that he'd left Blinman and wasn't going back?

He should've been excitedly telling them about Cooper and Damo. Sharing the two new people in his life who'd turned it upside-down in the most wonderful way.

His joy had faded—the bright, vivid rainbow colors of his eagerness muted to drab grays.

"We just miss you, son," Dad said. "You're such a help around the place."

Blake battled between a rush of pride and satisfaction and frustration that his parents knew how drawn he was to helping people—and they used that to guilt-trip him.

"Do you ever ask Adam or Richie to come back?" He knew his sister, Ella, had gotten her fair share of guilt trips when she'd moved to Adelaide. His older brothers had been gone for years, though.

Mum frowned and said, "They're in Queensland," as if he didn't know that. She laughed. "Don't reckon Heather or Julia would fancy Blinman."

Dad scoffed. "No way *Julia* would leave Brissie."

Blake clenched his jaw. His father always said her name with a hint of distain even though Blake's sister-in-law was lovely. He'd asked more than once what the issue was, and Dad had always insisted there was nothing. Blake suspected it was simply that she was a lawyer.

"And Ella's settled in Adelaide now with Griff and the baby," Blake said.

Mum sighed. "Yes. But there's no reason you can't come home!"

"Because I'm single? What if I wasn't?"

Ah, and there was that painful mix of discomfort and embarrassment with a hint of panic. Blake hadn't subjected Lance to a trip to Blinman, and his parents had always been too busy with the pub to visit him at uni in Melbourne. They hadn't even attended his commencement ceremony.

Awkwardly, Mum tried to laugh. "All right, so you're not coming home. Can't blame us for tryin'! Love, did I tell you what happened on Friday?"

"Oh, you won't believe it!" Dad said too eagerly.

Anything to avoid talking about the mere possibility that Blake could have a boyfriend. A partner. He'd told them after his first year in uni that he was gay, and after their initial disbelief and Mum's tears, it had been like this. They simply avoided the topic at all costs.

He nodded and listened to Mum go on about the ringers from the local sheep station getting up to no good, then said, "I have to be up early for work. Talk to you later." He forced a smile and disconnected.

They hadn't asked about his good news.

Blake wanted to ring Damo and tell him everything, but it wasn't fair dumping this on him when he had his own stress to deal with. Whatever that was. That Blake didn't even know was a stark reminder not to get ahead of himself.

Even if he and Damo were properly dating, it was early days. The last thing Blake needed was to go too fast and spoil it.

He could text Kat, but he hadn't replied to their latest messages yet. In fact, he hadn't even told them about Cooper. *Shit*. They had a lot to catch up on, but he wasn't in the mood to answer a million questions. He was best off getting to bed since his alarm would be blaring far too soon.

Chapter Fourteen

L OOSE HAIR STICKING to his sweaty cheek, Damo whipped his head around as the scream pierced the buzz of typical beach noise. He was used to kids screaming and shrieking while they played in the water or on the sand, but this scream made the hair stand up on the back of his neck.

He'd been patrolling the north side of the flagged area on foot, and he jolted to a stop, scanning the water. It hadn't seemed far away, but sound could play tricks. A violent splash just five meters out caught his eye. He threw down his radio and whipped off his sunnies and uniform shirt before grabbing the nearby rescue board and racing in.

The fully dressed kid was probably seven years old, and he was immediately climbing the ladder, clawing at the water as if he could pull himself up, going under just off the back of the sandbank, dark hair plastered to his face. His father was also dressed, and he flailed and tried to hold the kid up while going under himself. They were steps from safety, but panic had set in.

They were so close that Damo didn't even get on the board, instead shoving it toward them and yelling to hold on. He kept the board safely between them, and they clung on the other side, the boy sobbing. Pulling the board with the two patients clinging to it, Damo only had to kick once before he could stand on the sandbank.

"It's okay. You're safe." Damo motioned to them. "Stand up. You can stand."

They still clung to the board desperately, and Damo reached across to pry the man's fingers loose from the side rope. "Mate, *stand up*."

Kids were helpless and made crap life choices, so Damo didn't blame them for not knowing better. But he couldn't understand how an adult thought it was a good plan to go into the water in jeans when they couldn't swim a stroke.

He bit back the irritation and tried to smile, motioning upward with his hands. The man stumbled to his feet, pulling up the boy as well. Damo herded them onto dry sand, and the man bowed, shaking his hand and thanking him.

"Where are you from?" Damo asked.

"Japan. Thank you."

"No worries. Just stay out of the water if you can't swim. It's very dangerous to wear clothes." He pointed to the jeans, and the man nodded.

Damo crouched and looked up at the sniffling boy. "Did you swallow much water?" He mimed drinking and tried to get his point across. The kid's color was okay, and he'd only flailed maybe twenty seconds before Damo got to him, so he was probably fine.

But Jesus, that could have gone bad. He hated close calls, and with a kid it was even worse. Beachgoers who'd watched the rescue applauded, but Damo kept his focus on the shaking little boy. He wanted to give him a hug but instead explained to the dad about inhaling water and the danger signs before they went on their way, the boy managing a smile now.

Damo's walkie-talkie crackled where he'd left it with his shirt and sunnies, and he blew sand off it. "Central, had to move fast. Both patients look fine."

"Copy that," Ronnie said in the tower. "They were so close to shore, hey? Good work. Can you get up to north end? Croc's going to start chomping soon, and Foxy's dealing with a bag thief. Coppers are on their way. Mazza can swing by in the buggy for ya."

In the buggy with Mia a few minutes later, Damo tied his uniform shirt around his neck, letting his skin dry in the afternoon heat. Mia—who they mostly called Maz or Mazza—navigated around the clumps of families and umbrellas and tanners, sticking close to the water's edge. She cursed under her breath as a bloke walked right in front of the buggy, putting up an imperious hand for her to stop.

"*Mate*!" Damo shouted. "Sure, after you. It's not like we have a bloody job to do or anything."

"You right?" Mia asked as they drove on.

Damo physically shook off his frustration. "Fine."

"It's tough with kids. Confronting."

"Yeah. They're so helpless against the ocean. I wouldn't let mine anywhere near the water if they couldn't swim."

They parked at the north end, Mia on the mega telling tourists to go down between the flags. Sitting in silence, they scanned the water before Damo asked, "You want kids?"

Mia scoffed. "No idea. Not any time soon, that's for sure."

"How're things with whatshisname?" Damo asked.

She wore mirrored sunnies, but Damo *knew* she was rolling her eyes. She said, "You know his name's Tom."

"Right, so how're things with Tommo?"

"Excellent. Might introduce him to my parents. We'll see."

"Wow. Good on ya. They don't want you to marry someone Malay?"

She shrugged. "They want plenty of things. For example, they want me to be a doctor, not a lifeguard. Life is full of disappointment." She reached up for the mic, pressing the button with her thumb, the spiral cord swinging. "Swimmer in the red right in front of us! Come straight back to shore."

Of course the guy ignored her. A girl about Tabby's age building a sandcastle nearby approached, bucket still in hand. "Why don't you go get him now?" she asked in an accent Damo thought was maybe German.

Mia smiled at her. "Well, someone else could get in much more serious trouble while we're busy trying to convince him not to swim in the rip. From here, we're watching all sorts of people at once, so we wait to go in until we really have to."

The kid looked out at the man, then nodded. "Makes sense." She gazed at Mia with open curiosity. "Are there lots of girl lifeguards?"

"Unfortunately not. I'm the only one at Barking at the moment, but I'm hoping that'll change after the winter recruitment."

The girl nodded. "I hope so. Bye!" Then she was off back to her sandcastle, her parents napping under an umbrella.

"If you got pregnant now, think you'd keep the baby?" Damo asked.

This drew a frown. "Dunno. Why are you asking?"

He shrugged, trying to play casual. "No reason."

He failed, because Mia groaned. "Don't tell me you got someone pregnant. I know you've been getting laid lately, but I hope you're not that reckless."

"What?" He sat up straighter. "How do you know I'm getting laid?"

Mia pulled her sunnies down her nose and gave him a stare that said he was a complete boofhead. "You might as well hire one of those planes that flies banners over Barking with messages like 'Marry me, Bella' except yours would say, 'Damo's having sex with some chick he thinks he's in love with.' It's all over your moony face. Plus the spring in your step. You know you can't keep a secret to save your life."

Damo thought of a dark bedroom that stank of sweat and piss

and smoke, Dad hurling the remote at his head, Tabby crying behind him and Mum miles away at work. Locking that door tight, he tried to act offended.

"That's not true. I knew Foxy was gay for months before he came out on TV."

"We all knew that. Besides, Cody would have had your balls for breakfast with tomato sauce on top if you'd breathed a word. If any of us did. But obviously we didn't since that was major stuff. That was heavy. That wasn't you hooking up." She grimaced. "And seriously, tell me you didn't get her pregnant already."

"I didn't get anyone pregnant! There's no new chick."

"You're telling me you're not getting laid? Bullshit."

"I'm tellin' ya there's no new chick." Heart jumping now, he shrugged.

Telling Cody had been surprisingly easy. Cody was gay and his mate, and probably one of the least judgmental people he'd ever met. But Mia was his mate too, and while she had way more opinions than Cody, she'd be cool with it. Of course she would.

His throat was suddenly dry, but he got the words out. "I'm seeing a guy I met here. One of the clubbies. His name's Blake. Blake the bloke. I fancy him, and I think I'm bisexual. I still like chicks, but I like guys too, so now I'm seeing him, and you're right, I'm gettin' laid, and it's all been really good, and even though we just met, I like him heaps."

Out of words, Damo sucked in a breath and gulped from his water bottle, Mia watching him in silence, mouth open. He drank again, then added, "He's definitely not preggo, and neither am I."

Mia was silent for the space of a few more of Damo's thudding heartbeats before she said, "Wow," and looked back at the water, pushing her sunglasses back up her nose. "I thought I had you all figured out."

"I've got hidden depths, hey?"

A grin spread over Mia's pretty face. "I guess you do. Good on ya." She held out her fist, and he bumped it, exhaling in relief.

"You ever kiss a girl?" he asked.

She smirked. "Is this scientific research?"

"Absolutely."

"Yes, I've kissed a girl, but we were playing truth or dare, so it doesn't really count."

"Did you fancy it?"

Mia shrugged. "It was fun, I guess. And no, I'm not giving you any more details than that."

Damo scanned the surfers out the back, a giddy little flush in his chest even though he knew Blake was doing overtime at work. He was coming by around dinnertime, and Damo bounced his bare foot on the dash, trying not to let his mind jump to what he and Blake would do later.

Dinnertime. He realized with a groan that Tabby would be alone after school again with Mum working another double. At least Damo had gone to Woolies that morning and stocked the fridge.

Tabby would be fine, right? Besides, she was always banging on about not needing a babysitter. There was a roast chook and bag of salad, and icy poles in the freezer for dessert.

Shit. He still needed to tell her about Bremer Bay. He had to go home before he met Blake.

Considering he'd spent almost all his time at home when he wasn't working or surfing, it was ridiculous to dread it so much now. It had been years, but suddenly he was suffocating.

Maybe he should back out of going. It wasn't fair to Tabby. He was a terrible big brother. He—

Mia pointed. "Is there a head out the back? Fourth ramp."

Damo stood on the side of the buggy, peering beyond the swells, waiting for a flash of—"Yep. Reckon I'm going for a paddle." All thoughts of Tabby and home and Blake had to go.

The radio squawked, and yep, he was in.

~~~~

"TABS!"

Damo waited, then called again, "Tabs!" His long-sleeved wetsuit was unzipped to his waist, hanging down toward the lino floor. He'd caught a quick set to get his head on straight before coming home. He'd be meeting Blake back at Barkers soon, so he had to either tell her or cancel the trip.

"What?"

"C'mere!"

Standing at the kitchen sink, he picked up a plate from the soapy water and scrubbed at the dried-on sauce from last night's spag bol. Tabby's door opened down the hall with a creak, and she heaved a sigh as she entered the kitchen.

"What?" she repeated before tapping her phone.

"Just need to talk to ya." He scrubbed harder, trying to keep his voice normal even as his pulse jumped like he'd just spotted a tourist in a rip.

"Here I am. Yes, Dad had his meds. He's out of it today."

They'd never said it out loud, but Damo knew neither of them minded when he was dozy.

"Um…" Damo put the plate in the rack. The dishwasher had busted a year ago and now they kept extra pots in it.

Tabby stepped closer, putting her phone in her shorts pocket. "What?"

Jesus, he was leaving for two bloody nights. Mum would be home by eight the first night and off work the second. Why was he tied up in knots? "I'm goin' away."

Blue eyes wide, Tabby's lip trembled. "When?"

"Tomorrow. It'll—"

"*Tomorrow?*" Jaw on the floor, she stared. "Why the fuck didn't you tell me?" Hands balled, she blinked back tears.

"Whoa, whoa." Damo reached for her with wet, sudsy hands,
~~~~

but she jerked away.

"You're moving out tomorrow and never said a word?"

"Who's moving out? I'm going down to Bremer Bay for two nights. Then I'll be back."

Tabby blinked, shaking her head, her ponytail swaying. "Huh?"

"Bremer Bay. West of Albany? It's a five-and-a-half-hour drive, so we'll go down and stay overnight, then see the killer whales." Water from his hands dripped and splashed his bare feet. "'Course I'm not moving out. Where'd you get that idea?"

Tabby waved a hand at him. "From you! Why were you acting so nervous?"

"I wasn't!" he lied, feeling like the world's biggest pork chop.

"Why the hell did you make such a big deal out of it?"

"I didn't want you to be upset!"

"I'm not!"

Behind Dad's closed door, the volume on the telly rose. Tabby and Damo stared down the hall. She muttered, "Guess he's awake and we're being too loud for his royal *highness*."

"He didn't used to be like this," Damo said quietly.

Tabby clenched her jaw. "So you say. I wouldn't know."

"Come on, you remember. You have to." The awful, crushing sadness of Tabby barely remembering Dad before the accident stole everything made his knees weak.

Not answering, she focused on Damo. "I'll be fine. I'm not a baby. Mum's on days this week anyway."

Turning back to the dishes for something to do with his twitching fingers, he nodded. "She'll be home by eight tomorrow, and she switched a shift so she'll be home all day Thursday."

He'd held his breath asking Mum about her schedule. He couldn't—*wouldn't*—leave Tabby alone overnight.

Tabby shrugged. "Whatever. I'll be fine either way. Who are you going with?"

"Oh, just a mate," he answered way too fast. Face hot, he went at dried egg yolk on a fork.

"Why are you being weird again?"

"I'm not!" He desperately tried to think of something else to say. "I'll be stoked to see whales."

"*Okay*. You surfing?"

"Nah, not in Bremer."

Tabby rolled her eyes. "Now I mean." She motioned to his wetsuit. "You're not staying for dinner?"

"Sorry. I'll grab something later. There's food in the fridge for you."

She shrugged again. "'Kay."

"Sorry," he repeated. "I know I haven't been home as much."

"It's not like you can't go out. But you're acting weird."

"Am I?" He laughed, but it sounded fake *as*.

"Yeah, like, that? Was weird. I get you don't want to spend every night hanging with your little sister, but…"

Guilt gut punched him. "Tabs, it's not you. C'mere." She resisted, complaining that he'd get her wet, but he pulled her into a hug. After a second, her slim arms circled his waist. He said, "I'm just…"

Part of him wanted to spill it all about Blake. He could do it right now—just open his gob and let the words come out.

But he was going to be late. More than that, he still wasn't ready for his worlds to collide. He had no fear that Tabby wouldn't accept him as bi, but…

Bi. Bisexual. I'm bisexual.

He wanted to sit with it a bit more before he brought that truth into this house. Still, he hated lying, so he said, "I'm seeing someone new."

Tabby drew back with a grin, giving him a playful smack. "Why didn't you tell me?"

"I just did!"

"Okay, so who is she?"

It made sense Tabby assumed it was a chick—it always had been before. But Damo's stomach still tightened with a nervous rush, his throat going dry.

Yeah, he wasn't quite ready for this conversation at home.

"I promise I'll tell you soon, okay? I've gotta run."

"Fine. You'll cop it if you don't."

"Oh, I'm trembling!"

"You'd better be!" Tabby laughed, and the TV behind Dad's door got even louder.

Damo kissed her head again and started down the hall. "I'll tell him to turn it down."

"I don't care what he does." She made shooing motions with her hands. "You're late!"

Giving his sister a grin, Damo zipped up his wetsuit and escaped.

AN HOUR LATER, the current pulled hard around Damo's knees as he fought it. His feet sank into the wet sand, and he gritted his teeth as he splashed to shore, a wave frothing up to his hips. Blake was beside him with his board, laughing as he escaped the current's clutches too.

The sun kissed the horizon, and Damo knew they'd already pushed it by staying out for that last set. Dawn and dusk were riskier times than usual for sharks, and even though the odds were still slim, he'd promised Tabby years ago when she was small and went through an obsessive phase with sharks that he'd always be safely on the sand when the sun was going down.

It was mental to feel guilty now—it'd been forever since he'd made the promise, and Tabby surely didn't even remember it. But he still carried his board onto the dry sand and Blake followed.

There were only a few surfers left past the breakers, and the shutters were down on the lifeguard tower, everything locked up tight.

Most of the tourists had buggered off, packing up their umbrellas and eskies and sunburned kids, the long parking lot past the grass three-quarters empty. The sunset watchers were out, couples walking along the wet sand with the sea foaming around their feet, parked on towels on the beach and the grass, or sitting on the low stone wall along the edge of the beach. Not too many on a weeknight, and soon they'd be gone.

"You in a hurry to get going?" Damo asked. It was just gone seven, so still earlyish. Mum would be home soon, and Tabby knew he was out.

Blake watched the spread of orangey-pink across the sky, the soft light reflecting on his face, reminding Damo of how he'd looked wearing the red lippy. "That depends. What did you have in mind?"

And the way Blake said it made it sound like he definitely had something in mind.

Something sexy.

Damo shivered, his dick twitching. He willed himself not to pop a boner in his tight wetsuit. "I know a spot around the rocks."

Blake quirked an eyebrow. He opened his mouth, then paused. "You don't need to get home?"

It hung heavy between them in the salty air. Blake was no fool—clearly he knew there was something to do with home that Damo wasn't telling.

He said, "Not yet."

"You're sure? I understand if you need to get going."

And he *would* understand, which made Damo feel warm and fluttery. "Positive."

Blake gave him a smile. "Lead the way."

They tucked their boards into a sliver of space in the rocks locals had used for years as a hidey hole, then picked their way around the bend to the flat, barnacled rocks on the other side of the spit. There were no fishermen tonight, and Damo's pulse thrummed, the burning tug in his shoulders and thighs as he climbed up to the ledge satisfying after a long day working the beach.

He was aware of Blake following like there was an invisible thread between them. Like Blake was his surfboard, the leash reassuringly snug around Damo's ankle. They brushed against each other as they picked their way over the rocks before space opened up, the tug still there, coming together again a moment later.

Damo reminded himself to breathe.

The ledge wasn't high, but it was just high enough that the crashing waves foamed a couple of meters below. You had to know it was there—know exactly the right rocks to scale. The wind-smoothed stone was familiar under Damo's feet and hands, and he breathed a sigh of relief that the ledge was empty of other locals tonight.

He stood on the mostly flat surface, the rock still a bit warm from the hot sun. The evening wind ruffled his low, damp ponytail. The sky was red now, low clouds streaked with blood orange.

"Wow." Blake stood beside him. He craned his neck up, then leaned over the edge to look down. "Private little spot."

"Yeah, no one can see you here." Damo motioned up behind them. "The overhang is just enough. It's not a cave, but if someone climbed higher up, they wouldn't see us. And below, someone would have to be in a boat, I reckon. It's sweet as. Listen to the waves and feel like you've got the whole world to yourself. Me and my mates used to bring some tinnies and watch the stars come out."

"Smoke a few joints?"

"Yeah, if we could get our grubby paws on 'em."

"Talk about the meaning of life?"

"Oh yeah. Life according to Barkers' groms. Bunch of boof-heads."

Blake laughed quietly. "I had similar convos under the stars."

"With the best and brightest of Blinman?"

"You know it. Squid Allen and Bluey Jones are leading philosophical minds."

They chuckled, and Damo said, "I reckon we had the right idea, though. Sunsets and stars and mates. Maybe it's not the meaning of life, but it ain't far off."

After a few moments of silence as they watched the red sky, Blake asked, "You ever fuck here?"

The simple question punched the air from Damo's lungs like copping a wave and getting pushed under the whitewash. "No." His voice sounded reedy. *Needy.*

"You ever wanted to?"

"I... I don't know. Never came here with chicks. Don't know why. This was just the boys' spot. Mates."

"Mmm. And you never wanted to fuck your mates?"

His dick throbbed, pressing against the tight neoprene. Blake stood close enough on his left that Damo could sense the heat of his body, but they weren't touching. "I don't know."

"Did you talk about girls here? About tits and pussy and getting laid?"

Watching the light at the horizon fade, the red-tinged gray slowly seeping into black, Damo's throat went dry. "Yeah."

"Did you ever get hard just thinking about tits and pussy?"

"Sure. Plenty of times."

"Did you secretly wonder about cock too?"

Damo's breath caught, lust tugging at his balls, his toes curling on the rough edges of the rock. "I... Yeah. But I didn't let myself really think about it. I kept it out there." He motioned to the waves rolling in and crashing on the rocks below. "Not here. Not on land." He swallowed over his dry throat. "That doesn't make sense."

"Makes perfect sense." Blake trailed a finger down Damo's arm, a whisper on the damp material, then over his hand.

Damo's fingers twitched, lust simmering through his body. He grabbed at Blake, but Blake stepped behind him in a smooth movement, dancing out of his grasp. Now Blake's strong hands rested on Damo's shoulders, and Damo leaned back gratefully.

"Stars are coming out," Blake murmured.

Damo blinked up at the sky, tipping his head back to see a few twinkling lights, the moon rising behind them. "The really bright ones are probably satellites."

He didn't really give a stuff about the stars. All he could think about were Blake's hands heavy on his shoulders, and when Blake was going to touch more of him and *how* and *when*?

"I need—" Damo broke off, trembling. The wind carried the ocean mist, cool on his face.

Blake's breath was hot on his ear, his body pressing close. "I know. You need so *much*, don't you?"

Damo could only nod and try to make his lungs expand.

The slow snick and gentle tug of his wetsuit being unzipped sent a thrill shuddering through him, the air cool on his neck and back as the neoprene peeled open. As the zipper reached his tailbone, Damo tugged at one sleeve eagerly.

"No." Blake ran his big hands down Damo's arms firmly. "Not yet."

"But—" Damo gasped as Blake nipped an earlobe with sharp teeth.

"Not yet," Blake ordered.

Damo nodded, anticipation zipping over his flesh. He stood waiting as Blake slowly—*bloody* slowly—ran his hands back up Damo's arms. When he slipped them inside the wetsuit, his fingers wrapping about Damo's ribs, it was like the callused fingers were on his cock.

Damo could hear his own ragged breath over the hum and drum of the tide. His wetsuit hung open at the back, and Blake kissed the tops of his shoulder blades, pressing even closer now. His hands pushed up over Damo's damp chest to his collarbone, then down to his nipples.

"Oh, Jesus," Damo breathed as Blake caressed and teased the sensitive flesh. There was sand stuck on his skin, and the grit under Blake's fingers sparked zaps of electricity.

His body was strung tight, thighs clenched, hands in fists. He wavered like he was trying to balance on his surfboard. Blake was the wave supporting him, his lips soft where Damo's neck met his shoulder, then sucking hard.

Then one of Blake's hands dragged lower on Damo's stomach beneath his wetsuit, rough with the grit of sand.

Damo's belly quivered at the hard touch, then the gentle comb of fingers through his pubes, brushing the root of his straining cock. "Please," he begged, thrusting his hips.

But Blake's hand stayed on Damo's belly, his other fingers going back and forth between nipples. Tingles shivered over Damo from head to toe. Blake was so strong behind him, and Damo leaned back gratefully.

"Did you think about 'that arse business' we talked about?"

Damo's laugh was half a groan. "Hell, yeah."

He felt Blake's grin against the nape of his neck. "So, you're keen on the idea?"

"Who wouldn't be?"

Blake's laugh was warm and sweet against his skin, his hands sliding up to Damo's shoulders. He peeled down the wetsuit, Damo helping to tug his arms free. He didn't even realize he was reaching for his cock until Blake snatched up his wrist.

"You're not allowed to touch yourself." He squeezed hard.

And *shit*, did Damo like that. Knees knocking, he nodded.

"I'll take care of you," Blake whispered.

Damo moaned high and tight, nodding again, giving himself permission to go slack like he was bobbing in the water, letting soft swells lift him gently up and down, forward and back. Blake peeled Damo's wetsuit until it hung limply from his knees. Damo was about to lift a foot so Blake could take it off, but Blake urged him down.

The wetsuit cushioned his knees, and Blake tucked the upper half and slid it under for extra padding. Damo felt like he was kneeling on a folded yoga mat, and as he spread his fingers on the cool, salt-sprayed rock, he realized what Blake was going to do. His heart hammered, breath coming in eager pants.

"You want me to lick your arse?"

Any attempt at a smart answer died on Damo's dry tongue. "Yes," he croaked, moaning as Blake's hands spread over his cheeks.

"So pale and soft," Blake murmured. "Perfect for the moonlight."

Damo blinked at the silver glow of the rising moon skimming over the breaking waves, the real stars brighter and brighter as the night fully took hold already, the few clouds wisps of ghostly white.

He imagined how he looked—on his hands and knees, basically naked with his pale arse in the air and Blake pressing little kisses to the dip at the bottom of his spine.

Goosebumps rolled over his exposed body, the cool wind spraying salt he tasted on his lips. Blake tugged at his knees, spreading them wide, the thick, damp material tight now. The feeling of captivity from the constricting wetsuit and Blake's hands made him shudder. He hung his head, ponytail brushing his cheek and tickling his nose.

The first touch of Blake's tongue was so light Damo wasn't

sure it was real. Then it came again, a feather swipe along the edge of his arse crack. Blake spread him wide, cool air hitting his hole. Damo waited, locking his elbows to stop the shaking.

And waited.

"Chrissie's comin', mate!"

Blake laughed. "And you're being very naughty instead of nice."

"Uh-huh. Shit, I'm so hard."

"Mmm. You're beautiful." Blake circled his thumbs on the fleshy part of Damo's arse.

Damo had never looked at someone's arsehole before—not if he could help it. He squirmed, not even knowing what he needed—

"Oh, fuck!" he cried out. *That* was it. The rough drag of Blake's tongue from his balls to the dimple above his crack. Back down again. Harder, heavier, licking into his hole, his stubbly face buried in Damo's arse.

Waves frothed over the rocks with increasing thunder, Damo's heart pounding in time. He pushed back when Blake's tongue and mouth disappeared, moaning as Blake spit on his hole, the noise and wet *splats* deliciously dirty.

Blake brushed the leaking tip of Damo's cock as he brought a hand under him, pushing at Damo's lips with the order, "Suck."

Damo opened for him and sucked at the two fingers Blake shoved inside his mouth, licking and getting them as spit-soaked as he could, almost choking. When one wet finger worked roughly into his arse, Damo grunted and rocked.

His whole body was a raw nerve, nothing but sensation and release even while he was tensed and clenching. But he wasn't in control. There was nothing he had to do, nothing he had to think about. All he could do was ride the wave and give himself over to Blake.

Blake's face was back at his hole, stubble rough, tongue stabbing into him as he pulled at the rim with a finger. He ran his other hand up and over Damo's hanging head, fingers digging into his skull. Damo moaned, lifting his chin, wanting more.

Blake seemed to read his mind. He tugged at Damo's ponytail, and Damo practically screamed in pleasure. "Pull it," he begged hoarsely.

He wasn't sure Blake had heard him over the crashing surf below, but then Blake wrenched up Damo's head, yanking his ponytail. Damo stared up at the stars, pinned from all sides now. The ridge of discomfort along his hairline was tight and perfect, like he'd scraped his curls back too tightly. His back arched, Blake's tongue rhythmically pushing in and out.

He was being fucked.

Blake was undeniably fucking him with his tongue and finger, penetrating him more deeply than Damo had ever gone with his own fingers, or when Shaz had stuck the tip of her finger inside when she'd blown him the night the Dockers beat the Eagles in year twelve.

Damo was naked on the rocks, exposed and moaning, trapped in place and dying to come. The ocean surged in his veins, sea spray coating his skin. He didn't even feel the rock under his fingers now. He was flying even though he couldn't move, Blake's finger finding the exact right spot that set off fireworks. He let go of Damo's hair, and Damo's head dropped like a stone as Blake gripped his cock and stroked it.

"Fuck!" Damo lifted his head, his neck long and throat dry as he came. His orgasm ripped from his balls, his cry lost in the crash of the tide below, stars in his eyes. The pleasure was almost painfully intense, burning and building as he gasped and shook.

"That's it," Blake muttered against Damo's arse, stroking and licking inside him and milking Damo's cock until Damo could only whimper and fold over onto his elbows on the hard rock. Blake caressed his flanks with those big, warm hands, telling him how good he was.

When Blake eased him back up, kneeling behind Damo and supporting his boneless weight, his iron erection pressed against the small of Damo's back through neoprene.

Blake grunted as he reached up and unzipped his suit, twisting and squirming until he had the wetsuit peeled down to his own knees. Damo was spectacularly unhelpful, barely able to kneel.

Then Blake was pulling him close again, cock hot and hard against Damo's lower back. Damo loved the powerful throb of it the way he did the slip of a wet pussy. He wriggled and pushed, and Blake groaned.

"You need to come," Damo said, because he'd always been good at pointing out the bloody obvious.

"Oh, I will, baby."

Another thrill skipped over Damo's skin. He'd been *babe* before, but never *baby*. It resonated with some deep part of him, and as Blake spread his arse again and slotted his hot dick between Damo's cheeks, Damo squeezed around him.

"Yeah," Blake mumbled, gripping Damo's chest, pushing up into the cleft of his arse. He rocked steadily, and Damo could imagine his cock going right inside him. Suddenly, he felt unbearably empty.

"Fuck me," he gasped. "Do it."

Blake's thrusts in the cleft of Damo's arse stuttered as he groaned. "You want that? Want me to shove my cock inside you? Fill you up?"

"Yes. Yes, yes. Do it." He pushed back with his arse and tipped forward against Blake's hands spread on his chest.

Blake made an animal sound low in his throat, rocking harder, lifting up, his thighs flexing under Damo. "I will. But. Not. Now." He grunted the words out. "Won't. Hurt. You."

"Don't care. Fuck me." Even though he'd come, Damo's balls were tightening, his oversensitive dick throbbing.

Blake pressed his lips to Damo's neck. "I care."

For some stupid reason, tears pricked Damo's eyes, and he wanted Blake to fuck him more than ever.

"Squeeze around me," Blake muttered. "That's it. Gonna come all over you."

Then he did, the hot splashes raining over Damo's back and arse as Blake mumbled and shook.

Finally, Blake sat back, snaking his arms around Damo's waist. Damo's feet were going numb folded under him, but he didn't care. He grasped Blake's wrists over his stomach.

Looking out at the silver-tipped swells breaking past the sandbanks, the stars bending to the horizon, they caught their breath, the waves crashing and hissing. Jizz dried on his skin.

He twisted his neck to find Blake's mouth, the kiss clumsy and the angle awkward, but the sweep of Blake's tongue against his—tasting like sweat and sand and an earthy flavor Damo reckoned was *him*—was everything. They kissed slowly, deeply, and Damo drank him in until he had to stop and breathe.

Then they kissed some more.

And more.

Damo clutched at Blake's head, loving the burn of stubble on his face. They kissed until they gasped, and Blake pressed against Damo's cheek with chapped lips.

He murmured, "You're amazing."

Damo snorted, looking out to the dark waves and slumping against him. "You were doing all the work. I was just…taking it."

"Mmm. Taking it so beautifully." Blake stroked Damo's stomach with his thumbs. "It's not easy to let go."

"I like it." Damo swallowed, clearing his sandy throat. "I like how strong you are. How I could hardly move, and you were pulling my hair and holding me in place." His belly quivered to hear it.

Blake flattened a palm over Damo's stomach. "I like it too. I can't wait to fuck you. I'm going to make it so good for you, baby."

Damo's chest went tight, his head taking a spin. He could hardly breathe. "I meant it. You can do it now."

Blake laughed. "I appreciate the faith in my prowess, but I just came so hard I think it might be days." He nuzzled Damo's cheek, holding him even tighter. "Besides, we need a condom and lube. Need to take care of your virgin arse."

Virgin.

Even though he'd fucked chicks plenty of times, Damo *did* feel like a virgin all over again. It made his breath catch, and he grinned.

"You like the thought of me plowing your tight little arse?" Blake asked with a warm huff of a laugh.

"Yep." He remembered the hot press of wet tongue and fingers against his hole. "You think it's safe to do it without a condom?"

Blake tightened his grip around Damo's middle. "You want to fuck raw?"

"Hell, yeah. Don't have to worry about getting pregnant." He laughed. "I know you've heard that before, but I swear I won't get knocked up."

Blake was silent a moment, and Damo worried the joke had gone too far. Then Blake laughed, a full belly laugh that rumbled in his shaking chest. "Pretty sure Cooper won't get a sibling like this." He was silent a few moments. "When were you last tested, again?"

"At the holidays. Have to do a full exam every year for the insurance for lifeguarding."

"Okay. And I'm on PrEP, and I tested recently just to be sure." He hesitated. "We'd have to be committed and not seeing anyone else. And we just met, so we shouldn't rush."

"Guess not. But I kinda want to all the same."

Blake's chuckle was a warm kiss on Damo's neck. "Me too."

A horrible thought struck. "But you're not still seeing other blokes?" The question came out before he could shut his mouth. He hadn't imagined Blake hooking up with anyone else after their date at the club, and now he wanted to spew just to think of it. "We said we're boyfriends, right?" Jesus, he sounded like a dumb kid.

Blake squeezed him and kissed Damo's cheek again. "We are. I'm not into poly." He paused. "Do you want to see other people?"

"Nope."

"You can think about it. We both probably should when we're not in a post-orgasm haze. And if we decide to fuck raw, then it's our choice. An informed choice."

"Right." Jesus, he *really* wanted to do it. "I've never fucked without a condom. Even when my girlfriend was on the pill. She said it was too goopy, which is fair enough, hey."

Blake laughed. "Indeed."

Damo nodded so hard he bashed Blake in the face. He twisted around in Blake's arms so he could see his face in the moonlight. "Sorry! You right?"

Blake rubbed his forehead. "I'll survive." The wind gusted, getting colder as the day's heat faded. They both shivered, and he kissed Damo's shoulder. "We should get back. And in the meantime, it's…something to think about."

Damo groaned. "I know what that means. You're going to torture me with talk before you fuck me."

"Absolutely." Blake gave Damo's ponytail a sharp little yank, then grinned and swooped in for a messy kiss that went on and on until Damo was ready to start begging again to be fucked then and there.

They finally pushed to their feet, groaning and laughing, grimacing as they wriggled back into their damp wetsuits, zipping each other up. Damo led the way back down over the rocks, trying to concentrate on the path in the moonlight instead of wondering what it would feel like to have Blake's cock hot and hard inside him.

He didn't want to wait a minute. Not for anything. His life had been grinding along on its tracks, the weight of it heavier every day.

Nah, he didn't want to wait with Blake. He'd been waiting long enough.

Chapter Fifteen

As they turned back on the two-lane Great Southern Highway after lunch in Katanning, Damo asked, "What?"

Blake set the cruise control and glanced at Damo in the passenger seat. "Hmm?" He pushed up the visor now that the sky was clouded over.

"Whatcha smiling about?"

He hadn't realized he was, but sure enough, Blake was grinning. "Just happy. I love it when a plan comes together."

They were meeting Tasha, Tony, and Cooper in Bremer Bay to go whale watching, Damo was beside him, and the meat pie from the cafe in Katanning had filled his belly. They were making good time and would arrive at the hotel by five p.m.

Tick, tick, tick, tick. All the boxes were being checked off. He turned off the highway onto Broomehill-Gnowangerup Road and put on another classic rock playlist.

On the screen, a text from his mum appeared, but he ignored it, and the notification disappeared. He'd woken for work at three-thirty the morning after their video chat to find a screen of anxious messages from Mum.

She'd always been an early riser, so that wasn't particularly unusual. None of the messages were apologies—just her Wordle score and mundane notes about a new liquor supplier, his brother

Adam's upcoming birthday, and a few links about news she thought he'd be interested in.

And this was the way it went. Things would get awkward or tense or even angry, and they'd go on as though it hadn't happened. Blake had been tempted to ignore the messages or reply that no, all was not forgiven, but in the end, he'd given most of the messages a thumbs-up and had sent his Wordle score later that day. He'd made her wait hours, which was a petty rebellion.

Blake knew the day would come—and soon—that he told his parents exactly what he thought and how he felt, but with Damo beside him and "Carry On Wayward Son" playing, today wasn't that day.

They passed a ute coming west on the two-lane paved road, and as time passed, there was no one else as far as the eye could see over wheat fields and sheep farms with clusters of gum trees.

Damo tapped his bare foot against the dash. He never seemed to sit up straight in a chair, either curling or slouching and often propping up a foot.

"What're ya smiling about now?" Damo asked.

"Thinking about how cute you are."

Damo scoffed, then squirmed adorably. His hair was pulled back in a ponytail, and he fiddled with it. "You're pretty cute too."

"Though you know that if we get in an accident, you're going to snap your leg having your foot up like that."

Sighing, Damo lowered his foot and crossed it over his knee. "You're right."

Had that been too…lecture-y? "Sorry. Don't mean to be a killjoy."

Damo seemed taken aback. "You're not. You're looking out for me. I like it."

"Yeah?" Blake gave him a smile.

"Yeah." Damo smiled back sweetly, though there was a flirty twinkle in his eye. "I like it a lot. Oi, eyes on the road or we will have an accident."

A text flashed up on the screen on the console, and Blake tapped it. The automated voice read the message from Tash:

We're here! Made a reservation for all of us for dinner in the hotel at six. Btw, it calls itself a resort, but this is a glorified pub with a motel attached. Seems clean and friendly, though.

Blake dictated a response saying that was all good, and then Tash sent another message:

Coop says hi.

Blake's chest tightened. Those three words were momentous.

"Good sign, hey?" Damo said.

"Yeah. What should I say back?"

"Dunno. Don't overthink it."

"I'd never!" Blake gasped in mock affront.

Damo laughed. "Nah, wouldn't dream of it."

He quickly dictated a reply—even though he'd have preferred to think about it a bit more—saying he missed Cooper too and couldn't wait to see him again. Then he sent a follow-up, asking if Rosie was doing okay back in Freo with Tony's parents.

"There you go," Blake said. "I'm living on the edge. Speaking of which, how are you enjoying getting out of Barking?" He had the impression Damo didn't leave often.

"Love it. You can see forever."

"You never wanted to travel? Take a gap year?"

"Sure. Some of my high school mates spent six months in Bali."

Blake waited, then asked, "Why didn't you?"

"Couldn't. I… I had work." Damo shrugged but didn't elaborate. His foot jiggled, and he tapped the console screen as Tasha's reply appeared. The automated voice read:

Rosie was gutted when we left, but she's being distracted by lollies and going to Barking Beach again.

"No better place," Damo said proudly.

"Where do you go for holidays when you already live in such a great spot? Did your parents take you anywhere?"

Damo shrugged, but it was tense. "When I was a kid, we went to the Gold Coast and Brissie. Surfers Paradise was my fave, obviously."

"Of course."

"Tabby was little, and she loved Australia Zoo. Feeding the kangaroos and all that. I loved it too."

"How old is she now?"

"Thirteen going on thirty-five." Damo smiled tightly.

"What do your parents do? You've never really mentioned them."

Damo tapped his foot. "Mum's a nurse. Dad was a brickie, but he's been off work." Sitting up straight, he pointed through the windscreen. "Gettin' hilly out there."

Blake still wasn't sure what the deal was with Damo's family and had a lot more questions, but he went with the topic change. "Stirling Ranges, I think? Reminds me of home."

That thought prompted another—and Blake looked at the fuel gauge.

Belatedly.

A quarter tank. *Shit.* He should have filled up in Katanning, but it hadn't even crossed his mind. *How* had he not thought about it? Christ, he was beyond stupid!

"Fuck," he mumbled. At Damo's questioning glance, Blake confessed, "We should have filled up when we had lunch." Why hadn't he made a checklist for the journey? He should've mapped it all out.

Blake's gaze flicked from the empty road to the car's estimation of how many kilometers the fuel would take them:

175

Then he tapped the console screen to return from messages to the map, heart in his throat as he read the GPS distance remaining:

173

"*Fuck.*" He read the numbers to Damo, bracing for his reaction. God, Blake was *so stupid!* How could he have not thought about going to a petrol station in the only big town they'd passed through in hours?

Somehow, Damo...*laughed?* "Cuttin' it close, hey?"

"Way too close! What if something happens? We'll run out of petrol!"

"We'll be right."

"But... We barely have enough. We could seriously run out."

Damo shrugged—an easy, loose movement now—and gave Blake a smile. "No dramas. It'll work out."

"We haven't passed another vehicle since that ute. If we run out of petrol, we'll be stranded out here." He cringed to imagine what his dad would say. That he'd taught Blake better than that, for starters. Then Mum would chime in about—

Stop! They're not here. And they don't know everything.

"Someone'll come along."

Blake gripped the wheel, his gaze now flicking constantly between the road, the car's fuel estimate, and the GPS estimate. "It'll be dark in a couple of hours. Days are getting shorter. Maybe we should go back to Katanning."

"That'll add on more than an hour. We'll be late for dinner. It says we have enough."

He really didn't want to be late. Obviously, he could explain why to Tasha and Tony—but that wouldn't exactly speak highly of his responsible adultness, would it?

"We'll be right," Damo repeated. He was slouched again, his other foot crossed over his knee.

"But... I'm a moron! You're not pissed at me?"

Damo frowned. "What? It's not your fault. I didn't think about it either."

"I'm the *driver*. And I know better! I grew up in the bush. I know how isolated it gets. How did it not even cross my mind?"

"Even country boys make mistakes." Damo pressed his hand on Blake's thigh, fingertips brushing the skin under the hem of his long shorts. "It's okay."

"It's not! I'm putting you in danger." Every muscle in Blake's body was tensed, his knuckles white on the wheel.

"*Maaaate.* Come on. It says we have enough to get there. Tasha and Tony know we're coming. And there's gotta be a petrol station somewhere."

"There really doesn't, though. You don't know the outback."

"I'll check." Damo pulled out his phone and tapped it. After a moment, he muttered, "Crap. No signal."

Blake missed the warmth of Damo's hand on his thigh. Heart thudding, he tried the GPS on the car's screen. Nothing. The map was still showing their route, but it had obviously downloaded it earlier. There was no signal for any new searches.

"Look!" Damo pointed to a sign down the road. "Food and fuel in Gnowangerup. See? We'll be sweet."

Blake exhaled sharply. "Oh, thank god. I still can't believe I did that."

"We all stuff up sometimes."

"But—"

As they drove into Gnowangerup, a town clustered around the one main road, the petrol station appeared.

As did the signs proclaiming it now closed.

"All right," Damo said. "It won't be as cruisey getting to Bremer, but we're fine."

Blake searched the other buildings as they passed. Most shops were closed down, and they didn't see anyone except a lone little boy riding his bike. He had to be about Cooper's age. Blake was struck with a stab of shame. He was a father now, and he couldn't even handle filling up with petrol!

They drove on in silence. He wasn't sure when they'd paused the music, but it didn't feel right putting it back on now. Blake's eyes flicked over what was now his holy trinity until they reached Bremer Bay: the road, the mileage, the GPS estimate.

"You're really freaking out," Damo said.

"How are you not?"

"We're riding the wave. Either it's gonna smoke us, or we'll shoot out the barrel. Won't know 'til the end."

Blake forced an exhale and found a fond smile tugging his lips. "Zen looks good on you."

"Yeah?" Damo waggled his eyebrows.

"Oh, yeah. From the first time I saw you on Barking. Laughing with your red sunnies on. Zen surfer dude."

Damo's smile twisted, and he seemed unbearably sad for a moment. "I try. At least with the stuff I can't control."

Blake forced himself not to check the mileage. Instead, he asked, "Like what?"

Damo looked out his window, twirling his ponytail around his finger. "Lots of stuff." He glanced back with a cheeky grin. "Like, right now? I can't control that my boofhead boyfriend didn't fill up the tank."

Blake had to laugh—before his stomach fluttered. "I like hearing that. 'Boyfriend' I mean. I definitely do not like hearing that I didn't fill up with petrol."

"We're going to laugh about this later."

"If we're still alive, yeah."

Damo laughed, shaking with it, his cheeks pink. "The drama!"

"Look, the backpacker murderer killed men as well as women. I'm just saying."

"Mate! That got dark fast. You sound like my Auntie Shirl. She's obsessed with true crime. To hear her tell it, it's a miracle she hasn't been murdered yet and it's bound to happen any minute."

Blake snorted and dissolved into slightly unhinged giggles. "I suppose the odds of us encountering a serial killer are low."

"Probably have better odds of a shark attack out here." Damo's gaze caught on something ahead. "Do we turn up there?"

Blake slowed and turned right, heading south. They approached a town called Borden, though when Blake turned off and drove down the main street, it was a ghost town.

Damo whistled softly. "Nothing left. Bet this place used to be hopping."

It gave Blake chills. There were still a handful of houses that seemed occupied, although no one was about. They passed the husk of an old petrol station and looped back toward the main road.

"There!" Damo sat bolt up. "A pump!"

A single gas pump stood in the middle of a lot with an automated payment machine next to it. Blake's relief vanished as he pulled up and read the sign.

"Diesel only."

Damo threw his head back and laughed, and after a moment, Blake joined in. It felt good to laugh, and Damo was right—either they'd run out, or they wouldn't. The fuel estimate said they'd make it by the skin of their teeth, so here was hoping.

They continued south before turning east on the optimistically named Borden-Bremer Bay Road. They even passed another vehicle. The difference between the car's estimated mileage and the GPS shifted ten kilometers in their favor, and an hour and fifteen long minutes later, they drove into Bremer Bay, allegedly with eighteen kilometers of fuel to spare.

Blake drove directly to the gas pump outside the general store. Before he climbed out, he leaned over and kissed Damo breathless.

When they climbed out of the SUV in the hotel car park,

Cooper appeared at the edge of a grassy playground. Blake waved, his stomach tightening as he waited for Cooper to respond.

Which he did—waving with a beaming grin and running over. Blake wasn't sure if he was just happy to see Damo, but he'd take it as a win.

"Hey, buddy," Blake said, suddenly frozen. Was it too soon to give Cooper a hug? Surely. Wave again? Handshake would be ridiculous.

"Mate!" Damo lifted his hand for a high five, which Cooper gave enthusiastically.

"You came!" Cooper exclaimed. He was clearly thrilled to see Damo again, and Blake could relate. "You didn't have to work?"

"Nah, I switched a few shifts around. I cover for other guys all the time, so they owed me."

"Cool." Cooper was still smiling, and he said shyly to Blake, "Hi." He fiddled with the hem of his T-shirt, which had a bright orange stain splotched on it.

"Hi. It's great to see you again. How—" Blake's mind went blank. "Uh, how was the drive?"

"Boring."

"Coulda done with a boring drive ourselves," Damo said, giving Blake a wink. "But we're here now." He jerked his thumb toward reception. "Why don't you two hang out while I get us checked in?" He didn't wait for an answer, and briefly snagged Blake's hand, squeezing his fingers.

Blake watched him go, then turned to find Cooper watching him with an expression he couldn't read. "What?" Blake asked hesitantly.

"So, Mum said he's your boyfriend?"

"He is." He braced for a negative reaction.

But Cooper only nodded as if impressed and said, "Cool."

"How's the playground?" Blake motioned toward the empty jungle gym.

"Boring. No other kids around right now. But I had too much screen time in the car, so Mum and D—" Cooper scrunched up his freckled face, peering up at Blake hesitantly.

A wave of tenderness washed through Blake, along with an undeniable pang of longing. Would he ever be called "dad"? He said, "Your mum and dad said you have to get some fresh air?"

Cooper exhaled in clear relief that Blake wasn't upset. "Yeah. There were some girls here before, but they had to go." He nodded toward the adjacent caravan park. A family were grilling snags on a barbecue, and the fatty, salty, delicious smell drifted on the warm breeze.

"Come on, let's play."

Cooper's sandy eyebrows rose. "Yeah?"

"Absolutely! I'm not too old to have a play."

Sure, he did feel a twinge in his lower back as he stooped to get into the tube slide, but for the next twenty minutes, Blake and his son—his *son*!—ran around and played Coop's game of pirates. There was a whole story involving buried treasure, an invisible talking parrot, and a battle with another pirate ship, and Blake loved every second.

He'd spotted Damo unloading the car, and his phone buzzed in his pocket with a text telling him their room number. In the sand around the jungle gym, Coop pretended to dig, and Blake got on his knees to help. He hadn't playacted for so many years, and it was *fun*.

When Coop declared that they'd found the treasure and won, they high-fived.

"Hey, how about an ice cream?" Blake nodded toward the little kiosk near reception selling treats and drinks.

"So close to dinner?" Coop asked.

That tenderness returned, filling Blake with warmth. "I won't tell if you won't," he whispered conspiratorially. He was sure Tasha and Tony would understand. It wasn't a *bribe*, but Blake was eager to do everything possible to make Cooper like him.

When they were both licking chocolate Paddle Pops, they wandered on a path toward picnic tables where an older couple ate sandwiches and sipped plastic glasses of white wine.

Sitting on the top of an empty table, Blake and Cooper licked in silence. Perhaps not an *easy* silence, but not fraught. He'd take it.

"It doesn't bug you?" Cooper asked, chocolate smeared on the side of his mouth.

Blake passed him one of the napkins he'd grabbed. "What doesn't?"

"That… I call someone else 'Dad' and not you."

"No." He was grateful he could answer completely honestly. "Tony's raising you. He's been your dad. He deserves the title. I haven't earned it."

Cooper hummed, licking the ice cream with a serious expression. "Were you happy when Mum told you about me?"

"Of course!"

Cooper raised an eyebrow. "Really?"

Clearly he'd overdone it. Blake took a moment to find the right words. "Can we make a pact? No matter the question, no matter what—we'll tell each other the truth."

Nodding seriously, Cooper extended his hand, and Blake shook it. Coop's hand was small and sweaty, and it was wild to think that Blake and Tasha had created this whole human. He cleared his throat.

"Okay, totally honest: I was shocked when your mum told me. It wasn't something I'd ever considered for a second. That she might have gotten pregnant, I mean."

Coop wasn't too young for that word, was he? No. It wasn't as if it was a dirty word. Blake had so much he needed to discuss with Tash and Tony. He had no idea what was appropriate for eight-year-olds.

"That makes sense. She said she never even talked to you after."

"Right. It was just a one-time…thing."

Cooper rolled his eyes. "I know all about sex."

"Okay. Good. Er… Anyway, I was shocked when she reached out. But yes, I was happy. I felt all sorts of things. I was only sad to realize I missed out on you being a baby. I wish I could go back and watch you grow up."

With earnest seriousness, Coop said, "Don't worry. I'm not finished yet."

Affection filled Blake so completely he could barely breathe. "Lucky for me. So, yes, I'm thrilled you're here in this world. That you're…you. And that I'm your father." He quickly added, "I meant what I said about Tony. He's your dad, and I completely respect that. But I'm really, really happy."

Cooper seemed satisfied with this answer. After another lick of ice cream, he said, "Me too. It was weird. Not knowing who you were. Like, Mum told me who you were, but…"

Blake nodded. "I get it."

"Honestly?" Coop scrunched up his freckled nose again, and it was the cutest thing ever. "I was nervous to meet you, but you're nice."

I'm nice! He wanted to run a victory lap with his fists in the air.

"And Damo's *really* cool."

Blake grinned. He would take any and all bonus points his cool boyfriend provided. "He is."

"You're cool too!"

His heart swelled. "Thanks, mate." He winked. "But I know Damo's way cooler than I am."

Cooper laughed. "So, it's okay if I just call you Blake?"

"Absolutely! Whatever you're comfortable with. I haven't earned anything else—but I want to. I know you live on the other side of the country, but I want to visit, and we can video chat, and talk on the phone if that's something kids even do anymore?"

"You can talk on phones?" Cooper frowned, but couldn't quite resist laughing at his own joke.

Blake kept his expression blank. "Yeah, instead of texting on the screen, you hold it up to your ear, and you can actually hear human voices through it."

"Whoa." With chocolate still staining the corner of his mouth, Cooper grinned. Then his eyes widened, and he jammed the rest of the ice cream in his mouth, sucking it down to the stick and mumbling, "Mum's coming!"

Blake motioned to Cooper to wipe his mouth as he thrust his own half-eaten ice cream behind his back. Coop giggled, and Blake couldn't stop smiling.

〰〰〰

AS DAMO SLURRED a question around his toothbrush from the door of the bathroom, white paste frothing in the corner of his mouth, Blake's heart swelled.

Hair wet and curly from a shower and only wearing his boxers covered in sharks, Damo had one bare foot propped on his shin and a shoulder against the doorframe.

It was so wonderfully domestic. Blake had to remind himself to slow down while he strained to leap full speed ahead.

Damo was watching him, clearly waiting for a response. Blake asked, "Sorry, what was that?" He peeled off his tee to hop in the shower himself.

After turning to spit in the sink, Damo said—much more clearly—"D'ya get seasick?"

"Oh! Tash mentioned that the tour operators said to take ginger tablets tonight and in the morning. She bought us a box." He fished it out of the bag from the chemist. "I'm not prone to it but apparently it gets rough out there."

"Don't think I've ever been seasick, but can't hurt." Damo popped a couple of the tablets.

After Blake swallowed his down with a gulp of water, he said, "Nice undies, by the way."

Hand on hip, Damo struck a pose. "Pressie from my sister." His smile vanished, and he grabbed his phone, muttering, "What time is it? Let me just text her."

He tapped out a message, then waited, fingering the purple cord around his neck while watching the screen with a furrow between his brows.

"Everything okay?" Blake asked. He stripped off and waited.

"Yep!" Damo answered too brightly. Then something appeared on his screen that had him visibly relaxing.

What was the deal with his family? In the shower, Blake puzzled over it. Maybe Kat would know. He was overdue answering their latest teasing texts, but it didn't seem right to ask behind Damo's back…

Towel around his hips, he watched Damo through the open bathroom door. Damo wandered the room, skirting the two double beds, texting with someone and smiling to himself.

The room was average—white walls with a few generic beach prints, blue bedspreads, hideous brown carpet, old wood dresser with small TV on top.

Blake asked, "All good?"

"Yep," Damo answered genuinely. His whole body tensed when he wasn't being honest, that loose, easy vibe disappearing. With a smile, he glanced up—then his gaze caught on Blake's wet chest. Adam's apple bobbing, Damo said, "Uh-huh."

"I didn't say anything else." Blake bit his lip to keep from laughing.

Damo's eyes swept up and down Blake again. "Huh?"

"I'm sorry, am I distracting you?" He fingered the knot in the side of the towel.

With that glorious crooked grin, Damo muttered, "Diabolical." His gaze flicked to the beds, then back to Blake, then back to the beds. "Is it… We're going to sleep in one together?"

It wasn't what Blake had expected him to ask, and he paused. "Yeah, unless you don't want to? We can sleep separately. No pressure."

"No, I want to!" An adorable blush climbed Damo's bare chest. He fiddled with plugging in his phone on the side table between the beds. "You're going to laugh."

"I won't. What is it?"

Damo rolled his eyes, though seemingly at himself. "Just not used to sleeping with someone the whole night. Only done it once, and—" He snapped his mouth shut. "Not used to it, like I said. I know, it's pathetic."

Blake came around between the beds and sat on one. He wanted to take Damo's hand, but was that too much? "I'm not laughing. There's nothing wrong with that." He was dying to know *why* but waited.

Still standing between the beds, Damo fidgeted. "I haven't actually been away from home for a night since I was a kid."

"Okay." Blake wanted to beg Damo to just tell him what he was hiding so he could *help*. "Why is that?"

"It's just my family."

"Are your parents…strict?" It seemed odd given Damo was twenty-two and worked full time. And he'd never mentioned anything at all about being religious.

"Nah, nothing like that." Damo crossed his arms over his bare chest.

"You can tell me," Blake murmured. "Whatever it is."

"It's not, like, some deep dark secret." Damo scoffed. "Except I guess it is because I made it that way. I should just bloody tell ya already."

"I'm listening."

Exhaling loudly, Damo sat heavily on the side of the opposite bed. Their knees were almost touching, but not quite. "It's not *bad*. My old man's not a serial killer or anything. But I've always kept it separate. And the one time I didn't with my ex-girlfriend, it… Well, it went to shit. Wasn't her fault, but after that, it was easier to keep home in its own box. I didn't want to talk about it. Eventually, people stopped asking, and it was easier to keep going that way."

"Okay." Blake's mind raced trying to figure out what it could be.

Damo fingered the purple cord around his neck, his gaze down. "I just wanted to keep you to myself for a bit." He motioned to the room. "I wanted to escape with you."

Blake ached to smooth away Damo's frown and keep him safe and happy. "I'm all yours. I understand having family stuff." He laughed thinly. "I brought you back to my place and interrupted us to text my mum."

Who can't even bear to say the word "gay" out loud.

Damo's eyes met his. "But that's how I knew you were…I dunno. That I could trust you. And I do." In a rush, he went on. "My dad had an accident at work when I was fifteen. He was a brickie, and he fell off a ladder. It was bad. Broken back and other bones. Worst was that he hit his head, though. Never been the same."

"God. I'm so sorry." Blake did reach for Damo's hand now, relieved when Damo gripped his fingers.

Foot tapping, Damo tried to smile, his eyes flicking around the room again. "Mum's a nurse, and she works a lot of hours. Dad's disability payments are nothing compared to what he used to make. I have to stay close to home to help out. Not just with money. Tabby shouldn't have to deal with Dad, but she does these days. She insists she's not a kid, but she is. I should've pushed back harder. Kept her away from it."

"It's not your fault."

Damo didn't respond to that, instead saying, "He should have had a safety line on, but you know blokes like my dad. I mean, you don't know him, but…"

"I know what you mean. I grew up with plenty of them."

"At first, we were just thrilled he was alive. I figured he'd be back to normal in no time. My dad was tough. He'd barely ever had a cold. 'Course he'd be right. But he just wasn't himself anymore. Wasn't Dad."

"Mm," Blake murmured, waiting patiently for Damo to find the words.

"Not that anyone who'd gone through that hell would be the same. Still, I kept waiting. I'd wake up and think: Maybe today's the day Dad'll get up without Mum's help. Maybe it's the day he'll laugh again. Smile. Anything. It was because of the TBI. 'Traumatic brain injury.' I'm sure you've heard of that. Duh, obviously."

Damo crossed and uncrossed his legs. "The doc called it 'emotional lability.' I remember looking it up on my phone and reading as much as I could about it. It just means mood swings, pretty much. But there's all this other stuff too. Aggression, inflexibility." He spoke like he was quoting a textbook. "Obsessive and egocentric behavior. All these words Google spewed up. What they mean is he acts like a fucking prick."

Before Blake could repeat that he was so, so sorry, Damo's eyes glittered with tears and he exclaimed, "And I know it's not his fault! I know it. But he left us. He should've fought for his family. He should've worn the bloody safety harness! I'm so mad at him."

Blake squeezed his hand. "I would be too. It's not your fault. It's totally understandable."

Adam's apple bobbing, Damo said thickly, "I should've told you. I'm sorry."

"You don't have to be sorry. This isn't about me."

"Still should've told you. I don't even know what I was afraid of. I kept it separate for so many years. It became this *secret*, and I'm not even sure why."

"It's out now. It's okay. It's not a secret now." Relief that Damo had trusted him with the truth flowed like honey in Blake's veins. "I can help. You have so much to worry about at home. Way more than I realized. I'm here for you. You've done your best."

Damo's eyes met his. "You can't know that." He swiped his eyes.

"I can." Blake stroked Damo's white knuckles with his thumb. "I see you help people every day at Barking. Even from a distance, I could tell how sweet and generous and brave you are. You risk your life to rescue others, and then you talk to them and make them feel better. Make them laugh and smile when they're clearly embarrassed or afraid. That's why I was drawn to you. It wasn't just that you're gorgeous."

Damo rolled his eyes, but he couldn't stop from smiling. "Am not," he mumbled, and Blake wanted to kiss him senseless.

"Are too. That day I got up the nerve to ask you out, I just couldn't resist. I had to know you."

After ducking his head and squirming, Damo looked up with a beaming smile. "Glad you did. Not just because *you're* gorgeous. Though you are. Because you said you'd take care of me. And you have."

Clutching Damo's hands, Blake vowed, "I will. I promise."

Damo lunged forward and kissed him, their mouths opening and hands tangling in each other's hair, knees knocking. Blake wanted to climb inside him and hold him safe and close forever. Damo's trust was such an incredible gift. It made him feel so damn *good* about himself. He vowed to earn it every day.

Breathing hard, Damo broke the kiss. "Can we stop talkin'

about it now?"

"Uh-huh." Blake had so many questions, but they could wait. "Are you sure you're good sleeping together? I don't mean fucking. Just the sleeping part, since you're not used to it."

Damo wiped his wet lips. "Yeah. I want to sleep with you." His Adam's apple bobbed. "And I do want you to fuck me, but could we just sleep tonight?"

"Of course." He forced his hands away from Damo's thighs. "I'll be a perfect gentleman."

"Let's not get carried away!" Damo laughed, grabbing Blake's hands. "Not gonna waste a whole night alone."

Blake slowly stroked Damo's knuckles with his thumbs. "We'll have more. Lots more."

For some reason, this made Damo blush prettily. Then he said, "Still, we're here, and I don't want to think about home anymore tonight. I wanna sleep with you. In the same bed. All night. And mess around. Maybe not, like, all the way, but, you know." His gaze dropped. "Have I mentioned I want to lick your nipples pretty much constantly?"

Blake leaned back, pulling Damo on top of him and threading his fingers through his damp hair. "My nipples are all yours."

Chapter Sixteen

As the catamaran pitched over the Southern Ocean's choppy waves, Damo held on, grinning. He loved the sea spray in his face and the wind in his hair—though he'd knotted his ponytail into a bun. A few strands escaped, tickling his cheek.

"Too good!" he said to Blake in the chair beside him on the upper level.

Blake smiled and nodded. "Awesome."

"You right?" Blake's smile had been a little shaky.

"Totally!"

Damo wasn't quite sure he believed him. "We can go down if you're feeling crook." The boat staff had explained that the lower level was better for sea sickness, so Tasha and Tony had insisted to Cooper that they stay there.

"No, I'm fine! We took our ginger tablets. Hey, dolphins!"

They crowded to the railing—getting there with lurching steps—with a few other passengers as the captain pointed them to the dolphins on the starboard side. The pod jumped in the dark waves, and if anyone could watch dolphins in the sea and not feel that life was bloody good, Damo didn't want to know them.

The day was gray, so he kept his sunnies hooked to his shirt under his jacket. It was tempting to try to take pics, but the last thing he needed was to drop his phone into the ocean as the boat rolled. He'd leave it to the professional photographer on board who'd be emailing the pictures.

They'd been warned to always be holding on to a railing at all times, so Damo kept one hand on the metal and the other snaked around Blake's waist as they watched the three dolphins leap and play.

When he'd woken that morning sprawled on his stomach in bed with Blake's arm over his back and warm breath on his shoulder, Damo hadn't wanted to move a muscle.

It had taken a few seconds to process where he was and remember that, for the first time in seven years, he wasn't waking in his old twin bed with creaky springs.

And that he was naked with another bloke. Blake the bloke. His *boyfriend*. It had sent butterflies flapping through his tummy, and he'd tried to hold onto the joy without letting the guilt in.

All he could do was try, right?

At least he'd come clean to Blake about his dad and what it was like at home. Well, he hadn't gotten into the nitty gritty, but that could wait. He hadn't planned on saying anything, but suddenly, it had felt right.

The words had tumbled out, and he was glad of it in the light of day. Blake had understood the way Damo'd expected. And they'd gotten off and laughed, and Damo had slept like a baby in Blake's arms.

It was a far cry from the awkward, uncomfortable night with Shaz at home when he'd barely been able to relax enough to doze, lying awake for hours, rigid in his own bed until it had gone from bad to worse. Poor Shaz had only wanted to get closer to him, but neither of them had been ready.

Was Damo ready now? He was getting there, at least.

As the dolphins broke away from the boat, Blake cleared his throat. It was only a little sound, but Damo frowned. "Let's go down."

"I'll be fine when we get out there." They both gripped the railing as the boat pitched.

"It's at least fifty Ks out to the Bremer Canyon, mate. We've got an hour and twenty to go at least." Damo pointed to the staircase in the middle of the catamaran. It was a few steps down, then a turn and a few more, then the last steps to the main deck.

"Want to go down?" a young crew woman asked. She held out a hand. "Give me your bag."

Blake did, and as they stepped away from the railing, the deck heaved and they toppled forward. The rail at the top of the stairs jammed into Damo's side, and he laughed. "Southern Ocean is going off!"

Blake's answering smile was half-hearted, and he didn't argue as another crew member below on the stairs told him to sit and go down on his bum.

Damo did the same, asking the girl, "Is it always this rough?"

"Oh yeah. It was worse yesterday." She held up a white plastic bag with a hard plastic rim. "You need one?"

"Nah, I'm right."

When they reached the bottom deck, he realized half the passengers were puking their guts out. The main deck had benches at the back and several rows of metal chairs. There was an indoor cabin with plush seats as well, but Damo reckoned people would feel even sicker in there without the fresh air.

Tasha and Tony were bent over in their chairs holding vomit bags while Cooper spewed into his. Blake almost lost his balance trying to get to the seat beside Coop, and Damo dove after him, grabbing Blake's arm to steady him.

Cooper hiccupped, his eyes shiny with tears. "But—but—we took the tablets."

Blake wrapped an arm around Coop's shoulders. "I know, buddy. The water's just too rough."

Crew members went around collecting puke bags and passing

out new ones. They offered little cups of water and advised people to sip slowly and keep their eyes on the horizon. Damo had to look away as Tasha hurled again into a fresh bag.

Inhaling slowly through his nose, he watched the steel gray line of the horizon and tried not to listen. He'd never been seasick, but it was tough listening to it. He held a cup of water for Coop, watching Blake try to keep it together. He motioned to a crew girl nearby for a bag.

Blake reached for Damo's knee beneath the hem of his boardies. "Okay?"

Damo nodded. "It's for you."

"I don't need it."

He had to laugh. "You're gonna."

Blake tried to fight it—he really did. He comforted Cooper, murmuring encouragement, all the while breathing harder and harder. Tasha and Tony would lift their heads and check in on Coop before apologizing and crumpling again.

Lips sealed, Blake's nostrils flared, and Damo pushed the bag into his hand. "S'okay. Go ahead and spew."

Blake shook his head sharply, keeping his focus on Coop. He was gentle and reassuring, rubbing Coop's back slowly as the poor kid had another vomit.

It wasn't *sexy*, but somehow it was? Damo watched from the chair across from them, wanting to kiss Blake and tell him how much he liked him.

Because he liked him *so much*.

Damo spotted the moment Blake lost the battle, and he thrust out the bag, perching at the edge of his chair so he could squeeze Blake's knee as he hurled up brekkie.

As the journey continued, he monitored Blake, Cooper, Tasha, and Tony, handing off used bags to the crew and holding water for them and encouraging small sips. On the benches at the stern, some people were huddled under blankets, heads down and eyes shut, utterly miserable.

"We'd better see some damn whales," Tony moaned.

Cooper's bleary eyes widened. "What if we don't?"

"We will!" Blake insisted, looking a little gray. "The captain has a plan." He chanced some water. "I'll make sure we see some whales," he told Cooper.

Of course, Blake had zero control over the whales, but Damo loved that he wanted so much to give his son the experience.

Damo went into the cabin to fetch dry biscuits for everyone to nibble, and as they neared the canyon where the killer whales hunted and the boat slowed, he made cups of tea.

Blake sipped his and gave Damo a weak smile. "You must be part mermaid."

"Got the hair for it," Damo replied with a wink.

Blake's smile widened, and he snagged Damo's fingers as they looked at each other.

"You two are disgustingly cute," Tasha said before sipping her weak tea with a smile that turned to a grimace. "How many more hours will we be out here?"

"Uh, I reckon five or six?" Damo answered with a wince.

"We have to see the whales!" Cooper whined.

Of course it was never guaranteed, but Damo didn't say that. "We will, mate. I can feel it."

"He's one with the ocean," Blake said. "He knows."

Damo would've felt like a right dickhead if the whales had stayed away, but they showed up not long after. First, there were a few in the distance, and Damo maneuvered Coop to a prime spot at the side of the boat, holding him steady as they crossed the deck. Now that they weren't moving as quickly, it was more stable, but the boat still pitched.

With Coop in front of him and Blake at his side, Damo watched the killer whales surface. Even though the whales weren't super close, they had a great view. It wasn't just a few dark blobs on the horizon—the whales were clear as they surfaced.

The boat hunted for more whales, and when they spotted some, the marine biologist on board told everyone to make noise to attract them. They hooted and hollered, Cooper bouncing on his toes and practically screaming in excitement, his upset stomach forgotten.

Blake and Damo shared a smile, and Damo couldn't resist stealing a kiss. Blake's eyebrows shot up. "I must taste terrible." He glanced around. "And there are people here."

Damo shrugged. "Just had to kiss ya."

"I'm not complaining." Blake grinned, then stumbled as the boat turned.

Damo steadied him, and they kept Cooper in front of them at the railing. Of course, the whales were first on the other side of the boat, but soon enough the animals appeared right in front of them.

Gasping and pointing, they watched the whales roll and play and made more noise to keep them interested. The whales seemed content to hang out, having a cruisey morning.

Eventually, they disappeared under the surface, and the boat looked for another group. There were wraps and fruit for lunch, though even Damo didn't have much of an appetite. He ate the sliced pineapple and berries off a skewer, watching the horizon again as more people got sick.

"Not out this far too often," he said to Blake. In all four directions, there was only the gray sea and cloudy sky.

"It's a strange feeling, isn't it? Not just the nausea."

Damo laughed. "Yeah. Like, it's a bit scary on one hand." He was farther away not only from land than he'd been in years, but the farthest from home. *Ever.*

That thought predictably made him feel guilty, but with no mobile signal at sea, he couldn't text home even if he wanted to. It was out of his hands.

Breathing in the salt air and watching birds ride the air currents calmed him. He added, "The birds are so far out, but they can still get home when they want to. It's weirdly comforting? Anything's possible. *Everything* is."

When Blake didn't say anything, Damo turned to find him watching him, Blake's brown eyes full of—what? Tenderness? Feelings?

Love?

It was so hard to breathe, but Damo managed to ask, "What?"

Blake only smiled and said, "I know exactly what you mean."

〜〜〜

"YOU SURE YOU don't want to go to the bar and grab a beer or something?" Damo called. After showering off the day on the boat, he'd climbed naked under the covers in the hotel room. The small lamp beside the bed cast most of the room in shadow.

Through the half-open door to the steamy bathroom, Blake answered, "Don't want to tempt fate. My stomach finally feels back to normal. Go ahead, though."

"Nah. I'm good." Relieved, he settled back against the pillows he'd stacked up. It'd been a long day out on the choppy seas, and now they could relax and maybe…do more than relax?

Damo twisted his hair around his finger as the butterflies flapped in his belly. They were alone and sharing a proper bed, and when would they get the chance again? When—

Bolting up straight, Damo grabbed his phone. Shit. How had he forgotten to check in with Tabby once they'd returned to land? They'd come back and…

And it hadn't even *occurred* to him. What the hell was wrong with him?

He scrambled to open his messages. Nothing from Tabs, which loosened his shoulders a fraction. She'd have texted if it'd gone pear-shaped. Of course she would.

Wouldn't she?

But how had he not texted her? After watching people spew all day, now he was the one feeling sick to his stomach. He tapped out a message and hit send. Waited.

And waited.

"Damo?"

He glanced away from the screen, where bouncing dots meant Tabby was finally replying. "Huh?"

Blake's voice came from the bathroom. "You right? I asked if you're sure you don't want to grab dinner."

"I'm sweet. We can have a big brekkie tomorrow. I had an extra sausage roll on the boat since most people weren't eating. And a chicken pesto wrap on the way back." He barely knew what he was saying and hoped he sounded normal.

The dots bounced, and he jiggled his foot under the blanket. *Come on, come on…*

Relief *whooshed* through him as Tabby's message appeared:

We're fine. Same old shit. Did you see the whales?

Laughing, Blake called, "You have a cast-iron stomach."

"Yup." He quickly replied to Tabby and promised to see her as soon as she got home from school tomorrow.

Then he switched off his phone.

Everything was okay. He'd gone away, and the sky hadn't fallen. He and Blake had one more night together in this peaceful, faraway bubble, and he wasn't going to spoil it.

Damo cleared his throat. "So, uh, I was thinking…"

"Hmm?" Blake asked, still out of sight in the bathroom.

"Well, see, I reckon we could—"

Jaw dropping, Damo stared at Blake in the open doorway. Towel slung low around his hips, eyes popping with dark eyeliner, and cherry lippy on his mouth.

Blake arched a brow. "You were saying?"

"You expect me to know words when you're lookin' like that?"

Blake bit his lip in a way that was—what was the word? Sexy, yes. Hot as hell. But there was another word…

Coy. That was it!

Blake popped an eyebrow. "You like what you see?"

"Don't ask stupid questions, mate." Damo was half-hard, and he hadn't even touched himself. Not that he wasn't attracted to Blake all the time—*duh*, he totally was—but the makeup reminded him of that first night. The nerves and excitement and thrill of it all, going to that club alone and finding Blake waiting with makeup and that sheer shirt showing off his nips.

"Did you bring makeup to, to…" Words felt impossible. "Seduce me?"

Trying not to laugh, Blake caressed his nipples and batted his eyes. "Is it working?"

Damo swept off the covers and motioned to his fully hard cock. "Seems like."

"Mmm." Blake's gaze traveled over Damo. "I'd like to say this was all part of a brilliant plan, but I happened to have some makeup in the bottom of my toilet bag and I was in the mood for a bit of glam after feeling shit on the boat."

"I like it. That you're not afraid to look…girly. I mean, you don't! Not in a bad way. It's just most blokes are…"

"Choking on toxic masculinity?" Blake suggested.

Damo pointed. "That's it. You're not afraid. It makes you even more manly." The confidence was such a turn-on.

Out of words, Damo reached for him eagerly. Still wearing the towel, Blake straddled him, and they kissed. The lippy was sweet and a little sticky. Damo knew it would be all over his face in a minute and didn't care even a little. The friction of the towel against his cock had him groaning, and he reached for Blake's nipples.

"D'ya happen to have lube in that toilet bag?" he asked breathlessly.

Blake sat back, watching Damo carefully, the eyeliner making his eyes incredibly intense and sexy *as*. "I do." He traced his fingertips up Damo's arms and across his collarbones. "What are you thinking?"

"I'm thinkin' ya fuck me already."

"You're sure? I don't think I have condoms."

"Oh, I'm sure. You're taking those magic pills, right?" Damo joked, then added seriously, "And I know I don't have anything." He reached up and swiped at a smear of lippy on Blake's chin. "I trust you."

As Damo's heart tripped, Blake watched him for what felt like an eternity.

Finally, he said with a gravelly voice, "I trust you too." He bent and caught Damo's mouth in a long, slow kiss, running his thumb over the purple cord necklace.

His skin on fire and dick so hard it was about to snap off, Damo kissed Blake like his life depended on it. They were going to fuck. Like, *properly*. He was going to have a cock in his arse, and he just hoped he wouldn't blow his load before it was even in there.

With their stubble rubbing together, Blake rutted against him with the damn towel still in the way giving even more friction. "God, I want you," Blake moaned into Damo's mouth.

Damo gave him a playful shove. "Go on, boy."

Laughing, Blake hopped up, tossing the towel and disappearing into the bathroom. Stuff clattered as if he'd dumped his toilet bag on the counter, and he returned gripping the small bottle.

He stretched out over Damo fully, heavy and hard—and the sexiest thing *ever*. "Have you thought about this?" he asked in a low voice that Damo felt right down in his balls.

"Hell, yeah. Especially since that arse business." He wriggled his legs apart, and they both moaned as their hard shafts rubbed.

"Do you know how you want it?"

Obviously, Damo knew there were different positions, but… "Dunno. How do you want me?"

Adam's apple bobbing, Blake dived in for another kiss. "Every way I can get," he mumbled against Damo's lips. "But I want to see your face the first time."

Damo nodded. "Yeah. I like that. So, I can just, like…" His legs were wide, but he wasn't sure exactly what to do next.

After a sweet kiss, Blake shifted back and sat on his heels. He slicked his finger and circled Damo's hole, watching him closely. He teased and tickled, pushing in and then retreating until Damo's thighs shook. Blake's finger felt huge, and Damo was both nervous and excited.

He was completely exposed, and he couldn't imagine doing anything like it with anyone else. He'd never been this…open before. Not just because his legs were spread.

He blurted, "I reckoned I was pretty good at sex, but mate, I don't think so."

Laughing, Blake pushed the tip of his finger inside to the knuckle. "You don't give yourself enough credit." He dropped his gaze, his eyes dark. "I wish you could see your pretty little hole opening for me."

"Yeah, nah, not that flexible."

Laughing, Blake leaned over and kissed him again, then started fucking him with his finger, crooking it in just the right spot.

"Fuck! Never thought a finger in my arse could be this good. Not that it was bad before, but holy shit."

Lips at Damo's ear, Blake whispered, "I'm going to make it so good for you, baby."

"I know. Just do it already." He grasped at Blake's ribs.

Shoulders shaking with laughter, Blake crooked his finger even deeper. "I will." His smile faded. "Look how hard you make me."

The shiny head of Blake's cock was deep red and wet. Damo brushed the tip with his finger, then sucked the salty drop. "Just think how hard you'll be stuffed inside me."

He groaned. "Oh, I have. Trust me."

"I do." Damo pushed up on an elbow, desperate to taste. "I trust you."

Between messy kisses, Blake slicked himself and lifted Damo's arse, pushing his knees back to his shoulders. "You're more flexible than you give yourself credit for."

Damo was laughing when Blake pushed his cock at the tight ring of muscle, and he broke off with a gasp. "Okay, so dicks are a bit bigger than fingers, hey?"

"I'd like to think so." Blake nuzzled Damo's cheek. "Breathe. It's okay. We can go slow."

"Stuff that. Just get it in me already."

They laughed and kissed, and Blake still took his bloody time. But soon enough, he was past the tight entrance and pushing all the way in slowly, slowly, slowly until his pubes tickled Damo's arse.

"Okay?" Blake asked, his brow furrowed.

It took a second to inhale fully, as if Damo'd been pinned under a breaking wave for too long. Then he exhaled with a nod. "Feel like I'm gonna burst." He grabbed at Blake's arms. "Like my skin's on fire. In a good way. Hurts, but…I like it."

"Do you want me to move?" Blake's skin was flushed, his muscles tense.

"Yeah. Fuck me proper. I can take it."

The first real thrust almost made Damo scream. Blake hesitated, but Damo nodded, grasping for his hips with clumsy fingers and urging him on.

Blake's powerful, sure movements had Damo's toes curling. He was so full, and his dick strained, rubbing against his belly. "Can't. Believe. I've got. A cock. In me," he whispered between grunts. "*Your* cock."

"You like it, baby?"

"Fuck, I love it. I love—" Damo broke off. Wasn't it too soon to be in love? He had no clue.

Blake kissed him roughly, rocking his hips harder and faster. Damo was bent in half, Blake so incredibly heavy on top of him— *inside* him. He dug his nails into Blake's shoulders, back arching at the tug of pressure as Blake leaned a spread hand on his hair.

Immediately, Blake lifted his hand, slowing his thrusts. "Sorry. Are you—"

"Pull my hair." Damo panted. "I like it. Ow! Not that hard."

Blake loosened his grip and tugged experimentally on the damp strands. "Good?" He'd stopped moving inside Damo, though he was still big and thick.

"Not enough."

He tried again. "How about this?"

"*Fuck.* Just right."

"Guess I'll call you Goldilocks."

"Call me Snow White and the seven bloody dwarfs as long as you keep fucking me."

With a grin, Blake thrust powerfully, keeping the pressure on Damo's hair. "Let's see. Sleepy? Doc? Grumpy?" With each name, he rammed into Damo.

The pleasure and pain were almost too much, but not quite. Damo squirmed his hand between them, jerking himself desperately, but Blake batted his hand away and started stroking.

"I've got you, baby. Let's see. Sneezy? No. Dizzy? Bossy? How about Frothy?"

"Fuck, fairy tales have never been so hot," Damo gasped, the pressure in his arse joined by his tightening balls. "I'm gonna—"

Blake tightened his fingers in Damo's hair, and Damo came with a shout, trembling and gasping, his head thrown back, the delicious, perfect pressure tugging on the roots of his hair.

White-hot pleasure crashed through him, and he saw dark spots and bursts of light. He thought he really would get dizzy.

Chest heaving, he was completely drained, like every drop of jizz he'd ever had was now sprayed between him and Blake. "I…" He tried to speak. His eyes were still practically rolling back in his head.

Blake's fingers were hot on his chin, and Damo blinked up at him as Blake asked, "Can I come inside you?"

"Fuck, yes."

Planting his hands beside Damo's head, Blake rocked into him, sweat shining on his forehead, his eyeliner and lippy smudged to hell but still sexy. Even sexier.

When he came inside Damo, he shook and grunted and curled over him, emptying and moaning. Damo wrapped his wobbly legs and arms around him, caressing Blake's spine until they were a sweaty, sticky mess.

When Blake finally shifted and slipped out of him, he pushed up on one hand, still half covering Damo. "How do you feel?"

His arse was a bit sore. Damo reached down to tentatively touch his wet hole. "It's…loose. Like I've had a great big cock shoved up it."

Blake laughed softly. "Do you like it?" He seemed a bit nervous waiting for the response, his eyes intent on Damo's.

Damo's first instinct was to make a joke, but he simply said, "Loved it."

Blake's long exhalation tickled Damo's nose. "Good."

"Feel a bit slutty now. In a nice way." His body ached, and his arse would definitely be sore in the morning, but it turned out he liked being well-fucked. More than *liked*. It was almost as if he hadn't realized something was missing, and now he knew.

Did he *ever*.

"Oh, that's the other dwarf," Blake said. "Slutty." They laughed, and Blake stroked Damo's wet hole with the barest touch. "But no, I think Goldilocks fits you best. Goldie."

"Guess that makes you the three bears."

Laughing—Damo *loved* how much they laughed together—they kissed again. He knew they should probably move and clean up, but for now, everything was just right.

"CAN WE? CAN we?" Cooper asked, practically bouncing in the back seat. He'd told his parents he wanted to drive back with Damo and Blake, and Blake hadn't stopped smiling the whole way. Damo loved to see it. He loved—

Slow down, mate! Stop thinking about love!

"I say we can," Damo replied. "We'll text your mum." He asked Blake, "Wanna catch a few waves?" as Blake took the Barking exit off the highway. "We can show Coop the ropes."

"Always. Don't have my board, though."

"You can borrow one. It's…um, my dad's old one." His chest tightened. Dad would never surf again, so what was the harm? He cleared his throat. "I've still got one of my old ones too. Coop can use it."

Damo actually had every surfboard he'd owned since he was a grommet stacked up in the shed out the backyard. He hadn't been able to part with any of them. He ran through them in his head. His lime flowered longboard from when he was a grom would be perfect.

"Woo!" Cooper shouted. "I'm going surfing!"

They drove down into the Illawarra Valley suburb past streets of houses that had spread out from the original industrial area of garages and storage companies. Then up the hill past power lines. Kids played in the park after school, and Blake slowed as a few chased a rugby ball close to the verge.

The Indian Ocean appeared as they crested the hill, the Barking neighborhood spreading out below them with solar panels on roofs gleaming in the late-afternoon sun. The skies had cleared when they were halfway home, and the clear blue water glittered.

As much as he'd loved getting away, Damo's heart swelled to see the familiar houses and cafes of home, and of course the water called to him, but…

Between them and the beach, a black cloud seemed to rise up. The comfort of being home in Barking vanished.

Blake had slowed, apparently remembering where Damo lived. 'Course he did after how Damo had acted when he'd tried to take him to his house.

Blake asked, "Do you want me to drop you at the corner? We'll wait for you at the beach."

Damo exhaled through a wave of affection. Blake wasn't going to push. But maybe… Maybe it would be okay? They were approaching Damo's street, and his mouth went dry. For a long moment, he was frozen.

Then he said, "Nah. Turn at the corner. You can meet my sister." His pulse raced. Was he really doing this?

Maybe he'd just built it up in his head since the accident. Maybe it wasn't such a big deal. He could park Blake and Cooper on the porch and bring Tabby out. Hopefully, Dad wouldn't be shouting inside. Even if he was, Blake knew the truth now.

Blake's face lit up. "We'd love to meet her." He pushed the blinker and turned right—

And the new, shiny hope and happiness growing in Damo drowned in an icy flood of fear.

Chapter Seventeen

THE AMBULANCE SAT in front of a small house with a faded, rickety blue porch. Blake could imagine the yellow towel hanging there, telling little Damo it was time to come home for dinner. Back then, perhaps the garden had been tended and not overgrown with dried husks of plants.

Blake had barely come to a stop behind the ambulance when Damo flew out of the passenger seat. He disappeared inside so quickly Blake had to blink and take a second look. With no idea what was happening, he had to make sure it was safe.

"Can you wait in the car?" he asked Coop. "Come sit up front. I'll leave the keys so you can control the window." Wait, was *that* dangerous?

Was it the wrong thing to do? With the windows up, it would be too hot in minutes, but with the keys, what if someone tried to steal the car with Coop in it? Or what if someone tried to kidnap him?

"Actually, no," Blake said. "Come with me."

Neighbors were gathering to gawk, though none approached the house. The wood door was the same faded, peeling blue of the porch and stood ajar. Blake pushed it open cautiously and called, "Damo?"

Stepping into the tile foyer, he was aware of shouting from

deeper in the house to the left. To the right, a barefoot young girl in a footy uniform who had to be Tabby sniffled and frowned at him from the living room, which was crowded with a dining table covered in stuff.

"Who are you?" she demanded.

"I'm Blake. I'm—I know Damo."

"Oh. Are you a lifeguard?"

"No. I'm a garbo."

"Ew!" She scrunched up her red face. "Doesn't it stink?"

"Uh, sometimes." Blake stood there uselessly looking at Tabby while raised voices pulsed through the house. He belatedly added, "I'm a clubbie too. I met Damo at the beach. This is my son, Cooper."

Tabby crossed her arms and muttered, "Sure, whatever."

Blake's gaze flicked over open Amazon boxes, stacks of flyers, a few water bottles, a purse, an empty flowerpot, textbooks, a dirty plate, a footy uniform slung over a chair.

Still in the doorway, Coop said, "Garbo's an awesome job!"

Tabby rolled her eyes. "If you say so, kid. Like I care."

Seeing the nosy neighbors staring, Blake ushered Cooper a few steps in, and Coop asked, "What's going on? Why is the ambo here?"

"For my dad," Tabby muttered, her jaw tight, fingers twitching into fists.

"I'm sorry your dad's sick," Cooper said quietly.

She snapped, "I don't care if he's sick. He's always sick. I don't care!"

"Oh," Coop mumbled. "Okay. Where's Damo?"

"Look, let's, uh…" Blake had to take control of the situation. "Coop, can you stay here with Tabby?"

"How do you know my name?" she demanded.

"Damo's really cool," Coop said to Tabby.

"I know!" Her eyes narrowed. "Wait, how do you know my

brother again?"

"He came with us to Bremer Bay," Coop said.

"Why would he go away with *you?*"

Blake held up his hands. "Okay, let's take a breath." Tabby's face was going redder, and the last thing anyone needed was for her to start yelling.

But an instant later, fresh tears filled her bleary eyes. "Why didn't I get to go?"

"I'm sure Damo wanted you to come!" Cooper said, clearly eager to soothe her hurt feelings in a way that made Blake so proud. "But I have this week off school. You probably had to go to school, right?"

Tabby whirled around, her thin shoulders shaking. Blake squeezed Coop's shoulder and whispered, "Can you wait by the door? Don't go outside."

He nodded solemnly, shooting a worried glance toward Tabby. Blake approached her and cleared his throat.

"I'm really sorry you couldn't come with us. What happened with your dad?"

Sniffing loudly, her back to him, she motioned violently toward the other side of the house.

Passing an eighties-style kitchen with dishes piled up in the sink, Blake followed the sound of shouting down a hallway to the bedroom at the end. Pausing in the doorway of the bedroom, he took in the scene.

Two female paramedics crouched beside a man on the floor by the bed. One of them said sternly, "*Rod.* You need to calm down. We're here to help you, mate."

"Fucking bitch!" The man—Rod, who had to be Damo's father—gripped her arm with what seemed to be surprising strength as she gasped.

"Dad!" Damo wrenched his father's fingers free, and the woman stood and backed away.

The other paramedic was on her radio, asking for backup for a violent patient, and it was chaos as Rod punched wildly in the low light of the musty room. Blake wanted to charge in and pull Damo to safety, but the paramedics were blocking the door.

The blinds were drawn against the daylight, the room lit only by a muted TV and a weak lamp on the side table. The table was crammed with an ashtray, an empty plate with crumbs on it, and lollie wrappers: Red Frogs and Minties. There was faded carpet on the floor.

Before Blake could call to Damo and do something to help, footsteps approached behind him. Two cops filled the hall. Though the young men were likely average sized, their presence seemed huge somehow with their blue uniforms, shiny badges, hats with white and blue checkered stripes, and big utility belts holding radios, handcuffs, tasers, a few other things Blake couldn't recognize. And, of course, their guns. He squeezed against the wall to let them pass.

He heard Damo ask, "You right? Did he hurt you? I'm so sorry. Fuck."

The older woman said, "We're good, darl. Not your fault." Beyond the cops, Blake glimpsed her squatting down again next to Damo's father. "Rod, we're here to help you. You've had a fall, and you caught the back of your head on the dresser."

"Think I don't fuckin' know that, you stupid cow?" He lashed out with his arm, but the movement was weak this time.

"You're not helping anything," one of the cops said, looming over Rod. Blake couldn't imagine the cops would help either, but he didn't blame the paramedics for requesting backup.

"We need room to work," the other paramedic said, one of the cops backing out of the doorway and motioning for Blake to move.

He returned to the foyer just as a harried woman in scrubs who had to be Damo's mum burst in, skidding to a stop in her

Crocs and staring at him, then Cooper, who'd dodged the opening door.

She looked down the hall toward the bedroom, then turned back and said to Tabby, "Tell your friend to go home."

"Mum, I'm almost fourteen! He's not my bloody friend," Tabby shouted, swiping her eyes with staccato movements. "Damo knows them."

Frowning, Damo's mum asked Blake, "I'm sorry, who are you?"

God, he hated lying in front of Cooper, who looked at him in clear confusion. "Blake. I'm a mate of Damo's. And this is my son."

How odd to say those words aloud. Weeks ago, he hadn't even known his son existed, and Damo had been his fun beach crush. Now, he and Cooper were inside Damo's house in the thick of a crisis he could only begin to understand.

He added, "I'm sorry. We were—"

Damo's mum—Blake realized he didn't know her name—was already brushing past him, and he didn't finish his sentence since he didn't know what to say. He followed her without conscious thought, drawn back toward Damo.

He had to see him. Had to hold him and tell him it was all right. He felt the way he had watching Damo struggle with the panicking Irish patient. He had to do something to make it better.

But there were already too many people crowding the back bedroom, and he could hear Damo's mum's voice rise. As much as he wanted to help Damo, he needed to get Cooper away from this stressful, terrible situation and safely back to Tasha and Tony. He'd text Damo that he'd be back very soon.

Turning, he glimpsed a small bedroom through an open door. A twin bed with messy covers sat in the corner under a window. Damo had mentioned he was messy, and the evidence sat right in front of Blake.

Clothes were piled on the floor with two blue lifeguard shirts on top. He went inside, automatically picking up the laundry. That was something he could do! That would help, wouldn't it? Damo had said Blake was welcome to clean up after him when Blake had told him about the issues with Lance.

Was there a laundry bag? He could get Cooper out of here and still help from afar. He'd bring the clothes back later, washed and pressed, and Damo would have one less thing to worry about.

A Macca's cup and empty McSpicy wrapper sat on the carpeted floor by a video game controller, an old TV sitting on a dresser under a tacked-up poster of Stephanie Gilmore in a bikini holding her surfboard. Her windswept blonde hair was actually quite similar to Damo's.

"What are you doing in here?"

Gripping the haphazard pile of clothing, Blake turned at Damo's ragged question. "I was just—these are dirty, and—"

He glanced down the hall. "You can't be here! I thought you were gone!"

That felt like a slap. "Of course I'm here. I wasn't about to just drive away and leave you."

Damo's beautiful eyes glistened with tears. "I don't want you to see this."

"It's okay. You told me about your dad. I wasn't going to just leave."

Squeezing his eyes shut, Damo shook his head. "It was one thing to tell you! Telling and, and, *seeing* aren't the same. I never wanted you to see this! To see how we live."

"Baby, I want to help." He clutched the clothing, desperate to pull Damo into his arms but not wanting to make everything worse somehow.

Rubbing his red face, Damo laughed brokenly, and Blake's heart squeezed. "You must be regretting it." He grabbed the laundry, and his uniform shirts fell to the carpet. "This wasn't how it was supposed to be. Fuck!"

Another paramedic, a dark-haired man this time, appeared in the hall. "Damo?" he asked with raised eyebrows. Blake recognized him as one of the particularly good-looking Barking lifeguards.

"Just fucking great," Damo muttered. "Invite everyone over! Come on in and see how pathetic I am!"

Raised voices echoed from the main bedroom, and Damo threw the laundry to the floor and bolted past the paramedic, who watched him with concern and followed.

When the hall was clear, Blake hurried in the other direction. Damo had made it clear he should go, and as much as he hated it, Blake clearly wasn't helping. In the foyer, he called goodbye to Tabby, who ignored him, and led Cooper outside.

With shaky hands, Blake tapped the screen on the console and pulled up the address of the rental house where Tash and her family were staying. Heart thudding, tasting bile, he drove.

After a few minutes, Cooper said, "I guess we're not going surfing."

"No. Sorry, buddy."

"That's okay. How's Damo?"

"He's upset right now. But he'll be good." He would. He had to be. Blake needed Damo to be happy and laughing again like he needed oxygen.

After another long silence, Cooper said, "It's really cool that you can surf. Can I watch you before we go home?"

"Absolutely." Despite everything, Blake allowed himself a moment to be proud. His son thought he was *cool*. Or at least that he was cool-adjacent. "Thanks for defending my honor as a garbo."

"You get to drive big trucks. It's totally cool." He hesitated. "Why don't you know Damo's family?"

Blake couldn't quite say the naked truth—*We barely know each other.*

Was that the truth? It didn't feel like it. He didn't care if it was too fast. He *knew* Damo. Not all of him—and he didn't expect to in only weeks. But Blake was falling in love deeper than he'd ever expected.

"Uh…Blake?"

He snapped back to attention, giving Coop what he hoped was a reassuring smile as he slowed for a light. "Sorry, I was miles away. I haven't actually met Damo's family before today. We haven't been dating very long. Also, he's not out to them yet." That was unequivocally the truth, at least.

Coop frowned. "Why not?"

"He wasn't ready."

"But he wanted us to meet his sister. Even though she's kind of mean."

"I guess he was feeling ready today, but then there was so much chaos… And I'm sure Tabby was just stressed. It was a lot to deal with."

"That's true." Cooper shifted in his seat, kicking his feet in front of him. "Maybe I can meet her again. At a better time."

Blake nodded, hoping he'd be able to meet her again too— and that he hadn't completely ruined everything.

Chapter Eighteen

"WHAT'RE YOU DOIN'?"

On his knees on the kitchen lino wearing his boxers, Damo jerked his head up to find Tabby in the doorway in the oversized Dockers T-shirt she sometimes wore to bed. It brushed her knees and had been Dad's once upon a time.

Damo glanced up at the kitchen window to see the sky brightening beyond the reflected glare of the overhead light. He tried to smile. "Ya snuck up on me! Just, you know. Cleaning the floor."

Tabby's hair was messy from sleep, and she tucked it behind her ears. "Why don't you use the mop?"

"Can't find it. Should be in the broom cupboard, right? Dunno where it went."

Probably lost in the shocking mess you call home.

He stood and rinsed the sponge he was using, the soapy water turning gray. After scooping up some suds, he knelt at the next section of floor. It wasn't the most efficient way to clean the floor, but he was getting the job done.

"Have you been cleaning all night?"

"Nah. Just woke up early and figured I'd do the dishes and tidy up a bit."

"Have you heard from Mum?"

He scrubbed at a sticky stain of...something. "Texted after

midnight. They admitted him to the ward. Talking about some kind of rehab."

Tabby snorted. "As if he'd do that."

"Yeah."

Damo didn't have it in him to defend their father. He knew in his head that it wasn't Dad's fault. The accident, the pain, the addictions, the abuse he hurled at them.

It still *hurt*.

On tiptoes, Tabby picked her way across the floor and boosted herself up onto the bench beside the sink. Damo scrubbed, moving onto the next square. The floor was faded by the sun and hadn't been changed since he was little.

"Who was that guy? Blake? He said he was a mate of yours, but you've never mentioned him before." Tabby asked.

Damo's throat suddenly felt like he'd gotten a mouthful of sand.

The two days away had been so bloody good. Hanging with Cooper, the drive together—even with the stress over the petrol— sleeping together in the same bed and waking up with Blake's elbow in his ribs, not wanting to wake him even though Damo's arm was cramping.

Being fucked like that. Giving up control and being on the edge of pain—but knowing it was safe.

His phone sat on the bench, and he could feel the weight of the unanswered text waiting for him like a wave pinning him to the reef.

Hi. I'm so sorry for earlier. How's your dad? Are you okay? I'm here for you.

What did Blake have to be sorry for? He'd only wanted to help. Damo was the one who'd stuffed up everything. He'd been selfish and gone away, abandoning his sister—and look what happened.

He'd been off fucking and cuddling and having fun. He never

should have left. Never should have thought he could have more.

He'd been too embarrassed to answer. What could he say? He'd stared at the message on his lock screen until the text from Mum had arrived and he'd had to open his phone to answer.

Then, he'd stared at Blake's message some more, trying to cough up the right words. Or any words. He'd given up at two and slept for a few restless hours, dreaming of paddling out for a patient but not being able to get any closer.

He'd finally jerked awake after watching the faceless person drown over and over and over.

He could feel Tabby's eyes on him but didn't look up. There was another stain on the floor, and he scrubbed at it with jerky movements. God, he couldn't even imagine what Blake had thought seeing the house. Seeing Damo's room.

Prickly humiliation crawled over his skin like the tiny ants they couldn't keep from going after crumbs. They came in through the drain and the cracks in the foundation, no matter how much repellent Damo sprayed.

Scrubbing harder, he cursed himself and squirmed with a toxic mix of embarrassment and shame. Not to mention heaps of regret. He wanted to shrivel up and die remembering yelling at Blake in his room.

Fuck, that *room*. What must Blake think of him?

"Is he your boyfriend?"

Damo looked up so quickly he tweaked his neck. Feet dangling where she sat on the bench, soles dirty from the goddamn floors that needed to be mopped properly, Tabby watched him with a serious expression.

"Why d'ya say that?"

She shrugged.

"Yeah, he's my boyfriend." In the end, it hadn't been hard to say at all. "At least, I hope so. Not sure after yesterday."

"I wasn't very nice to him. Sorry."

They could just toss that on top of the mess Damo had already made. "S'okay. Yesterday was…bad."

"Really bad." Her voice quivered on the second word.

In one movement, Damo dropped the sponge and leapt across the damp floor to hug his sister where she sat on the bench. She didn't fight, folding against him like a balloon with a hole in it. Her tears wet his chest, and all he could do was hold her tight, her knees digging into his belly.

"I'm sorry I left," he said when he was sure he could speak without sobbing himself.

"It's not your fault," she mumbled against his shoulder. "You can't be here all the time. It's *his* fault."

Damo sighed and rubbed her back slowly. Her hair tickled his nose. "He's in so much pain."

"I know, but… It's not *fair*."

"It's not. It's really, really not."

After a minute, Tabby lifted her head and swiped at her red eyes. "Does Mum know? About Blake."

"Nah. Maybe if Dad gets help, she… She could be here more. Really *here*, I mean. You know?"

Tabby nodded. "Yeah." She sniffed loudly. "Your boyfriend's cute. He's old enough to have a kid?"

"Yeah, had him young."

"I was a bitch to both of them." Her lip wobbled. "I'm sorry."

"We're all bitches sometimes, right? If he's still talkin' to me, you can apologize."

"Why don't you ring him?"

"I think he'll be at work now. Or, no, it's Saturday." He tried to remember if Blake had mentioned if he was scheduled for a clubbie shift or if he was rostered off since Cooper was in town. "It's his day off. Don't want to wake him too early."

Face scrunching, she said, "That sounds like an excuse."

"Oi! That's enough out of you. Don't need dating advice from my little sis." Especially when she was right. "Do ya have a clean uniform for footy practice? Come on, chop, chop." He lifted her down off the bench the way he had when she was younger, and she didn't roll her eyes or complain.

"Yeah, yeah," she muttered.

He grabbed her wrist. "Love ya, Tabs."

Her face brightened a few degrees. "You too."

Alone in the kitchen, Damo thumbed open his phone and stared at the text from Blake.

And realized he'd somehow accidentally responded to it hours ago—

with a thumbs-up emoji.

A bloody thumbs-up emoji!

Of all the emojis, he'd hit *that* one? 'Course he had because he was the biggest pork chop in the entire universe. What was he supposed to say now?

Anything would be better than a *thumbs-up*, but his whirling mind was somehow blank at the same time, and he had to make sure Tabby was okay and get to work.

Damo stared at the stupid little thumb and felt even more ridiculous than he had before.

〰〰

AS HE MADE his way down to the water, Damo distractedly nodded at a few locals he knew, not slowing down to chat. He stood in the shallows, the waves reaching shore with a *boom* and then retreating with a *whoosh*.

Matching his breath to the rhythmic thunder and hiss, his toes sank deeper and deeper into the sand. There wasn't a cloud in the sky and the sun was already strong on his face. He loved Barking in the mornings before the crowds arrived.

He only had ten minutes before his shift started but he had to take a second to…what was the word? Recenter? No. Re…something. What was it? Blake would know.

Not just because he'd gone to uni. He knew things. He had his shit together. He had actual art on his walls! In frames! He had a kid. He was a grown-up.

And Damo had to put on his big boy pants and send a proper reply to Blake's text—or just ring him even though he barely ever actually talked on his phone.

He still cringed to think of how he'd yelled at Blake. Told him to get out. He wanted to bury himself in the sand.

On his way to the tower, he stopped short. The clubbies were setting up their sunshade and chairs. Kat was there, and Damo looked for the now-familiar shape of Blake's body—his broad shoulders, cute ears, strong calves, magnificent arse, slim hips…

It had been less than twenty-four hours, but Damo had missed him so damn much.

He couldn't spot Blake among the yellow and red uniformed clubbies. Maybe he was rostered off to spend the day with Cooper. Blake had surely mentioned it, but Damo couldn't remember. He'd barely slept, and he'd have to chug one of the mediocre coffees from the machine in the lifeguards' kitchenette.

When he jogged up the stairs to the tower, he mumbled a prayer and pushed open the door with its sign instructing the public to only knock for emergencies.

But because the universe bloody hated him, of course Mark was leaning forward in the roller chair at the long benchtop under the windows, scanning the water with binoculars. He was only a casual lifeguard, but he just *had* to be on the roster today.

Mark usually kept himself to himself. He wasn't one to go drinking with the boys, and Damo realized he didn't know much about him. Meanwhile, Mark had seen the shitshow of Damo's house in all its glory.

"Hey!" Cody greeted Damo from his seat by the far windows.

"Hiya." Bracing, Damo waited for Mark to look at him.

Mark did, taking his eyes off the water for two seconds at most before asking, "How are you?"

What did he mean by that? "Fine! Everything's fine." Damo practically shouted it.

Frowning, Cody glanced over. "What's up?"

Heart tripping, Damo fiddled with his sunnies, which were now hooked over the neckline of his T-shirt. "Nothing!"

Looking dubious, Cody turned back to the beach. Damo's gaze cut to the lineup of surfers out the back at the north end. The swells were up, and they were forecasted to only get bigger.

Even though he knew Blake couldn't be out there—that surf was already too much for his skill level—Damo still searched for him. As much as he wanted a glimpse, it was a relief Blake wasn't there.

"You going to join us, or...?" Cody asked in a teasing tone.

Damo tore his eyes from the surfers and escaped to the change room with a choked laugh. He shoved his stuff in his locker and shook out his wrinkled uniform shirt.

If he'd gotten over his embarrassment and let Blake do the laundry, he wouldn't be rocking up to work with the uniform that smelled the least offensive. He hadn't been able to think straight in that moment.

Now, the idea of Blake cleaning his clothes for him and folding them neatly—because no doubt Blake would make everything perfect and fresh smelling—sent warmth flowing through him.

Before he locked up his phone, he checked again. Nothing from Mum or Tabby, which was good. Also nothing from Blake, which made him want to spew. Why would there be after Damo's *thumbs-up?*

The change room door creaked open, and his heart plummeted as Mark appeared wearing his usual calm, serious expression. With his thick eyebrows, did he ever look unserious? He was probably in his late thirties, and his dark hair was graying at the temples. He was hot, which Damo had never let himself think about before—and definitely shouldn't have been thinking about now! He needed that coffee.

"You right?" Mark asked quietly with a glance behind him.

"Yeah, 'course! All good. Everything's fine. Nothing to worry about. Sorry to bother you and the other ambos. We're good. We're—" Damo was babbling, and he shut his gob.

Mark smiled sadly without teeth. "It was no bother. That was a confronting scene. You did the right thing to ring for help. I'm sorry your dad's so unwell."

Shrugging, Damo kicked his locker shut and spun the dial on his padlock. "It's fine. Is what it is. I don't talk about it much."

"I won't mention it to anyone."

"Right. Thanks." He spun the lock again, not meeting Mark's kind, serious gaze. "He had an accident when I was a kid. Never got better. Now the docs are sayin' something about rehab, but there's no way he'll do it, so..."

"If you ever do want to talk, I'm here." Mark laid a warm hand on Damo's shoulder.

His steady manner was similar to Blake's, and Damo flushed again with shame. Fuck, he had to message Blake properly. "Thanks."

"Are you sure you're up for working?" Mark asked.

"Just had days off. I can't chuck a sickie."

"Needing time for a family emergency isn't pretending to be sick."

"Mark?" Cody called distantly. "Got an allergic reaction out here."

Mark and Damo snapped into work mode, hurrying out to the main area. Cody was helping a teenage girl with a swelling face onto the first aid bed, and as Mark joined them, Damo automatically jumped up the steps to the windows.

Didn't matter that he'd barely slept and Dad was in the hospital and he'd yelled at Blake. It was go time.

He picked up the binoculars with one hand and rang triple-zero with the other, cradling the phone on his shoulder. "Ambulance, please."

He knew Mark would administer the epi-pen in the meantime but they still needed the ambos. While he spoke to the operator, he surveyed the water. Just in the time since he'd come to the tower, the crowd had swelled and would only get bigger.

Lowering the binos, he spoke into the radio with his free hand, jabbing speaker on the phone on the bench. "Central to orange buggy. There are three heads out the back just north of the flags. Got a little flashy there. Might be worth a paddle."

In typical Barkers fashion, everything was going off at the same time. It was early in the day for rips to be popping up, but with the big swells, that water needed somewhere to go.

"Copy that, Central," Mia said over the radio.

The woman on the phone asked, "Is she still conscious?" and Damo yelled the question to Cody and Mark before telling her she was.

Staring through the binos again, he said into the radio more forcefully, "Yeah, Maz, you're in. No way they can get to shore. Backup's on the way."

He sent Cody out to help Mia, and Mark could handle the girl while Damo took control of the tower. Everything else—Dad, Blake, even shitty coffee—had to wait.

Chapter Nineteen

"WELL, LOOK WHO'S making an appearance!" Kat said with a wink as Blake and Cooper approached the clubbies. "Thought you were away or something?"

"Yeah, I was," Blake said as he jammed the bottom of his surfboard into the sand. "Sorry I haven't been in touch this week."

Standing from their folding chair, Kat shrugged, though Blake sensed with a wince that they were a bit hurt. "Who's this?" they asked, smiling at Cooper.

"Well, it'll surprise you, but this is Cooper. My son."

Cooper lifted a hand in a wave. "Hi."

Jaw on the sand, Kat stared between them, looking like the personification of a "shocked" meme. "Yeah, that was unexpected! Hiya, Cooper. I'm Kat. How ya goin'?"

He grinned. "Great! We're going surfing."

Blake looked out at the swells again, putting what he hoped was a comforting hand on Coop's shoulder. "I'm not sure, mate. It's looking fierce already."

He'd wanted to see the conditions close up before renting a board and wetsuit for Cooper, and there was no way he could take him out surfing today.

Kat nodded. "Yeah, gnarly swells today."

"But you promised," Cooper whined. "And you're all ready!"

He motioned to Blake's short-sleeved wetsuit.

"I also promised your parents I'd keep you safe and sound." He squeezed Coop's bony shoulder. "Don't worry—we'll still have loads of fun."

Another clubbie, Billy, looked up from his folding chair. "If you're into sandcastles, my kids just started building the Perth bell tower. They're about your age. I'll bring you over if you want to join in?"

Coop looked up at Blake. "Can I?"

"Sure! I'll have a chat to Kat and come over in a little bit. No swimming without me, okay? And keep your hat and rashie on."

Billy's kids were digging near the water between the flags, only about ten meters away, so Blake felt okay about letting Coop go. He watched the kids say hello, aware of Kat's gaze boring into him.

"Uh, since when do you have a kid? You never mentioned!"

"I just found out. Right after the first night with Damo."

"Wow. Seriously?"

"Yup. It's been a lot to process." His board leaned where it stood in the sand, and he propped it against his shoulder.

"I guess so. I was going to say, you kept that under your hat. Having a whole kid and all." They laughed awkwardly. "I thought I'd gotten to know you pretty well the past few months."

"You have." He turned to face them. "I'm sorry I haven't been in touch lately. It was shitty of me. I should've at least texted back. Even if it was only a thumbs-up or something."

Kat screwed up their face under the brim of their red uniform cap. "Thumbs-up? Nah, I think silence was better."

Blake sighed, the knot in his stomach tightening. "Yeah." He'd been happy to get anything from Damo, but it hadn't been particularly reassuring. He'd immediately looked for him when he and Cooper had arrived, but hadn't spotted him yet.

"Right, you're forgiven for temporarily ghosting me. Don't let it happen again, and you can make it up to me by explaining how the hell you have a kid." They went up on tiptoes in the sand and added, "Keeping an eye on that family clinging to the camel floatie. Have a feeling they can't swim."

Blake clocked them. "At least they're between the flags. Been a busy morning so far?"

The radio beeped, and as Kat listened to a message, Blake watched Cooper and Billy's kids pack wet sand into bright plastic buckets. Billy returned and muttered, "Bloody sandcastle's gonna look like a pointy dildo, but it'll keep 'em out of trouble for a while," before taking his chair again.

Standing in the shade from the tent and not blocking Billy's view, Kat belatedly answered Blake, "You can see it's going to be chockers by lunchtime." They lightly slapped his arm, gaze on the water. "Spill it. You said 'parents' to Cooper. What's the story?"

Blake explained, answering a few of Kat's and Billy's questions. It felt good to talk about Cooper openly. He'd tell Rocky and the guys at work next week. He was officially a father.

Tash and Tony had let him take Coop to Barking just the two of them, and he watched his son laughing and playing with Billy's kids with a surge of pride.

"Did you think about having kids before?" Kat asked, nodding to Billy as he went to fetch more water from the clubhouse that sat on one side of the grassy area beyond the boardwalk.

"Yeah. Not concretely, especially once I realized I'm gay. But distantly." Digging his toes into the cool sand under the warm top layer, he added, "When I came out to my parents, my mum kept wailing that I'd never have children."

Kat grimaced. "Yikes. Now you can rub it in her face that she was wrong."

He laughed weakly. "Suppose so. I haven't told my parents yet. I wanted to make sure Cooper would be interested in a relationship with me."

"Seems like it." Kat elbowed him lightly. "You're doing a great job. Stop worrying. And stuff your parents if they don't like it."

"I'm sure they'll be thrilled." So why was he dreading telling them?

Kat lowered their voice as a few other of their fellow clubbies approached. "And Damo went with you to Bremer Bay?" They grinned.

"Yeah, it was great. Amazing."

"Really? You should tell your face."

"No, it was."

God, he wished they could go back to that hotel room when it was just the two of them. Damo had told him about his dad's accident, and Blake had felt so close to him. Not to mention being inside him for the first time.

"Then what happened?" Kat asked, frowning and scanning the water.

Blake watched Cooper digging a moat around the phallic tower. "There was an emergency with Damo's father when we got home. Ambos were there. I tried to help but did a shit job of it."

"Ah. Damo's never liked talking about that. He and my younger brother were in the same year at school. I remember after the accident, Damo seemed to act like nothing'd happened."

Blake glanced from Cooper to that family on the floatie. Even between the flags, the waves were bigger than usual for morning. "Yeah. He didn't want to tell me about it at first. He did though—in Bremer Bay. But then he was upset I went into the house, and now all I've heard from him from my apology text was an emoticon."

"Let me see."

With a sigh, he showed Kat the screen with just the last message on it. And the thumbs-up.

"Oof. Maybe he didn't know what to say?"

"Or maybe he never wants to talk to me again."

"Nah. Not his style. You should—" Kat squinted to the right. "It's going off north of the flags. And speak of the devil! There's your man."

My man.

Blake desperately wanted that to be true. Holding up a hand to shield his eyes, he peered over the growing crowd to see Damo running in with a rescue board, his golden hair gleaming in the sunlight.

God, Blake loved him so much.

He didn't care if it was too fast. In that moment, with Barking Beach surging around him, people and crashing waves, salt filling the air under the sun's power, he was floating outside himself, watching Damo almost in slow motion.

My man.

He peered out farther to spot the patient Damo was going for and realized there must have been a flash rip. Two people had likely been drawn to the calm channel of water, not realizing it would pull them out.

Déjà vu swallowed Blake in one gulp, his stomach dropping as he crashed back to earth, watching Damo paddle out toward the two drowning people. Heart thudding, he remembered how that Irishman had panicked.

That time, he'd been close enough to help. Now, he was too far away, and as Damo reached the patients—they were near in the impact zone.

Billy's wife, Trish, scanned with binoculars and spoke into her radio. "Copy that." To Billy and Kat, she said, "Lifeguards are under the pump. It's going off again, so be ready to get wet." She squinted at Blake. "You're not on shift, but if you want to lend a hand—"

Blake scooped his board under his arm. He slowed a step as he neared Cooper, shouting, "Stay here! I'll be right back."

Blood rushing in his ears, he veered north, leaping over sunbakers and splashing into the water, watching the incoming swell, the water like quicksand as he tried to run through it.

He strapped the leash around his ankle and timed the shore break, tossing down his board and paddling hard. He'd never gone in for a real rescue as a clubbie, and adrenaline coursed through him with a roar.

Damo was in trouble. He was in *danger*, and Blake wouldn't—couldn't!—stand by and watch.

He caught the rip, the surge of the water frightening. It was hard to see Damo and the patients beyond the rise and fall of the growing swells… There!

Off to the right, he glimpsed Damo in the water, gripping his big rescue board and yelling at the patients in the water. It was just like before, and Blake swam sideways out of the rip toward them, kicking as powerfully as he could.

A massive wall of water loomed, and Damo tugged at arms and legs, helping the two women on the board. The woman in front slipped off with a cry, and Damo rolled the board under the curling wave.

Blake gulped in a breath and duck-dived under, pushing his board down and coming up with burning lungs.

Another wave barreled toward them, and Damo helped the women on the board as he looked back at the incoming set. Blake was close enough to hear him.

"Get on here. You're right. Come on." He directed one to the back of his board and pointed to the other and patted the board in front of him. "Quick!"

Damo had it under control, and Blake gripped his surfboard, realizing his mistake in charging out. Damo was paddling forward, and their eyes met.

Wide-eyed, Damo shouted something lost in the water's roar—and then his board surged up as he caught the wave. It was too late for Blake to catch it, and he pushed his board down to dive under.

It was too late for that too.

Ricocheting violently under the surface, Blake ordered himself to relax. He'd wiped out on waves before, and he knew what to do.

Except the waves were never this big, and he'd barely had time to gasp in a breath before being pummeled.

He whipped back and forth like he was in a washing machine, the pressure on his lungs and diaphragm already too much. His board banged into his hip, and he kicked hard, reaching up for the surface—

Coral scraped his outstretched hands, ripping into his knuckles.

Wrong way!

His body was ready to snap with tension, white spots behind his eyes, and he forced himself to go limp, letting the water bring him to the surface for sweet, sweet air—

Another wave crashed on his head, slamming him down. The leash yanked on his ankle, digging into his flesh as the vortex of water tossed him and his board back and forth, up and down.

He breached the surface and gulped in a breath, salt on his lips before another wave hit, trapping him in the impact zone.

Chapter Twenty

SPITTING OUT A mouthful of saltwater, Damo rode the wave with one of the patients' arse in his face, tightening every muscle to keep the rescue board steady as they neared shore.

He could taste bile as he glanced back, praying to see Blake behind them. There was only frothing water.

Damo had to get the patients to dry land. They tumbled off in the shallows, and he urged them up. "Go, go!"

Kat was suddenly there helping one of the women as Damo practically dragged the other to dry sand.

"I'll check them out!" Kat shouted. "Blake got smoked!"

Dragging the rope handle of the rescue board, Damo spun and raced back into the water, searching for Blake in the impact zone. Head down, he punched through a wave, his shoulders burning as he paddled hard.

Fuck, fuck, fuck!

Where was he? Damo's heartbeat thundered in his ears, as he searched. He knew all too well that getting held down by big sets was brutal. Blake could hold his own in the surf, but not in these conditions. If he'd had a head knock…

The swell period was getting longer, which gave Damo precious seconds to sit up and search. Of course that meant the sets were getting even bigger.

Suddenly, Blake appeared, gasping in a breath. Damo paddled for his life and grabbed Blake's bare arm, hauling him over the rescue board. The relief of feeling that warm skin and hearing his ragged breaths had Damo's head spinning.

"I've got ya! Hang on tight!" He ripped off the leash around Blake's ankle, freeing his surfboard.

Both dragging Blake into position and turning them to face shore, Damo glanced over his shoulder. He'd ridden these waves all his life, and he waited a heartbeat. Then another.

Then he paddled fast, fast, fast—and they caught the wave, the force lifting them into the air in a spray of white water. Another day, he would have screamed for joy.

Not today.

Then they were in the shallows and tumbling off the board, and Damo wedged his shoulder under Blake's and locked his arm around his waist, dragging the rescue board with his free hand. The feeling of Blake's familiar body against him was reassuring.

He's okay. I got him.

Damo lowered Blake to sit on the dry, hot sand and crouched in front of him, ignoring the curious onlookers. "Did you swallow water?"

Blake blinked at him, panting softly, his face red.

"Oi! Did ya hear me?" Damo demanded. "Did you swallow water?" He brushed back wet hair from Blake's forehead, wanting to hold him and kiss him and make him good as new—and shake him for being out in too-big conditions.

Blake shook his head but looked down at his leg and poked the long slash in his wetsuit on the outside of his right thigh. "Shit."

Damo leaned in and eyed the gash, his heart going *boom*. He lifted his head and shouted, "Kat! Tell Central to call an ambo! Fin chop! Big one."

"Shit," Blake repeated, then started and peered around with

wide eyes. "Where's Cooper?"

Icy fear licked Damo's spine. "Is he in the water?" The thought of Cooper out there made him want to spew. He held down Blake's shoulder, not letting him up.

"No. Making a dildo castle…" Blake jerked his head left and right.

"What? Did ya hit your head?" Damo's pulse raced. Blake had to be heaving with adrenaline to have not even realized he'd been cut at first.

The wetsuit was compressing the cut, so Damo left it alone, not wanting to get his grubby, sandy hands on it. He held his left fingers in Blake's face. "Look at me. Focus. Where did you last see Coop?"

"Making a sandcastle with Billy's kids. A tower."

Damo exhaled as he said, "We'll find him. No dramas. Look at me." He peered closely at Blake's eyes. "You didn't bang your head? Let me feel." He gently prodded Blake's skull through his soft, wet hair, not feeling any bumps or wounds at least.

"Don't think so," Blake said. "I have to find Cooper!" He tried to get up, but Damo kept him down.

"You need to stay put," Damo ordered, gripping his shoulder.

Kat called, "Cooper's here!" and guided him over, stopping a couple of meters away.

"Hey, Coop!" Damo said, managing a smile through his relief. "No worries, mate. He'll be right."

"Hey, buddy." Blake smiled up at Cooper. "Sorry I ran off like that. Got a little banged up, but I'm fine."

Cooper's cheeks were blotchy, his eyes red, and Damo would've hugged him if he thought he could let go of Blake.

"Great parenting," Blake muttered under his breath. "Full marks." Louder, he said to Cooper, "I'm sorry. I wasn't thinking."

"You can say that again." Damo's relief that Blake was relatively okay gave way to a surge of frustration. "You can't be surfing in these conditions. And before you say you're not a grom, you're still not an expert. Not even close. These swells are too big for you."

"I had to help you."

Damo looked up sharply from Blake's wound, which thankfully wasn't bleeding too much despite the deep gash. "What?"

"There were two patients. The other lifeguards are busy, and Trish said we had to lend a hand. I'm not on today, but I saw you and…"

Damo blinked at him. "You were rescuing *me*?" He wasn't sure whether to throttle Blake or kiss him. "I've done plenty of double rescues. You don't need to protect me."

"I know, but the day we met, you were in trouble and—"

"And I would've handled it! That was a fluke. And yeah, it was awesome that you came to my rescue that day, but I'm not a, a—" He waved his free hand.

"Damsel in distress?" Blake suggested.

Damo pointed at him. "Bingo. I'm not that. Look—" He broke off and glanced away. They'd gathered quite an audience now, and he called out, "Back up! He doesn't need you all watching."

"You heard him!" Kat shouted. "Move on!"

"Bugger off!" Cooper yelled.

Bystanders giggled, and Blake and Damo shared a laugh that released a bit of the tension. With Kat and Cooper keeping a perimeter around them, Damo swallowed hard and spoke softly.

"I love that you want to take care of me. And I know it was hectic yesterday at my house, okay? I was a mess. But not here. I know this beach. I'm bloody good at my job."

Blake nodded. "You are. I just panicked seeing you out there alone."

"How d'ya reckon I felt having to take those two patients in and leaving you in the impact zone?"

Blake winced. "I'm sorry."

"Good. Wiggle your toes for me?"

He did, thankfully.

Damo added, "I thought my last words to you might've been a bloody thumbs-up."

Blake snorted a laugh and dipped his head. "Can I see?"

"Nope. Head up." He tapped under Blake's chin.

"Bossy," Blake murmured with a grin that quickly faded. "How bad is it?"

"Yeah, look, it's a pretty good cut. You'll probably need a few internal stitches as well as on the outside. Good thing you were wearing your wettie." He exhaled a long breath. "Could've been worse. Could've hit an artery. And lucky you didn't fin chop your bloody head. Can't believe you did that!"

Kat added, "Yeah, when Trish said we clubbies needed to help out, she meant getting overwhelmed people in from the flags, not racing out to rescue a professional lifeguard."

"I wasn't thinking!" Blake insisted. He gave Damo a smile. "Just feeling."

Damo's heart fluttered, and he couldn't hide a smile. It was okay. Blake would be okay. *They'd* be okay. This was too good, and even if they both acted like pork chops sometimes, they'd figure it out. Had to.

Kat asked, "Whaddya reckon, Cooper?"

"My teacher, Mrs. Georgiadis, would say he's an 'enthusiastic learner' like my best friend Kyle, but that really means you're a handful and need to listen more."

A few remaining onlookers close enough to hear giggled, and Damo had to give Coop a grin. "Roasted!"

Smiling, Blake reached out toward Cooper. "Nailed it on the head, mate. You sure you're okay?"

Hesitantly, Cooper knelt beside Blake and took his hand. "I'm fine. It was scary for a few minutes. Though you looked really cool paddling out. Like a real surfer."

"Thanks, buddy. I'll get there. With lots of patience. And listening."

Damo was relieved to see the buggy approach, horn blaring as it drove across the sand. Mia and Lachlan hopped out, Lachlan flying toward the water with a rescue board. Damo glanced behind him. Was he taking too long looking after Blake?

No, he'd be doing the same for anyone with a fin chop. Without thinking about giving them a kiss and cuddle.

Mia said into the radio, "Yep, bad laceration. Doesn't look like it hit an artery, but he'll still need that ambo." She snapped on gloves and passed a pair to Damo, saying, "Ambos are close," before glancing up at Coop. "You right, mate?"

Cooper nodded. "He's my…this is my…Blake."

Mia said to Kat, "Want to show him the buggy?"

They nodded and led a reluctant Cooper away, and Blake whimpered—letting go of the brave face he'd clearly been putting on as the adrenaline faded.

Damo was pretty sure in that moment he was in love. Head over bloody heels.

He carefully peeled up the wetsuit hem, his gut clenching to see how deep the gash went.

It was *deep*.

The fat of Blake's flesh looked like red jelly with paler cubes like cottage cheese. It wasn't natural to see under the skin like that. Damo had seen bad fin chops over the years, and this was up there.

He cleaned the wound and pressed a thick white pad to the gash as Blake groaned. "Sorry, babe," Damo murmured.

Mia's eyebrows shot up. "Wait, is this…?"

"He's my boyfriend." Damo looked at Blake uncertainly. "That is, if he still wants to be after the spray I just gave him."

"Yes!" Blake gritted his teeth. "Definitely." He glanced around and gave Damo a questioning look.

Damo cleared his throat and announced loudly to the onlookers who'd crept closer, "He's my boyfriend!"

There. He'd said it out loud at Barking—and it felt bloody fantastic. Blake the bloke was his boyfriend, and anyone who didn't like it could get stuffed.

A few people clapped, and he could hear someone say, "Aww."

Smiling, Mia poured the vial of gas into the green plastic dispenser. "Great to meet you. Wish it was under better circumstances. Here, suck on that, mate. Slow, deep breaths into your lungs."

Cody jogged over, dripping wet. "How ya going here? Think we're back under control. Jet Ski picked up a ton of people out the back. We took down the flags. No more swimming until the conditions change."

Damo glanced at the water. There were still some people in who'd likely refused to get out, and of course the surfers wouldn't dream of missing the huge sets. But at least the lifeguards could breathe for a minute. He prayed the kooks were staying on dry land and leaving it to the experts.

Blake screwed up his face. "Been better."

Cody said, "Tastes gross, hey? Weirdly sweet?"

Nodding, Blake inhaled from the plastic tube, grimacing. "What's it called again?"

"Green whistle?" Cody asked, turning to scan the water. "Methoxyflurane. It's an analgesic gas."

Mia tightened the bandage on Blake's thigh. "Careful or you might declare your undying love like Cody did."

Damo squeaked and held up his hands, staring at Mia. Of all the bloody things to say!

She said, "Kidding!"

"Still rubbish at jokes, mate," Damo muttered. He glanced up at Cody with a grin. "Worked out pretty well for you and Liam, but."

"What?" Cody's laugh was awkward and high-pitched. "I mean, it's fine! It's great, yeah."

Mia peered up suspiciously. "Why are you being weird?"

"I'm not!" Cody kept his eyes on the water as he flushed.

Mia frowned. "Mm-hmm." She turned as another buggy approached. "Ambos are here."

As Mia jogged to the other buggy, Cody dropped to his knees and hissed at Damo, "You're not supposed to tell anyone!"

"I didn't! *You* made it weird!"

Cody glanced at Blake. "No telling him until the whistle's worn off. Loose lips."

"Who, me?" Blake laughed and touched his mouth. "My lips are still here. Not loose."

"There it is," Cody said as he stood. "The whistle works its magic. Feeling cruisey now? Yeah you are."

Blake giggled, and it was *adorable*. That Damo couldn't kiss him was epically unfair. He reluctantly stood as the paramedics took over, taking off his gloves and slinging an arm around Coop's skinny shoulders.

"Doing okay, mate? Bit scary, hey?"

"Yeah. I'm better now. He was really worried about you."

Warmth curled through Damo. "Yeah, seems like. Are your mum and Tony about?"

"Uh-uh. They're at my grandparents' house. Can I go with him in the ambulance?"

Damo nodded. "I've got your mum's number, so I'll give her a ring and let her know."

Cooper peered up at Damo seriously. "You're sure he's going to be okay?"

"Yep. Not gonna be rescuing anyone for a while, but he'll be right. See?" He motioned to Blake's sweet, goofy smile. "All good."

Blake waved up at them, and they waved back as he said, "Goldie, I feel it in my *cells*. In the mitochondria."

"Keep sucking on the whistle, mate," one of the paramedics said. "That's it."

Blake did, then added, "And the lysosomes and the centrioles..."

"What?" Damo asked with a laugh. "You speaking another language?"

"I *was* good at biology," he said.

Damo and Cooper laughed, and Blake seemed pleased as punch.

Kat returned and offered to sit with Cooper in the front of the buggy as Mia drove. With Damo's help, the paramedics got Blake on his feet—well, *foot*—and he hopped a couple of steps as they shifted him into the back of the buggy.

Damo sat behind him, eager to have the excuse of keeping Blake upright to spread his hands over Blake's ribs. As they slowly made their way through the crowd, Mia leaning on the horn and Kat shouting at people to move, Blake leaned back against him, and it took every single bloody ounce of willpower not to nuzzle the nape of his neck.

Once he was on the stretcher ready to go in the back of the ambulance, Damo snagged his fingers and gave him a squeeze. "I'll come to the hospital after my shift."

"You're not coming?" Blake gripped his fingers. "I'll miss you so much."

"I'll miss you too." Even with the flags temporarily down, there were far too many people on the beach who'd be tempted into the cool water for Damo to leave early. He nodded to Cooper. "Coop's going to ride with you."

To the paramedic, he asked, "Going to Fiona Stanley in Murdoch?" She nodded, and Damo said to Blake, "Maybe they'll even put on the lights and sirens."

"*Ohh*, cool!" Blake said with complete sincerity, and everyone laughed.

And on the clock or not, Damo had to kiss him.

Chapter Twenty-One

"H EY, MATE," BLAKE said as Cooper and Tasha joined him in the curtained cubicle in the emergency department. "Thanks for coming, Tash. I'm really sorry about this."

Her smile was tight. "Accidents happen." She eyed his bandaged leg, which was propped on pillows. "How are you? Did they stitch you up?"

"Not yet. Waiting my turn. There was a bad accident on the highway, apparently." He smiled at Cooper. "You okay? I know it was scary to ride in the ambo."

"Nah, it was awesome." His grin faded. "I mean, not that you got hurt."

"I know what you mean."

Tasha said, "Hey, bub—are you hungry? I am." She gave him a credit card. "Can you grab me a Cherry Ripe from the vending machine out there? You can get something too."

With a delighted gasp, Coop vanished beyond the curtain, and Tash's eyes blazed. "Seriously, what the hell were you thinking?" she hissed to Blake. "Coop said the surf is massive today."

"I know. I wasn't going to go in! But then I saw Damo out there with two patients, and… I had to help him. I couldn't just stand there and watch."

Shoulders loosening, she sighed. "I understand that, but he's a professional lifeguard! You're a country boy who learned to surf. Your son could've watched you die today."

Tash's quiet words were a gut punch. The pressure around his lungs roared back as if he was trapped under the crushing force of the waves again. Tears flooded his eyes, and he had to look down at the blue pattern of the scratchy hospital gown he wore.

Finally, he managed, "I'm sorry." His throat was like sandpaper. He couldn't meet Tash's eyes. "Do you… Can I still see him? I know I messed up." He wouldn't blame her and Tony for taking Coop home and being done with Blake. What kind of father would be so reckless?

She exhaled noisily and took his shoulder with a warm squeeze. "Don't be silly. 'Course you can see him again. You're his father—along with Tony—and he'd be gutted if you disappeared."

"Really?" Blake looked up as hope swelled. "So, he likes me?"

She smiled. "Yes. He really, really likes you."

"He's such a great kid. I just…I love him so much already. Is that strange?"

"Nope. That's parenthood." She winked as Cooper returned.

"Cherry Ripe for Mum," he said as he passed her the chocolate bar. "Violet Crumble for me, and I wasn't sure what you like, so I got a few." He emptied his pockets and put a mint Breakaway, Twirl, and packet of Sherbies.

"It's my lucky day!" Blake exclaimed, though he had to blink away more tears, touched that Cooper had thought of him. "I love them all. Do you fancy sharing the Sherbies with me?" He patted the side of the gurney by his good left leg, biting back a grimace as he shifted over. "Climb aboard."

When it was time for Cooper and Tasha to go, Cooper stood unmoving for a moment, then threw his arms around Blake's neck. "I'm glad you're okay," he mumbled.

Blake barely had time to hug him back before Coop disappeared through the curtain, which was probably for the best because Blake might have burst into tears.

Tash kissed his cheek. "You don't have to be perfect. Just don't be a fuckwit."

"Can I get that on a T-shirt?"

She grinned. "I'll tattoo it on your forehead."

WHEN DAMO PULLED back the curtain, still wearing his lifeguard uniform, bubbly warmth spread through Blake despite the throbbing in his thigh. "Shouldn't you be working still?"

"Hazza came in to take my last couple of hours. Figured I'd get your car keys off you, go home and shower, and come back to pick you up." Damo closed the curtain behind him and came around the left side of the gurney. "No stitches yet?" he asked before kissing Blake softly.

"Should be soon. I should've thought to give the keys to Tash. She didn't think of it either, but I think she was focused on getting Coop out of the hospital."

"No worries. I'll come back and pop up to see Dad before I get you home. It's not far. Got a taxi. Just had to see you again."

The mention of Damo's father had his heart sinking. "I'm so sorry. I didn't even ask earlier how your dad is."

Damo slid off his left thong and sat on the side of the gurney with his leg folded under him. "You had a fair few other things on your mind. That was a gnarly fin chop. I would've been screaming bloody murder. But yeah, Dad's...I dunno. He'll probably be sleeping. Mum said she'll fill me in when I get home."

"You shouldn't have to come back and pick me up. I can call Kat."

"You know you don't have to always be taking care of me, right? I can take care of you too."

Blake had to smile. "Thank you. I'm sorry I stuffed it all up today. I wanted to help."

"I know. It's one of the best things about ya. It's not that I don't appreciate it, but we don't want clubbies charging out and getting in over their heads. Then we have to rescue you, and it takes us away from the beachgoers."

Blake squirmed with shame. He *knew* this. It was part of his training as a clubbie. Why had he been so determined to rush in without thinking? "I just want you to keep liking me."

Damo blinked. "What, you think I'll like you more if you risk your neck for me?"

"Well…yeah?"

"*Maaate.*" Damo squeezed Blake's bare knee on his uninjured leg gently. "That's not the only reason I like ya. Sure, it was hot when you came to my rescue when we met. And I really liked what you said that night."

"Which part?" Blake asked a bit too eagerly.

With a little smile, Damo leaned close and whispered in his ear, "I'll take care of you." His hair brushed Blake's cheek, breath warm.

Blake caught his mouth in a kiss before Damo sat back. "And I want to. I will."

"I know. You spent three extra years in the middle of nowhere to help your parents." He shuddered dramatically. "Away from the water. Put your life on hold to be a good son. I've got a lot of family shit to deal with, but at least I still have Barkers. I'd lose it otherwise."

"Trust me, I came close."

Damo frowned. "Why'd ya stay? Did they really need you for that long?"

Blake shifted, wincing at the pain in his leg. "Can you pass me the water?" Damo handed him the plastic cup, and Blake drained it. "Thanks."

"You right?"

"Yeah. Keep forgetting to drink water until my throat dries up."

After a few beats of silence, Damo said, "Still wondering why ya stayed so long."

"Oh. I don't know. You know how it is with family."

"Yeah, I do. I don't have a leg to stand on, but I feel like you don't really want to answer?"

A denial immediately sprang up, but Blake stopped it on his tongue. Damo was right—it made him uncomfortable to think about it. Uneasy. *Hurt.*

He was silent a few moments, the warm weight of Damo's hand on his knee comforting. Finally, he said, "When I came out during uni, my parents didn't react well. My siblings did, and they told Mum and Dad to get over it. It was awkward with them for a while, but eventually, things between us seemed to get back to normal. Except they really didn't want to talk about anything remotely queer. If I tried to bring up my boyfriend? Forget it. It wasn't as if they said out loud I couldn't talk about it. But it was clear how uncomfortable it made them."

"Shit. I'm sorry." Damo traced a semicircle on Blake's knee with his thumb.

"Then Mum had the stroke, and I was the only one who could stay for longer than a few weeks to help out around the place. That had always been my role anyway. My brothers had moved away by the time I was in year eight, and Mum and Ella had rowed a lot. I was good at helping. Smoothing things over."

"Mm."

"And something about being back there—being home—fixed the distance between us. They were so *grateful* and loving, and I needed that. I guess I needed to be needed. Worthy. I felt loved again."

"But not, like, completely?"

It was true, as much as Blake hated hearing it said out loud. He nodded. "As time went on, we stopped talking about it completely. Not *it*. *Me*. Who I really am. In Blinman, they could pretend I'm not gay." He laughed harshly. "And I let them because it felt too good to be loved."

Blake rubbed his face. "Wow, saying it out loud like that makes it sound pretty fucked up, hey?"

Damo shrugged. "Look who you're talkin' to. We're all fucked up in our own way."

"They're not bad people! They try. Well, once in a while. Not enough. Not nearly enough."

"You don't need to do that with me, okay?" Damo gazed at him seriously. "Yeah, it's awesome when you're brave and responsible and all that. You stepped right up for Cooper. I feel like I can trust you."

Blake nodded eagerly, taking Damo's hand. "You can. I promise."

"But I like you for more than that."

It was cringey and needy, but Blake had to ask, "What else?" He winced. "You don't have to answer that."

"Why not? I want to." Smiling, Damo squeezed his fingers, their palms warm where they pressed together. "You're smart. You're funny. You're sexy as hell, with makeup and without. We can always have a laugh, even when we're…" He waggled his eyebrows adorably. "You know."

Blake grinned, glad he'd asked.

"You love the water like I do. You won't complain if I want to spend all day at the beach. You'll be right beside me paddling out."

"I can't think of anything better."

"That's 'cause there is nothing better."

Excitement rippled through Blake despite the throbbing in his leg. "I want to make plans with you. Surfing and grabbing a coffee and going to a movie." He hesitated. "I know it's hard, though. With your dad."

Damo gripped his hand. "It has to change. I'm going to talk to Mum. I've been out of the house more since I met you than I have in the past year. I can imagine us driving down to Margs for the weekend. I dig your music. Never listened to classic rock much before, but I love it. I can picture us with the tunes going, stopping for fish tacos by the water. Talking about nothing but everything. You know?"

Blake's heart soared, his breath caught in his throat. He loved him—so quickly and fiercely. This was what he'd felt on the beach in the green whistle's joyous haze that he'd tried to explain. Love for Cooper—his *son!*—and Damo that was brand new yet life-changing. It filled every pore. Every cell.

"I know," Blake rasped before drawing Damo close for another long, hopeful kiss.

Chapter Twenty-Two

"WHAT HAPPENED?" TABBY asked with a frown. She'd appeared in the hallway from her room the moment Damo had come in and kicked off his thongs. Had she and Mum had another row?

Walking back into the house, that familiar heaviness pressed down painfully. Part of him wanted to turn on his heel and run back out into the sunshine.

"Sweetheart?" Mum asked from where she sat at the dining table wearing jeans and a tee instead of the usual scrubs or a nightie. Her hair was in a ponytail as always, the dark roots stark. She'd cleared a square of space, and papers sat on the old wood.

When had they last actually eaten at that table? Years ago now. Mum frowned at him too and turned on the chair like she was about to spring into nursing action.

"I'm fine," he said.

"No, you're not," Tabby insisted. "You look like shit."

"Surf was pumping today. It was full on with rescues."

"And?" Tabby demanded.

She knew him too well, which made Damo feel good. "Blake got hurt. Fin chop."

"Oh! Is he okay?" Tabby asked. She tugged nervously on the hem of her footy jersey.

Damo nodded. "Missed the nerves and arteries in his leg. They're stitching it up."

Mum asked, "Is that your friend from yesterday?"

Damo nodded. "I have his car keys, and I'm gonna pick him up after I shower. I can look in on Dad, too." He should've already, but he was dreading it.

"He's not there," Mum said.

Damo and Tabby stared at her. For a terrible moment, Damo thought he might be dead, and another mess of feelings gut punched him—grief and regret and relief and even more terrible grief.

Mum held up the top sheet of paper. "Intake for the rehab center in Perth. He's been transferred, and I'm taking the paperwork over shortly. It's a twelve-week program under the Mental Health Commission."

Wide-eyed, Tabby whispered, "He agreed?"

"He did. Frankly, he didn't have much of a choice."

Damo and Tabby shared a glance. "What does that mean?" he asked.

Tears welled in Mum's eyes. "We can't do this anymore. It's too much for all of us. Especially you two." A sob escaped. "It hasn't been fair at all."

Damo rushed to his mother's side, crouching at her feet. "Don't cry. It's all right. We'll manage. We always manage."

"You shouldn't have to manage!" She shook her head as tears slipped down her cheeks. "You've both shouldered far more than you should have." She beckoned Tabby close and drew her against her side. "I didn't want to face it. I'm sorry. I've let you both down."

"You haven't!" Damo insisted. Fuck, he hated seeing her cry. "You've done your best. It's not your fault."

"I'm the parent. My best should have been better."

"It's not like you magically become perfect when you have

kids," he said. He thought of Cooper and how clueless he would be if Coop was his son. "You're doing everything you can. You work so much."

"Don't cry, Mum," Tabby pleaded. "Is it because of what I said?"

"No, darling! You were right." Mum pulled Tabby into a hug and rubbed her back.

Damo wasn't sure what they were talking about, but he could guess. "Wow. Rehab." It was good news. Amazing news! Still, dread returned. "What happens after that, though?"

Setting Tabby on her lap even though she was too big for it, Mum said, "A care home. He's been on the waiting list for more than a year. I didn't think—I kept hoping..." She smiled sadly. "This event bumped him up on the list. He has to complete rehab, then they'll take him on permanently."

Damo tried to process what she was saying. "A year? You were planning this?" He was grateful and relieved and surprised and guilty and, and, and...

"I know it's a big step. To not have your dad at home any-more. I didn't want to say anything until he actually had a spot. But we can't go on like this."

Damo's chest was too tight. It had seemed endless. His world narrowed in to this house and Dad and the beach. Two halves of his life and nothing else. Mum working and sleeping and hardly ever really *here*.

But she'd been trying to make it better. His eyes burned, his throat thick. "I wish you'd said." He'd needed the hope. Hadn't had it until he met Blake.

Mum brushed back his tangled hair. "I'm sorry, bub. I didn't want to disappoint you more than I already have if we couldn't get a spot."

"S'okay. You did your best. But how are we going to pay for that?"

"We have to sell the house."

Tabby shot up off Mum's lap as Damo rocketed to his feet. "What?" they demanded in unison.

Mum smiled sadly. "It'll be worth at least a million now. The land alone this close to the beach."

"So some dickhead can tear it down and squeeze in another ugly McMansion?" Damo asked. "Yeah, nah."

His heart raced at the thought of the house—with all its memories and misery—not being theirs anymore. Being *gone*.

"You really want to stay here?" Mum asked. "You haven't thought about getting an apartment or sharing with your mates?"

"I haven't!" It was the truth—he'd never even entertained the idea because it had simply been impossible.

But now, he thought of waking up in bed with Blake? He could have that every night. They could come home to each other and drink a beer and make a stir fry and laugh and talk about their days. They could kiss and fuck and go to sleep in *their* bed.

He could have that. They could do life together.

"But where will we live?" Tabby asked.

Mum blew out a long breath, her cheeks puffing. "Well, after we sell the house—which won't be right away—we can move in with your Auntie Kirsty."

Tabby's voice rose so high the neighborhood dogs had to be having seizures. "In *Quinns Rocks?*"

Damo had to hold in a shudder. "Forget about north of the river—that's practically Broome!"

"You know very well the Northern Beaches are an hour away. It's the top end of Perth, and they're extending the train lines. There are all sorts of new housing developments going up. We can live with Auntie Kirsty for a year and figure out which area we like best. It's cheaper there. We can't afford Barking anymore."

"I'll have to change schools!" Tabby wailed. Damo squeezed her shoulders.

"I know, sweetie," Mum said. "I'll have to find a job at another hospital. It'll mean change for all of us. But we need it." She took a shaky breath. "We can't go on like this. It's…" Her voice caught. "It's crushing us. Including your dad. He needs more help than we can give."

They all knew that was true.

In the silence, Mum added, "The care home's in Mindarie. A ten-minute drive from Quinns. In the meantime, we can drive up to visit."

Tabby demanded, "What about Damo? He can't leave Barkers!"

Standing, Mum gazed at him with damp, blue eyes so much like his own. "That's his choice." She took his hand. "I only want the best for you. I've let you give up far too much already. Both of you." She jerked with another sob, and Tabby and Damo moved in unison to hug her, the three of them holding each other until they could speak again.

Damo's phone buzzed, and he read the text from Blake saying he was being discharged. His head spun. "I need to shower and pick up Blake."

"Sorry, how do you know him?" Mum asked. "I thought I knew all your mates from the beach."

"He's a new clubbie," Damo said. His heart thudded. "And he's my boyfriend now." It really was getting easier, and he smiled despite everything.

Mum's eyebrows shot up. "Oh! I… Oh!" She blinked at him. "I'm sorry. I didn't realize. I should've. How long have you…" She shook her head and pulled him into another hug. "That's wonderful, sweetheart."

"Thanks, Mum." He breathed out and squeezed her tightly. "I still like chicks too, for the record. I'm bi."

Smiling as she pulled back, Mum said again, "Wonderful. I'd love to meet him and—was that his son? I want to meet them again properly."

Tabby asked, "Are you going to sleep over at Blake's to look after him?"

"No," he said automatically. "I'll be back, Tabs. Don't worry."

"But you should. Stay over at his, I mean. I'm okay." She sniffed loudly. "I promise. And Mum's here with me."

Mum held Tabby against her side. "How about we get some takeaway and watch a movie?"

Tabby brightened. "Really? Can we get hot dogs from Run Amuk in Freo?"

"Definitely," Mum said. She smiled at Damo. "Go on. We'll see you tomorrow."

The two nights away in Bremer Bay had seemed like a miracle. Now he could just…leave again? "But…"

Tabby rolled her eyes. "Are you still here? On yer bike!" She gave him a playful shove.

They laughed some more, and then Damo thought of Dad and wanted to cry. He reckoned none of them knew what to think or how to feel, veering from tears to laughter and back again in a blink. But one thing he knew for sure?

He couldn't wait to sleep in Blake's bed.

〰〰

BLAKE GROANED AS he sat on the side of the mattress in his boxers. "Maybe I can just take a quick shower. Stick my head in."

"Mate!" Damo could tell Blake wasn't going to be an easy patient. "You're not going against doc's order on my watch. She said forty-eight hours until you can get the stitches wet." He took the crutches and propped them against the table beside Blake's bed.

The bedroom was clean and spare like the rest of Blake's unit. Holding a queen-sized bed with gray and blue doona, a small TV on the wall across from it, a closet, window with pale curtains, and an armchair in the corner that somehow wasn't piled with dirty laundry. A framed picture of the sun rising—or maybe setting—over an endless ocean hung on the wall over the bed.

Damo helped Blake sit back against the padded gray head-board and prop his bad leg on pillows. "You right?"

Blake nodded. "Are you sure you don't have to get home? I don't want to take you away from your family."

"No worries. Mum and Tabs are good, and I can't do any-thing for Dad tonight while he's getting settled in rehab."

"It's not fair that you go from caretaking at home to looking after me."

Damo kissed him softly. "Reckon you'll be a much better patient. Besides, it's like a holiday getting out of the house again so soon." He hurried into the kitchen and poured a glass of water for Blake, asking, "Hungry?" as he returned.

"God, no. But I guess I'll have to have some toast with the meds." Blake took the water. "Thanks. Sit with me. I promise I'll tell you when it's time for more painkillers."

Damo walked around to the other side of the bed and careful-ly lowered himself. "You must think I'm a dickhead calling it a holiday to be here when you're injured."

"Nope. Not even a little bit." Blake took Damo's hand and kissed the inside of his wrist. A sweet brush of lips that made Damo shiver. "How do you feel about your dad going to rehab? And a long-term facility?"

"The thought of him being in a care home should be awful, but…"

"I'd think it would be a relief. Partly, at least."

Damo whispered, "Isn't that wrong, though?"

"It's human. It doesn't mean you don't love him. It's okay to be relieved. He needs full-time care. It's not fair to you or Tabby or your mum to have to take that on."

"It's not fair to Dad that he had the accident. Even if he wasn't wearing the bloody harness."

"I know. None of it's fair." Blake held Damo's hand, threading their fingers together.

Damo's shoulders slumped. "If they move north, I don't know what to do. I don't want to leave Barkers."

"Move in here."

"What?" He sat up straight with an awkward laugh. "That green whistle must be lingering. I can't move in."

"Why not?"

"You'll be sick of me in a week!"

Blake watched him, steady as a rock. "I won't."

Damo opened and closed his mouth, then smiled. "It's not going to be for months anyway. Fixing up the house to sell, waiting for the new school year."

"We won't rush into anything." Blake grimaced down at his leg. "I've learned my lesson." He nudged Damo's shoulder, his bare skin warm against Damo's arm under his T-shirt. "How about we stop trying to be brave and take care of each other. Within limits. I know you're not a damsel in distress."

"Sounds good. I'm taking care of you tonight, and you're not gonna argue."

"Aye-aye, captain. Or are you the doctor in this scenario?"

"I'm just your boyfriend. Don't think either of us are up for playing doctor tonight."

"Well, the night is young," Blake drawled with a wink, and they laughed. For the first time since the car ride home from Bremer Bay, Damo was able to really breathe.

～～～

MUMBLING TO HIMSELF, Damo stretched—and hit warm flesh.

He jolted, opening his eyes to find Blake smiling down at him where he sat against the padded headboard, the covers around his lap. He reached for a remote and muted the surf competition playing on the TV.

Damo sat straight up. "When did I fall back asleep?" He'd woken at dawn to make Blake vegemite on toast and coffee, and they'd had breakfast in bed. "Are you right?"

"I'm good. Heaps better."

Damo snorted. "I've had a fin chop, mate. I know how much it hurts. And I can see the bruises coming out." He pointed to Blake's chest. "There on your ribs. Up on your shoulder. I know there are more on your back. Have to be."

"Okay, it hurts like a son of a bitch, and yeah, I got a little banged up. But I'm home in bed with you, so, yeah. Heaps better. Plus, the painkillers are working."

"Sorry I conked out."

Blake brushed Damo's mess of hair back from his face. "You clearly needed the rest. Don't worry—you still have a couple of hours before your afternoon shift."

"Have enough water? Do you need to piss? Want another coffee?"

Blake shook his head.

"Sure you're okay?"

"I'm okay."

Damo still sprang up, filled with the need to do *something*. "More brekkie?"

"I promise I'm good," Blake said with a soft smile. "Though I don't mind the view."

Realizing he was naked, Damo laughed, striking a model pose.

"Oh, yeah. Work it, baby."

Damo crawled back onto the bed and peeled away the covers to reveal Blake's body. Being so casually naked together was sexy in a way Damo wasn't used to. The comfort of it made Damo's heart ache. In a good way.

"Let me check your bandage," he said before he got choked up over having their soft dicks out.

"How did I get this lucky?" Blake asked.

Damo pointedly eyed the stitched wound as he opened a fresh bandage. "Look, you're the one with the uni degree, but I don't think that word means what you think it means."

Blake chuckled, and Damo redressed the wound. Waking up with Blake had been different this time—Damo had made sure to keep to his side of the bed since Blake was injured, and the last thing he wanted to do was flail during a dream and kick his wound or something.

Waking up with Blake was still incredible—even with the flood of guilt that had been partly eased by texting with Tabby about the latest *Married at First Sight* even though he didn't watch it. Anything she wanted to talk about was good by him.

Mum said they couldn't visit Dad in rehab yet, and Damo had to admit he didn't mind waiting. In the meantime, Blake was the only thing he was going to let himself worry about. For the morning, at least.

The skin around the laceration was bruised and red, and he was glad Blake had gotten the good painkillers. He wished he could go back and keep Blake safe on the sand. Take the fin chop himself.

"Sure it's not too tight?" he asked.

"It's just right, Goldie."

Damo's cheeks heated. "Glad to hear it, Bear." When he was finished, he kissed Blake's raised knee and curled beside him, resting his cheek on Blake's outstretched left leg.

Idly tracing patterns on Blake's shin, hair tickling his fingertips, he sighed. It had been a hell of a couple of days, but for the first time since he was a kid, the future truly felt…possible.

"The things I want to do to you," Blake murmured.

Damo grinned. "Yeah?"

"Oh, yeah." Blake caressed Damo's hair. "*Everything.*"

Before he could remind himself that Blake was injured and this wasn't the time for it, Damo asked, "Like what?" It was just talking. No harm, right?

"I want to fuck you again, obviously."

"Duh."

He could hear the smile in Blake's voice as Blake said, "Get you on your hands and knees. You remember the cave?"

Damo's breath hitched. "It's really a ledge, but yeah," he whispered. No harm, his arse.

"Open you up with my mouth again. My tongue. Get you ready for my cock." He tightened his fingers in Damo's hair. "Make you scream. You'll come so hard, won't you?"

He could only nod against Blake's thigh.

"I want you to fuck me too. Make me beg for it."

Damo lifted his head to find Blake watching him with a grin. Damo swallowed hard. "Suppose that sounds all right." He put his head back down, because if he kept looking at Blake's gorgeous face and the heat in his eyes, he was going to have an…issue. "Not for a few weeks at least, though."

"Good thing we have plenty of time."

Damo tightened his hand on Blake's knee. "Yep."

"I want to watch you ride me. Your hair loose. Your skin flushed that pretty pink. Watch you straddle me and sink down on my cock. Think you can take every inch of me?"

"I did before." *Annnd,* he was hard, and he ached to press the heel of his hand against his dick.

"You did." Blake smoothed his hand over Damo's head, then traced the shell of his ear. "Such a good boy."

Damo sat up because he'd come soon just from Blake's fantasies and fingertips on his ear. "What're ya doin'? You're in no state."

"No, between the pain and the meds, I don't think I am." He

eyed his soft cock ruefully—then raised a brow. "But you clearly are."

"Diabolical!" Damo groaned. "Give me a minute."

"Why?"

"Because I'm—" He motioned to his dick. "And you can't."

"But you can. Let me watch."

The rush of heat filled every pore, and Damo could only make a strangled sound that might have been, *gorgleguuuuh.*

"Can I watch you, baby?"

Nodding, Damo asked, "Just like this?"

"You can't ride me yet, but will you use your fingers?"

He practically lunged for the lube before realizing he didn't know where it was. Grinning, Blake directed him, and Damo straddled Blake's outstretched ankle, sitting back on his heels. He couldn't sit over Blake's hips yet, but he liked the warmth of Blake's calf against his inner thigh where they touched.

With slick fingers, Damo pulled back his foreskin and teased the swollen head of his cock. With his other hand, he pushed his middle finger into his hole.

"Bit like rubbing my belly and pattin' my head."

So sexy!

But Blake laughed and watched…adoringly? Was that a word? Whatever it was, it made Damo's heart swell. And when he crooked his finger and hit just the right spot, his dick grew even more in his grasp.

"Fuck, that feels good," he mumbled.

That first night, he'd been too awkward to finger himself while Blake watched. Now, the heat of Blake's eyes on him turned him on in a way he didn't expect, and he only wished Blake could reach to tug his hair.

"You're so beautiful," Blake said. "I could watch you all day."

Damo shuddered, his balls tingling. "Appreciate it, but I won't last that long."

"You need to come, baby? That's okay. You can come."

He couldn't work jerking his cock and his finger in his arse at the same time, so Damo pulled out his finger and squeezed his nipple hard. Arching his back, he came, shaking and moaning, eyes closed, every little bit of his body lit up with bliss.

Also coming all over Blake as it turned out, which made his balls seize up again at the sight. His performance had also worked magic on Blake, whose cock stood up, straining and almost purple.

Damo knelt on Blake's good side and leaned over carefully, sucking him down as far as he could before choking. He moaned around the rigid, hot shaft as Blake twisted Damo's hair in his fist, pulling too hard, then not hard enough, and then just right.

When Blake came into his mouth, he groaned, his body rigid. Damo swallowed, then lapped at the jizz that dripped from his lips. Panting, he lifted his head. "Did it hurt?"

Blake was wincing, and he was clearly about to say it hadn't bothered his leg. Then he nodded. "Not too bad, though. Well worth it."

"Yeah?"

Blake gave him a big thumbs-up, and it took Damo a second to get it. "Fuck off!" He laughed, shoving at Blake's shoulder playfully, making sure not to jostle his leg. "Let's not make my humiliating thumbs-up emoji a thing."

"I can't make any such promises."

"Guess you are lucky after all, because if you weren't injured, I'd tackle you. I'm an expert tickle fighter. Tabs'll tell ya. You don't know who you're messing with."

A grin spread over Blake's face, and he pulled Damo in for a long, wet, dirty kiss. "I can't wait to find out."

Chapter Twenty-Three

"HIYA!"

"Have a good week?" Blake asked. He shifted his leg carefully, his feet on the coffee table on a pillow, his elbow on the arm of the couch. It'd only been a few days, but he'd go mental holed up in his bedroom, and the midday light in the living room was bright.

His gaze flicked to the painting over the TV, and he took a deep breath. He'd always found the curl of azure water comforting, and now he smiled and remembered Damo peering closely at it that first night.

"Can't complain," Mum said, pointing her phone down at the kitchen sink and the pile of potatoes she was peeling. "Doing a gratin."

"That's new."

She shrugged. "Reckon we need to try a few new things around here." As the camera shook, she shouted, "John, Blakey's on the phone!"

Blakey.

His eyes burned with a sudden swell of emotion, and he blinked rapidly. Wouldn't do to get emotional before they'd even had the talk. Still, he found himself blurting, "You know I love you, right?"

The view on the camera suddenly shifted to Mum's wide eyes. "What's happened?" she demanded. "Are you ill?"

Dad's voice said distantly, getting louder as he neared, "What's up, darl? Blake's crook?"

"Are you?" she asked again. "What's going on?"

"Nothing! Well, not nothing, but I'm not sick. I'm fine."

"Is it cancer? You're so young!"

"I'm fine!" Blake had to laugh, some of his nerves easing.

Dad's cheek appeared over Mum's shoulder, his wiry hair curling over his ear. "I'd ask if you're in some kind of trouble, but that would be a silly question with you."

"I had a little mishap in the water the other day. I—"

"You and that surfing!" Mum exclaimed. "It's too dangerous!"

"As you can see, I'm perfectly fine," Blake said calmly. "The fin of my board cut my thigh, and I had to get a handful of stitches." Two handfuls, but that would only upset them. "I can walk around my apartment without the crutches now, and it's only been a few days."

"No head injury?" Mum demanded.

"Nope." He knocked his skull. "Still thick as ever. Just like yours."

"The cheek!" she exclaimed, fighting a smile.

"What about work?" Dad asked.

"I'll have to take time off again to be sure I can drive safely. A few weeks. The council won't take any chances. Rightfully so." It had to be his right leg that got cut. Of course.

Dad frowned. "Why were you off already?"

"Took a week's holiday."

"For anything special?" Mum asked. "Wasn't to visit home, apparently."

Blake ignored the jibe. He'd rehearsed this speech, but in the moment, it all flew out the window. He blurted, "I have a son."

For an endless moment, his parents simply stared at him.

Then Mum said through a tight smile, "Little early for April Fool's."

"His name's Cooper, and he's amazing."

Dad's bushy eyebrows rose, and he was silent a few beats. "This isn't a stitch-up." To Mum he added, "He's not joking, darl."

Blake nodded. "It's true. I have a son. You have another grandchild."

Mum clapped a hand over her mouth, eyes brimming with tears. Then she exclaimed, "I knew it!"

For a moment, he couldn't make sense of it. Then his heart plummeted. *Don't say it. Please.*

"I knew it wasn't true! See? You just needed to find the right girl."

"*No*," he gritted out. She was still talking in a rush, and he didn't want to hear it. "No!" he shouted.

Mum's mouth gaped, but no more words came out, thankfully. Dad cleared his throat. "Don't talk to your mother like that."

"I'm gay!" He was still shouting, and he didn't care. "How many times do I have to tell you? I'm gay. I'll never not be gay."

Mum asked stiffly, "Then how do you have a son? What are we supposed to think?"

"He's eight. It was one time with a girl, and it helped me realize I'm queer. Which I told you years ago."

They half laughed awkwardly. "We know."

"But you don't accept it. Not really. Look at how you just reacted when you thought I was straight after all! Even though queer people can and do have kids all the time. Which I've told you."

Mum was pale. "I didn't mean anything by it. It's fine that you're—" She waved a hand.

"Gay. You can't even say it. We talk around it. But I had a boyfriend in uni and I have one now. I wear eyeliner and lippy when I go dancing. I volunteer at the Pride parade every year."

"Makeup?" Dad asked, his bushy eyebrows close in bafflement.

"Yep. Why not? Because it's for girls? Screw that. It's fun. I like it. I'm queer, and you can't keep on pretending it's not true. If we're going to have a relationship, you need to acknowledge the truth. Acknowledge *me*."

As his parents blinked at him uncertainly, tears filled his eyes. "I'm gay, and I need you to love me the way I am."

Tears spilled down Mum's cheeks. "Oh, Blakey. Of course we love you."

Voice gruff, Dad said, "We just worry. We—"

"*No*. There's nothing to worry about. Not anything more than the worry you have for Ella and Adam and Richie. You don't get to use that as an excuse."

They opened their mouths to speak, Mum wiping her eyes, but Blake cut them off.

"I'm gay, and I have a boyfriend, and I'm going to talk about him. His name's Damo, and he's a lifeguard, and he's amazing. I love him, and I won't let him live…in the margins. Unsaid. *No*. He deserves more than that, and so do I. I won't be quiet anymore."

"Oh, son," Dad whispered hoarsely. "You never said…"

"I shouldn't have had to!" The words punched out of him, the hand holding the phone shaking. "You should've loved me the way I am. I wanted your approval, and I let myself derail my life for it. No more. Do you understand?"

They nodded stiffly.

After they stared at each other in silence for uncomfortably long, Blake swallowed hard. "Okay. Do you want to hear about my son?"

"What kind of question is that?" Mum demanded. "'Course we bloody do! Did you say eight years old?"

Blake quickly filled them in, adding, "I totally understand why Tasha didn't tell me. I'm not angry with her."

Dad frowned thoughtfully. "Squid Allen's cousin? Can't recall."

"Suppose I don't blame her for not wanting to get tangled up with a bloke she barely knew," Mum said. "But we've all missed out on so much."

"We'll make up for lost time now," Blake said.

"Too right we will." Mum nodded vigorously. "Another grandson! When's Cooper coming to visit?" she asked. "Or we can go visit Tasha and Cooper in Sydney. We'll get the Connors to run things here for a week. Or we'll just shut down."

"Narelle Holbrook volunteering to go to Sydney of her own free will?" Blake asked with a wobbly smile.

"For my grandson, I'll brave that godforsaken city."

Tears pricked his eyes. No matter what, he still loved his parents. "Thanks, Mum. But Tash and her husband said they'd love to come to Blinman."

"No one *loves* to come to Blinman," Dad said. "But we appreciate it. When can we expect you all?"

"School holidays, I hope. They just went back to the East Coast."

"Must've been hard to see him go. Can we see a photo?" Mum asked.

"Of course, and yeah, it was tough. But we've been video chatting every day. It's been good."

Mum fought tears. "You'll be such a bloody good dad, Blakey. Cooper's lucky. You were always a good boy. Wasn't he?"

Arm around her, Dad gave Mum a squeeze. "He was. The best."

"And we love you," she added. "Gay and all. We'll... We'll do better."

He nodded. "Okay, you're going to make me cry too."

She wiped her eyes. "And don't you think for a second we've forgotten that you nearly killed yourself surfing. What've you done to yourself?"

Reluctantly, he angled his phone down at his bandaged leg. "It's really not bad. I promise."

"Crikey," Dad muttered. "Wouldn't want to see a serious injury."

Mum ordered, "Take off the bandage. I need to see it properly."

"*No.* I promise, you don't need to worry."

"Who's taking care of ya?" she demanded. "You're living all alone. Unless… What did you say his name was?"

"Damo. Yes, my boyfriend's taking care of me."

"A lifeguard, you said? Sexy blokes, they are."

"Oi, I'm standing right here." Dad lifted his chin. "Sexier than a country publican?"

"Never." She pulled down his chin and smacked a kiss on his lips, and Blake smiled. They weren't perfect, but they were still Mum and Dad. They'd promised to do better, and he'd hold them to it.

〰️

"SURE THIS IS a good idea?" Damo asked.

"Positive. I'm walking better. Slow and steady."

Damo didn't seem convinced, but Blake kissed his cheek before grabbing his keys from the little shelf by the door. "I've got my brave lifeguard boyfriend to help me. And I'm using my crutches."

The flight of stairs down to the ground was still tricky, but Blake was determined. He was antsy in his apartment and needed to get some proper fresh air.

Damo stood below, peering up at him, determined to catch

his fall. He was so sexy and beautiful and Blake had to stop and kiss his lips this time.

A smile tugged at said lips, and Damo said, "We'll miss sunset at this rate."

Once Blake was in the passenger seat of his SUV with Damo behind the wheel, taking them down the coast road toward Barking, Blake played with the radio. The sun was lower in the sky, but still bright, and he rolled down his window as "Ventura Highway" came on.

"Good one," Damo said.

They listened in peaceful quiet, reaching the beach just as the song ended. The crowd had thinned, and Damo found a spot in the car park. Even though Blake had been getting around his unit without the crutches, he humored Damo and used them to cross over to the beach, carefully going down one of the ramps to the sand.

Families were packing up, but there were still a fair few people scattered over the beach. Damo spread a blanket and put his arm firmly around Blake's waist as Blake lowered himself. He wanted to protest that the wound really was improving and he didn't need to be treated with such care.

He didn't, though. The weight of Damo's arm secure around him as they settled on the blanket was too good.

They sat as the sun slowly dipped toward the horizon. Damo waved and said hello to people he knew, and a few lifeguards stopped briefly on their way past on patrol.

Blake watched Liam Fox dig up a dangerous current warning sign and pack it onto the trailer on the back of his buggy. He moved on to the flags, yanking them out of the sand. The end of another day at Barking. As wild as the beach could get, it was wonderfully peaceful after hours.

"You were so lucky to grow up here," Blake said. "Not that the country didn't have its charms."

"Outback's beautiful in its own way," Damo agreed. "But there's nothing better than Barkers."

"Doesn't look like we'll get much color," Blake said after the sun had disappeared beyond the sea.

"Not much." Damo shrugged. "Still awesome. No such thing as a bad sunset in my book."

"No?"

"Nope." Damo gazed out at the pale orange horizon. Waves washed over the sand, the tide coming in, and gulls cried. "Some are splashier than others with the color, like a big wave rider doing tricks on their board—handstands and alley-oops. Tonight's like an old bloke who still paddles out to catch the small swells, even though he had a hip replacement and his hotshot days are forever ago. He still catches some sweet rides."

"No bad sunsets," Blake agreed. He hooked his pinkie over Damo's where they leaned on their hands.

"We get so many good ones here, but I still hate missing even one." Damo exhaled sharply, a sardonic twist to his lips. "I remember when I was a grom, I stayed at the beach even though the yellow towel was out at home. I *needed* to see the sunset. It was pink and orange and red and *epic*. Even when the sun was gone, the colors stayed for ages, getting darker and darker as the night took over. My dad got so aggro. I was late for dinner and still wet in my boardies. I remember him sayin', 'Watching the sunset? What for? There'll be another bloody sunset tomorrow!' And I tried to explain that it wouldn't be *this* one. That it was gone forever and would never, ever happen again. That every sunset was like a fingerprint."

"That's poetic." Blake stroked Damo's pinkie.

Damo smiled crookedly. "It is, hey? Very poetic. Dad just looked at me like I was a boofhead and told me to eat my bloody dinner." He laughed sadly.

"I'm glad you still love sunsets."

"Every single one." Damo glanced around. "You reckon they think we're boyfriends? Or that we're just mates enjoying the view?" He only seemed curious, not nervous.

Blake glanced around at the few dozen remaining people. "Dunno. They probably haven't thought about it. Too busy with the sunset to worry about us."

Though Damo had announced Blake was his boyfriend after the fin chop, Blake realized they'd never engaged in PDA at the beach out in the open.

"If I kissed you, I doubt they'd care one way or the other."

Damo's crooked smile was beautiful. "Since you're my boyfriend, I reckon you should kiss me at sunset."

"I reckon." Blake's heart *thump-thump-thumped* against his ribcage. "Seems like the thing to do. Being your boyfriend and all."

He brushed back a stray curl from Damo's cheek, tracing his cheekbone. Damo watched and waited, lips parted and blue eyes dancing, the golden, fading light caramel on his face. Blake caught his bottom lip, their stubble scraping, mouths opening on a sigh.

It was slow and sweet, and Blake thought maybe kisses were like fingerprints—each their own perfect sunset.

Epilogue

One month later

IT WAS FULL-ON bizarre to see Dad outside in the sunshine. It was already cooking at ten in the morning, and his wheelchair sat in the shade under an awning. He puffed on a cigarette. A few other patients walked around the yard over half-brown grass.

Damo's heart thumped as he crossed the courtyard and passed a rock garden. Until two weeks ago, the last time he'd seen his father had been getting loaded into the ambulance that night, screaming and cursing. The first time Damo had visited the rehab center, Dad had been in bed, withdrawn and sullen.

Now, sitting outside, he wore trackies and one of his old T-shirts—this one from New Zealand with the All Blacks logo. That trip had been Mum and Dad's honeymoon. The paleness of his skin was even more stark outdoors, even in the shade.

"Hiya!" Damo said, keeping his tone light. He stood there awkwardly by the wheelchair. Should he try a hug? They hadn't hugged since before the accident. At first, Dad had been in traction. Later…

There wasn't any hugging.

"Ya just gonna stand there gawping?" Dad asked, though his tone was lighter than Damo could remember in ages.

"Yeah, nah." He pulled over a patio chair. "How ya goin'?"

Dad grunted.

"Nice to be outside, hey?" Damo thought of all the times he and Mum had tried and failed to convince Dad to let them help him out to the porch.

Another grunt.

"Did Mum tell you Tabs scored six behinds in one game?"

"That's good." Dad exhaled a stream of smoke and tapped his cigarette into a half-full ashtray. "Is she..." He seemed not to know what to say, or changed his mind. "She doesn't wanna come here." It wasn't a question.

"Not yet." Damo kicked off his thong and tucked his foot under himself. "She will."

Dad grunted, then looked up, his lip curling. Damo followed his gaze and waved back to a man in slacks and a buttoned shirt who called out, "Beautiful morning, isn't it?" before walking into the building.

"Shrink," Dad grumbled. "Wants me to go on meds."

"Ah, yeah?" Damo asked, trying for a neutral tone.

"They won't give me the pills I need, mind you. Says I'm 'depressed.' Told him he would be too."

"Fair enough. Can't hurt to try, though. How's the physio going?" They'd had multiple therapists try home visits over the years, but they'd each only come once. Mum had done her best to encourage Dad to do his exercises. For a few years, at least.

Dad muttered something under his breath, and Damo didn't ask him to repeat it. At least he didn't have a choice now. Along with the drug and alcohol rehab, physical rehab was part of his program. He coughed and fumbled with his cigarette, dropping it to the pavement.

"I've got it." Damo bent and carefully handed it back to Dad even though he wanted to stub it out, take Dad's pack off him, and flush them down the toilet the way he'd fantasized as a kid. Which was probably bad for the environment, but he'd always hated the stench and smoke.

Dad's bare feet were dry, the heels cracked. Damo would mention it to Mum to see if they could get some of that ointment they'd used in the past.

"How's your…" Dad waved a hand. The tips of his fingers were yellow from the nicotine. "Friend. Boyfriend."

"He's good." Damo smiled, nice little butterflies flapping in his belly. He reckoned the "honeymoon phase" as Mia called it would wear off soon enough, but he hoped not.

He'd told Dad the week before with Mum there for backup. Hadn't needed it, which was a pleasant surprise. Dad had only nodded and said it was good Damo was happy.

Now, Dad was silent, and Damo's smile slipped. Was he about to say something shitty about Blake? Quickly, Damo started talking. "His leg's healing well, and he's back at work. I've told him he's not allowed to go surfing without me if it's over a meter. Even though I know a fin chop can happen anytime. We all get one eventually. His was a doozy, though."

"His what?"

"It was a fin chop," Damo repeated. "Not quite as gnarly as that one your mate Kevo had. Remember that?"

Dad's brows met. "Maybe."

"It was the back of his heel. He was lucky it didn't cut through his Achilles. That kook went right over top of him, and Kevo almost made it under except his foot came up. It was the worst thing I'd ever seen. At least at nine years old."

"Mm. But what's his name?"

"Kev? Um, Preston, I think."

Dad's voice rose in sudden agitation. "No, your boyfriend!"

Going rigid, Damo quietly said, "Blake."

"Right." Dad exhaled, sitting back and repeating, "Right. I couldn't remember."

"No worries. He's still new."

"But I want to remember."

Throat tight, Damo nodded. "Thanks." That bit of effort… It was the first time in years.

A young woman bustled out of a smaller building and said brightly, "There you are, Rod. Having a nice visit with your son?" She didn't wait for an answer. "It's time for art class in the studio. Paints today. I think you'll really enjoy having a play with the watercolors."

The idea of Dad *playing* or painting anything but walls was wild to Damo. "Sounds fun, hey? I've got to get to Barkers for work anyway."

Dad grunted, and the woman waited for him to say more. When he didn't, she gave Damo a kind smile and wheeled Dad away.

Damo had to admit he breathed more easily now that he was leaving. He took a few steps, then heard Dad call his name. He turned and waited.

Dad asked quietly—almost pleadingly—"Will I see you again?"

"I'll be back next week. Maybe I'll bring Blake with me to say hello?"

"Good."

That one simple, hopeful word echoed in Damo's head, and he was smiling again as he headed to Barkers.

***

"SHOREY'S GONNA GET him. Gone. Gone!" Hazza cried out through laughter.

In the tower, they were all laughing as Ryan nosedived with a patient even though the surf wasn't high. Their laughter paused for a moment until they saw that Ryan and the patient—a teenage boy who'd gotten in over his head—were okay.

Damo scanned the water with binos. "Rookie move."

Lachlan shook his head with a grin. "Can't wait to tease him about this one."

Teddy said, "As your boss, I should discourage any and all teasing, but mate, that was shocking." His mobile buzzed, and he left the tower.

The day had turned so hot that the crowd had thinned a bit while people went for lunch and found aircon. They'd be back after three and keep the lifeguards busy as until sunset. In the meantime, the sand and unprotected skin were burning.

"How's your boyfriend?" Lachlan asked.

"Yeah, good. His leg's so much better. He's great. Amazing, really."

Lachlan chuckled. "Glad to hear it."

"Don't mind him," Cody said, giving Damo a slap on the back. "He's in the honeymoon phase."

"Must be nice." Lachlan cleared his throat and looked suddenly uncomfortable.

Damo and Cody shared a glance before Damo asked Lachlan, "What about you, mate? The chicks must be knocking down your door."

Lachlan's eyebrows shot up. "Girls? I'm queer. Thought everyone knew by now."

"Wait, what?" Damo exclaimed. "Yeah, nah, I would've remembered that, mate! Good on ya. We're taking over."

They all laughed, though between the full-timers, seasonal, and casual lifeguards, there were at least two dozen on the roster.

Cody said, "My impression was that I was the first out lifeguard here? Weren't you at Barking for some years before me?"

"Oh, I definitely wasn't out the first few years. Not with my boyfriend being—" Lachlan broke off and cleared his throat. "Guess I wasn't properly out until law school, and it never came up here with the boys. Figured Ryan might've said something while I was gone, but of course he wouldn't."

"Cool," Cody said. "Seeing anyone now?"

With a shrug, Lachlan said, "Nah. Too busy," and peered intently at the north end.

Damo had to think that he'd have been a damn sight busier before as a lawyer, but he didn't let that thought trip out of his mouth for a change.

Lachlan said, "Is there a head out the back? Two?"

Damo followed Lachlan's gaze. "Ah, yeah. I see 'em. Can't swim a stroke. I'll go." He raced down the tower stairs and fired up the waiting buggy as Cody hopped in beside him.

The day passed in a rush of rescues, chasing a bag thief, and helping a lost kid find his parents. After pack-up, he changed into his shorts and singlet, leaving his thongs by the ramp before walking down to the water's edge as the sun disappeared in a splash of red. A familiar person was outlined by the pink sky.

"Hey, Bear," Damo said, sinking his toes into the wet sand as cool water washed in.

"Hey, Goldie." Blake curled Damo's hair around his fingers and drew him in for a soft kiss.

"Dreaming of catching a few waves?"

"You know it. Soon. And yes, I'll be careful."

"Damn right you will."

"My mum wants me to promise not to surf at all without you there."

"Tell her I'll be there every chance I get. How are they?"

"Pretty good. Maybe we can do a video chat with them so you can say hello? They say they want to meet you."

"Yeah. That'll be good." It made him nervous, but he'd do his best to charm them. Like Dad, they were making the effort. "How's Coop?"

Blake beamed. "Great. Passed that math test he was worried about with flying colors."

"Sweet. Tell him congrats."

Blake gazed out at the horizon. "You're right, you know. There are no bad sunsets."

It wasn't as spectacular as others, but Damo nodded since he *was* right. "Glad you can appreciate my wisdom."

Blake chuckled. "Always."

"Having dinner with me and Tabs?"

"Wouldn't miss it."

Warm fingers clasped, they crossed the sand and picked up their thongs. Walking across the grass, Damo nodded to a few locals.

He made sure he was always there overnight with Tabby if Mum had a night shift, and he tried to stay over a couple of nights a week regardless. Funny that even though it would always be home in one way, he was already thinking of it as "staying over" when he was there.

Being with Blake—sharing a bed and bathroom and morning kisses—was feeling more and more like home every day.

They had dinner—Tabby's spag bol special that she'd learned from Damo—and when Blake had gone and Damo finished the dishes, trying to keep things neater than before, he put on a load of laundry.

Blake had cleared out half the drawers for him at his place—which would be their place within the year—and Damo packed up a few more things to bring over. Then he flopped onto his old narrow bed, the springs squeaking.

His phone buzzed, and he laughed as he looked at the screen and sent the same back. Damo never reckoned he'd be saying *I love you* with a thumbs-up emoji.

With Blake, everything was possible.

**Read more of the Lifeguards of Barking Beach
in book three featuring Lachlan's story. Coming soon!**

About the Author

Keira aims for the perfect mix of character, plot, and heat in her M/M romances. She writes everything from swashbuckling pirates to heartwarming holiday escapism. Her fave tropes are enemies to lovers, age gaps, forced proximity, and passionate virgins. Although she loves delicious angst along the way, Keira guarantees happy endings!

Discover more at:
KeiraAndrews.com